Praise for Inferno's Heir

Book 1 of the Inferno's Heir duology

"A mesmerizing debut fantasy."

—Rebecca Yarros, #1 *New York Times* bestselling author of *Fourth Wing* and *Iron Flame*

"*Inferno's Heir* is an absolute delight. Teia is the kind of character you'll follow anywhere—devious, driven, and full of emotion. The world is so rich and intriguing that I sank into it and never wanted to leave."

—Marie Rutkoski, *New York Times* bestselling author of *The Hollow Heart*, the Winner's Trilogy, and the Kronos Chronicles

"*Inferno's Heir* is just like its protagonist: destructive, deceptive, and heart-wrenching. Wang creates a world where heroes and villains are two sides of the same coin and fates unfold with the flip of a playing card. Prepare to fall in love—and fall apart—in this dark fantasy done right."

—Vanessa Le, author of *The Last Bloodcarver*

"Full of court intrigue, assassinations, prison breaks, and heists, this is a dangerous and riveting story that's part *Six of Crows*, part *Game of Thrones*, and part *The Poppy War*. I adored Teia, the novel's relentlessly fierce, morally gray heroine, and rooted for her even in the most impossible situations. Absolutely recommend if you're looking for a book to devour in one sitting."

—Jamie Pacton, bestselling author of *The Absinthe Underground* and *The Vermilion Emporium*

"A stunning concoction of political intrigue, found family, and nail-biting tension. *Inferno's Heir* is destined to be a book people obsess over."

—Jaysen Headley (@ezeekat), global top 5 BookTok influencer

TEMPEST'S QUEEN

TEMPEST'S QUEEN

BOOK TWO OF THE *INFERNO'S HEIR* DUOLOGY

TIFFANY WANG

Published by Violetear Books, an imprint of
Bindery Books, Inc., San Francisco
www.binderybooks.com

Acquired by Kevin T. Norman
Edited and designed by Girl Friday Productions
www.girlfridayproductions.com

Cover illustration: Dan Funderburgh
Cover design: Charlotte Strick

ISBN (paperback): 978-1-964721-44-6
ISBN (ebook): 978-1-964721-46-0

Library of Congress Cataloging-in-Publication data has been applied for.

First edition
10 9 8 7 6 5 4 3 2 1

Printed in China

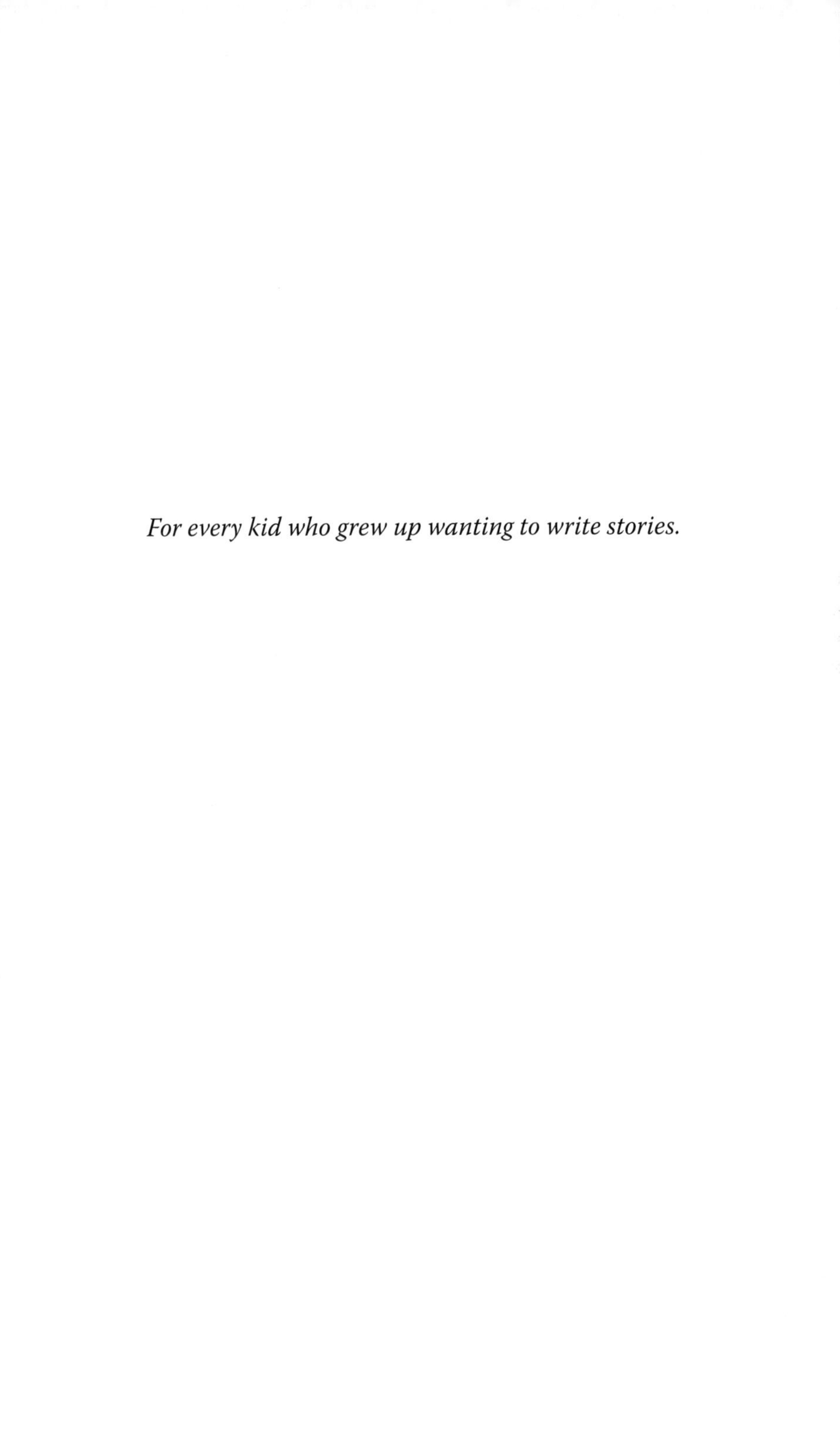

For every kid who grew up wanting to write stories.

Chapter One

The clouds had cleared when Teia Carthan emerged onto the deck of *The Inferno.*

It was a pretty sight. Beautiful, in fact, to even the most hardened sailor. After days of rough water—winds beating at the ship's hull, rain pounding down in heavy sheets—the Dark Sea had finally calmed. The moon hung fat and round, poised gracefully against the velvet sky. Stars streaked overhead, trailing gold as they vanished against the horizon.

All across the length of the deck, *The Inferno*'s crew had abandoned their usual duties. They sprawled in hammocks or stretched out against the furled sails, clinking glass bottles in lively celebration. Someone huffed away on the flute, until his companion begged for mercy. Another belted a folk song at the top of his lungs, his voice cracking on each note. The night was young, the energy electric. Anything seemed possible, against the backdrop of the ocean.

Teia, however, had no time for such pleasantries. She felt the attention of the crew as she strode by, the red hem of her cloak brushing at her heels. Six months after her coronation, the whispers still followed. She suspected they'd linger forever, but Teia didn't mind. It was the price to pay for her name becoming legend, for the title that sang against her ears.

Highness.

She heard it now, piped cheerfully from atop a mast. A second later, Enna van Apt dropped down from her perch. She moved with a natural ease, like she was a dancer and the boat her stage.

"Evening, Boss," the thief said. "You're not joining the celebrations?"

"I wouldn't call a bottle of rum and a few scales on the flute a celebration."

Enna surveyed the crew with a practiced eye. "Not just that," she put in. "Lucen's taking song requests."

Teia glanced toward the hammocks, to where the reedy sailor warbled out yet another chorus. "Interesting," she said. "Is that what we're calling it?"

The ship swayed under them, the ocean bobbing in agreement. Enna kept her footing, rocking easily to the rhythm of the waves, but Teia stiffened. She might have inherited her mother's ability to control water, but the open sea was an entirely different beast. There had been multiple days of the journey where she'd lain in her cabin, fervently wishing for the sweet comfort of land.

Unfortunately, Enna was annoyingly perceptive. "You're not going to hurl again, are you?"

"That was one time," Teia said sourly. Leave it to Enna to recount her most humiliating moment. "I'd never been on open water before."

"Are we keeping count? Because it was four times, actually. Twice when you got on board and once after that meeting with Ket." She sidestepped a stray bucket. "Oh, and that incident after dinner, too, when you excused yourself to your cabin early—"

Teia didn't bother asking how Enna knew she'd knelt over a

basin in absolute misery, cursing the day she'd stepped foot on this damned boat. Despite three locked doors and a hallway between them, Erisia's best thief had her ways.

She settled for lifting her hand to where the seamen had begun milling around their companions, lighting brass lanterns for the impromptu festivities. Teia focused on the threads of heat, which swam around her lazily. She gave them a quick tug, and the threads went careening every which way, directed toward the many lanterns aboard *The Inferno.*

The ship brightened, illuminated as the lanterns sprang to life. All around Teia, sailors gasped in awe. Several sank into bows. The fellow on the flute lowered his instrument, while another dropped a full deck of cards, scattering them in the sudden breeze.

Enna lifted her foot delicately, trapping a card before it fluttered out of reach. "All right," she said. "Now you're just showing off."

The corners of Teia's mouth ticked upward. "That was an afterthought," she replied. "When I'm showing off, you'll know."

Ahead, close to the ship's massive wheel, a figure watched on from the new light of a lantern. Somebody else might have struck up a conversation, eager to curry favor with Erisia's monarch, but *The Inferno*'s grizzled captain wasn't one for wasting words. He simply set down his spyglass and ran a thumb over his graying beard.

"Highness," he said.

"Ket," she answered.

"Enna," Enna chirped. She pointed to herself, looking terrifically pleased, before fluffing out her black curls.

The captain huffed a laugh. "No map tonight?" he said to Teia, eyeing her bare hands.

Three weeks on the water had made her predictable. When she hadn't been violently ill in her cabin, Teia had taken to carting a map of Shaylan around with her. She spent her free time interrogating each of the sailors on their knowledge of the kingdom, learning all she could about the different cities.

It was strange hearing about the place that Teia's mother came from. Shaylan and Erisia hadn't been at war in years—yet, in the Golden Palace, Teia had been raised on a steady diet of whispers. The Shaylani were barbaric and sneaky and devious. They were people without morals. They killed indiscriminately.

But such animosity hadn't tainted the sailors aboard *The Inferno*. Perhaps it was a by-product of traveling between the kingdoms, with Ket and his crew escorting merchants across the sea on a biannual basis. When Teia had asked about Shaylan, she'd been enthusiastically regaled with stories about Paifan, the capital city set deep in the valley, bordered on three sides by towering chains of mountains. Chusun was another favorite—the small fishing community with an array of docks and an ample number of pleasure houses. And one evening, when the weather was clear, Ket had spent an entire night telling her about Okkan. She'd listened to him describe the city's rugged shoreline, the cliffs that fell away in sheer, black swaths.

Tonight, the map of Shaylan was hidden from sight, tucked into a leather pouch that she wore on her hip. "I heard you sent for me," Teia said. "Is something amiss?"

Ket chuckled as he held up the spyglass. The golden barrel was cut with the outline of the Serkawr, the sea beast that had supposedly helped found the Five Kingdoms. "Why don't you see for yourself?" he said, motioning toward the horizon.

At first, all Teia saw was the black shine of water. She twisted impatiently at the spyglass's metal knob, skimming past the ship, before her gaze landed on a faint strip of lights, twinkling in the far distance. Her breath caught. She lowered the spyglass hastily, her voice wary as she said, "Is that—"

"Shore," he finished proudly, as if presenting his firstborn. "We'll be at Paifan within the hour."

She should have thanked him. Instead, Ket's estimation stirred something within Teia, rooting out any response. Excitement crackled through her—but there was fear, too, a hesitation that had lain dormant for months, ever since she'd first concocted her plans to sail for Shaylan.

What will I find when I get there?

It had been over twenty years since an Erisian royal had entered the kingdom of water. Last time, Teia's father, Ren, had come to sign a treaty that ended a decade of war. He had left with an uneasy peace between Erisia and Shaylan, a ship packed with diplomatic gifts—and a blushing new bride, bursting with hope for what was to come.

He and Calla—Teia's mother—had been enamored from the instant they met, slipping notes between meetings, sneaking away for quick moments alone. But while their love had endured until their deaths, Teia couldn't imagine the Shaylani people would be particularly thrilled to receive her. Was Ren perceived as a blackhearted villain—one who had duped the future empress of Shaylan into leaving her home? Had Calla been remembered as naive and foolish, someone who'd relinquished her throne for the man she'd adored?

Teia had carried her questions across the Dark Sea, reciting them like prayer, holding each in her heart. Yet now, she stuffed the thoughts down, somewhere beneath the surface. There was only one person in the Five Kingdoms she might have confided in, one person she'd have laid her fears bare to. But he was gone, swept away with the bones of her past, and so she faced Ket with a steely conviction, spine straight, shoulders firm.

"Our papers are ready for entry?"

"We've received confirmation from port. The Shaylani know we're coming."

"And the trunks?" Over fifty had been stashed in the hold, filled to the brim with offerings. Salt, linen, dried fruits. Several crates carried more-precious cargo, including rubies extracted from Erisia's mines.

Teia's advisers had been skeptical. General Samos Miran, especially, had questioned the trunks' necessity, but Teia had been adamant. Whenever she thought of the speech she'd prepared for the Shaylani, a miserable jolt flared through her.

Beautiful palace. Thank you for having me. By the way, before I forget—Cornelius Lehm, the leader of the Erisian rebel movement, is trying to summon the Serkawr. Yes, the one from myth. Yes, the one that's sacred to the Five Kingdoms. Oh—and he plans on using members of your own court to do it.

Goddess. Teia had rehearsed the words a hundred times, and she *still* sounded mad to her own ears. If it took a few jewels to soften up the Shaylani nobility first, then so be it.

Beside her, Ket was nodding diligently. "We'll prepare the trunks as well, Highness," he assured her. "There's nothing to be concerned about. My men and I—"

All at once, the captain's voice died in his throat. His focus flitted beyond her, anchored over her head. She saw disbelief reflected in the blue of his eyes—and when Teia whirled around, she sincerely wished she hadn't.

The wave rose straight from the sea, pulling itself into a black wall of water. It surged above them to crest over the ship's tallest mast, stretching upward to dwarf *The Inferno.*

Any merrymaking died as the ship went quiet. The crew stared. *Teia* stared. And for one wild instant, as the wave dragged to its peak, she thought, *The Serkawr.* The sea beast had risen from the depths. It had heeded Lehm, locked into the desires of its new master. It wanted revenge, and it was here to collect.

Just as quickly, her senses came hammering back. *The Inferno* might be on the Dark Sea, but this was no monster, draped in scales and dripping poison. No—this was the ocean. Her lifeblood, her kin.

This was her death, headed her way.

Teia threw out her hands. She grabbed for every trail of heat, coaxing them from the sailors and the air and the lanterns beaming against curved iron hooks. A flickering grid expanded over one edge of the ship. As it lengthened to meet the wave, Teia flattened herself against the opposite rail.

"Brace yourselves!" she yelled to Ket and Enna. She heard a muffled response, a scream from her left—and the roar of the water as it crashed aboard, triumphant in its descent, dousing the barrier of flames to rip apart *The Inferno.*

Chapter Two

The Dark Sea swallowed Teia whole.

She'd never felt water like this before—cold and unforgiving, ready to devour. The current shoved her under, tendrils snaking around her arms, her legs. Beneath the surface, there was nothing but thick, inky darkness.

Give up, the water whispered. *Give in.*

Shut up, Teia thought back. She refused to drown now, so close to land. She hadn't endured all those ghastly weeks on the ocean—a majority of which she'd been stuffed in her cabin, sick to her stomach—only to perish here, mere miles from Shaylan.

She squeezed her eyes shut, prodding at the water. But while Calla could have parted the Dark Sea with a single motion, Teia's abilities were far less developed. The waves laughed at her scornfully. They batted away her pleas, tossing her about to solidify their stance. She was a rag doll lifting against the tide, sucked into the depths and spat back out.

As she broke into open air, scanning furiously for survivors, Teia saw the remnants of *The Inferno*. The ship had been destroyed, the deck splintered in two. Broken mast pieces floated just out of reach. A sopping red banner was tethered to a loose slab of driftwood.

Yet that wasn't what drew Teia's attention. A girl was clinging to an overturned trunk. One hand grasped at the filigreed gold edge; the other clutched the handle of an ice pick, jammed deep into the polished wood. She was coughing violently, wet hair tangled over her eyes.

"Enna!"

The water remained choppy, eager to pull Teia under. She fought with each stroke as she swam forward, catching one of the trunk's wide straps. For a terrible moment, she almost lost her grip on the slick leather. The Dark Sea jeered in glee, before Enna lunged to the side. The thief grabbed for Teia, fingers wrapping around her wrist.

"Damn ocean," Enna rasped. "Remind me to never sail again."

Teia heaved herself onto the trunk. It sank a few inches lower, but bobbed persistently against the surface. She cursed, spitting water from her mouth, shaking off the heavy fabric of her cloak. It disappeared into the sea, engulfed by the deep. At least the leather pouch with Shaylan's map was still on her waist.

"Ket?" Teia said.

Enna shook her head. "I don't suppose we could swim for shore?" she said hopelessly.

It was an impossible distance, the shore not yet visible without a spyglass. Teia swore. She lifted her arm, reshaping what little heat endured around her and Enna. A respectable circle of flames formed beside them. Teia forced it upward, and it ricocheted into the sky, lighting their place in a fiery halo.

She held tighter to the trunk, shivering against the cold. *Where did the wave come from?* she thought furiously. Teia didn't believe the Shaylani would try to drown her outright—but the wave could have been one of the kingdom's wards, unintentionally triggered by *The Inferno.* Ket hadn't mentioned anything, but there was no other explanation for what had happened. Before the wave, the water had been calm, the skies clear.

Either way, though, its source hardly mattered now. All around Teia, the current was shifting, contorting with newfound urgency. A rush of concern overtook her.

"Did you feel that?" she said to Enna, as dread pooled in her stomach.

"Feel what?"

The water was gathering now, moving swiftly as it centered on a single spot. A haze of droplets linked themselves together, one after another. They joined and writhed, quivering in their ascent, combining to climb into the air.

"Oh," Enna breathed. "You mean *that*."

The new wave rose sluggishly. Ten feet—twenty—thirty. Its shadow fell across Teia and Enna. Any farther, and it would douse their beacon, which hovered above them diligently.

"Teia?" Enna said nervously. "If you have one of your brilliant plans ready, I'd love to hear it."

"Ah," Teia said. "Hold on?"

"*Hold on?* That's it?"

At that exact moment, a gong cut through the night. The sound was deafening against the emptiness of the Dark Sea, echoing so loud that the water around them rippled. Teia twisted back in shock, at the same moment Enna said, "Is that a *ship*?"

Not just a ship—but one with somebody at the helm, feet planted above the silver figurehead. His dark hair blew wild against the howling wind. When he leveled one arm, a pale hand swept forth from a sloping sleeve.

Time seemed to slow. The wave, which was now taller than the last, stilled. It shivered at its apex, as if poised to fall.

Then it carved itself apart, tearing into two. Water sloughed away on either side, tumbling down like twin waterfalls. And while the force alone should have destroyed the trunk, casting Teia and Enna under, a shimmering shield of water appeared just above them. They heard the thunderous roar of thousands of gallons crashing against the shield—but inside their makeshift shelter, everything was oddly calm.

Enna swore, shattering any temporary peace. "I guess we found the Shaylani?"

"I think the better way to phrase that," Teia said, "is that they found us."

"They saved us. I take it that's a good sign?"

"I don't believe in good signs."

"Of course you don't," Enna said, before glancing down at her sodden clothes with a sigh. "I love being disheveled when meeting foreign dignitaries."

"You've never met any foreign dignitaries."

"Untrue. I've stolen from at least five."

Overhead, the cascade had stopped. As the protective shield of water fell away, melting back into the ocean, the ship drew nearer. The intricate figurehead was fashioned in the likeness of a woman, a dragon nestled around her shoulders. Lanterns gleamed from the hull's many windows. Blue sails stretched proudly against the mainmast, with geometric patterns embroidered down the centers.

A ladder was dangled over the side of the ship, woven from coarse black rope. Teia seized the bottom rung. She began the painful climb upward, her steps labored as she reached the top. The warm glow from the deck had just come into view—the crew pressing dangerously close to the edge, a shaggy black dog bounding about happily—when a hand caught hers, helping her balance, hauling her aboard.

The young man before Teia was simply dressed. His plain white robes fluttered against the breeze, and a jade bracelet looped around his wrist. *Not that it matters,* Teia thought. He didn't wear any finery, but she identified him at once. Who else could move with such careless confidence? Who else could cast aside the waves, as if the Dark Sea was merely a nuisance?

Teia dipped her head. "Li Yuwen," she said, as he bent again to the ladder to pull Enna onto the schooner. "It's a pleasure."

The crew broke into vigorous whispers, taken aback by her informality. A boy around Yuwen's age even dared to dart forward, pushing rounded spectacles higher on his nose. He muttered something in Yuwen's ear but was quickly waved off.

The Emperor of Shaylan inspected Teia. He reached behind his head, grasping for a silver hairpin, before catching it between his teeth. He tied back his hair neatly, the ends brushing his waist, and then he paused. He smiled.

If Yuwen had any sense, he'd fire his royal portrait artist immediately. The painting he'd sent Teia scarcely did him justice. In person, there was something ethereal about his features, his brown eyes set against a narrow face, a dimple creasing his cheek. He appeared younger than his twenty-two years, as he nodded ever so slightly, raising set knuckles toward his forehead.

"Teia Carthan," he said in lilting, accented Erisian. "Welcome to the kingdom of Shaylan."

Chapter Three

If there was anything to be said about this country, it was that the Shaylani were exceptional hosts.

Teia awoke to the smell of roses, which wafted from an ornate stone diffuser. As she pushed herself upright and flung off the quilt, light checkered through the patterned window shutters. It lit upon the lacquered furniture scattered throughout the room, the woven slippers placed beside the bed. A porcelain tea set rested on the desk. It had been delivered to Teia the night before, with a dozen tea sachets stashed within a jewel-encrusted box.

She padded over to the wardrobe and pulled back its heavy doors. An assortment of Shaylani garments had been prepared for her arrival, all sized to her exact measurements. She dressed slowly—a high-necked tunic dyed the palest blue, a skirt that matched in color. Two cranes had been stitched on the back, circling over a vast ocean.

The sight of the embroidered waves sent grief crackling through her. Teia's fingers stilled on the skirt, her thumb curled around one of the waist's satin ribbons. *Ket,* she thought. *The crew.*

Yuwen had commanded his men to search for any survivors from *The Inferno*—but hours later, Teia received a note slipped under the door, penned in the emperor's narrow hand. There was no one left alive from the wreckage, with the bodies swept out to sea or else forced beneath the current. Ket and his sailors were gone, added to Teia's endless list of ghosts. She could almost envision them in the room with her, their bloated arms stretched her way, features distended from the salt.

I did this, she thought, and the pain that struck next hammered straight into her chest, lodging above her heart.

Because, after all, it had been *Teia* who'd insisted on coming to Shaylan to deliver her warning about Lehm. She'd fought against the will of her advisers, challenged every minister who argued that a letter would suffice. And while she knew it was what needed to be done, she'd just traded the lives of seventy Erisians to arrive where she was now.

She had to succeed. She *needed* to.

The road behind her was paved with bodies—but so, too, would be the path ahead, if she failed at her current task.

Teia gave herself another minute, releasing a long breath, adjusting her collar. When she was ready, she reached for her pouch first, which hung from a pearl hook beside the bed. Miraculously, its contents had survived the Dark Sea, thanks to the thick coat of wax she'd slicked against the leather. The map was more or less intact, but it was the square of folded parchment that Teia grasped at.

She undid it carefully, scanning to ensure each word was still legible. Her signature had been scrawled neatly at the bottom. A scarlet seal was pressed beside her name, bearing the coiled form of the Serkawr. The decree had been one of Teia's first acts after she'd assumed the Erisian throne. She knew it was foolish to bring it across the Dark Sea, but she couldn't bear to part with it—not now.

Not yet.

She rolled up the document tightly and stuck it in her boot for safekeeping. She inhaled once more. Then, because she could delay it no longer, Teia stretched toward the circular window, her hands unsteady. Before she could falter, she threw aside the shutters.

She'd caught glimpses of Taijin Palace the previous night, when the carriage had rattled through the gates. Yet in the daytime, Teia admired the true sprawl of the complex, made of a dozen spacious courtyards and three times as many buildings. Each hall was fashioned with overhanging eaves and magnificent painted walls, held aloft by pillars twined with thin swirls of silver. Craggy trees reached for the sky. In the far back, rows of mountains loomed over the palace walls. The one in the center had a diamond-shaped peak, which disappeared into the wispy clouds.

But most extraordinary of all were the canals that ran through the palace grounds, connecting its different buildings. Yesterday, they'd resembled black stretches of ink, opaque against the darkness. Now, sparkling water threaded through the complex, maneuvering around stone walkways and marble bridges. Golden koi glistened in the channel. Lily pads jostled the surface.

From Teia's place at the window, Taijin Palace seemed to float on water.

Wonder crested through her, followed by a tightness in her throat. The ache for her mother was always there, wedged somewhere Teia could not reach. Today, though, she felt its sting more sharply than usual, like a knife taken to her ribs.

Calla had loved Shaylan. She'd spoken of her old home fondly, with an ease Teia had rarely seen. How many times had she described the flowering trees, shedding pink petals against the wide-set walkways? How often had she recalled the bustling canals, the clamor of the courtyards, the scent of mooncakes as they drifted from the kitchens?

What would she say, if she knew Teia was here today?

Teia could have remained there endlessly, caught in her own thoughts, if a knock hadn't spiraled from the staircase. The sound shook her into action. As she snapped the shutters closed and treaded cautiously down the wooden steps, she wondered who was at the door. A servant, in all likelihood, or a guard. It was fairly early—a gong bellowed in the distance, marking the top of the hour—but perhaps the Shaylani were early risers.

Instead, Teia opened the door to the Emperor of Shaylan.

"Teia," Yuwen said. His blue robes were decorated with dragons darting through gray plumes of mist. The silver sash around his waist matched the pin tucked in his hair, which was set with three twinkling star sapphires. "Did you sleep well?"

"Very much so." Teia didn't care for small talk, but for Yuwen, she'd make an exception. After all, he *had* fished her and Enna out of the Dark Sea. "The diffuser is a nice touch."

"I wanted to make the space more personable. I had it custom built once I received your letters asking to visit Shaylan. Roses aren't usually cultivated here, but I read about common perfumes in Erisia. If you don't care for the scent, I can have it switched out—" He broke off, a flush rising on his pale cheeks. "My apologies. I've been told I ramble."

"No more than anyone else."

"It's just—" Yuwen hesitated again, wavering. "It's good to meet you is all. It's been a long time since I've had family in Taijin."

Family. It was strange to hear such a word, uttered so casually from the mouth of a stranger.

"Cousin," Teia said, and Yuwen's face brightened at the acknowledgment, his features lighting with a grin. She didn't expect he'd remain this happy when he heard what she'd say next. "The wave from yesterday . . ."

His smile dimmed. "It wasn't one of Shaylan's defenses," he assured her. "But the Dark Sea can be dangerous. Unpredictable. There are occasions when even our ships are pulled under by a rogue wave."

Somehow, knowing this was even worse. Had Ket and his sailors died because of an *accident*? If Teia were more adept at controlling water, could she have saved the men who'd sworn to follow her?

She was so embroiled in her thoughts that she barely noticed Yuwen gesturing toward the walkway. A boy lingered behind him, half-hidden in the shadows. As he emerged into the bright slant of sunlight, folding neatly into a bow, Teia recognized the rounded spectacles perched atop the narrow nose. "You were on the ship last night."

"Jin is my adviser," Yuwen provided, which took Teia aback. He couldn't be older than twenty. Then again, age hardly indicated effectiveness. Teia herself had rewritten Erisian law so she could rule at seventeen—and things had gone quite well, up until this disastrous journey to Shaylan. Not to mention Jura's advisers had all exceeded him by decades, but each had been more useless than the last.

"It's an honor to meet you, Highness." Jin's posture was razor straight, his cropped hair flattened with absolute precision. His Erisian was similar to Yuwen's, meticulously honed by an instructor—clean, exact, and deliberately formal.

"Charmed," Teia said, before turning back to the emperor. Her message about Lehm hovered on her tongue, but she cast a quick glance at Jin, unsure how much she should say. "Yuwen—I was hoping we could speak privately."

"About?"

"The reason for my visit."

The emperor's tone warmed. "Ah, yes," he said. "I must say, Cousin—I read each of your letters a dozen times over, searching for clues. You were superbly vague."

In truth, Teia had tried numerous times to compose a message about Lehm's intentions with the Serkawr. The end result was a small mountain of crumpled drafts that spilled from one of the mahogany drawers of Teia's desk. If Lehm could fake his own death and steal back the Morning Star—the jewel needed to raise the Serkawr—who was to say he couldn't intercept a few pieces of mail?

Her lips thinned, as an image of the rebel leader rose to mind. "It's a talent of mine," Teia said crisply.

"No doubt one of many," Yuwen said cheerfully. There was something about his endearing optimism that needled Teia's skin, similar to a scratchy tunic on a sweltering day. People like this didn't tend to bode well for her. "I actually know just the place for conversation, if you wouldn't mind a short walk—"

"Is someone giving a tour?" a voice drawled. "Because if so, I insist on a stop at the Shaylani treasury. I've been told the imperial jewels are astonishing."

Both Yuwen and Jin started. Enna had popped up behind them, her footsteps silent against the stone path.

"Have you been there this entire time?" the emperor gasped, clutching at his chest.

"More or less." Enna stretched out her arms with a yawn. "By the way, Boss," she added, spinning nimbly toward Teia, "have we thought about importing some Shaylani beds to Erisia? My back feels excellent."

Teia cleared her throat. "This is Enna," she said, by way of introduction.

"Chief adviser to the queen," Enna tossed in smugly, as she extended her hand. It was the best way to explain her presence on the journey, although she'd nearly keeled over in laughter when Teia had first proposed the title.

Jin took her outstretched hand. "Jin," he said seriously. "And I'm afraid the treasury is off-limits. We've had some recent encounters with thieves—"

Enna's ears perked up. "Thieves?" she interrupted. "As in the Society of Thieves?"

"You know of them?"

Teia resisted the urge to elbow her. "They're a group that began in Erisia," she put in, before Enna could start singing her organization's praises. "I'm sorry you've had trouble with them. I was told they'd expanded across the Five Kingdoms."

Jin scowled. "Scoundrels—the whole lot of them. Lowlifes, who do nothing but pilfer from others."

The smirk slid off Enna's face. "Excuse me?" she said.

"It isn't only Taijin they've struck in the past few months. Two weeks ago, they stripped a fleet of our warships bare. They took everything on board—cargo, weapons."

"It could have been worse," Yuwen supplied gently.

"They cut holes in the sails to steal the insignia on the fabric."

"Very thorough," Teia said dryly.

"*Too* thorough," Jin bit back. "I've told Yuwen he's too soft on them—"

"They left the crew unharmed, Jin," the emperor said. "What

would you have me do? Put warrants on their heads? See each of them hanged?"

"If you take no action, they'll abuse your kindness."

"There are other ways to earn respect. I'm not my—" Yuwen's voice cut short, crumbling in the center—and just like that, all of Teia's old instincts came roaring back. It was a feeling set in the pit of her stomach, honed from the many years she'd spun her influence in Erisia, lurking within the passageways. There was more that could be uncovered here: a secret to be unearthed, a wound to be pried open.

Despite the urge to remind Yuwen about her request for a private audience, it was Teia's curiosity that won out.

"Do you mean Li Feng?" she said delicately, and the former emperor's name seemed to curdle in midair. Teia had heard rumblings about Yuwen's father, but never anything more than rumors. In Erisia, nobody had conducted proper intelligence on the Shaylani in years; with Jura wreaking havoc on the country, there had been little time to dwell on international affairs. The most Teia knew about Feng was that he'd had a tremendous temper.

Apparently, there was some truth in the gossip. If possible, Jin's expression grew even stiffer. "Yes," he said shortly. "Yuwen assumed the throne two years ago."

"And?"

"And all of Shaylan is better because of it."

Teia cocked her head. As she glanced from the emperor to his adviser, she chose her next words carefully. "Were your parents nobles under Feng?" she asked Jin.

"No. They were employed at Taijin, rather than members of the court. I became a noble when Yuwen selected me as an adviser."

"Jin and I came up together," Yuwen said. He offered Teia a smile, hastily redirecting the conversation from his father. "We used to drive the palace staff mad. Once, I convinced Jin to sneak away during one of our lessons. He was always outstanding, no matter the subject. History, economics, astrology—"

"You were better at philosophy," Jin said.

"Unfortunately, nobody considers reciting proverbs as the pinnacle of intellect." Yuwen sighed in mock disappointment. "Anyway, we decided to break into our botany instructor's room, to see if we could pinch his notes for our exam—"

"*You* decided—"

"I suggested an idea, which I recall you accepted."

"It didn't go well?" Enna said.

"Not in the least," Yuwen said happily. "It turns out our instructor was a regular lecher. We found him tangled in an—ah—*unbecoming* position. The woman was the wife of a local official."

"What did you do then?"

"Why," Yuwen said, "what any normal person would do, of course."

"Yuwen," Jin said. There was a slight note of amusement in his voice. "You *fainted*."

It was the kind of story that couldn't be tortured out of Teia, much less one she'd offer freely before a foreign dignitary. "You *what*?"

"It wasn't my fault," Yuwen said indignantly. "I was tired, all right? All those exams wore me out."

"You were so still that I thought you'd died," Jin countered, his lips tugging upward as he turned to address Teia and Enna. "Imagine me bent over him, nearly in tears, with my botany instructor and his *mistress* both huddled under a bedsheet—" The adviser stopped suddenly. The smile evaporated off his face. "Not that it matters," he finished rigidly. "It's a silly, useless story. We were young. Children who deserved a good thrashing."

For a second, sadness flickered across Yuwen's features. He opened his mouth, before closing it again. "It was a different time," he said at last. The sentence rang with a false merriment. "The past is the past."

A long beat of silence followed. It was clear there was more there, but Yuwen's expression told Teia it wasn't the proper moment to pry. Perhaps it was just as well. She wasn't there to collect information about the Shaylani, scuttling about like a spider behind walls. Instead, she'd come to provide a warning, a message that needed to be shared.

Teia cleared her throat pointedly. "Er," she said. "The reason for my visit?"

That same strange melancholy still tinged Yuwen's demeanor. He considered Jin once more, his gaze lingering, before wrenching his eyes back to Teia.

"As I was saying before," the emperor said bracingly, "I know a place we can talk."

"Close to here?"

"It's a quick stroll through Taijin."

At this, Jin nodded. "If it pleases you," he said evenly, as he bent into another perfect bow. He beckoned Teia and Enna toward the end of the walkway, where a bridge curved over a glistening strip of water.

Teia gave him a curt smile, but Enna shot Jin a glare as she passed. It was clear she hadn't forgotten his earlier comment about the Society of Thieves. Teia could hear her grumbling faintly under her breath, barely audible over the dim chirp of crickets.

"If it pleases me," Enna mumbled, "I'll nick the robes off that adviser's back and throw them straight into the canal. Seems to me he could use the change in disposition."

Chapter Four

It seemed an entire city had been crammed behind Taijin's silver walls.

The bridge opened to a wide gravel path, dotted with courtiers who strolled between flowering trees, chattering away in Shaylani. They hefted colorful parasols over their shoulders, intricately painted with picturesque valleys or foaming oceans, each design lovelier than the last. Music floated from the top floor of a spiraled pagoda, accompanied by soft snatches of laughter. Pink petals blanketed the ground, swirling in the breeze, filling the air with a perfumed scent.

Enna sniffed at a blossom, pulled a face, and immediately broke into a fit of sneezes. "Goddess," she moaned. "I think I'd prefer to visit the desert next time."

"These are from Okkan," Yuwen said proudly, as he balanced a petal on the curl of his fist. "When Taijin was first constructed, my ancestors brought a batch of saplings to the palace."

Teia's mind flew to the map of Shaylan, laid neatly on the table within her chambers. Okkan had been built along the upper coastline, positioned beside a dense forest that led to the country's largest mountain range. "My crew told me stories about the city," she said, and she felt another twinge of regret at the memory of *The Inferno*'s sailors. "Is Okkan close to here?"

"It's about two days by horse, following Niisha Mountain." Yuwen lifted his hand toward the palace walls, where the diamond-shaped peak rose in the distance. "Tell me, Cousin—is street food of interest to you? If so, Okkan has the best fried oysters I've ever tasted. On occasion, you even get to keep any pearls that have been found inside—"

Jin clucked his tongue disapprovingly. "Of all the merits of Okkan, you choose to start with the *oysters*?"

"What?" Yuwen said. "Is there something more?"

"What about the central pagoda worshipping the Goddess? The royal visits to the cliffside? The sacred grove these saplings were culled from?"

Yuwen dismissed all this with a quick shake of his hand. "That too," he said. "But have you tasted a freshly grilled oyster?"

"I'm allergic to shellfish."

"One of your fatal flaws." He flashed a smile at Teia. "Like I mentioned," he said, "the food is what Okkan is best known for—"

"Incorrect," Jin muttered.

"But there's also history here and there," Yuwen continued, unabashed. "Legend says that the Serkawr once walked Okkan's shores, which is how its cliffs were formed. Farther out from the city, there's a grove of trees several miles away. It's said that everywhere the sea beast stepped, a new sapling sprang to life. These trees come from that original crop. They stay in bloom all year round—even during winter."

Enna sniffled. "Oh joy," she said.

Teia, in comparison, felt better than she had in all her days of travel. It was peaceful here, far different from the chaos of Erisia's

Golden Palace. Water ran cheerfully in the canals. Koi fish shimmered beneath the clear surface, their scales glinting like copper pieces against the sun.

I could get used to this, she thought.

One bridge later, and all illusion of tranquility melted away.

The music vanished, as did the gentle notes of conversation. The walkway widened into a stone courtyard, which was choked full of people. There were far more servants now—men and women in long white robes who carted wicker baskets and wheelbarrows as they wove through the bejeweled courtiers. They scampered deftly around the nobility to disappear within a terraced building, which was adorned by fresh plots of magnolias.

Teia shaded her eyes. A bronze statue towered in the middle of the courtyard, with a line of people wrapped around the wide pedestal. Servants and courtiers alike shuffled forward. They bent low before the statue, or else touched two fingers to their lips before setting them gingerly to the polished base.

"What are they doing?"

"Paying their respects," Yuwen answered. "There are some who visit several times a day."

Enna blinked. "Is that the Goddess?" she said, maneuvering closer to the statue.

Teia knew Armina was worshipped throughout the Five Kingdoms. If the priests were to be believed, she was the reason each country retained powers over a separate element. Fire, water, earth, metal, air. Later on, when infighting broke out among the founders about who would rule, Armina interfered once again, halting the civil war by sending the Serkawr to keep the peace. After that, the five founders had learned their lessons. They'd settled into an uneasy truce, before starting their own separate kingdoms.

Back at home, Teia had seen countless statues of the Goddess, fashioned from gold, wreathed in rich velvets—but the sculpture before her was different from any Erisian interpretation. Here, Armina was shown with the curved eyes of a Shaylani, armor fitted over her flowing dress. The Serkawr was wrapped over Armina's shoulders, its scaled hide spilling down her torso. While its maw was drawn back in a snarl, revealing hundreds of daggered teeth, the Goddess appeared serene. She rested one hand on the sea beast's tail, fingers cupped against the spiny ridges.

"It's good to see her," Enna said quietly. When Teia glanced over, the thief was smiling, radiating happiness at the sight of the deity's statue. She sidestepped the many offerings heaped around the metallic base, before bringing both hands to her forehead in prayer.

Yuwen and Jin followed suit, while Teia stood to the side, shifting uneasily in place. She didn't harbor a single shred of faith, but she decided to stretch forward anyway, where she gave the statue's foot a tentative pat. It seemed like a healthy compromise, just in case the Goddess really *was* listening.

"Is everyone in Shaylan devout?"

"Most are," Yuwen said. "Here, we have a saying—that there are few who don't have something to pray for."

"I'll keep that in mind," Teia said.

"The statue has been a good deterrent. There have been times when officials have stopped fighting, solely because they can see Armina through the assembly chamber windows." Yuwen pulled back his hand, pointing to the tiered ornamental building. Its double doors were decorated in motifs of dragons, inlaid with shining mother-of-pearl. "Luckily, the governors don't gather often. The Hall of Eternal Wisdom usually stands empty, aside from matters of state."

Now *this* was some common ground. "Droning speeches and dithering officials?" Teia said.

"Worse and worse each year. We have twelve governors in total, each overseeing a region in Shaylan. Every single one of them has an opinion."

"Better than fifteen."

"*Fifteen* governors?"

"We call them ministers, but I imagine they serve similar purposes." There were some days when Teia was ready to commit murder, as she waited for each one to deliver their updates.

"The endless joy of being a ruler," Yuwen said. "At least we have some distance here. The governors reside in their own regions, so they're rarely called back to Taijin. These next few weeks are an exception."

"You're throwing a banquet?" Enna said eagerly.

"Close. We're making preparations for Kashan."

"Kashan?" Teia repeated. The clipped consonants felt clumsy against her tongue.

"The Festival of Lights," Jin translated. "It's a time of great reflection."

"Come now, Jin," Yuwen said with a grin. "You make Kashan sound so *dull*."

"Well, that's the original purpose, isn't it? To mark when Shaylan was founded—to pay our proper respects."

He gestured to the Hall of Eternal Wisdom's steps. A bronze statue of a woman stared back at them—smaller than Armina's, but still large enough to overlook the throngs of people. She had a stirring face, with deep-set eyes above a lowered brow. She lifted a saber in one hand, and a sphere of water in the other.

"Mei," Teia said.

"You know of her?"

Too well, Teia thought sourly. Mei might have established Shaylan, but she'd also secretly summoned the Serkawr alongside Eris, Erisia's first ruler. Yet for all her research, Teia hadn't been able to uncover *when* this might have happened—perhaps after the sea beast had been commanded by Armina to stop the civil war between the founders. "I've heard stories."

Enna appraised the statue. "She looks friendly," the thief said dubiously.

"She started a kingdom with nothing more than the clothes on her back," Jin said. "She isn't meant to invite you to tea."

"I would hardly accept. I don't fancy poison in my cup."

Jin looked ready to leap at Enna, but Teia let out a hasty cough. "Yuwen," she said. "You were saying about Kashan?"

Yuwen scratched his head thoughtfully. "I suppose reflecting on what Mei did is part of the holiday, but nobody takes that as Kashan's original purpose anymore. You'll see. It's a time of food and drink and dancing."

He nudged at Jin, who remained stoic as ever. "I don't dance," the adviser intoned.

"It would do you some good," Yuwen said jovially, as he returned his attention to Teia and Enna. "Kashan is the largest celebration of the year. There are nine straight days of festivities, starting with the initial banquet." He nodded to the magnificent gates beyond the courtyard, with three arched entrances and an elevated watchtower. "We keep the palace gates open during the evenings. The entire city comes to feast with us. We set up tables—some right here in this courtyard. Everyone gets fantastically drunk on berry wine and white liquor, and nobody gets a lick of sleep."

"Ghastly," Jin said.

"You're heaps of fun," Enna told him.

He straightened his spectacles primly. "Thank you," he answered, as a gong rang out past the courtyard. It was followed by a short burst of drums, which thundered over Taijin, sending a flock of birds roosting on Armina's statue into a panic.

Teia glanced around. "Is that also for Kashan?" she said. Nobody else seemed the least bit concerned. One of the courtiers in line to pray released a long yawn, her fan fluttering over her mouth.

"In a sense," Yuwen said. He was already weaving through the line, angling to the other side of the courtyard. "This is good timing. The drills happen to be on our way."

"He's not going to show us some military barracks, is he?" Enna murmured to Teia. "Because I have a list of things I'd rather see instead."

Teia held back a grin. "Are you continuing your petition to tour the Shaylani treasury?"

"Or the royal museum. I heard they have an entire set of solid-gold furniture there, right down to the matching chamber pot. *Solid gold.* Astounding, isn't it?"

"Sounds impractical."

"Only for those who lack imagination."

"Untrue," Teia said. "For instance, I can imagine exactly what happens to us if the Shaylani discover you've raided their museum."

"Begrudging respect?"

"If we end up being tossed back into the Dark Sea, I'm going to be extraordinarily unhappy."

They followed the emperor and his adviser along one of the glistening canals, winding through the flourishing pink trees and masses of courtiers until they arrived at another courtyard. A large group stood at one end of the square, clad in simple black robes. Behind them, three rows of drummers were arranged on a set of wide stone steps. In perfect synchronization, the drummers lifted their sticks, muscles bulging against the trimmed sleeves of their tunics. A steady beat ricocheted over the courtyard as two of the black-robed figures began to move.

The woman had shorn hair and tanned skin; the man had a thick neck, set over a barrel-shaped body. Both had the snarling image of a dragon inked above their right brows, the patterned tail snaking down to their jaws. They faced one another, stooping into bows. Then they lifted their hands, and twin ribbons of water unfolded in the air.

"What are they doing?" Enna said.

"More importantly," Teia said, "who are they?"

The drums grew louder, pacing out a frantic rhythm. The figures struck, their coils of water lashing out. Teia watched in fascination as the woman flexed her fingers. Her ribbon split into five, each aiming for the man's neck.

"The Naga," Jin said. "Imperial guards, who answer only to the emperor."

"As for what's happening," Yuwen added, "consider this a dress rehearsal. They typically showcase their skills during Kashan on one of the later nights. Usually, each Naga specializes in a particular affinity, so they'll cycle through their best fighters."

"What's an affinity?" Teia asked, as the male Naga deflected the blows, slipping around the woman to send his own coil forward.

"My instructor used to explain affinities as the talents we're born with. When we're young, we gravitate toward certain skills—causing mischief, eating mooncakes. It's the same concept with water. I can learn to change the temperature of water, to mold it into ice, but it's not what comes naturally."

Jin snorted. "I don't think Instructor Lao used mischief and mooncakes to describe affinities."

"He should have. He was terribly boring. I used to pray Armina would strike him down."

"Yuwen—"

"Don't worry. I always did penance after. Not *much*, mind you—"

"Yuwen—"

"Is there an affinity that describes drowning people?" Teia interjected. It wasn't a particularly graceful way to introduce her powers, but she found herself thinking of the men she'd killed. She could no longer recall their faces—just the gleeful chuckle of water as it rushed into their lungs, creeping higher with each second.

Jin considered her statement. "I believe the term for that is *internal manipulation*."

Before them, the duel had come to a searing halt, with the female Naga's ribbons dissolved to shreds, puddles of water flecking the courtyard. She set her hands together, lowering her head in another bow. Her opponent did the same, and as one, they melted back into the crowd.

The little girl who stepped forward next couldn't have been older than six. She bore no dragon tattoo, but exuded the same determination as the guards before her. When she spread her arms, spears materialized in her palms, wrought from solid ice. Someone wheeled forth a dummy, stuffed with straw, painted with a garish red smile.

Teia's next question came a smidge too eagerly, leaping from her lips. "Can all affinities be taught?" she said, as the little girl pierced her spears straight through the dummy's belly.

Jin and Yuwen exchanged glances. "All except one," the

adviser answered slowly. "But only to Shaylani who can control water."

Enna frowned. "I thought everyone here felt some pull to water."

"For most, it's a subtle draw," Yuwen told her. "Maybe they feel more comfortable at sea, or find peace in a rainstorm. But in order to *manipulate* water, to bend it to your will . . ." The emperor shrugged. "Most of the nobility can. Some of the commoners, as well. But compared to the full population, there aren't many who have the connection required to do so."

Teia remembered the wave he'd parted with a single motion, the ocean ceding to his will. "You're able to."

"Family trait," he said, grinning shyly. She should have returned his smile, accepted whatever offer of friendship it might have held. Instead, Teia's chest tightened. She remembered the cold of the Dark Sea, the way the current had scoffed when she'd tried to command it.

Give up. Give in.

A bitter taste filled her mouth. "Couldn't have described it better myself," Teia said.

Enna still didn't seem convinced. "The Shaylani who *do* have powers," she said. "They all end up here?" She gestured to the little girl, whose spears had now morphed into serrated knives.

"Only if they want to," Yuwen assured her. "Being selected to train as a Naga is one of Shaylan's highest honors, and I'm not one to conscript soldiers. Besides," he added, his voice quiet, "I don't want to be feared by the people I lead."

The girl attacked with a cry, power compressed behind each step. When she rammed the weapons upward, the straw head popped clean off the dummy. It rolled toward Yuwen, who stopped it expertly with his heel. He kicked the dummy's head back to the girl, and she giggled. Her weapons evaporated, as she scooped up the head like some large, macabre ball. When Yuwen gave her a wink, she dissolved into laughter.

In the months since she'd assumed the throne, Teia had learned what type of ruler she was—fair but stern, just but removed. She wasn't the kind to kiss babies or coddle children, bursting with unbridled charm. Jura had drawn people in with his magnetism, only to torment them behind closed doors. Sometimes, Teia remembered her half brother's distorted grin, his scarlet robes flung around him, a set of gilded cards flashing in his fist.

Do you want to play a game?

She banished the memory with a shudder, blinking hard to clear her vision. Teia wasn't Jura. She never wanted to be.

But as she watched Yuwen bestow the little girl with a round of applause, an odd sting plucked at Teia's chest. Was this who she might have been, far from the clutches of the Erisian court? In another life, did she, too, wear a weightless smile, cheerful and untroubled, carrying on without a care in the world?

They left the Naga to their drills, but Teia heard the steady beat of drums long after the guards faded from view.

Chapter Five

The pavilion they stopped in was every bit as isolated as Yuwen had promised.

The wooden structure was suspended in a glittering pond. Canals fed in from the far edges, before snaking onward to course through the remainder of Taijin. The water was so clear that Teia could see the orange koi bumbling beneath the surface. They paddled languidly among the white lilies, swimming through the muddy roots.

The entrance of the pavilion was lined by rows of gray-barked trees, identical to the ones Yuwen had recognized earlier from Okkan. Flowers burst from the branches in shades of pink and blue, blossoms scattering loose with the wind. As they ducked inside the pavilion, Enna descended into another fit of sneezes.

Jin brushed off his robes pertly, before examining the emperor. "Yuwen," he chided. "You have a flower in your hair."

"Do I?" Yuwen said. He reached upward, patting errantly at the spot next to his ear. "Here?"

A small smile graced Jin's lips, even as he heaved an exasperated sigh. "Stand still," he said gently. He stretched high on his toes—and, suddenly, he and Yuwen were inches apart, framed by a backdrop of flowers, petals drifting down like rain. As the adviser slid his fingers into the emperor's hair, working the bloom free, Teia saw a tremor pass through Yuwen. His eyes slid shut, if just for a moment.

Jin didn't seem to notice. "How many times has this happened now?" he said ruefully, pressing the blossom into Yuwen's palm.

"Every time I take a walk, apparently."

"One day you'll spot these yourself."

"Maybe, maybe not. Until then, I'm glad you're so vigilant."

Jin huffed a laugh. "Happy to be of service," he said. He moved toward the pavilion's marble bench, utterly oblivious—and when his back turned, Yuwen's gaze softened. Longing cut across his face. He looked at Jin like he was the sun—too bright to withstand, impossible to ignore.

In one instant, Yuwen tore his heart wide open.

It was a scene Teia observed with enormous interest. She didn't much care for love, but it had its benefits. Back in Erisia, she'd blackmailed her fair share of ministers with the lives of their mistresses. The results spoke for themselves.

She wondered if Enna had also witnessed what she'd just seen. But when she twisted around, she found the thief was busy scooping armfuls of petals over the side of the pavilion, mumbling in vindictive pleasure as they floated into the pond.

Yuwen tucked the blossom into his pocket. Then he, too, sat beside Jin, his blue robes creasing neatly beneath him. "Please, Teia," he said, all traces of yearning wiped away. "The floor is yours. I've been racking my brains about why you've finally decided to visit."

She made a mental note to return to the question of Jin and Yuwen later, when there was proper time to assess what had happened. For now, she had a speech to give, one she'd practiced incessantly before the mirror, until her voice ran dry and her sentences blurred together.

If her cousin thought this was a social visit, he was about to be sorely disappointed.

Teia started from the beginning. She spoke of infiltrating the Dawnbreakers, meeting Cornelius Lehm, and receiving the strange request to steal the Morning Star. It had never become public knowledge that Lehm colluded with Jura in an attempt to raise the Serkawr, and so Teia provided the same amended version she'd given to her advisers: that she'd discovered notes in the rebel leader's private study, where he'd laid out the three things needed to call forth the sea beast.

Commoner's flame, noble's water, and the Morning Star. Even now, it sounded like the opening line to a terrible riddle.

When she was done, neither Yuwen nor Jin reacted. In fact, the emperor was remarkably calm as he said, "Lehm wants to summon the Serkawr?"

"You don't seem surprised," Teia said. When she'd learned about the rebel leader's plans, she'd almost put a dent in the nearby wall.

"I'm processing," Jin replied. His arms were so tightly crossed that he must have lost all circulation.

Yuwen straightened one of his silver hairpins. "Oh, I'm surprised. But I've heard a variation of this story before. Not the part about Lehm," he added quickly. "But in Shaylan, there's an old saying that the Serkawr has always been destined to return—that it will answer to whomever summons it from the sea."

"But Lehm doesn't have any affinities," Jin said. "No fire, no water—no elemental gifts at all. If he's using others to bring forth the Serkawr, wouldn't the sea beast answer to them instead?"

Teia didn't think mythical creatures cared much for

technicalities. Apparently, Yuwen didn't either. "What if Lehm begins the ritual needed to call the Serkawr?" the emperor said. "This is all speculation, of course. Jin, you've heard the same legends I have. But if those are to be believed, there's an incantation at the start of the ceremony, which is how the Serkawr will know Lehm as its master."

Jin's face was bleak. "Wonderful," he said.

"Splendid," Enna grunted.

We're doomed, Teia thought. *Completely, utterly doomed.*

By this point, the adviser had risen from the bench, where he paced unhappily around the pavilion's cramped perimeter. "There are artifacts that support the Serkawr's rise," Jin said grimly. "The Seascript, for one, although I always thought it was an exaggeration."

"Me too," Yuwen admitted.

Enna raised her hand. "The Seascript?" she repeated, her expression brightening as it did when she stumbled across something worth taking. "What's that?"

"It's one of the oldest surviving texts in Shaylan," Yuwen said. "A record of our kingdom that dates back to Mei herself. The first portions were made from her personal journal, before being added onto by each generation of historians."

"Sounds precious."

"That's an understatement." A wisp of water had appeared in Yuwen's hands. He toyed with it absently, pulling at its edges. "Teia. You think Lehm is in Shaylan?"

"I know he is. Our scouts last spotted him in Ismet. By the time word was sent to the dockmaster, the schooner had cleared the port. The ship's itinerary was bound for K'val, but it had been chartered to make a stop at Shaylan."

"Where?"

"Chusun."

"That's only a half day from here. He could be in Paifan, and we'd not even know it."

"He already has Kyra Medoh," Jin said, and Teia glanced at him, pleased. The adviser might be finnicky, but he was an excellent listener. "She's loyal to him, and provides commoner's flame. That means if just one of our nobles cooperates with Lehm—"

"The Five Kingdoms will fall," Teia said. "We'll be under the thumb of a zealot."

"I see why you didn't put this in a letter."

Yuwen's brow puckered. "Lehm might have Kyra and the Star," he said slowly, "but it doesn't necessarily mean he's won. There are stories that say the sea beast can only be summoned at the proper *shi*."

"Shi?" Enna said.

"It's an old Shaylani word. There's no direct translation into modern tongue, but it equates to *location*."

It was the first shred of good news Teia had received on the subject. "The Serkawr can't be raised on a whim?"

"Not according to superstition. If the *shi* isn't correct, then nothing will happen—but I don't know much more than that. The rest has been lost to legend."

Teia hesitated. "What about the Seascript?" she said.

"What about it?"

"What else does it say on the Serkawr? If there are parts from Mei's journal, surely there's more information."

Yuwen blushed. "There is, but I've never read it."

"You've never read Shaylan's most important relic?"

"It's dense enough to sink a ship," the emperor said defensively. "Imagine a bound book, packed with decades worth of information." He paused. "I might not have read it, but Ba did. He used to tell me that the Seascript contained more knowledge on the Serkawr than any other document in existence. The *shi* it needs to be raised, how the Serkawr could be defeated—supposedly, it's all there."

Teia was on her feet before he'd finished. Her mind whirled with possibilities. Hope crested in her chest.

Lehm was already in Shaylan—and if he was as resourceful as he'd proved to be, the rebel leader would have uncovered the importance of the Seascript. If Teia could destroy it—keep anyone from learning the location where the Serkawr had to be raised—it was a far better bet than convincing every Shaylani official to steer clear of Lehm.

There was no easy way to suggest that Shaylan's most valuable artifact needed to be set aflame. "Yuwen," Teia said sweetly. "Do you happen to have the Seascript in the palace library?"

The emperor winced. "We *did*," he said.

His tone didn't sound promising. "But?"

"But it was stolen several years back."

Enna made a nervous humming sound. "Er," she said. "By who, exactly?"

Jin lobbed a pebble into the pond. It startled the school of koi, which fled immediately from the scene, bubbles splashing to the rippling surface. "The Society of Thieves," the adviser said with a scowl.

In the span of a minute, Teia's plan came apart at the seams, unraveling at a dangerous rate. Enna had long described how the Society kept their possessions heavily guarded, stored deep in the bowels of their elaborate safe houses. Yet Lehm had all but waltzed into the division in Erisia, snatching the Morning Star from their grasp. She didn't have much confidence in the Society's retention abilities.

Goddess. She'd entered the conversation with one problem and was now leaving with two.

"Did anyone read the Seascript before it was stolen?" Teia demanded. If there were historians who'd leafed through the text, she wouldn't put it above Lehm to torture them for information.

Yuwen nodded reluctantly. "When it was in the palace, the Seascript was kept under lock and key. A handful of scholars had access to it, but it's impossible to learn what they might have known."

This would have been reassuring, if not for the ominous tint in the emperor's voice. Teia narrowed her gaze. "Why? They don't like visitors?"

"They're dead," Jin said bluntly. His face was a mask as he leaned back against the stone railing. "They were killed by Feng—every last one of them."

"What?"

Shame mottled Yuwen's features. An uncomfortable flush spread down his cheeks. "Ba commanded a purge in the last few years of his rule," he said softly. "Scholars, historians, archivists. He burned any books that he disagreed with, too, including texts derived from the Seascript. Anything considered a threat was destroyed."

"A threat to what? He passed the throne to you, didn't he?"

The water in Yuwen's palms burst. He shut his eyes, tipping his head toward the pavilion's painted ceiling. "He didn't," he said. "Not willingly."

The admission sank into Teia. She wondered if she'd misunderstood at first, as she peered at Yuwen quizzically. "You deposed your father."

"You didn't know?"

It was a humiliating thing for Teia to admit. For all her

digging into the Shaylani court, the last complete records she'd unearthed had been coated in dust, stuffed unceremoniously in General Miran's overflowing cabinets. She'd heard that Emperor Feng had stepped down, of course, and the throne assumed by his only son. But she'd always expected it had been a peaceful transition of power, the torch handed from one generation to the next.

A *coup*. Teia took in Yuwen with new respect. Maybe they had more in common than she'd originally thought.

The Seascript posed an issue, but it was a complication that could be addressed later. For now, the easiest step was to speak to the court. If she could persuade them of Lehm's duplicitousness, it would help buy her some time.

"Let's say the Seascript isn't relevant," Teia said briskly. It was amazing how confident she sounded, despite the riot in her head. "I came to warn your court about Lehm."

Yuwen looked relieved by the change of subject. "The governors," he said. "You can speak to them before Kashan. I can call them to the Hall of Eternal Wisdom before the feast begins."

Jin snorted. "The governors aren't known for their blind belief. They might be familiar with the legends, but they'll also want proof of Lehm's intentions."

Even in the Dawnbreaker base, there hadn't been some magic confessional, a diary where the rebel leader had recorded each of his thoughts. "I wouldn't have crossed the Dark Sea for nothing," Teia said tightly.

"I know," Yuwen said, his voice kind. "But Jin is right. The governors will need more than just your word. They'll be wary of you, Cousin. It wasn't too long ago that our countries were at war."

"Besides," Jin said, "many in the court hold poor opinions of Ren."

"Because he was Erisian?" Teia said.

Yuwen folded his arms before him. "Some, perhaps. But most dislike him because he spirited your mother to Erisia. Calla was beloved here. The day she left, it was said that the crowds could be seen miles from shore."

"She would have ruled Shaylan if she hadn't married Ren," Jin said roughly. "Feng was the younger of the two siblings. He was never meant to take the throne."

Sadness slashed through Teia. She had always known Calla stood to inherit a kingdom—but here, in the very palace her mother had once roamed, the knowledge came with a jagged edge.

What had Calla given up to follow Ren to Erisia? Her family. Her birthright. It was unnerving to think of her mother as she'd once been—someone not much older than Teia, set to inherit a kingdom. Someone with a future written in gold, who had chosen a different path.

"I'll be on my best behavior," Teia said blandly. "Take any questions the governors might have."

The emperor shook his head. "Trust me, Cousin. The court will ask for indisputable proof. They'll *require* it." He rose to his feet, optimistic until the end. "Not to worry—I'll think of something. After all, we still have four days before the start of Kashan."

Four days didn't seem like nearly enough time to dredge up *indisputable proof,* but Teia supposed there were no better options. "Are you sure the governors won't listen to a rousing speech?" she said miserably.

At this, Yuwen's lips twitched. "They'll listen," he said. "But I can't be blamed if one falls asleep at the table."

Chapter Six

Teia spent the next two days wandering through Taijin, waiting for Yuwen's brilliant solution.

At first, it was agonizing to be sitting on her hands. Yet if she was being truthful, there was some small part of Teia that enjoyed the tranquility, this unexpected calm in the eye of the storm. In this new pocket of time, she discovered the hidden lake caressing the guesthouses, the sticky wedges of honeycomb offered by the kitchens, the musicians who played atop the pagodas and switched between different songs upon request. One afternoon, she even ventured into Paifan. The capital city was just past the arched gates, and Teia had been accompanied by one of the Naga. The guard had lingered behind her like a grim, hulking shadow as she'd explored the dusty streets, taking in the mule-drawn carts and rows of hawklike vendors who peddled everything from spices to candy.

But for all the sights she'd seen in Shaylan, Teia was especially fond of the space outside the Hall of Eternal Wisdom. When she perched on the marble steps, she had a marvelous view of both Taijin's main gate and the central stone courtyard. At the base of Armina's statue, the servants were busy preparing for Kashan. They hauled out stacks of dishes, decorative wreaths, and iridescent silk tablecloths. Glassware caught the late-afternoon light, rainbows reflecting against the rims.

"Boss?"

Teia glanced back. Enna stood several feet away, blinking out at her suspiciously. "What are you doing?" the thief said.

"Spectating."

"Is that some kind of coded message?"

"Am I not allowed to appreciate my surroundings?" Teia nodded at the silver ornament dangling from Enna's pinkie. "You didn't steal that, did you?"

"I would never," Enna said, although a smirk had flitted over her face. "A servant gave it to me. Apparently it's for Kashan."

It was one of the silver strands that had been affixed to nearly every available surface in the palace. Teia had woken that morning to find the desk, the wardrobe, and the foot of her bed had all been decorated by an overzealous servant. The chamber resembled a jewelry shop for how radiantly everything had sparkled in the sun.

She inspected the five charms threaded on Enna's ornament. "Stars," she mused, noting the pointed shapes. "Is that why Kashan is called the Festival of Lights?"

"Beats me."

"You didn't ask?"

"I was distracted."

"Meaning you found something to steal?"

"I have incredible self-control," Enna said. "But, honestly—who keeps a clutch of jewels out in the open? These nobles wouldn't last five minutes in the Flats." She puffed out her chest, deep in thought, before brightening. "Jewels aside, Yuwen sent for you. He says he has a plan on how to convince the governors about Lehm."

Teia was off the steps in an instant. "You should have led with that."

"I tried to." She raised her voice to Teia's retreating back. "He's in his chambers. Says to go straight there!"

Yuwen resided at the far end of Taijin, close to the pavilion where they'd spoken about the Serkawr. As Teia approached the building, she examined the thick silver columns that held up the tiled roof, carved with motifs of shells. A dragon mural crested above the door. Two Naga had been posted beneath, but neither of them reacted as Teia walked by. They were as motionless as sculptures, their black robes arranged around them.

She found Yuwen within an expansive room, studying something with immense concentration. Velvet curtains had been drawn over the rectangular windows. Lanterns hung down from the beamed ceiling.

"What's that?" Teia asked, and the emperor dropped the box he was holding. Dried flowers tumbled onto the plush rug, covering the floor in wilted shades.

"Teia!" he gasped. "You startled me."

She bent down to help him sweep up the blossoms. As Teia scooped several flowers into her hand, she paused. One in the center seemed fresher than the others, its petals tinged a lively pink.

"Yuwen," she said. "Is this from the pavilion?"

He blushed a fantastic shade of magenta. "I'm fond of plants," he said, hastily dropping the other flowers into the wooden box. He opened his palm for the remaining few blossoms, but Teia stayed where she was, inspecting her discovery. Her mind flashed back to Yuwen and Jin, the adviser untangling the blossom from the emperor's hair.

How many times has this happened now?

Every time I take a walk, apparently.

"Have you been saving these?" she said. "You and Jin—"

Yuwen's grip tightened on the box. "He's my adviser," the emperor said. His voice was unusually short. "My friend. Nothing else will ever come of it."

"But—"

"Teia. Please."

After a moment, she relinquished her hold on the flowers. He set the blossoms into the box delicately, before moving it aside. "Enough about me," Yuwen said. He walked over to a large blue armoire, and undid the brass lock. Inside, the shelves had been removed, leaving behind a hollow space.

A silver pedestal had been placed within. The base had been sculpted to resemble the twist of a wave, widening out near the bottom. The reflective top was perfectly flat, save for a divot in the middle, which held a shimmering sphere.

"Splendid," Teia said. "You want me to play catch with the governors?"

"This isn't a toy," Yuwen said. "It's a memory."

"A—what?"

"In Shaylan, there's always been the belief that water holds memory. It sees all. It remembers." Carefully, Yuwen removed the sphere from the pedestal, before bringing it up for Teia to see. Silver trails swirled beneath the transparent surface, moving in lazy circles. "If you can show the moment you discovered Lehm's schemes, maybe that will convince the governors of what he's planning."

"A *memory* is going to do all that?"

"You sound uncertain."

"I'm naturally inquisitive."

"All memories carry an air of authenticity. Once it's captured in this form"—Yuwen raised the sphere delicately—"it can't be tampered with. It stays exactly the same as when it was first preserved."

Teia's brow folded. "But what about before that?" she said. "Memories are subject to interpretation. We could witness the same scene, but remember very different things."

Yuwen smiled ruefully. "Are all Erisians so hardened?" he said. "Memories are about far more than what someone remembers. They also reflect *intent.* If you can show what *you* believe as truth—a moment preserved in time—then that may be enough to sway the governors. At the very least, they'll know you aren't here for a nefarious reason."

"Why else would I have come to Shaylan? To gorge myself on mooncakes? To steal your throne?"

But even as she spoke, Teia could appreciate the weight of Yuwen's words. The emperor had been right, back in the pavilion—the echoes of war lingered between both their kingdoms. It certainly did in Erisia, and so she couldn't fault the Shaylani governors for being skeptics. Teia would be the same, if another one of the Five Kingdoms' monarchs came knocking on her door, claiming a sea beast was about to rise from legend.

She didn't like the idea of Yuwen poking around in her mind, rooting for a specific memory. Yet if that was what it took to provide the governors with proof—to dismantle one of Lehm's avenues to the Serkawr—then she supposed there was no other choice. From the way both Yuwen and Jin had described them, it didn't seem the officials would be moved by any typical argument.

"All right," Teia said, with the enthusiasm of a condemned man. "Am I able to sit down for this? Or is it better if I'm standing—"

To her surprise, Yuwen shook his head. "Don't look at me," he said. "I'm not able to extract anything."

"The sphere you're holding—"

"Was made for me by a Memory Keeper. That's what we call anyone with this particular affinity."

"You didn't learn?"

"I couldn't if I tried. You have to be born a Memory Keeper—not trained, not taught. They all have a silver streak in their hair." He lifted his elbow awkwardly, indicating the space just below his ear.

Teia hadn't noticed any unusual hairstyles, but many in Taijin wore decorative headpieces. This might simply have been something she'd missed. "Fine," she said. "Which part of the palace do they stay in?"

Yuwen drew a thin breath. "Well," he said. "There are no Memory Keepers left in the palace."

"Not a single one?"

He shook his head once more, and Teia felt her patience wither.

"All right," she said curtly. "If they aren't in the palace, then where are they?"

"There's one at the Archive, about a day's journey from here. Think of it as a library for memories. It's a relatively new fixture—about a year old. We used to house memories in Taijin until . . ." He trailed off, his face clouding over. "Never mind," Yuwen finished weakly. "But if you need a Memory Keeper, you can find Hebei at the Archive."

Yuwen wasn't exactly filling Teia with confidence, and this plan seemed sparser by the second. If a stranger was about to go digging through her thoughts, she wanted more assurances than the emperor's say-so. "What's so persuasive about a memory, anyway?" Teia said, nodding at the sphere cupped in his hands.

Yuwen glanced down. He appeared to be debating his next move, before he let out a sigh. "It may be easiest if I just show you."

When he raised his palms, the sphere floated into the air. It glimmered in the lamplight until the ends began to pull apart, widening like sheets of taffy. Pictures bloomed within the water's surface, moving on their own accord. Slowly, the images brightened in color, shedding their silvery pallor.

A man exited an ornate carriage, flanked by a handful of Naga. He had a handsome face, kissed by laugh lines, dimples creasing his weathered cheeks. His robes were patterned with dragons, while a ceremonial headdress rested upon his brow, the front decorated with minuscule jade pieces.

Teia's eyes widened. The resemblance was uncanny, even framed within a memory. "Is that . . ."

Yuwen's tone had become somber. "My ba," he said.

She hadn't thought Feng would be so *tall.* The former emperor towered into the sky, as formidable as Armina's statue—but when a child's giggle rippled from the water, Teia paused. "How old were you in this?" she asked.

He didn't look at her. "Six?" Yuwen said. "Maybe seven."

In the memory, a grin split Feng's face. He hurried forward with a laugh, sidestepping soldiers and officials alike. He must have reached Yuwen, setting his son onto his shoulders, because the view suddenly shifted to overlook the crowd. Taijin's terraced gate soared in the distance. Somehow, Feng's headdress had been knocked askew. It lay in the dirt, the jade beads glistening in the muck.

Swiftly, the image dissolved, before re-forming into something new. It was a memory that must have occurred shortly after the first. Feng was dressed in the same clothes, but he was now sitting within a cluttered workshop, hunched over a wooden bench. Buckets of green paint crowded the table, some with brushes stuck haphazardly upright. There were colors that Teia hadn't known existed, shades of green so vivid they nearly glowed.

"Were you masquerading as a forest?" Teia said lightly.

"I used to love the color green," Yuwen said, his tone hoarse. "When Ba found out, he purchased boxes and boxes of green paint. He had them imported from Ismet at the beginning of each month, or custom-made from different dyes. Whenever he returned from his travels, he used to bring me gifts. Toys and trinkets—things we would repaint together."

Feng held up a small wooden object, his lips pursed in thought. It was a toy dragon, Teia realized, speckled in green paint. When Yuwen clapped his hands in delight, paint coating his chubby fingers, Feng's mouth lifted in a smile. He looked at Yuwen with undisguised pride, like the sun and the moon were caught in his eyes. Very gently, he leaned over, planting a kiss on his son's forehead.

The memories came one after another, a waterfall of movement and activity, each blurring into the next. Feng, sneaking Yuwen pastries at a banquet. Feng, sprawled at the base of a massive oak tree, loosening kites into a cloudless sky. Peals of laughter drifted from the water, reverberating into the chamber.

"That's enough."

Teia had almost forgotten Yuwen was beside her. The emperor was pale, as if he'd shaken hands with a ghost. The memory retracted, compressing back into a sphere.

"I'm sorry," he said, without looking at Teia. "I only wanted to show you one memory. I didn't mean . . ."

His voice was fragile, a sentence away from splintering. She felt a twinge of sympathy for Yuwen as he wrapped his palms protectively around the silver sphere.

But stronger still was Teia's interest in the former emperor. Meticulously, she began to parse through what she knew about Li Feng. There was the way Yuwen faltered whenever his father was mentioned, his hesitation as he recounted the coup. She thought of what her cousin had said in the pavilion, as the sun sparkled down on the pond, and her question came in a rush, filling the space between them.

"Why are there no Memory Keepers in Taijin?"

Yuwen looked stricken. "I've welcomed them back since Ba's rule," he stammered. "But they don't trust my word. They don't trust *me*."

"At the pavilion, you said there was a purge. Your father—"

"Yes."

The lamp sputtered faintly, tingeing Teia in a sickly glow. "What did he do to them?" she said softly.

Anger contorted Yuwen's features. He stared at the silvery sphere, as if searching for an answer. "He wasn't always like that. I need you to know that there was a time when he was different. He was *kind*."

"And then?"

"Toward the end, he changed. He became more distrustful—paranoid of his own advisers, afraid to venture outside. Ba didn't just want power—he wanted to *become* it. He was going to rewrite history, with his reign as the beginning. He would build a dynasty, greater than any that once came before."

Power twisted and corrupted. It chipped away at even the best person. Teia had never claimed to be above it—yet Yuwen's words stirred something in her, forcing an image to mind. She could picture the scarlet Carthan crest, with the family motto scrawled beneath the twining form of the Serkawr.

Power incarnate. It was a phrase that she'd learned to live by, etched into her very bones. As Teia listened to Yuwen, she had a sinking suspicion she knew what came next. "The Memory Keepers stood in Feng's way."

"All of them did—the archivists, the recordkeepers. Anyone who might have knowledge of the past, who would dispute his glorious rule." Yuwen swallowed. "When he issued his decree, there was nothing that could be done. He corralled the Memory Keepers within the palace and had them executed before him, one by one, so he could verify they had been killed."

Goddess—it seemed madness really *did* run in the family. *Both sides of the family,* Teia thought grimly. Jura and Feng would have gotten on wonderfully. "Is that why you moved the memories to the Archive?"

"What little we had left. Ba destroyed nearly every memory that had been preserved within Taijin. In the span of a few days, almost everything was gone."

She tried to picture hundreds of years of history lost to the whims of time. An instinct, a feeling, clawed into her chest as Teia scrutinized the silver sphere. "When you deposed your father, it wasn't because you wanted to rule."

His laugh was embittered. "Surely you understand, Cousin. What sane person wishes for the weight of the world?"

Teia had. She fancied herself perfectly sane as well, although she admitted there was some room for argument. Perhaps those sound of mind didn't infiltrate a rebel movement, storm an impenetrable prison, and concoct the death of their murderous half brother.

"You led the coup to spare your kingdom," she said instead.

"I was content as I was. I always had been. I would inherit the throne at twenty-five, as Shaylani tradition dictates. I would enjoy what time I had left, outside the obligations of court. As it turns out, happiness can be found outside of crowns and thrones."

That sounds like a myth, Teia thought. But what she said was "Do you regret it?"

Yuwen walked back to the silver pedestal, setting the memory down tenderly. "Sometimes. There are people who don't support my reign. The Red Mountain, for instance, would choose my ba in a heartbeat."

"The Red Mountain?"

"A rebel group, which formed after I took the throne. They claim things were better under Ba—lower taxes, higher wages."

"Even with the purges?"

"Everyone has their own priorities," Yuwen replied. "But I'm afraid unhappy subjects are the burden of any ruler. The Red Mountain is small, and the governors haven't reported much activity in their regions. As long as there's no violence, who am I to quell any stray dissenters?"

Naive, Teia thought. Then again, she didn't think Yuwen would much approve of her tactics with the Dawnbreakers. "Erisia had its own rebel movement."

"Had?" Yuwen repeated. "They're no longer operational?"

She ignored the twinge in her heart. "I made my stance on rebellions clear."

The emperor's response was a weary sigh. "I often wonder if this is my own doing," he confided. "If I hadn't exiled Ba—if I hadn't left him alive—I doubt the Red Mountain would have anyone to rally behind."

The admission caught Teia by surprise. She was convinced

she'd heard him incorrectly, as she said, "You chose to exile your father?"

"There was debate about it, when I announced his imprisonment—arguments from every official in my employment, families who begged for his execution."

"You couldn't do it."

"He wasn't a good man, Teia. I *know* that. But he's my blood—and no matter how hard I try, I carry him with me."

It was a loose end that remained unresolved—a moment of weakness, an act of love. And for one terrifying second, Teia nearly told Yuwen that she understood. This flavor of grief was one she recognized—it matched the wounds that she bore, scarred deep against bone. She thought about confiding in him about the last six months, the ghosts that trailed each of her steps.

Alara. Tobias. Kyra.

"Sometimes," Teia said, "we're shaped by our circumstances."

"Our circumstances," Yuwen provided, "and our families."

There was that sadness again, carving into each word. When Teia observed Yuwen, she caught dark circles beneath a thin layer of powder, his eyes glittering as he rotated toward the oil lamp. With a twitch of his fingers, a water droplet formed in the air. It quivered above the wick, before dousing the flame with a hiss.

She wished she had more to offer—words of comfort, a gentle hug. But in the end, Teia was quiet. Her ghosts were her own. She'd learn to exorcise them eventually, far from the grandeur of Taijin Palace.

Instead, she gathered her skirts and dipped her head. She reached for the door, the bronze handle glistening against the mahogany frame.

The silver memory shone behind them as they exited the room in silence.

Chapter Seven

It was an exceedingly unpleasant carriage ride to the loneliest place in the world.

Aside from Teia, Jin, and Enna, there wasn't a single soul on the pebbled beach. The shore was blanketed by a gray cloud of fog, which wrapped Teia in its embrace. A graveyard of black stones stretched beneath them, tumbled smooth by the sea. As she stared into the haze, her skin stinging from the tiny pricks of mist, a pillared building rose out from the water, gleaming with a dull luster.

"*That's* the Archive?"

"That's it," Jin confirmed.

There was no bridge, no road through the choppy bay. Several abandoned boats had been flung against the shoreline, swathed with moss and speckled in barnacles. The one farthest away was tangled in the remnants of a fishing net.

Enna kicked viciously at a stray pebble. "Remind me again why Yuwen isn't here?"

The emperor had seemed genuinely regretful when he'd sent them off that morning, like he was missing out on some grand adventure. But despite how much he'd bemoaned not being able to accompany them, Teia was certain he had received the better end of the deal.

"Yuwen is welcoming governors for Kashan," Jin said. Then, a disapproving tint coloring his tone, he added, "I already mentioned this in the carriage."

"So sorry," Enna said, not sounding the least bit apologetic. "I only listen to people I find interesting, and I'm afraid you don't quite meet that criterion."

The adviser scowled. "Must you be so *rude*?"

"I'm honest."

"You're an adviser to your queen. A *representative*."

"So what do you represent?"

"Honor. Integrity."

"The merits of inducing someone into an early sleep?"

"With manners like that, you're no better than a common thief."

"If you want, I'm happy to show you just how similar to a *common thief* I can be—"

"Enna," Teia interrupted. The other girl had a dangerous glint in her eye, the kind she wore before jamming her ice pick into someone's ears. Before she and Jin could devolve into another round of arguments, Teia said, "This Memory Keeper—Hebei. He lives here by himself?"

Jin directed one last glare at Enna. "The groundskeeper is on the island as well, along with his little boy. But aside from that—yes. The emperor has offered Hebei housing in Taijin, but he continues to refuse."

"He likes the isolation?"

"He prefers it."

"It must be the ambience," Teia said. Of all the places to keep memories, Yuwen couldn't have chosen somewhere happier?

"The building used to be in a better state," the adviser offered. "It was once a nobleman's manor—he had it built entirely out of silver to demonstrate his wealth."

"Respectable," Enna muttered. "I can see why the Society of Thieves likes it here."

Jin glanced back. "What was that?"

"I said it's magnificent what a *society* can accomplish." She offered Jin a terse smile. "I like your earrings. Very pretty."

He reached up with a frown, tugging at the jade stones. "When the nobleman was killed in the Ten Years War, the manor was left empty until Yuwen purchased it. By then, most of the silver had tarnished. The groundskeeper was brought in for restorations, but it's a massive task."

"The Ten Years War?" Teia said. "What's that?"

"The war fought between Shaylan and Erisia. I believe you know it as the Shaylani War."

She hadn't considered that the Shaylani might have christened the conflict with a different name. It was a time before her own, when both countries set out to lay claim to the Dark Sea. The result was years of battle, thousands dead, and a flimsy peace accord, in an attempt to prevent another decade of fighting.

Yet even after all the lessons she'd received on the war, Teia had never understood why the sea was something to be conquered. As she peered again toward the Archive, standing tall against the unwavering fog, she wondered how memories had been stored before. She imagined a cozy wing of Taijin Palace, lamps beaming from hidden corners, silver spheres arranged on rosewood shelves, stretching as far as the eye could see.

"All this because of Feng," Teia murmured.

She'd meant the statement for just herself, but Jin recoiled at the name. "Yuwen told you?"

Teia nodded. "You knew his father?" she asked. The adviser's parents might not have been in Feng's court, but Jin had grown up with Yuwen. Surely he'd had some interaction with the former emperor.

Emotion broke through Jin's face, shifting like the tide, too fast for Teia to read. A moment later, his expression had calmed. "What I think of him isn't important," Jin said. "All that matters is that he's gone."

He stepped forward, leveling both hands to his chest. As he set his palms together, an odd moment of quiet blew over the bay. The water seemed to still in anticipation as Jin's brow creased, wrestling with an invisible force.

When he spread his arms apart, the water split in two.

It wasn't the same control that Yuwen had exhibited in the Dark Sea, but a narrow walkway slithered through the center of the bay. Water lifted back from the muddy stretches of silt, falling aside reluctantly. The Archive beckoned, a beacon against the raven-black waves.

"Go," Jin growled, his arms trembling. "I can't hold it for long."

They hurried through the muck—Enna and Teia in front, Jin at the rear. As they kicked their way past brown clumps of seaweed and fat white shells, the sea closed quickly behind them, washing over the path. Teia could feel the water's disgust as it regained its form, its irritation at being shunted aside. If Jin lost his focus, even for a minute, they would be buried beneath the crushing weight of water.

She tried to banish an image of *The Inferno*'s crew, dragged into the frothing deep. *I'll succeed,* Teia vowed, as she pressed forward, mud clinging to the soles of her shoes. *I'll honor their memories if it's the last thing I do.*

When they finally took the remaining few steps onto dry land, Jin dropped his hands. The tide rushed over the path, roaring in approval. The adviser staggered, panting, waving off Teia's offer to help. "Fine," he wheezed. "Just need . . . a minute."

After he had recovered enough to rise, they trudged up the paved road, picking their way across the worn cobblestones. It was overrun by weeds, stray thistles poking at Teia's ankles, but there were small signs of life here and there—proof of the groundskeeper and his son. A wooden top lay discarded in the patchy grass. A pile of brambles had been heaped beside an overturned bucket.

"What a place to grow up," Enna mumbled to Teia. "At least we had activities in the Flats. What does the kid do here? Talk to grasshoppers?"

"Some people would prefer that to the company of criminals."

"Nonsense. It's excellent character development."

At the entrance of the manor, oil lamps burned within elaborate metal sconces, keeping away the chill that enveloped the rest of the island. Two Naga stood before the wooden door. Their black robes flapped in the howling wind. Their tattoos were visible in the light, the tail of the dragon flickering as they moved in unison, blades made from water forming in their grasps.

Jin called out to them in Shaylani. They exchanged a few tense words, before the adviser pointed toward Teia. The Naga on the left inspected her, his affect flat, before uttering a cursory grunt.

Jin gestured to Teia. "You're free to go. He says that Hebei is waiting inside."

She ascended the weathered stairs with Enna at her heels. Yet when the thief treaded onto the first step, the Naga to the right extended his sword, blocking her way. Jin listened intently as the man spoke in a guttural voice.

"It's customary that only the person seeking a Memory Keeper's service should venture into the Archive," the adviser translated. "He asks that only Teia proceed."

"Customary for who?" Teia said.

Jin relayed the message to the Naga, who shrugged. "Apparently those are the orders he received."

Normally, Teia would have respected tradition. But she was about to enter the home of a dead noble, where she'd allow a stranger to comb through her thoughts. There was self-sufficiency, and then there was stupidity. Teia liked to think she knew which was which—and although she didn't dole out trust freely, Enna van Apt had grown into the exception.

Teia lowered her chin at the Naga. "Move," she snapped. And after a long moment, the guard did, falling aside to allow Enna to pass.

The door was marked with the stamp of a seashell, which had long been chipped away. Teia gave it a firm push. It creaked aside, the hinges squeaking in discordant symphony. Inside, the main hallway was completely dark. A single strip of light shone out beneath the square frame of another door, glowing at the end of an elongated corridor.

"On second thought," Enna said thinly, "I would have been just fine staying outside."

They crossed the stone tiles, the air heavy with the stench of mildew. Teia felt for the handle of the second door—and when she pulled it aside, a gasp slipped through her lips.

The room was as large as a banquet hall, with a grand staircase extending down to the main floor. At the bottom, rows of silver pedestals filled the space, each with a sphere resting in the center. They cast the chamber in their glow, reflecting dreamscapes on the ceiling, bathing the place in an unearthly shine.

Teia descended the stairs in twos, her heart thudding with wonder. The pedestals were marked with individual dates. Below, a row of Shaylani characters had been notched into silver—presumably a description, although Teia couldn't decipher what they meant.

If each sphere was a memory, a moment in time contained within water, what traces of her parents could she find here? Yuwen had said most of the memories had been destroyed by Feng, but had someone managed to save one of Calla? Teia hated the hope that squeezed into her chest, the odd lump that rose within her throat.

For a few minutes, Teia was utterly consumed by her task, lifting spheres from the podiums. These were all memories of strangers, people she'd never seen before. Figures draped in gold-threaded robes and intricate jewelry, who erected statues and stood over applauding crowds, sweeping aside the tide as they roared in triumph—and yet every image sent a searing hunger gnawing against her.

One of the men had Teia's nose, another the shape of her eyes. The woman who'd parted the tide had Calla's wry smile.

These are my ancestors, Teia thought. *My history.*

All her life, she had never known herself to be surrounded by family.

"Boss," Enna said. The thief was in another row, examining one of the spheres. "Have you seen this one?"

Teia wound closer. The date on the pedestal was from just two years before, but the sphere in front of Enna glistened brighter than the rest, with great swirls of silver clouding beneath the surface. As Teia stooped toward it, something jolted within her, a shock that stung through her veins. She heard the water call out, compelling her. It had a memory to show her—a memory she needed to see.

Come, it wheedled. *Look.*

"Boss," Enna said warningly, as Teia reached out as if in a trance. "Are you sure you want to do that—"

The sphere rose off the pedestal, hovering toward Teia. At her touch, it ascended into the air, unfurling eagerly to present an image. The scene grew clearer, sharpening into view, and Teia's jaw dropped.

"Oh," Enna said. "Is that Taijin?"

It *was*—and yet the palace was in flames, with bodies strewn on either side of the ruined hallway. Blades had been embedded into the walls. Paintings were slashed and statues tipped over. The images jerked unsteadily, as if the memory holder was limping down the corridor. A trail of blood spotted against the floor, leading to a set of massive iron doors.

At the memory holder's command, water twisted outward, melding into a battering ram. The doors flew open to reveal a vast chamber. Wide blue pillars flanked a wooden throne, set before three massive panels. The two on either side showed Armina and the Serkawr, while the one in the center featured a snarling dragon. It was adrift in a sea of clouds, a pearl clutched in its claws.

And there, sitting atop the throne, was Li Feng.

He appeared older than he'd been in the other memories. Wrinkles etched into his face. A gash extended from his forehead to his chin, bloodying the neck of his elaborate blue robes. A heap of water writhed above his palms, reshaping into different beasts—a tiger, a snake, a lion.

Yet when Feng saw the memory holder, his expression

crumpled. Water collapsed back to liquid, as his arms fell to his sides.

"Yuwen," he whispered. *"Heshen?"*

It was a word that Teia understood, drawn from the rudimentary phrases she'd learned before traveling to Shaylan.

Why?

Yuwen didn't answer. When he snapped his fingers, water swelled before him. It assumed the form of a dragon, its body filling the length of the room, spilling out the doors. Horns sprouted atop its head, as it released a low growl.

From the throne, Feng hadn't moved. *"Heshen?"* he said again. *"Heshen?"*

Yuwen's hand rose. He must have wiped at his eyes, because everything flickered, images stuttering with black. Yet when the scene cleared once more, Teia could see the blood smeared in Yuwen's palm. It had been muddled by an odd reflectiveness, which beamed against his skin.

Tears.

Then he lowered his hand, and the dragon surged forward, aimed straight for Feng.

A choked cry flew through the Archive, echoing off the chamber walls. Teia cursed. The memory faded, the sphere returning to its original form. She set it back on its pedestal quickly, before rotating toward the stairs.

There was nobody there.

"What was that?" Enna rasped. A dagger peeked out from her fist. Her stance was wary, braced for attack.

"That way," Teia hissed. There was a door she hadn't noticed before, hidden beneath the base of the staircase.

Together, they crept along, approaching the door slowly. It had been left ajar, with an oil lamp burning on the table. It illuminated the calligraphy scrolls that bunched in the corner, the overturned pot of ink that pooled onto the tile.

There, his head resting on a sheaf of papers, was the body of a man.

He was facing away from them, unmoving on the desk. A single streak of snowy hair protruded through his black curls. A jade bracelet dangled from his wrist. As Teia padded forward, stretching high to overlook the body, she could see the foam that trickled from the man's mouth, dribbling down his neck.

Goddess.

The Memory Keeper had been poisoned—that much was clear. The offending teacup rested on the floor, broken shards crunching beneath Teia's feet. But it was like nothing she had seen before, as she assessed the thick, porous substance that coated Hebei's front. The linen fabric had sizzled away from the foam, revealing clammy skin beneath.

Teia knew the Dawnbreakers' calling card when she saw it—and there was only one person in the Five Kingdoms who could have created such a poison.

"Enna," Teia said. "We have to go—"

Then came the click of a revolver.

"You move," came a voice, "and I'll put a bullet in your skull."

It had been an amateur decision to keep her back to the door, and more foolish still to think this wasn't a trap. Teia went rigid. After the last six months with her phantoms, she knew who the voice belonged to—the soft dip in tone, the iron will beneath.

Kyra Medoh had returned.

Chapter Eight

Kyra." Teia's voice was calm as it rustled through the room—a minor miracle, considering the adrenaline that coursed in her veins, raking embers through her blood. A thousand questions cluttered her mind, but none more urgent than the weapon clasped in Kyra's hand. "Put down the gun."

Kyra's laugh was hollow. "I listened to you once, Teia. What makes you think I'd do it again?"

"Because you're not going to shoot me."

"Um," Enna said. "I wouldn't be so sure about that, Boss."

Teia flicked a look at Enna. "It's true," she said smoothly. "You might want to put a bullet in my head, but I'm betting Lehm told you not to."

"Maybe he did," Kyra said. And Teia was struck by how *empty* she sounded, her voice drained of any warmth. "But you're not the only one who knows things, Teia."

Teia bit down on the inside of her cheek. "Such as?"

"Such as how you freed me from the catacombs. Such as if you wanted me dead, you would have left me to rot in the Golden Palace." She let out a hollow chuckle. "You *cared* about me, Teia. You still do. So even though you could drown me where I stand—incapacitate me by some other means—you won't. I know you won't."

She was right. With enough internal convincing, Teia might have spurred herself to action. Yet for a girl who had concocted more schemes than she could count, her mind had gone frighteningly blank. She couldn't remember a single step of the plans she'd made for being confronted by the Dawnbreakers, washed away by the horrible cold that pressed into Kyra's tone.

Stupid, Teia thought fiercely, as she cocked her head to the side. "All this for a stalemate?" she said. "If you wanted to say hello, we could have sat down for tea." She rotated cautiously, her hands drawn before her. It was the first time she'd seen Kyra in over half a year.

The rebel champion had always been slight, but now her face was gaunt, cast in shadow. Her fitted jacket clung to her form, her black hair braided to her waist. There was something behind her eyes that hadn't existed before, something hard and unyielding.

"You don't get to make jokes," Kyra said. "Not after what you did."

"Noted. But since we've established you're not going to shoot me—"

"What about Enna?"

Teia froze. "What *about* her?"

The thief shifted uncomfortably. "If it's all the same to you," she said, "I'd like to be left out of this."

Kyra ignored her. "It's just as you said, Teia," she continued. "Lehm wants you alive—so you come with me. You go quietly. And if you move out of turn—if you so much as snap your fingers—I'm going to shoot Enna instead."

"About that," Teia said. She kept her focus trained on the

barrel of the revolver, reflective against the light. "I wouldn't do that if I were you."

"And why is that?"

"Easy," Teia said. "You don't know when to duck."

She was already in motion, grasping for the threads of heat around them. In one movement, Teia compressed the threads into a woven knot. Before Kyra could react, Teia flung the spurt of fire forward, knocking the rebel champion off her feet.

Kyra went flying back, skidding out of the room. But in that span of a second, as smoke petered into the space, the revolver discharged, the shot cracking through the air. Enna buckled with a shout. Terror arched through Teia, as she threw herself sideways, positioned squarely before the thief, gazing down at her frantically.

"Enna—"

"It's just a graze," Enna panted. Sweat glistened on her forehead as she pulled herself upright. "She has awful aim."

Teia cast a look at the door—but Kyra had disappeared back into the Archive. Quickly, she stooped down, ripping a strip of fabric from her skirt. "I didn't think she'd shoot you," Teia said roughly. The admission stung of failure—a calculation she hadn't accounted for—but Enna wasn't one for holding grudges.

"I didn't either," the thief said, as she accepted the makeshift bandage. "I'll be fine, Teia. Go!"

Teia managed a nod before sprinting from the room. As she glanced around the main chamber, the spheres glimmered out at her prettily. "Kyra!" she yelled, her own voice rippling back to her.

She was lifted in the air, blown sideways in an explosion of flames. Teia's vision spotted white. Suddenly, she was on her front, struggling for breath. Before her, a row of pedestals had been overturned, marking where the blast had struck. Without the podiums to help maintain their shapes, the spheres had imploded, puddles of water seeping into the floor.

The sight sent a vibrant anger thundering through Teia. She rolled aside just in time, as Kyra sliced down in an arc of fire. Her flame caught harmlessly on the stone. She wrenched back toward Teia, her lips drawn in a growl, a new flame sculpting above her hand.

"I've thought about this every day since your guards dragged me into your throne room. Since you had me paraded like a dog in front of your court, while you admitted you'd given up the Dawnbreakers—"

Kyra cast the flames forward, as Teia threw out both hands. The tips of her fingers tingled with warmth. She staggered to her feet, and the ball of fire melted at her touch, deflating into a heap of sparks.

"Whatever Lehm has told you is a lie," Teia said. "Listen to me, Kyra. He wants the Serkawr. It's why he brought you to Shaylan—"

The rebel champion didn't slow. With each step she took, she hurled another bolt of fire. Teia seized hold of each one, deflecting the blows as they came. One of them landed on the staircase, engulfing the steps in flames. Pedestals collapsed, crashing to the floor. More memories burst around them, showering them in water.

Teia feinted, swiping out her left arm, but Kyra merely drew her flames around a pedestal. Fire engulfed the stand, lifting it high. The rebel champion threw it at Teia, who was a second too slow to react. The pedestal caught Teia on the shoulder, spinning her off balance. She landed hard on the floor, dazed, pain lancing down her arm. By some miracle, nothing had broken.

Teia heaved herself upward, feeling for her shoulder. Blood dripped from a fresh cut on her forehead.

Fine, she thought between gritted teeth. If Kyra wanted a fight, then that was what she would get.

As the rebel girl leapt her way, Teia seized the heat in the air. She met Kyra's flame with her own, crimson on maroon. When Kyra lashed at her, Teia ducked down, before aiming a fiery strike. Kyra stumbled back, her jaw beginning to swell. She slammed her hands together, and a wall of flames materialized above Teia, a second ceiling that lifted high, hovering precariously before heaving downward.

Heat bent toward Teia, wrapping her in a dome. Fire shielded her, as Kyra's wall fell. There was a moment when everything went red, an odd ringing settling into Teia's ears. She could have believed this was death, as she cleared her shield. Cautiously, she gripped tight to the heat, searching the smoke for signs of movement.

There.

Teia fashioned her flames into a hissing viper, its head as large as her torso. When she saw Kyra once more, blurred against the smoke, she sent the snake forward with all her might, speeding faster than any bullet. The rebel champion gasped. She crossed both arms before her protectively, but the snake slammed into her, pinning her down.

Then Teia was on top of her. As she snatched for the water within Kyra, anger swept away any rational thought.

She shot Enna. She wants me dead. She wrecked the Archive.

Rage painted over Teia's vision. Water shouted with glee, twining between her fingers. The liquid in Kyra's lungs reacted to Teia's will, just as it had when they'd first met in the Golden

Palace, all those months before. Yet there was more, too, just beneath the surface—tiny pinpricks that had emerged throughout the rebel champion's body. Each was a note of water within her blood, her veins. They sang out at Teia. They dared her toward them.

When Teia reached for the glowing points, Kyra's arms went still. The rebel girl was alive—her eyes wide with fury, her legs thrashing as she choked on water. But even as she kicked feverishly, squirming beneath Teia, her hands had flattened to the ground, as if kept in place by invisible tacks.

It was an interesting phenomenon, but Teia didn't have time to dwell on what it might mean. A voice had broken into her mind, louder than the rest. Its whisper wrapped around her, roping against her throat. *Kill her,* it murmured. *End it.*

Teia had allowed her feelings to win once before. She'd let the Dawnbreakers go, and look where that had led. Hebei was dead, along with any possible chance of convincing the governors. Yet without Kyra—without commoner's flame—Lehm couldn't raise the Serkawr. What did it matter if he wormed his way into the Shaylani court? What did it matter if he found the Seascript? The Five Kingdoms would be safe. *Erisia* would be safe.

Kill her. End it.

It would be so easy. One pull, one twitch of her fingers. As the Archive danced with flames, memories evaporating in the blaze, Teia stared down at Kyra. The chamber was alight with the sounds of a wildfire. The crackle of embers. The rasp of flames.

The wail of a child's scream, as it cut through the blistering inferno.

Chapter Nine

At first, Teia thought it was a diversion. A trick, to throw her off guard.

But when the cry came again, Teia remembered what Jin had said about the manor's inhabitants. The wooden top she'd seen outside, strewn carelessly in the grass.

The groundskeeper is on the island as well, along with his little boy.

Panic overtook Teia, even as some part of her resisted. *No.* She was so close to a resolution—to stanching the threat that haunted her nightmares. As she stared down at Kyra, a new resolve beat against her temples, sounding out a frantic rhythm. *Kill her. End it.*

I can't.

Maybe it was a truth Teia had known all along, from the second she'd heard the rebel champion's voice. Because this was *Kyra*. Here was the same girl who'd split scones with her over breakfast, who'd whispered stories about her childhood and murmured dreams about the future. Their friendship was hollow, flayed open by betrayal—and yet it hovered over Teia nonetheless, threatening to crush her.

She clenched her jaw, determined to stamp out this final

thread of weakness. But when it became clear that she couldn't, her hands refusing to move, her pulse hammering in her chest, it was almost a relief to loosen her stance. Fine. *Fine.* Not all her plans had to end in murder, even if some of her best ones did. A child might be trapped in the blaze, but that was nothing more than an unfortunate casualty. Teia would distract Kyra, find Enna, and leave this cursed manor behind. They could return to Taijin and concoct a story, something about Lehm killing Hebei, which wouldn't necessarily be *false.* The Memory Keeper hadn't confirmed Teia's fears on Lehm, but his death might spur the Shaylani.

Except Teia had the sudden image of being much younger, when Jura set her aflame in the palace gardens. The vision of her half brother was so real, so terrifying, that she winced, glancing again toward the blaze. Teia had used children in her schemes before, blackmailing parents and maintaining leverage, but what would she become if she turned tail for safety as a child burned in the fire she'd helped create?

Jura was gone, dead and buried, but she hadn't killed him to walk in his shadow.

Dammit, Teia thought. She drew back the water quickly, emptying Kyra's lungs and pushing away from the rebel champion. Of all the days for her to develop morals, why did it have to be this one?

As she rushed for the stairs, something whistled past her. Teia rotated back, severing a halo of fire before it could make contact. As the two halves disintegrated, the embers winking to dust, she saw Kyra advancing on her, summoning for new heat.

"You don't get to run, Teia," the rebel girl growled. She had recovered remarkably well from a near drowning—or maybe she was propelled by the same bout of adrenaline that crackled through Teia.

"There's a child in the manor, Kyra. We have to go find him—"

"Since when have you cared? Since when have you cared for anyone but yourself?"

"I did what I had to!" Teia roared. "But are you going to let someone die because you want revenge? Have you really changed that much?"

"I didn't change! You did! You—"

There was no time to argue ethics. Teia spun her hand outward, releasing a spurt of fire. It caught Kyra across the stomach, sending her staggering. As the other girl went to her knees, winded from the blow, Teia hurried up the staircase, tearing through the flames to enter the hallway.

All around her, fire clawed up the walls. It danced against the floor, racing down the corridor. She could see the main entrance far to her left, a pinprick of light wavering through the gaps. *Where is Jin?* Teia thought suddenly. Surely, the adviser must have noticed the commotion by now. Had sounds of the fight been contained within the main chamber? Did he think she could take care of herself?

If she left to find Jin, she'd lose whatever precious minutes she had before the flames reached the groundskeeper's son—and so Teia sped on in the opposite direction, forging deeper into the building. Smoke lodged within her chest. It drifted up her nose. She doubled over in a fit of coughs, eyes smarting from the fumes.

Unwittingly, she thought of something her father had once told her when she'd first come into her powers. Ren had sat with her on that sprawling green lawn, the sun glimmering down from a clear blue sky. He'd taken her hand, teaching her about the different strands of heat, showing her how to weave a flame.

We're Carthans, he'd told her warmly. *And Carthans have never been afraid of fire.*

Now, soot streaking her face, her clothes melting off her back, Teia wished for Ren. She wasn't afraid of *fire,* but the consequences of what came next. Inside the manor, the flames had spread too far and too fast. Even as she evaluated the threads of heat, Teia knew it was impossible to extinguish the blaze alone. There was no beginning and end to the strands. Everything had melded into an indecipherable heap, like old jewelry matted in a drawer.

How was she going to find a child in this mess?

"Hello?" Teia called. Her shout was lost in the flames, barely audible to her own ears. She tried again as she soldiered on, checking each of the rooms, breathing into the collar of her robes. "Are you there?"

From around the corner, there came a stifled sob. Teia quickened her pace, flicking aside a patch of flames. "Hello?" she said once more and was rewarded with a quavering voice, spoken from behind a closed door.

She pushed it aside to enter a cozy room, with just enough space for a few simple furnishings. A bed had been squeezed beside an open chest of toys. An assortment of books and dolls littered the floor. A handmade kite rested on the desk, shaped like a massive koi. Patchwork quilts in every color were stacked on a wooden chair.

The little boy was around eight years old. He'd wedged himself between the bed and the wall, his knees bunched to his chest. When he saw Teia, he scrambled up, running to her with a wordless cry. Before she could object, he'd fastened his spindly arms around her waist, sobbing into her robes.

She took him by the wrist and lugged him into the hallway. Teia's throat blistered as she tried to swallow, gauging the flames that lapped hungrily toward them. High against the ceiling, she spotted the jumbled threads of heat, overlaid like a crooked web against the yellow tongues of flame. As the boy clung to her legs, Teia combed through the strands. When she grabbed several in her hands, they resisted fiercely, stubborn to the end.

Come on, Teia thought, planting her feet against stone. Her head spun, heavy from the clouds of smoke.

This time, when she yanked at the threads again, a sliver of fire vanished, cutting a swath through the hallway. Teia jerked her head toward the path. "Run," she managed.

The flames bellowed in anger, but the boy seemed to understand. He started to sprint through the narrow pathway, as Teia moved shakily behind him, straining to keep the flames at bay. Her muscles trembled from exertion. She had never tried to control so much at once, and she felt its weight press against her, sinking her to the floor.

She had gone to one knee when she heard the little boy shout. Through watering eyes, Teia could make out the end of the hallway, the door that led to the exit—and the bubbling flame that had escaped her command, leaping to meet the child.

He cowered back in fear as the flames rose higher, sensing a victory. But as they crashed down over the little boy, a figure appeared from the blackened staircase, vaulting over the ruined banister. She thrust out her arms, and fire peeled away, forced back toward the ceiling. The boy gawked up at Kyra. He was dazed but unharmed, awed as she lifted her voice.

"Go!"

As he pitched himself out the door, Teia fought to stand. Fire arched around Kyra in a golden fold. She saw the threads as well—the shining points of the web, beautiful against the din. As the rebel champion seized a portion in her grip, the web sputtered ever so slightly. The flames around them dropped in height.

Teia stretched, regaining her hold on the strands. Warmth surged through her limbs. The colors flashed in harmony: red and orange, yellow and blue.

Together, as one, Teia and Kyra *pulled.*

The strands of heat snapped, like strings plucked off an instrument. As Teia reeled back, her legs shaking, the flames shrank to nothing, disappearing into thin air. The manor became eerily quiet. There was nothing left besides smoking lumps of ash, smoldering gently on the ground.

Teia met Kyra's gaze. "I thought you didn't believe me," she said.

"I didn't. I still don't."

"Then why—"

"Do you want to know what happened that day your military broke into our base?" Kyra's voice was hard. "They kicked open the doors. They fired bullets into the ceiling, and the chandelier came crashing down. Someone was crushed beneath—I couldn't see who. All I saw was his arm twitching under the crystal, but there was no path to help, not with all the people in the way."

Despite warning General Miran to proceed with caution, Teia had always known that there would be casualties when storming the Dawnbreaker base. She'd read the reports, too, ruminating over each page obsessively, combing through the sentences and demanding more details. In some twisted way, maybe she'd hoped to do penance—like possessing knowledge of the raid might lessen the knot in her stomach.

"Kyra—"

"I came back for that boy because I'm not watching someone die again while I stand aside and do nothing. But to *believe you,* Teia?" She jutted out her chin. "When your soldiers put me in shackles and dragged me away, I wished for death. I prayed for it, because it was better than being tortured for secrets. But then I kept picturing you and Tobias and Alara—and even when they brought me into the palace, I swore I wouldn't say a thing. Not a word, no matter what they did. And when I saw you standing there like a monarch—a *queen*—"

Her black eyes bore into Teia's, searching through her soul. "Tell me," Kyra rasped, "are you even sorry for what you did? Do you ever think of us, when you're sitting on your throne? Do you laugh about how foolish we were to trust you?"

Her words cracked a dam within Teia. In an instant, she thought of all the things she longed to tell Kyra. How the past six months had been a mass of endless nights and awful dreams. How Teia had lain awake in her chambers until the sun kissed the sky, or else jolted awake in a cold sweat, charred trails raked down the length of her blankets, the Dawnbreakers' faces blooming like bruises against the dark.

Teia should have retreated. She should have fled. Emotions collided within her, shoving a knife into her ribs. She hadn't expected to feel such *sorrow,* so thick and heavy that it nearly smothered her.

I'm sorry, she wanted to scream. *I'm sorry.*

Yet how could she, after all that she'd done? It would have added insult to injury, provided a false layer of truth after the dust had settled. Teia still agonized over betraying the Dawnbreakers—but while her sins were inked in blood, she had accomplished what she'd promised. She had bettered Frisia. She had chosen her country.

For all those sleepless nights and horrendous dreams, she had never once regretted taking the crown.

So Teia did what she was best at. She collected her thoughts and lifted her head and pushed away the throbbing ache in her chest. "I meant what I said," Teia managed. "Everything I told you back in Erisia is true. Lehm betrayed the Dawnbreakers to Jura. He wanted us to fail during our run for the Morning Star."

Kyra scoffed. "Is that why you're in Shaylan? You're chasing that idiotic rumor about Lehm and the Serkawr—"

"It's not a rumor. He needs both water and fire to bring it to shore. He's going to align himself with the Shaylani court, which is why he brought you here."

"I didn't have anywhere else to go," Kyra said coldly. "Don't forget that you were the one who banished me from Erisia."

"You have every right to be angry—I know you do. But if Lehm manages to sway the Shaylani, he's going to summon the Serkawr to destroy the Five Kingdoms. It's why he had you poison the Memory Keeper who lives here, so I couldn't bring proof back to the palace."

"I didn't poison anyone. I slipped him a sleeping draught to keep him out of harm's way."

A hysterical laugh fell from Teia's lips. "You don't honestly believe that, do you? Hebei is dead, Kyra. And that little boy would be, too, if you hadn't had your magnificent change of heart—"

"*My* change of heart—"

Just then, a rustling came from behind Teia, the tread of bootsteps crunching over debris. She spun around, steeling herself for another attack. There must have been a back entrance to the manor, one that remained unsecured—but when she glanced into the hallway, there was nobody there. The corridor remained empty, save for the scorched lumps of furniture.

And yet Kyra must have seen something. The rebel champion—who'd been so eager to capture Teia—hesitated. She cast Teia one final look, brimming with hatred. She stalked past her without another word, her braid coiled down her back.

A few seconds later, Kyra Medoh was gone, swallowed into the charred remains of the once-lovely manor.

Chapter Ten

When Teia hobbled outside the manor, she discovered a body slumped in the dirt.

She recognized the trim cut of his hair, the pale green robes flung around him. As she hurried over to Jin, stopping to retrieve his spectacles from a patch of dirt, Teia glimpsed the bloody gash across his forehead.

Goddess, she thought, dismayed. Then, with absolute certainty: *Yuwen is going to have my head.*

"Don't worry," someone called out. "He's fine. Kyra didn't have the decency to finish the job."

Enna was slouched by one of the bent willows—disheveled, disgruntled, and very much alive. She stowed away her dagger and sauntered over to Teia. Without preamble, she said, "How was your chat with Kyra?"

Heartbreaking. Horrific.

"Fine," Teia said. "How's your arm?"

Enna patted the top of her bicep carefully. A thin layer of red had seeped through the makeshift bandages, but she seemed to be in decent spirits. "Better. Did I tell you about this handy trick I learned from the Society of Thieves?"

"How to steal the wheels off a moving carriage?"

"That too," Enna acknowledged. "But more recently, a former healer taught me about blocking different nerve points."

Teia lifted a brow. "Don't people usually do that when attacking others?"

"And?"

"And you did it to yourself?"

"Why not?" Enna said. She poked at her right arm for good measure, and it flopped limply against her finger. "It's temporary, it's convenient—and I can't feel a thing on this side now."

"You're right," Teia intoned. "Very handy." She frowned. Jin was out cold, but the Naga who'd been guarding the manor were nowhere to be found. "Were the Naga here when you escaped?"

"No. I made a lap around the manor before you came out. There's nothing here but crickets and grasshoppers—although, if you want my opinion, the Naga are probably halfway back to Taijin by now."

"They *ran*?"

"Think about it, Boss. This is the kingdom of water. You're one of the emperor's guards, posted on this terrible ink stain of an island. You're bored. You're tired. You're wondering when you can break for your next meal—"

"Is there a point here?"

"The *point,*" Enna said indignantly, "is that when a girl shooting fire out of her hands charges you out of nowhere, wouldn't the natural instinct be to bolt? Even if the Naga are the best of the best, that would be enough to spook anyone."

"I suppose."

"You don't sound convinced."

"I'll believe it when I see it."

"Well, how's this for believing? I didn't see the Naga, but there was a kid that made it out of the manor. I think he's the groundskeeper's son—his da met him at the bottom of the path." Enna whistled. "That little boy must be the luckiest bastard alive. He sprinted right out of the flames, and didn't have a scratch on him."

"A miracle," Teia said flatly, just as Jin released a groan. The adviser's eyelids fluttered. He rolled onto his side, feeling gingerly at his forehead.

"What—?"

"Kyra Medoh," Enna said promptly. "Be thankful that she just bashed you over the head. She shot me."

"She *shot* you?"

Bludgeoning someone didn't seem like Kyra's style, but perhaps the rebel champion had changed tactics. Teia handed the adviser back his spectacles. "What do you remember?"

"I don't know. I was here, waiting for you to return. Someone hit me from behind." Blood beaded down his cheek, crusting the side of his jaw. "Kyra—she ambushed you?"

"She also killed Hebei. And the Archive . . ." Teia didn't want to think of the smoking remains within the manor. "It's destroyed, Jin."

He'd grown paler with each new piece of information, until his coloring resembled a sheet of paper. "Anything else?" he said weakly, as he slid the spectacles back onto his nose.

Teia thought about sharing what had happened in the Archive, when she'd warped the water inside Kyra, trapping her arms in place. For some reason, this didn't seem like the appropriate time, particularly with what she intended to show Jin next.

She pulled a jade bracelet from her pocket and placed it in Jin's hand. The green stones were bound together in a clustered formation. A pattern of three interlocked spheres was stamped along the silver clasp.

Enna rose on her toes, peeking over Jin's shoulder. "Did you happen to go shopping, Boss?"

"No," Jin said quietly, examining the bracelet. "This was Hebei's. It was a gift from Yuwen, after he agreed to take up residence in the Archive."

Teia had gone back for it before she'd exited the manor, stepping past the toppled pedestals to enter the Memory Keeper's study. She'd wriggled it loose from the dead man's wrist, recoiling from the clammy feel of his skin. "If the governors want proof of the danger Lehm poses, I intend to bring it to them."

"Smart," Enna remarked. "I would hate to share carriage space with a corpse."

Jin simply looked dazed. "We have to return to Taijin," he said. He sounded utterly miserable about the task ahead. "When Yuwen finds out . . ."

It wasn't *only* the dead Memory Keeper or the razed Archive, although that certainly would have been enough. Teia glanced around. Despite Enna's theories on what had happened to the guards outside, an uneasy feeling needled into her.

"Jin," she said. "Were the Naga with you when you were attacked?"

"Yes." He brushed off his robes, swiping away traces of dirt. "You haven't seen them? I assumed they'd gone inside the manor—"

"Would they have run after Kyra struck you?"

"Never," he replied instantly.

"Are you sure?"

"The Naga wouldn't flee. It's in their training, their beliefs. To abandon a fight would be a fate worse than death."

The sinking sensation grew. If what Jin said was true, then things were about to become infinitely worse.

"Kyra wouldn't have been able to overcome two Naga," Teia said slowly. This she knew with absolute certainty. The rebel champion had improved in the months they'd been apart. Yet barring some divine act from the Goddess, she lacked the skills to overpower two of the emperor's imperial guards—and even if she had, where were the corpses?

Jin hesitated. "What are you implying?" he said. The words came out stiffly, like the adviser's own honor was being called into question. "The Naga are loyal to the emperor, sworn to serve until their last breath."

"Everyone is loyal, until their allegiances change," Teia said. "Yuwen sent word ahead that we were coming. And I don't think it's a coincidence that Kyra happened to be lying in wait at the Archive. You're telling me she crossed the bay, entered the manor, and laid this ambush, all without help?"

"Are you saying the Naga *allowed* Kyra inside?"

"I'm saying we need to get back to Yuwen as soon as possible," Teia said. "One way or another, there are traitors within Taijin Palace."

They retraced their steps back through the fierce waters of the bay and the pebbled beach, until at last they came to the forest. Birds hooted from hidden knotholes, and pinecones crunched beneath their shoes. Felled logs and overgrown shrubbery made it impossible for a carriage to travel the lumpy path, which was why they'd braved this portion on foot.

The coachman didn't look at all surprised to see Teia, Jin, and Enna stumbling from the forest in various states of disarray, their clothes streaked with blood and ash. He merely stowed his book, dipped into a bow, and reached over to unhinge the carriage's glistening door. They collapsed silently onto the upholstered seats, each claiming a different corner of the carriage.

Jin and Enna drifted off at once, but Teia stayed awake, staring at the heavy baseboard across from her. It had also been decorated for Kashan, with suspended silver stars nailed above the top. The board itself had been fashioned like the head of the Serkawr, a design that Teia found both deeply ominous and vaguely sacrilegious. She hoped it wasn't an omen of things to come, a sign of the journey ahead.

The carriage was quiet for the remainder of the day, until the sun had slipped below heavy clouds. When the mountain shifted into darkness, the coachman stopped at an inn for the night. The gnarled building was tucked among a dense thicket of trees. A cracked statue of Armina guarded the stoop, sculpted with a pristine smile.

"Is making a stop necessary?" Teia protested, as they were welcomed by a hunched innkeeper, old enough to predate the sea itself.

"The horses need to rest," Jin said, as he counted coins for the old woman. She watched him closely, scooping each silver piece into her withered fist. "If they give out from exhaustion, we'll have to hike the rest of the way back to Taijin."

"I don't hike," Enna informed him. She was observing the coins with great interest, although she scowled as the innkeeper swatted toward her. "Watch it!"

When the old woman was satisfied nobody was trying to cheat her, she gestured them in with a heft of her cane. They dug into a late meal of stewed pork and fragrant rice, before following the rickety stairs to their individual chambers. The innkeeper accompanied them up the steps, a weathered tray balanced expertly on the crook of her arm.

"Tea?" Jin translated. He accepted a cup, as did Enna. Teia didn't move.

"You don't want any, Boss?" Enna said. She took a delicate sip from the steaming cup. "It's good for the complexion."

Teia had a vivid image of Hebei lying dead in his study, the broken teacup shattered on the floor. "I'll survive," she said, as she swept into her room and shut the door behind her.

The space was small but tidy. A clean basin of water had been set on the table, and a flattened bamboo mat substituted for a bed. Teia drew a cloth from the stack by the wall and plunged it into the basin. She washed herself methodically, sopping up dried blood from the earlier fight. Plain cotton robes had been hung in the wooden wardrobe; she shrugged them on quickly, before undoing her boots. The rolled parchment she'd placed inside for safekeeping was still there, undamaged by the fire. Teia made a mental note to compensate the shoemaker handsomely for his services when she got back to Erisia.

She lowered herself on the sleeping mat, stretching onto the cool surface. Teia wanted nothing more than to forget the events of today, to pretend Kyra's face didn't linger in the dark.

She was just beginning to drift off when a knock puttered from the door, breaking through the quiet.

Teia had a feeling it was the innkeeper, back to offer her more tea. She lay motionless, hoping the old woman would continue on her way—but when the rapping came again, Teia sighed. She kicked away the blanket reluctantly, already speaking when she yanked aside the door. "I'm fine as I am—"

Teia's voice died within her throat.

Standing in the hallway was a girl with golden curls cut

stylishly to her chin. A familiar belt was fastened around her waist. She was dressed in traditional Shaylani robes, a gray cloak tied over the lapis fabric.

The overlapping collar was just low enough to see the scarred edges of the Carthan crest, branded into her tanned skin.

"Hello, Teia," Alara said. "I think it's time we had a talk."

Chapter Eleven

Teia blinked hard, scrubbing a palm over her face. "Alara?" she said.

Alara didn't smile. "Who else?" she said. "Can I come in?"

She strolled into the room before Teia could answer, moving the washbasin to settle on the edge of the table. Her expression was unreadable. She waited expectantly for Teia to follow, her legs crossed at the ankles with the elegance of a royal.

Teia shut the door, keeping a wary gaze on the other girl's belt. Some of the dangling bottles were made of frosted glass, but others were transparent, so Teia could see the colorful assortment of powders within—reds and greens and purples, able to blind or maim or suffocate. She wondered what mixture Alara would choose to use on her, what lethal combination might best uphold the Poisons Master's title.

She briefly considered running for the exit, but decided it was pointless. If Alara was here, out in the open, that meant Teia had already ingested some quantity of poison. It was only a matter of time before she fell choking to the floor, her blood congealed to an unseemly texture.

Silence swelled between them, as Teia considered her

manner of death. At last, she shoved the thought aside and eked out a tepid "How have you been?"

Alara's laugh was stilted. "Six months, and that's all you have to say? How do you think I've been, Teia?"

"Good, I hope."

"After you raided the Dawnbreaker base and exiled me from Erisia?"

Maybe *good* hadn't been the proper answer. Teia bit her lip. "How did you find me?"

"There are only so many paths for carriages to take once you leave the bay. I assumed you'd want the shortest route back to Taijin—and if you were resting for the night, this is one of the few inns that had vacancy."

Teia remembered the rustling from the burnt corridor, the way Kyra had snapped to attention. She should have known that the rebel champion wouldn't have abandoned her mission for anyone else. "You were at the Archive?"

"Why wouldn't I be?"

"I thought I'd have seen you."

"It wasn't my fight."

This was an assassination attempt *for sure*. "So you're here to kill me," Teia said.

"You don't sound worried."

"I know how thorough you are." She paused. "What did you slip into my food? The same type of poison you used on Hebei?"

For the first time, uncertainty broke through Alara's features. "I said I was at the Archive. I never said I poisoned the Memory Keeper."

Now *this* was unexpected. "If you didn't poison Hebei—" Realization struck Teia, anchoring her to the spot. She thought about how Kyra had insisted that she'd spared the Memory Keeper. "Kyra went rogue."

"Not exactly. She acted on Lehm's orders."

"Which you weren't privy to?"

Alara's gloved hands fiddled with one of the leather pouches on her belt. "It's been happening more and more," she admitted. "I didn't know she'd be at the Archive until I found her gone. Lehm had taken a vial of toxin I'd been working on. He fed her some nonsense about how it was a sleeping draught and sent her off to the island alone."

"Is that why you're here? To confirm she's not an *intentional* murderer?" Teia fought the absurd urge to burst into laughter. "If that's what you want, I'm happy to help. She might have shot Enna and destroyed years' worth of memories, but Kyra Medoh is as purehearted as ever."

There was a tired edge to Alara's tone. "She's angry, Teia. I'd say she has every right to be."

Just like that, shame compressed into Teia. Any fight drained out of her. What was she doing, bickering over ethics with the Poisons Master? For all Kyra had done, Teia had been the one to put the Dawnbreakers through hell—the passage of time had done nothing to diminish her actions.

If these were going to be her last minutes, she'd rather spend it with some modicum of grace.

Teia plodded across the room, sitting tentatively beside Alara. "How long do I have?" she said quietly.

Alara tugged at a lock of her hair. "Teia," she said, appearing very much like she might regret what she'd say next. "I'm not here to kill you."

"You're not?"

"I meant what I said. I'm here to talk. I *did* put something in the teapot, but it's only a powder to induce sleep. I know you don't take tea, and I thought we could use some privacy."

That explained the snores that reverberated through the walls, sending ripples pooling within the basin. "You want to talk," Teia repeated carefully. She was afraid she'd misheard, or else was on the receiving end of some frightfully unfunny joke. "About Kyra?"

"About Lehm."

Hope crested inside Teia. "You believe me?" she said.

"I don't trust you. I might never again. But I don't think you would be here without reason." Alara's sigh was weary. "I heard what you said to Kyra back in the Archive. She told us something similar months ago, when we first left Erisia—about Lehm betraying the Dawnbreakers and trying to raise the Serkawr. She wrote it off as nonsense, just like I did. What Lehm might have wanted wasn't relevant anymore. He was dead. I *saw* him die before my eyes."

"He took some kind of potion before the military raided your base—one that slowed his heart to replicate death."

"I know," Alara said sourly. "It was a prototype I'd had in my lab. He'd neglected to mention that he was borrowing some. When he found us in Ismet three months later, I swore I was seeing a ghost."

"An unwelcome one."

Alara grimaced. "Maybe for me—but Kyra was ecstatic. It was like every holiday had been rolled into one, including the obscure ones that nobody celebrates."

"Husking Day?"

"The costumes don't even make sense," the Poisons Master complained. "What farmer goes about her day shucking corn in checkered skirts?"

"It's tradition."

"It's blasphemy." Alara smoothed out her filmy robes, reassured that she was far from the horrors of plaid. "Within a day of Lehm reappearing, he told us he'd commissioned a ship. We were going to Shaylan—all of us."

"What for?"

"He said he would demand an audience with Shaylan's emperor, and ask for the resources to remove you from the throne."

Lovely. "You went with him?"

"I wouldn't have, but Kyra followed without question."

"I'm glad my downfall is such a core motivator," Teia said. A frown deepened her features. "You've spent months with Lehm. What's changed?"

The Poisons Master fidgeted at the long strings of her cloak. The ends were braided with tiny black beads, shaped like miniature leaves. "I've made my own observations—little things Lehm does that don't make sense. He's paid others for information, but nothing related to Erisia. Mostly old scrolls and relics, artifacts that date back to when the Five Kingdoms were founded."

The Seascript. "He's doing his research," Teia murmured.

"We've traveled to cities in Shaylan, too—Chusun, Meng'an. He says we're there to meet allies, but he disappears for days at a time. I've trailed him before to learn where he goes. He visits libraries, or sorts through public records."

"He reads Shaylani?"

"Enough to get by. When we were in Meng'an, I asked the scholar at the library what he was seeking. She said he searches for the same subject each time."

"The Serkawr."

"Yes."

"And you've told Kyra this?"

Alara gave a dry chuckle. "Have you *tried* convincing Kyra of anything? Once her mind is made up, she has to be the one to change it."

"She won't listen to you?"

"She won't listen to anyone. I was hoping what happened in the Archive might sway her, after she discovered she'd poisoned Hebei—that maybe it would erode some of her faith in Lehm."

"It hasn't?"

"Not enough." Alara's fingers fiddled absently with her belt. She drew a breath, as if preparing to dive into icy water. "Teia. Lehm's planning something."

Trust was in perpetually short supply with Teia. But tonight, it felt especially precious as she gripped the side of the table. The Poisons Master had ample reason to despise her, starting with the brand scorched into her chest—and yet here Alara was, offering knowledge that Teia would be a fool not to accept.

"Tell me."

She listened intently to Alara's explanation. When the Poisons Master was finished, Teia found she wasn't surprised. She could scarcely fault Lehm for concocting a scheme. Plotting was in his nature, just as it was in hers. What she hadn't realized was how brazen the rebel leader was prepared to be. If this was war, he was willing to take the battle above ground.

Luckily, Teia had her own safeguards in place. "I took precautions," she said cagily, and Alara's golden brows lifted.

"Which means?"

It was a risk, confiding in Alara. For all Teia knew, the Poisons Master could be funneling information straight back to Lehm, a double agent with a hidden agenda.

But Teia was also aware of Alara's allegiances. She'd never been fond of the rebel leader, even back in Erisia. And it was clear the Poisons Master cared deeply for Kyra. Every time she spoke her name, a spark lit behind Alara's expression. She wore her feelings like a new coat, cast proudly around her shoulders, on display for all to see.

When Teia was done speaking, Alara shook her head. "You're the same as always," she said wryly.

"Is that a compliment?"

"I'm not sure yet." The Poisons Master pushed upright. "I can do what you asked for. But if you hurt Kyra—"

It's far more likely she'll hurt me. "I won't," Teia said.

Alara's gaze was steady. "I hope you mean that," she said pleasantly. "Because if you don't, I'll take your tongue first. It's one way to prevent any more lies."

Teia resisted the urge to clamp her teeth together. She knew a promise when she heard one. "What a rousing visual," she answered politely. She rose to her feet as well, accompanying Alara as she walked toward the door.

"I've been told I have a way with words." Alara rested her hand on the door's latticed panel. But before she could pull it open, she paused, rotating back toward Teia. "Teia. I heard you poisoned Jura."

"I did."

A smile flitted across Alara's face. Her hand strayed to the brand beneath her robes. "Did it hurt?"

Teia thought of her half brother's final moments, the fear reflected in his bloodshot eyes. Of all the emotions he might have experienced, she was aware of at least one. "Yes."

The smile grew. "Good," Alara said, satisfied. Then, almost casually: "I forgot to mention. There's someone else who wants to talk to you."

The door slid aside.

Teia came face to face with Tobias Rennert.

Perhaps some part of her had known he was there all along, even during the conversation with Alara. It was foolishness. It was instinct. It was a surety that sounded as true as her own pulse.

He was as beautiful as she remembered. She'd traced his features inside her mind a thousand times, the details she'd held close. The pearly scar notched along his neck, the lean cut of his jaw. She'd almost forgotten how tall he was, so that the top of her head barely grazed his shoulders.

Neither of them spoke. Neither of them *breathed.*

"Ah," Alara said. "I'll give both of you a minute."

She darted soundlessly from the room, the door closing behind her. Teia almost begged her not to go. In that moment, she would have given every coin in the Erisian treasury to have kept Alara's company.

"Teia."

Tobias's voice was a rasp. He was so close that she could have touched him. She nearly *did*, her hand lifting in a fit of insanity, reaching toward his face.

"Tobias."

He wrenched away from her, stepping back like he'd been burned. His expression contracted in pain, a veil shuttering behind his torrential eyes. "Don't," he snarled. Already, he was turning away, grasping for the door. "I don't know what I was thinking. This was a mistake."

She'd thought her heart healed in the past months, bandaged and smoothed over. Except now, watching Tobias walk away, Teia saw through her own lies. Something inside was splintering again, fissures snaking toward the surface. She wanted to carve herself open. She wanted to disappear.

Tobias rounded the corner. He vanished down the hall without a trace—but still she heard his parting words, echoing like a curse against her ears.

"You should have killed me in Erisia. Anything else would have been better than this."

Chapter Twelve

Taijin's majestic gates greeted Teia the following day, as the gilded carriage came to a stop before the palace's main entrance.

The barred metal grates that normally covered the arched openings had been thrust aside, lifted in preparation for the first night of Kashan. Even so, a half dozen guards checked the carriage from the ground, while others milled atop the stone watchtower, scanning for any potential threats.

The carriage was waved through, the horses nudged down the gravel path. But before they could continue into the stables, the driver suddenly came to a screeching halt, so hard that Enna nearly flew into Jin's lap, before scrambling back with a disgusted expression.

The thief lifted the velvet curtain that covered the window, tugging back its embroidered corner. "Er," she said. "I think it's for you, Boss."

She held the curtain aside for Teia to peer through the glass. A knot of people had clustered around the carriage—twenty or so soldiers in total, with an additional four Naga tucked in the middle. Unlike the gray-robed soldiers that hovered nervously on the sides, sporting pearl-handled sabers and slender silver axes, revolvers drawn and at the ready, the Naga carried no weapons. Their dragon tattoos shone beneath the late-evening sun. The wind ruffled through their shorn hair.

In the front was a page boy, wearing garish, forest-green robes that Alara would have taken offense to. "Highness?" he squeaked, in heavily accented Erisian. "Emperor Yuwen requests your presence at the Hall of Eternal Wisdom."

She cranked down the window and stuck her head through the opening. The page boy shrank back, knocking his elbow against one of the Naga.

"He sent for me?" Teia said sweetly. "What for?"

The page flushed. "It's not my place, Highness," he stammered, offering a quivering bow. "Please—if you may."

"One minute," Teia answered. She ducked back into the carriage, dread prickling up her spine. The page boy was nothing more than a formality. Teia had spent far too long in the Golden Palace to let a veiled demand go unnoticed.

She glanced over at Jin, wondering if he had any insight. The adviser merely shrugged. "If the emperor has asked for you," he said, with an earnestness that made her want to fling him out the window, "there must be a reason."

If he said so.

The Naga were waiting, not to mention the small horde of soldiers behind them. Teia blew out a breath before descending the carriage as elegantly as she could, with Enna steps behind her. They'd just begun to follow the page boy when Teia turned back. Jin was still in the carriage, holding fast to the door.

"You as well," she told him. "I'll need your testimony for what happened outside the Archive."

Together, they curved around the main grounds, past the courtiers and pavilions and rows of flowering trees. The Hall of Eternal Wisdom came into view, as did the colossal statue of Armina, beaming over the rooftops. At her feet, low-set tables had been laid out for the banquet. Silver chopsticks etched with constellations balanced atop each bowl.

The entrance to the Hall of Eternal Wisdom was shrouded in a layer of mist. High above, water flowed from an opening near the roof, which was fashioned to resemble a roaring dragon. The waterfall crested down in a steady stream, before maneuvering around the door to tumble gracefully into fitted gutters.

"Very pretty," Teia said, and the page boy gave her a wan smile. He guided her down the ornate corridor, until they stopped at a pair of metal doors, connected with a conjoined circular handle. When the page boy sank into a bow, Teia didn't wait for him to rise. Instead, she seized the metal rings, yanking them back to stride into the chamber.

Any chatter died to nothing.

The gray-robed soldiers remained by the door as the Naga pushed on, flanking Teia's group. On either side of the walkway, curious onlookers were crammed onto long wooden benches. Bushels of flowers burst from porcelain vases, and another statue of Armina towered next to the pews.

At the front of the chamber, thirteen figures were framed before a painting of a raging storm. They were arranged on an elevated wooden dais, gathered around a half-moon table—twelve governors in identical blue robes, with Yuwen in the center, sitting upon an opulent throne.

The emperor's attention flew to Jin. Aside from that, he was deathly still. His robes were cast in cerulean. His headdress was dotted with milky pearls, resting low upon his brow. Slowly, his gaze dropped back down, to where a silver-haired man stood before the dais.

Teia's pulse began to race. Adrenaline flooded her veins as she forced herself onward, her footsteps ringing against the blue-tiled floor. As Teia stopped before the dais, drawing back her shoulders, she cast a steady look to her left. She paused.

"Hello, Lehm," she said evenly.

Cornelius Lehm appeared no different than he had six months before, when she'd last seen him in the Dawnbreaker base. His hair had been neatly trimmed, his beard equally well maintained. Despite the balmy heat, he'd forgone Shaylani clothing for a familiar pressed greatcoat, with a linen shirt peeking out beneath the gray folds.

Next to Teia, Enna gritted her teeth. "Lehm," she spat, her voice coming out in a growl.

Lehm acknowledged them both with a tight smile. "Enna," he said, before his eyes jumped to Teia. "Halfling."

Reason be damned. Teia might be thrown out of Shaylan for setting Lehm aflame in front of the court, but she'd address the consequences later. At the very least, she would have dispatched the root of her problems.

But as soon as Teia pulled for heat, she knew something was wrong. There was a strange sheen to Lehm, a dewy aura that surrounded him. Teia hesitated. She scanned the governors on the platform, before pivoting back to examine the spectators. Someone here was shielding Lehm, protecting him from her flame.

She had no choice but to relax her stance, folding her arms before her. But when Lehm shifted aside to reveal his companion, Teia's breath hitched.

"Kyra?" Enna said, her fingers flying to her arm, teasing at the bandage.

There was a smugness to Kyra, an air of anticipated victory

that Teia didn't like one bit. Cuts flecked the side of her face. Silk clothes clung to her lithe form. "Don't mind me," Kyra said coolly. "I'm here as a character witness."

Teia lost hold of her temper. "I wasn't aware that you were interested in toppling governments outside of mine."

"Oh, hardly. I'm here to provide a warning."

"It's customary in Shaylan for the court to grant an audience for all those who request one," Lehm added. His pale gaze gleamed out at Teia. "Excellent practice, don't you think?"

"I wasn't aware such courtesy applied to traitors."

At this, Lehm clicked his tongue. *"Traitor,"* he said, "is such a derisive term."

"You incited a rebellion against the Erisian monarchy."

Kyra released a cough. "Last I looked," she provided, her tone taking on a nasty edge, "this is Shaylan, not Erisia."

Yuwen raised his hand. *"Enough,"* he said. Although he spoke no louder than normal, his voice echoed throughout the assembly chamber, reflected back on hidden surfaces.

"I quite agree," Lehm said smoothly, as he glanced toward Teia. "I've heard the most fanciful stories over the past months, Halfling. Something about me seeking to raise a mythical beast from legend with the help of the Shaylani court?"

"I wouldn't be so eager to speak about lies." Teia withdrew Hebei's bracelet, feeling the cold jade against her skin. Yuwen stood in interest, and Teia reached upward to set the bracelet into his open palm. "If you're feeling so talkative, why don't you tell the court why you decided to kill Hebei?"

Yuwen's hands shook. He held up the bracelet for the governors to see, the officials leaning forward. "This is Hebei's," he confirmed. "He was known to never take it off."

"It doesn't prove cause of death, Emperor," Lehm interjected.

"For all we know, Teia Carthan murdered this man herself to frame me."

"What possible reason would I have to do that?" Teia said.

"Forgive me if I don't believe you. You seek to tarnish my reputation. You want the court to dislike me, to distrust me. You know what I've traveled to Shaylan to say."

"Do I? Because as far as I can tell, your sole purpose here is to bore me into submission."

Lehm's mouth twisted into a sneer. Beside him, Kyra shuffled eagerly from foot to foot.

"Bold words," the rebel leader said, "from someone who seeks the Shaylani throne."

Whatever Teia had been expecting, it hadn't been *this.*

The room broke into an uproar. A governor pounded his fist on the table, as another jumped to her feet. Behind Teia, Jin stifled a gasp. Members of the audience dissolved into a chorus of whispers, sleeves rustling as they bent toward one another. They cast tepid glances at Yuwen, who sat motionless in his seat, his fingers clamped around Hebei's jade bracelet, each knuckle strained paper white.

Bold words, from someone who seeks the Shaylani throne.

It was a ludicrous claim, one bordering on absurdity. While Teia had always hungered for Erisia's crown, she'd never once wanted Shaylan's. She had no desire to rule a kingdom that was entirely unfamiliar, a place that wasn't home, despite its connection to her mother.

But the charge had been laid, strung with words that dripped like poison. Even as she gaped at Lehm, Teia felt the vitriol of the room, the wrath of the governors. Calla's legacy might have provided her daughter with some measure of goodwill, but any trust was fraying fast, unraveling before her eyes.

"Cousin," Teia called out, speaking over the clamor of the audience. She addressed only Yuwen now, taking him in, trying desperately to convey what was truth. "Just a few minutes ago, Lehm spoke of proof. Now, you'll find he has none to offer. I have no desire to lay claim to Shaylan."

Lehm dismissed her statement with a wave of his hand. "She's lying, of course," the rebel leader said airily. "But I wouldn't expect you to take my word for it."

A figure from the audience stood, shaking back his gray hood to reveal his face. This newcomer was a stranger to Teia, an Erisian with golden hair and sun-weathered skin. He had a spiraling Serkawr design inked along his collarbone, the standard for all naval members. When he parted his cracked lips, his teeth were stained yellow, the front two bent apart.

Wait.

She had seen this man before, in a dim warehouse under very different circumstances. It had been when Teia first met the Dawnbreakers. After she had arrived at the safe house, one of the men—*Fader,* Teia remembered—had been intent on killing her, before Alara had thrown him from the room.

She hadn't encountered him again after that initial meeting, nor had she given him a second thought, in all these past months. *What a mistake,* Teia thought grimly, as Fader cleared his throat. Like an actor trotting onto stage, his bearing molded into one of grave concern. His forehead wrinkled dramatically.

"It's true," Fader said heavily. "I was part of *The Inferno*'s crew. I heard Teia Carthan speak about conducting reconnaissance in Shaylan."

Teia's anger flared, as she thought again about the men who'd drowned in the Dark Sea. How dare he use them against her, distorting their memory with falsehoods? She almost leapt for

Fader right then and there, but a faint shred of lucidity held her back. How would it look to the Shaylani if she set him on fire as he began his testimony? Thanks to Lehm, they already thought she had something to hide. The last thing she needed was to appear completely mad.

"When Teia caught me," Fader continued, rolling up his sleeves, "she threatened my life. She burned a warning into my flesh." He revealed a peeling burn mark on the cusp of his arm, and a murmur seeped through the room. "She ordered me overboard, but the rest of the crew revolted. It's why *The Inferno* sank so quickly—she'd started to set the ship aflame when the wave struck."

Goddess. Had Lehm been tailing Teia, keeping a close watch on *The Inferno*? There had been no devious plots to overthrow Yuwen, no raging blaze that consumed the crew, but how else could he have known that the ship had sunk in the Dark Sea? How else could he have fabricated such a story for Fader?

Unfortunately, Teia had far greater problems than deciphering Lehm's tactics. Yuwen was staring hard at Fader, his eyes clinging to the burn on his arm. "How did you escape the wreckage?" he said. "My guards searched the surroundings but found no survivors."

"By the Goddess's grace, Emperor. I couldn't explain a miracle if I tried—but the next thing I knew, I was being pulled out of the water. Cornelius here found me. He persuaded me to speak today because it was the right thing to do."

"The right thing—" Teia broke off, swallowing the obscenities that rose in her throat. "This man is a fake, Yuwen. A Dawnbreaker I met when infiltrating the rebel movement. Lehm brought him here to frame me."

Jin blinked. "Emperor—" he began.

"She's speaking nonsense," Lehm cut in. "I'd never met this man before I found him on shore, half-drowned and badly injured. I'm happy to invoke even the Goddess's name, if that would prove my sincerity."

"It wouldn't," Teia snapped, as another tide of whispers descended upon the chamber. "You could be kneeling before Armina herself and still speak in lies."

Lehm's face shone with a cruel sort of glee, a craftiness that only the best politicians ever mastered. "Please," he implored to the court. "Tell me what's more likely. That I would somehow raise a mythological sea beast? Or that a new monarch, fraught with expectations from her advisers, would travel to Shaylan under false premises? That she would befriend the emperor and take advantage of his kindness, all to displace him from the throne?"

As soon as Yuwen hesitated, Teia knew that she'd lost. She saw it in his features, how his brows knit together as he sat back in his seat. "Teia Carthan," the emperor said. His tone was razored, an eon away from the levity she'd grown used to. "Cornelius Lehm presents compelling evidence."

"Emperor—" Jin said again. His voice was more urgent than before, but Yuwen shook his head.

"Has Lehm not provided proof, Jin? Has he not done as we require in the eyes of the law?"

Teia lifted her chin. "Is one witness all it takes to sway you, Cousin?" she said. "You sent me to the Archive for evidence of Lehm's deception, and yet you're willing to accept the first statement he presents?"

Yuwen pushed aside Hebei's bracelet, the jade screeching against the wooden table. "I can't deny what is fact, Teia. A Carthan has not stepped foot in Shaylan for decades. Before that, we were at war."

"And that's why you don't trust me?"

"There's little foundation to build on."

"Yet here I am, extending my hand in offering."

Yuwen's mouth thinned. "Your mother was family, as are you. In Shaylan, we cherish our own—the ties that bind, the respect between generations. But the role of an emperor is uniquely positioned. You might be blood, but my duty is to the good of Shaylan first."

Teia thrust a finger toward Armina's statue. The Serkawr writhed at the Goddess's feet, each fang chiseled to a point. "What about the Serkawr?" she said. "If he succeeds, both our kingdoms will fall."

"And if what Lehm says holds merit," Yuwen said, "you'll dispose of me and take Shaylan for your own." His robes settled around him in shades of blue, designs gleaming against the gossamer fabric. "My decision stands. The Naga will escort you and your adviser back to your chambers. I'll see to it that someone is posted outside."

For all the emperor's diplomatic language, Teia could read between the lines. "You're keeping us captive?"

"I'm securing both our positions."

"For how long?"

"Until I have time to consider the matter. I can send for another Memory Keeper. There's one living at the far end of the coast, about a two-week journey from here. She can see if your testimony holds—"

Teia stepped closer to the dais. "And what of Lehm?" she interrupted, as the Naga behind her tensed with unease.

"Cornelius Lehm," Yuwen said, "will be allowed the freedoms of any imperial guest."

He looked so self-assured in his decision. In some ways, Teia glimpsed the boy she'd seen in his chambers, the one who refused to execute his father, who carried a wide-eyed sense of good.

It was why she tried once more, desperate to have him see reason. "Yuwen," Teia said. Her words were strained, a message meant only for him. It was the closest she would come to begging. "Don't do this."

The emperor's face hardened. "Think again before you reprimand me, Teia. My hospitality is a courtesy, not a requirement."

Goddess. Couldn't anything ever be done smoothly?

Teia steadied herself. She called for the threads of heat, wrapping them around her fingers. "Enna," she said softly, and Lehm's head whipped around. *"Now."*

Smoke bloomed throughout the room as Teia shoved a palm outward. She narrowed her eyes against the gray billows, and threw a wreath of flames in the direction of the Naga, driving back the ones who'd been quick to react. Screams ricocheted within the chamber, magnified by the wooden panels. Someone shouted in fury, and a column of water burst through the air, casting a drizzle over the space.

An annoying, if wholly unnecessary, move. Teia knew where she was going.

She found who she was searching for, before doubling back down the corridor, towing her captive through the writhing masses. Somewhere to her left, the pews had caught aflame. At the door, Teia swept fire forward, aiming for the gray-robed soldiers. They fell like stones in a lake, and she darted by easily, pushing back one of the heavy doors, slipping into the safety of the corridor.

Under her hand, there came a whimper.

"Quiet," Teia crooned, and Jin flinched. Flames crackled over his right ear. They descended close to the base of his neck, eager for a taste. "Not a sound, Jin. I'd hate for either of us to do something we'll regret."

Chapter Thirteen

Enna appeared seconds later, stepping through the smoke.

Her arm was hooked around a struggling figure. When Kyra saw Teia, her eyes widened. Her arms dangled uselessly by her sides. She tried to speak, but Enna merely smiled, resting her dagger along the rebel champion's throat.

"I wouldn't try to scream if I were you," the thief warned. "I haven't forgotten that you shot me."

Kyra bucked, but it was clear she was defenseless. Whatever pressure points Enna targeted had done the trick—and while it was technically possible for Kyra to command heat without moving her hands, Teia had taken a gamble about the other girl's abilities. She'd improved since they'd parted ways in Erisia, but mastery was difficult without a proper teacher.

Teia studied Enna's dagger. "Move your blade lower," she advised, and Enna obliged. She shifted her knife to Kyra's stomach, just below her ribs. The rebel champion sucked in a breath as Teia nodded, satisfied. "Let's go."

She nudged her flame toward Jin's waist, before pressing her free hand against the door's handles. Blue fire burned beneath her palm, fusing the two iron rings together. Behind the door, the commotion had grown louder. Teia's amateur welding wouldn't hold the Shaylani forever, but it would buy them a few minutes.

Outside the assembly chamber, the hallway was blissfully empty. The walls were heavy with images of torrid oceans and raging storms. The statues seemed to follow their every move as Teia and Enna lugged their hostages onward. Jin was surprisingly cooperative, but Kyra resisted every step of the way, digging in her heels.

"Would you stop that?" Enna panted, before glowering at Teia, her tone brisk with exasperation. "Well, Boss? This is as far as we discussed after you stepped into my room last night. I hope your plan includes more than some casual kidnappings."

"Please," Teia said. "I thought you liked the excitement."

They burst into the courtyard, startling a pack of servants who were dawdling on the steps. One of them dropped a tray of glassware, while another tripped over his own feet, crashing down the stairs. Pastries littered the ground. Servants scrambled out of the way as Teia and Enna stumbled along, weaving through the tables. Dusk had swaddled Taijin in hues of blue.

In the distance, there came an odd rush of sound, the hum of a hundred voices that reached through the courtyard. Enna stiffened. "What's that?"

A smile ticked at Teia's lips. "Haven't you heard?" she replied. "It's the beginning of Kashan."

She had timed things best she could, dragging out her departure from the carriage for as long as she'd dared. In the days before visiting the Archive, Teia had spent a disproportionate amount of time strolling between the courtyard and the main gate, testing just how long it took to go from one end to another. She'd observed the watchtower installed above the gate, with its silver balcony and rotation of soldiers. She had watched as the guards practiced raising the metal grids, readying themselves for visitors into Taijin Palace.

Now, the first revelers were beginning to stream into the courtyard. Men carted children on their shoulders. Women were dressed in borrowed finery, their lips painted red, powder caking their faces. They beamed at the palace, the decor, kneeling in prayer before the statue of Armina, exclaiming over the dishes laid out on the tables. They were here to indulge, to celebrate, to stifle their sorrows in tankards of rice wine.

Thank the Goddess for Yuwen's generosity.

"This way," Teia hissed, and they joined the growing crowd, keeping their heads low. Beneath the flaps of their sleeves, Enna's knife was almost invisible, while Teia kept her pocket of flames close. To any wandering eyes, they were merely two couples, rushing back into the city.

Teia steered them toward Taijin's gate. There were even more merrymakers here than in the courtyard, bottlenecked against the entrance. Gray-robed soldiers marched across the top of the watchtower, illuminated by lanterns that hung from thick iron hooks. A banner flying Shaylani colors fluttered in the breeze.

With a quick tug, Teia sent a spark into the corner of the banner. It caught alight instantly, fire lurching up the fabric. There was a shout from the watchtower as Teia grabbed hold of the lamps too. When she doused the flames, the gate plunged into temporary darkness.

Chaos overtook Taijin's entrance. The crowd, so eager to explore the palace just moments before, now changed direction in a panic. Teia and Jin were caught in its midst, with Enna and Kyra behind them. It only took a few minutes to wriggle their way out, following the flow of people. Nobody spared a second glance as they emerged on the other side, with the soldiers by the gate trying to calm the stampeding crowd. As Teia and the others ducked into the shadow of the watchtower, she could hear the faint bellow of a gong.

When she saw the hooded figure approach, leading a spotted mare forward, Teia exhaled a sigh of relief. Kyra stared, but Enna waved weakly, as if testing out a greeting. "Alara," the thief said. "Your haircut looks nice."

"Thank you," the Poisons Master replied flatly. "I had ample time to style it after I was forced into hiding."

The thief winced, no doubt remembering the last time she and Alara had met. In her grasp, Kyra looked equally horrified, although for a distinctly different reason. "Alara?" she croaked. "What are you doing?"

The Poisons Master didn't meet her gaze. As she loosened two coils of rope, strung expertly around her belt, Teia glanced at the worn satchel over her shoulder. "You have what I asked for?"

"Three horses wasn't enough?" Alara said.

"Enna could steal three horses with her eyes closed. What about everything else?"

Alara held up a hand. "A map of Shaylan," she said, setting down a finger for each item she recited. "Dried rations, water-skins, and all the money Lehm squirreled away in our safe house. Don't worry, Teia. I came prepared."

With that, Alara and Enna hoisted Kyra onto the horse, before binding the rebel champion's limp arms to her sides. Kyra squirmed mightily, opening her mouth to scream, but Alara threw a cloak over her wriggling form. The cries became muffled, absorbed into the noise around them. The Poisons Master set to work with the second length of rope, as she looped the cord beneath the saddle, securing Kyra like a loose package.

From the swarm of people, another figure emerged, the reins of two horses threading through his fingers. Teia's breath caught. Even in a simple tunic and brown trousers, Tobias was striking, a boy who'd stepped free from a painting. The collar of his shirt puckered low, exposing the scar that snaked down his neck.

He stopped short when he caught sight of Teia, his eyes settling on Jin. "And this is?" Tobias said.

Teia wavered. She was suddenly all too aware that her elbow was locked around Jin's, that she held him in a way that pushed their bodies together. "Er," she said. "This is Jin."

"Wonderful," Tobias said with a grimace, turning without another word.

They mounted the remaining horses—Teia with Jin, Tobias behind Enna. Alara made sure Kyra's bonds were tight, before swinging herself onto the mare.

"This way," the Poisons Master said, snapping the reins smartly.

They galloped through the narrow streets, leaping over abandoned wagons, skirting around incoming visitors, who dove out of the way, muttering swears or shaking their fists. Teia had only walked Paifan's main road, its buildings jammed together like narrow rows of teeth, the stalls on either side painted in bright, vivid colors. Yet she knew the way north, guided by the diamond-shaped peak that loomed over the valley. Even in the dark, Niisha Mountain etched a hulking shape against the night, like a strange, unseemly beacon.

They had just reached the outskirts of the capital city, the terrain beginning to slope upward, when something landed in Teia's path.

Her horse reared in fright, almost bucking her off. As Teia

stretched around Jin, placing a hand on the horse's flank, she saw just what had caused their ride such alarm.

Ribbons of water twined before her, writhing like an injured animal. Before her eyes, they twisted into a misshapen form, a body that grew a gangly set of limbs. Its gaping maw peeled back, unraveling into a roar. Its antlered horns rose above her, scaled body widening over the dirt road.

When Teia glanced back, she already knew who had sent the beast.

Yuwen sat on a magnificent black stallion, his arm extended before him, cast in the pale light of the stars. Next to him, Lehm was saddled atop a smaller gray horse. His eyes hardened when he noticed Alara and Tobias, a vein twitching in his forehead. Tobias remained impassive, but the Poisons Master tossed her head defiantly, clutching tighter to the leather reins.

There were no Naga, no soldiers thundering up behind Yuwen. Out in the valley, away from the sparkle of the city, everything was eerily calm.

Yuwen spoke first. The silver designs on his sleeves glimmered. His gaze burned as he took in Jin, tracking the flame that hovered beside the adviser. "Teia," he said. "Have you gone mad?"

She didn't bother dignifying that with a response. Her cousin was free to draw his own conclusions. "Tread carefully, Cousin. You try to harm me, and I'll set Jin aflame. You threaten the others, and I'll do the same."

"What do you want?"

"Safe passage out of the valley." She dug her heels into the horse's side, rotating it toward Yuwen. "Tell your beast to stand down. I'm leaving."

"Leaving?"

"Lehm is lying to you, Yuwen. I won't be locked up like a prisoner while he roams free."

It wasn't a complete fabrication—but Teia had more than one reason for escaping Taijin. If Lehm wanted to raise the Serkawr, he needed Kyra Medoh to do so. And if he needed Kyra, then that was exactly what Teia was going to take from him.

The rebel leader's features darkened with rage. He, for one, could guess her true intentions. "If your plan is to run," Lehm said, "you're more dim-witted than I'd thought."

"Save your soliloquies for someone who cares. I'm not trying to be lulled to sleep."

Lehm's fingers flexed, as if longing to strangle her, but Yuwen curled his hand. Ahead of Teia, the beast gave an earsplitting shriek.

"I won't play your games," the emperor snarled. "As long as you have Jin, you won't be going anywhere."

Slowly, Teia tipped her head to one side. "All right," she said after a pause. "Fine."

"Fine?"

"Swear to me that no member of your court will entertain Cornelius Lehm, and I'd be happy to let Jin go. Swear before the Goddess that you'll drive Lehm from your kingdom, and I'll cross the Dark Sea for Erisia tonight. You have my word that you won't hear from me again."

She thought it a fair bargain, even with all that had happened. But when she saw Yuwen's expression, Teia could predict what his answer would be. If there was a single characteristic that bound rulers together, it was pride. She had injured the emperor beyond any normal repair, damaging his reputation within the court. Such a grievance couldn't be so easily forgiven.

"Don't test my patience," Yuwen snapped. "Do you really think you're in a position to make bargains?"

"I'd say so. You're still listening, aren't you?"

The creature made of water growled, as the emperor clenched both fists. "I'll say this once, Teia," Yuwen said. "If you stand down now, I'll offer you amnesty. I'll allow you to walk away. But mark my words—if you leave, I won't stop hunting you. Whether it's in Shaylan or Erisia, you'll never know peace. I'll make sure of it."

Peace. Was that the best he could come up with?

Despite the apprehension that lurked within her chest, the fear that fluttered at the corners, Teia's reply was a blank smile. It was one she'd sharpened to perfection, honed throughout her many years in the Golden Palace.

"I've never known peace anyway," Teia said. "Now—tell your beast to stand aside."

"And if I don't?"

The flame by Jin expanded, flattening into a shield-like shape. The adviser cringed, shuddering under Teia's hand.

"Yuwen," she said quietly. "We both know I've done terrible things."

As soon as Teia had taken hold of Jin, she had known how this conversation would end. And when Yuwen dropped his head, his dark hair sweeping over his brow, she knew that she'd won. Her cousin had come as a monarch, an emperor desperate to assert his position.

He would leave as a man, with his heart split wide open.

The emperor snapped his wrist. The beast he'd created lumbered a few steps, before its legs began to retract. It folded quickly, releasing a pitiful mewl. Within seconds, the creature was a caricature of itself, no larger than a house cat.

For the first time, Lehm's composure broke. "You're letting

them go?" he howled. His scream pitched louder with each word, radiating out into the valley. "You're letting the Halfling *go*?"

Teia ignored him. She adjusted her hold on Jin, taking care that Yuwen could see. Her fingers bit into the ridge of the adviser's shoulder. "If I see a single guard on my trail," she warned, "you'll have more than one corpse on your hands."

Yuwen followed each of her movements. A look of hatred had set onto his face. "Rest easy, Teia Carthan," the emperor said back. "Tonight, you've made an enemy out of Shaylan."

Chapter Fourteen

They raced into the night, cantering up the steep road that coiled toward Niisha Mountain. They had put substantial distance between them and Paifan already—but while Teia could no longer see Yuwen, she suspected he was still in the valley, frozen in place with that awful expression.

Rest easy, Teia Carthan. Tonight, you've made an enemy out of Shaylan.

It wasn't the first threat she'd heard; it wouldn't be the last. Teia had made a habit of cheating death, but tonight felt different, like she'd only escaped by the slimmest of margins.

At the front of the saddle, Jin shifted uncomfortably. "Teia," he said, and she leaned closer, straining to hear over the growing wind. "Where are we going?"

"You don't actually expect an answer to that, do you?"

Her reply seemed to vex him. The adviser drew himself up to full height—or as tall as he could get with her flames cupping at his waist.

"In Shaylan," Jin said, "all hostages are treated with dignity and respect."

"In Erisia," Teia said, "hostages lose their tongues for asking stupid questions."

That did the trick. Jin lapsed into silence, as Teia spurred the horse on. She pushed the others at breakneck speed, keeping Niisha's diamond peak in sight, stopping only so Alara could administer a sleeping draught to Kyra and Jin. Then they were off again, cantering along a series of curved roads that hugged a crumbling ledge. There were some parts where Teia could feel her horse's hooves skidding, inches away from an open drop. Other stretches were more serene, cradled between stony summits and towering crops of forests.

When dawn peeked over the horizon, casting the world in gold, Teia finally signaled for a stop. They'd come to a fork in the road, surrounded on all sides by a dense canopy of trees. The leaves were so thick that no light pierced through the branches, and so the way forward was cast in relative darkness, cut through with the shrill whine of bugs. Jin was starting to stir when Teia slid off the horse. She guided it farther into the underbrush, where a hidden grove sprouted away from the path.

When she finished hitching the horse to a nearby tree, Teia found Jin wide awake, his legs bound uncomfortably to either side of the saddle, his hands fastened to the horn. Before he could speak, Teia reached for the strands of heat, weaving a new flame in midair. It trailed Jin, not unlike a stray puppy, and the adviser winced, leaning as far as he could from the flame.

Leaves rustled behind her, branches snapping as the other two horses clopped into the grassy space. Enna jumped down, hopping from the stallion she shared with Tobias, pushing back her curls in a flourish. "I have to hand it to you, Boss. All these suicide missions, and we're not dead yet."

"You sound surprised."

"Awed," Enna said hastily. "I'd never think to doubt you."

Alara's spotted mare was last into the clearing. Kyra was still bound to the saddle, the cloak tucked over her writhing form as Alara dismounted the horse. "She's awake," the Poisons Master said dryly.

"Are we sure that's in everyone's best interest?" Enna muttered.

With his blade, Tobias sliced through the ropes tying Kyra down. He scooped her up easily, before lowering her to the ground. As he did, she kicked out a leg wildly, narrowly missing Alara.

Kyra threw off the cloak, her brow glistening in the early morning heat. Her arms stayed at her sides, drooping listlessly. Enna must have hit her harder back in the Hall of Eternal Wisdom than Teia had thought.

"Let—me—go."

"Gladly," Teia said. "Does over the side of the cliff work for you?"

At this, Kyra struggled harder. She was astoundingly uncoordinated as she flailed about, and Alara darted forward, pressing her gloved hand against Kyra's shoulder. "Stop," she said worriedly. "You'll hurt yourself."

"Don't touch me," Kyra hissed. She glared at Alara with such vitriol that the other girl took a step back. "I can't believe you, Alara. You're allying yourself with someone who shoved a knife in our backs."

"Did you consider I had no other choice? Six months ago, you never would have killed an innocent man. You never would have left a child to burn inside a manor."

"It was a mistake—"

"I don't think so. We shouldn't have come to Shaylan. We shouldn't have listened to Lehm."

"I thought you cared about the Dawnbreakers. About *Sai.*"

At the sound of her brother's name, an angry flush rose on Alara's cheeks. "Kyra," she said, her voice cold and terrible, "are you really going to use my *brother's death* against me?"

This, if nothing else, seemed to sober Kyra. "I'm sorry," she said. "I didn't mean—"

"Do you even hear yourself?" Alara snarled. "I know why I'm still here, Kyra—why I followed Lehm across a damn ocean. It's because of you. It's *always* been because of you. But I don't think you know what we're fighting for anymore—you haven't since we left Erisia. And if Teia is right about Lehm and the Serkawr . . ."

"How can you *think* that after what she's done? We had friends back in the base. *Family.*"

"I know. But for a while, Teia was family too."

The statement struck air from Teia's lungs. Kyra, as well, was momentarily stunned. "So that's it?" the rebel champion said, when she'd shaken off her disbelief. "You brought me here to—what? Convince me of Lehm's guilt? What does it matter when you're planning to flee Shaylan?"

"Who said anything about fleeing?" Teia said.

"There's hardly any other choice, is there? Yuwen will set his guards on you soon enough."

"Let them come. They'll keep their distance, especially with the leverage we hold."

She didn't miss the crease in Tobias's brow. "Him?" he said, nodding scornfully at Jin. "He looks like he's afraid of his own shadow—"

"Perfectly natural in a situation like this—"

"I don't see how he can be of help—"

"You've clearly never taken a hostage before—"

"Not to mention what happens if he doesn't cooperate—"

"I'm not going to *kill* him, unless you want the wrath of the Shaylani army coming down on us—"

"Excuse me," Jin said nervously. "Do I have any say in this?"

"Hush," Enna said. "Do you want Tobias to win?"

Teia had forgotten how astonishingly irritating Tobias could be. He knew just what nerves to pry loose, tinkering like a blacksmith in his shop. As he leaned back against a tree with a remarkable scowl, arms crossed over his chest, she could see the muscles corded beneath the thin fabric of his shirt.

"Is there something more you want to share?" Teia snapped.

"Plenty. Do you also plan on dragging Jin through all of Shaylan?"

"You're welcome to carry him if you like."

"That I'd pay to see," Alara said.

"Me too," Enna offered. "We could pool our funds."

"You can't keep your flame bearing down on him day and night," Tobias growled to Teia. "What happens once you have to rest, and he runs back for Taijin—"

"Excuse me," Jin said again, more forcefully than before. "I *want* to stay."

It was, perhaps, the only thing that could have plunged both Teia and Tobias into an uneasy silence. It became very quiet in the clearing, so that the warble of birdsong could be heard overhead.

Kyra's mouth dropped. "Excuse me?"

"It's a trick," Tobias said. "How long will it take before he drowns us in our sleep?"

"Five minutes," Alara guessed.

"Less," Enna said. "We shut our eyes, and instantly meet the Goddess."

"I can't drown anyone," Jin said indignantly. "I was never able to master internal manipulation. It's a difficult talent to learn."

Teia had never thought of her ability to drown someone as a *talent*, but it seemed like an optimistic way to perceive things. Truth be told, she was as taken aback as the others. It was the first time she'd captured a *willing* hostage.

"Is this because of the Serkawr?" she asked, remembering Jin's reaction when she'd first described Lehm's plan.

"Not just that," Jin said. "It's also Lehm—I don't trust him."

"He has that effect on people," Enna grunted.

"When he brought out his witness, he implied the man was a veteran in the Erisian navy. But the ink on his chest—the one of the Serkawr—was much too fresh."

"How do you know?"

"I used to visit the royal infirmary with my parents. There were some Naga who were there, healing from the tattoos they'd just received. The witness Lehm brought covered the edges with powder, but there was too much irritation for it to be older than a few days."

Had his parents been healers, visiting patients in the ward? Teia stowed the thought away as Jin continued. His next words were shaky but audible. They streamed out in a frantic rush, refusing to be stemmed. "Yuwen tries to be a good ruler. He's kind, compassionate. He wants to earn the respect of the governors, especially after his ba. But he can be too trusting—too eager to believe whoever is before him."

"Noble," Kyra murmured.

Naive, Teia thought.

"Then why not return to Taijin?" Tobias said. "Try to persuade him of how you feel?"

"The emperor is stubborn," Jin said. "He made a declaration

before the governors—a *public* declaration. It's not an easy statement to walk back on. But if I can help uncover proof of Lehm's deception, his intention to raise the Serkawr . . ."

Alara fixed her slate-gray eyes on Jin. "You're here to protect Yuwen."

"It's my duty as his adviser."

"Is it?"

"If Lehm summons the sea beast, all of Shaylan will suffer. And besides, I . . ." Jin swallowed. He appeared ready to collapse from the attention, if not for the ropes holding him upright. "I owe Yuwen this much."

So *this* was the by-product of all those yearning looks. Yuwen might have saved each flower Jin had ever pulled from his hair, but apparently the adviser was no less devoted. *The tribulations of love,* Teia thought, barely suppressing a shudder.

From his spot by the tree, Tobias remained unmoved. "I don't trust him," he said.

"Nobody is asking you to," Teia retorted. "Keep him bound, take a late watch, stay up at night, and act as his chaperone. One way or another, Jin stays."

Tobias's frown told her just how he felt, but Teia had other worries to contend with—chief of which was Kyra Medoh, who seemed equally as impassive as Tobias.

"Jin might have rolled over for you," she said, "but I'll do no such thing. Wherever you plan to go, I'm sure as hell not following."

"Are you certain about that?" Teia said.

"Positive."

As she gazed at Kyra, she could read every ounce of hatred in the rebel girl's features. There was no absolution for what Teia had done. She realized this now, more clearly than ever. She couldn't turn back the heavy hands of time—she had made her choices. She had accepted them.

Teia hadn't captured Kyra to plead forgiveness. Instead, she was here to do what she was best at.

Teia Carthan had come to strike a bargain.

She strode forward, ignoring Kyra's furious glare. "Before you think about making tracks back to Lehm, you might be interested in what I have to offer."

"I don't want anything from you."

Everyone wanted something. It was just about hitting upon that hidden desire, that long-lost dream. "Really?" Teia said. "What if you could come back to Erisia?"

To someone unsentimental, Teia's offer might have been woefully inadequate. On a good day, the capital of Bhanot was squeezed with far too many people, tourists and hustlers alike who flooded the cobblestone streets, shoved side by side along horse-drawn wagons. Con men set up shell games in narrow alleyways, their gold-capped teeth gleaming as they searched for their next victim. Plague houses rotted near the edge of the Flatiron District.

But for all its tears and cracks and flaws, Bhanot was home. *Erisia* was home. And Teia knew the rebel champion felt the same way. Kyra had been willing to lay down her life to better her kingdom. Such a love wasn't one that was easily diluted.

Kyra's eyes widened. "I don't care about that," she said haltingly, in a tone that wasn't the least bit convincing.

"You might not," Teia said. "But what about Alara and Tobias?"

She hated to invoke their names, hated the version of herself she retreated into, one that had been shaped in the twining tunnels of the Golden Palace. Yet decency had no place here—of that, Teia was certain. Even Tobias didn't argue, although his jaw flexed at her words. They might be at each other's throats, but they shared a mutual understanding. Despite their differences, they were tethered together by a common enemy—and the knowledge that, if Kyra refused to cooperate, it would make the journey that much more difficult.

The rebel champion sat back on her heels. Uncertainty lined her face as she glanced at Alara. "You knew about this?"

"Not this part."

"I'm taking creative liberties," Teia said. "You don't try to run. You stay—you help us. And even if we don't find anything—even if there's proof that Lehm is innocent—you, Alara, and Tobias can come home."

How many conversations had Kyra had with the others about returning to Erisia? Had they stayed awake late into the night, reminiscing about the view of Bhanot from the top of Sunset Tower, the blanket of lights that stretched out like a maze? Had they whispered about what they'd do if they ever went back, sampling the candied fruits in the market's wooden stalls, dodging harried merchants as they traipsed through the Financial District?

She didn't know. She didn't need to. When Kyra looked up, dark eyes blazing, it was the answer Teia had hoped to receive.

"Fine."

"You agree then?"

"Yes."

"You swear it?"

"I keep my promises." The insinuation was there, the words left unspoken. *I keep my promises—unlike you.* "And you?"

Teia nodded. "On my life," she said. "On my name."

It was a long second before Kyra inclined her head. "Fine,"

she said again. "I won't try to run, but I don't see how that helps."

"Why?"

"We've been wandering around for hours. You don't have a destination, much less a plan."

"Who said I didn't?" Teia said. "Have you heard of Okkan?"

"Is that a person?"

"A place. It's known for its grilled oysters."

"You're hungry?"

"Ravenous," Enna said.

Jin shook his head tersely. *"History,"* he said. "It's known for its history."

"What kind of history?" Alara asked.

"Okkan used to be the capital of Shaylan," the adviser explained. "It was built when Mei first founded the kingdom. Every royal goes at least once after they come of age."

Teia vaguely recalled Jin mentioning imperial visits back in Taijin Palace, although she'd assumed it was a casual affair. Perhaps the royal family had a vacation villa overlooking the Dark Sea.

"What do they go for?" she asked curiously.

"There's a ceremony that we have, where each royal goes to Okkan's cliffs. They stir the tide to prove their abilities. It's one of our largest celebrations, right after Kashan."

Alara pulled at a clump of grass. "Teia. We're on the run, and you want to go sightseeing?"

"I'm appreciative of my surroundings," Teia said. "It would do us some good to see Shaylan."

"And how is this supposed to help us stop Lehm?"

"Easy. Do you know what the Seascript is?" She was met with blank stares from the Dawnbreakers, although Enna sat straight up, her mouth flapping open. "It's a relic that was stolen from

Taijin Palace. Yuwen said it documents the history of the Five Kingdoms, dating back to when the Divine Five received their powers. There's an old prophecy that the Serkawr will rise, but it needs to be called at a certain *shi*—in a particular location."

Kyra's laugh was incredulous. "That," she said, "sounds like a rumor."

"I prefer *opportunity*."

"What do you want to do? Steal it back?"

Tobias ran a hand over the scar on his neck. "If Lehm doesn't know the location," he said, "he has no chance of raising the Serkawr."

"You agree with this?"

"It sounds saner than infiltrating Blackgate."

"To be fair," Alara said, "breaking into a prison is a low standard to exceed."

"You broke into a *prison*?" Jin said.

Enna propped an elbow on her knee. She had a vivacity to her, crackling with barely contained energy. "Teia," she said shrewdly. "Don't tell me this was your intention all along."

In truth, visiting Okkan had been a possibility since Teia learned about the Seascript. Yet when she and Alara had spoken at the inn, Teia had conveniently avoided mention of the relic. In some ways, she'd hoped things wouldn't come this far. She'd dreaded it.

There were too many moving variables awaiting them in Okkan, details that panned out of her control. At least she had some familiarity with Taijin Palace. Now, she was relying a bit too heavily on improvisation and good fortune.

If there was one thing about Teia's luck, it consistently seemed to run dry.

On the horse, Jin looked far less entertained. "You *do* know who took the Seascript?" he said.

Alara groaned. "Don't tell me . . ."

Enna grinned, rubbing her hands together. "All right then," she said, with barely contained glee. "Let's go pay the Society of Thieves a visit."

Chapter Fifteen

It took another full day before they arrived at Shaylan's northern shoreline.

As Teia broke through the gnarled reach of the forest, she never wanted to see another tree again—and yet as the horse came to a sudden halt, shuffling nervously on a jutting shelf of rock, Teia understood why Okkan had once housed the emperor.

She was on the edge of a sheer black cliff, one of many that ringed in an uneven semicircle, which extended toward the Dark Sea. The bluffs stretched upward from golden strips of sand. Far below, the waves crashed against the shore, before withdrawing in a roar. Steps had been chiseled into the side of the cliffs, leading to the wooden harbors braving the ink-black water, cluttered with fishing boats painted in pastel shades of green, blue, orange.

Okkan's skyline was no less astonishing. The city's sloped gray roofs pierced into the cloudless sky, broken apart by a scarlet building, its soaring eaves topped with crimson statuettes. To the west, a three-storied pagoda lifted above the horizon, with a sculpture of Armina balanced on its highest point. She overlooked the Dark Sea, her hand raised in a blessing, so lifelike that the breeze seemed to twine through her hair.

Teia slid from the saddle she shared with Jin. She'd untied

him after their talk in the clearing; although Tobias had argued they should at least bind his hands, Teia hadn't seen the point. If Jin did try to run, she knew from experience that her flames could outpace any man. It was how she reassured herself about his powers as well—that if the adviser tried to turn water against them, Teia and Kyra could overpower him.

Jin glanced at her in surprise. "You want a better view of the cliffs?"

She thought it more practical to explore on foot, since the potential fall made the horse skittish. But if she was being honest, it was more than that, as the adviser's earlier statement rattled loudly in her mind. "Jin," Teia said uncertainly. "You said there's a ceremony in Okkan, where every royal stirs the tide."

"Yes. It takes place close to here, actually." He pointed to a trampled section of the dirt road. There was a portion of the cliff's bluff that pushed out farther than the rest, with space for one person—maybe two—to stand in its center. "The imperial procession stays near the front, with crowds packed so tight that it's hard to move. There are always vendors mixed in with the spectators, selling candy and rice wine and sparklers, no matter how much the Naga try to shoo them away. There's usually music too—drummers who keep tempo, measuring the crest of the wave."

Teia could imagine the pulsing rhythm, moving in time to the rising water. She hesitated, wondering if she should ask her next question. "Does that mean my mother also participated?"

She'd expected a general response. *Yes. Of course.* But when Jin met her eyes, his face was bright with recognition. "She was one of the best. People still speak of how she stirred a wave as high as Okkan's main pagoda. It was the tallest one called in a century until . . ."

Jin's voice petered away, lost to the sea below. Teia narrowed her gaze. "Until who?"

"Until Feng." There was a bitter note to the adviser's tone. "He wasn't popular, you know. It's hard to be, when Calla was the one who'd been primed for the throne. But in Shaylan, might is respected. Rumor is that Feng practiced for months leading up to the ceremony. He knew he'd have one chance to win the kingdom over."

"It worked."

"For a while."

Around them, the wind had picked up, lashing furiously against them. The horse stomped in place, its mane tangled in disarray, and Teia tilted her chin toward Okkan's uneven horizon. "I'll be right behind you," she said to Jin. "You go on ahead."

His response was a wry shrug. "Not too far," he answered, as he nudged the horse with his heels. "Tobias said he's happy to acquaint me with his knife, if I'm ever out of his sight."

"Impossible. Tobias is never happy to do anything."

Jin continued down the path, leaving Teia to mull over what he'd said. As she crept closer to the steep drop of the cliff, the boats in the harbor were as small as toys. The air smelled heavily of brine. It was impossible to think that Calla had drawn water to this height, bending the ocean to her command.

What would she think if she knew my affinity? Teia thought. The first time they'd trained together, Calla had led her to the Dark Sea, where she'd instructed her to hold back the waves. Had she assumed Teia would inherit her abilities, able to part the tide? Had she been disappointed by how her daughter had struggled, the many weeks wasted on the rugged shoreline?

A sigh slipped through Teia's lips. And when she retreated reluctantly, turning away from the sea, she discovered Tobias standing a few feet away, watching her with an inscrutable expression.

The shock went straight to her head. "What happened to your horse?" Teia said, before instantly regretting it. *Goddess—what a stupid thing to ask.*

"Enna rode on ahead. I'm assuming Jin did the same?"

She glimpsed the others along the path, hovering at a respectable distance, yet close enough that they were certainly within earshot. She suspected they would be eagerly eavesdropping on her and Tobias, with Enna and Alara taking bets on the outcome.

"We'll catch up to them," Teia said.

"I'm sure we will."

"How was the journey over?"

"Good. Yours?"

"Fine."

"I'm glad."

Was small talk all they'd been reduced to? Was this the boy she'd once confided in about her family, the boy who'd made her laugh until her sides ached? Once, Teia had been able to read every emotion that flickered across Tobias's face. But the months had stolen away any familiarity, shrouding him in shadow.

I did this, Teia thought—and with that came a burning sensation, guilt wrapping around her ribs.

She stared across the chasm that separated them, the rift she'd created, searching desperately for her next words. "You used to want to visit here," she said quietly, beckoning out to the bluffs.

It was, clearly, the wrong thing to say. "How do you know that?" Tobias said stiffly.

"It was on one of your maps. You'd circled it, written your notes beneath."

He flinched, as if she'd reached out and struck him. "I'm not talking to you about this."

"I didn't mean—"

"To what?" he growled. "To split me in two? To make me the fool? Tell me, Teia—was it all for show? How many lies did you tell when we were together?"

"None when it mattered."

"So more than you can count."

"I never said that."

"You implied it."

"And you're inferring," she snapped. "I know what I did, Tobias—I *know.* What do you want from me? An apology? A reason?"

"I want to know why."

"Why I took the throne?"

His laugh was sharp. "I don't give a damn that you assumed the throne," he said. "You're ten times the ruler Jura ever was. I would have followed you into fire—I would have bent the knee. What I want to know is why you didn't trust me, after all we went through in Blackgate, after everything in the Temple of Past."

"I did."

"You didn't."

"I did!" The waves crashed below, enveloping the sand. "I trusted you, Tobias. More than anyone—more than myself."

"Bullshit."

"It isn't," she said fiercely. "I think of you. I always do—"

"That's the problem, Teia. I don't just think of you. You haunt me. You visit my dreams. And once I notice you, you kill me there too—slowly, without mercy."

He'd etched her into a villain with the tools she'd given him. But it was easier to burrow into the hurt, to nurse her pain like a tonic. "If you hate me," Teia said angrily, "then why are you here? Why come to Shaylan at all?"

"As opposed to . . . ?"

"Didn't you want to travel the Five Kingdoms? Explore different countries, see the world?"

"Do you really have to ask me that?" he snarled. "How could I go anywhere else, when I knew you'd be here?"

Emotion welled in her chest, threatening to drag her under. "And what would have happened if I'd told you about wanting the crown? How would things be any different? What would have changed?"

"Everything!" he exploded. "How can you not see that? I bled for you. I *cared* for you. And sometimes, somehow, I think I might even—" He broke off abruptly, brushing past her to stalk toward the edge of the cliff.

Her heart rose against her throat. "You might even *what,* Tobias?" she said, as she pivoted toward him.

"I don't know," he said harshly. His voice rang out over the bluffs, falling away against the shriek of the tide. Then, more softly, his tone shattered: "I don't know."

She knew who they were then, who they would always be. A rebel who hailed from the Highlands, searching for vengeance; a royal who'd clawed her way to a bloodied throne. There was no rest for the wicked, no gentle future for the likes of them.

Teia reached deftly into her robes. She withdrew the creased parchment she'd been carrying since Erisia, the one previously tucked into the leather pouch. Now, she held it up, tossing it over to Tobias. He caught it easily, an innate reflex, holding it away like it might bite him.

"Open it," she said.

Tobias's lip curled. "The last time I listened to you, I was exiled from Erisia." But he smoothed out the crinkled square anyway, studying the words before him.

The paper had weathered an extraordinary amount, from a dip in the Dark Sea to the battle in the Archive. Tobias scanned the page quickly, his hands trembling against the parchment. "What is this?"

"It's not a bribe," Teia said. And it wasn't—truly. She didn't intend to change his mind about her. But she had brought the decree across the ocean, borne by some wild hope that she might right a wrong.

She would never forget when Tobias had spoken of his parents. Isaac and Liana St. Clair, both killed by Jura. In the aftermath, Jura had gifted the mountainous lands they'd overseen to Devon Ralis, a brute of a noble who'd murdered both his past wives.

It was a story that had stayed with Teia, settling under her skin. When she'd assumed the throne, her opening act had been to strip Ralis of his title and place the Highlands under the leadership of an intermediary dignitary. After, she'd drawn up a separate decree in an act of insanity, although Enna had warned against it.

What's the point, Boss? It'll only lead to more heartache.

Apparently, Teia was a glutton for punishment. Tobias inspected the declaration as if he didn't quite believe his eyes. "You'd restore the Highlands to my family—to me."

"Assuming we don't die in Shaylan," Teia said, before nodding. "Yes."

"Why?"

"The Highlands belong to the St. Clairs. They always have."

He folded the paper to his chest. "I don't know what to say."

What could they have been if she hadn't ripped them apart? What might have happened if she'd chosen a different path?

It didn't matter. It never would. As Teia stared out at the raging water, it was almost a relief to know this was how things ended. They would retrieve the Seascript and learn its secrets. They would part ways as strangers.

"You don't have to say anything," Teia said. "I've always preferred silence anyway."

Chapter Sixteen

Okkan was the liveliest place Teia had ever visited.

The main road led directly to the enormous blue pagoda. Through its open doors, a statue of Armina could be seen inside. It rested upon a metallic altar, a mass of silver that rose behind the Goddess, engraved with designs. Outside, a line of worshippers snaked down the building's stone steps.

The path to the pagoda was bordered on either side by shops and stalls, their shelves crowded with an assortment of colorful trinkets: miniatures of the Goddess, silk paintings of mountains, glass bottles that supposedly contained powdered scales of the Serkawr. Deep blue banners fluttered from rooftops. Music tumbled through the air. Despite the early hour, shopkeepers were packed outside with sizzling pans of oil, squatting over charcoal grills, fanning open flames as they shouted out to potential customers.

While each stall differed in size, most had silver ornaments gleaming against their painted wooden counters. Ahead of Teia, Alara came to a screeching halt, before lifting one of the charms eagerly.

Jin nodded in approval. "The constellations have begun to change," he said proudly.

Teia tore her attention away from a nearby vendor, who dipped skewered fruit slices into melted vats of sugar. "I thought Kashan was a time of reflection."

"It is," the adviser assured her. "But there are certain stars that only show during this time of year, ones that brighten and dim throughout the nine-day period. It's said Mei looked to them for guidance when she first began her quest to found Shaylan."

"And?"

"And what?"

"Did she find anything?"

"Probably not," Tobias muttered. He'd been avoiding Teia since their conversation at the cliffs, which was just as well. If she had to meet his gaze, she thought the act might physically kill her.

Jin shrugged. "It's unclear," he said. "But on the final night, everyone stays awake to see the last star before dawn, which glows with a blue tint. The entire kingdom comes together, if just for one day."

"Is that why Kashan is called the Festival of Lights?" Teia asked.

"How else would it have gotten its name?"

Teia glanced at Enna. "Told you," she said.

"How misleading," the thief said back. "Why not call it the Festival of Stars?"

Meanwhile, Kyra surveyed the throngs of people. There had been some mild concerns about their group standing out, but there were plenty of tourists from the other kingdoms, mixed among the locals. A few feet away, a pale-haired Dvořákian was paying for a frosted cup of soybean milk. With each tilt of his finger, the coins flew directly from his pocket to settle into the vendor's hand. Nearby, an Ismetian man entertained his children, levitating a set of polished souvenir stones into the air.

"Just how are we supposed to find the Society of Thieves in all this?" the rebel champion said tartly.

Tobias eyed a porcelain bowl before one of the stalls. It was positioned carelessly on the edge of the counter, where tourists deposited silver pieces as payment. "Jingle a coin purse and wait for someone to appear."

Enna grimaced. "You used to run with the sellswords, didn't you?" she asked.

"What gave it away?"

"The glower," Kyra mumbled.

"The hair," Alara offered.

"The lack of creativity," Enna proclaimed. "All mercenaries think the same. Stab, slash, parry. There's no variation."

"As opposed to looting everything in sight?"

"Not *everything.* Most of us have excellent taste."

Jin glanced away from the silver decorations. "What do you mean *most of us*?"

"Most thieves. What else?"

"You're a *thief*?"

Enna blinked. "Oh," she said cheerfully. "Did I forget to mention that?"

"I thought you were an adviser!"

"Well, yes. I *advise* Teia to do something, and she usually ignores me."

Jin rounded on Teia. "You *know* she's a thief? And you brought her into Taijin?"

Enna was beginning to look distinctly offended. "What do you think we are—a bunch of vagrants with no morals?"

"You plunder and raid for fun."

"Royals impose crippling taxes on people who can't afford them," Enna answered. "I'd say my morals are just fine."

He opened his mouth, before snapping it shut. But while Jin had been temporarily chastised, Alara didn't seem convinced. "Mark my words," she said, wringing her gloved hands in front of her. "If someone cuts my throat inside the Society, I'm going to be *deeply* unhappy."

"Don't worry," Enna said soothingly. "We stopped cutting throats years ago. A knife in the back is far less messy."

"I thought thieves had honor," Kyra snarked.

"I wouldn't be one to talk. If I remember, you shot me unprovoked."

"My hand slipped."

"Yes," Teia said, "and if it happens again, I'm going to personally drown you where you stand. Now, if you're all done squabbling, can we get back to locating the Society?"

Around them, people jostled about in densely packed groups, nibbling on bits of grilled squid or sampling flaky bites of fish—and despite coins rattling in nearly every pocket, there wasn't a thief in sight. Teia had never *wished* to be robbed before, but there was a first time for everything.

She lifted her head toward Enna, who beamed back in return. "Don't worry, Boss," the girl said. "I told you I know how to get the Society's attention, didn't I?"

"You did," Teia replied, desperately wishing that the intelligence she had on the Society of Thieves—collected by her spies back in Erisia—extended further than a general location. "But most of your plans involve setting something on fire."

"Once."

"Twice. Remember when you broke into the Minister of Tourism's estate?"

They both paused, reminiscing on the moment.

"You're right," Enna conceded with a roguish grin. "It *was* twice."

The thief shepherded them away from the tangle of vendors and pushcarts. They loped closer to the center of town, where lanterns had been strung between the narrow lanes, suspended from the eaves of each building. The occasional shrine peeked out from folded stoops, where offerings of fruit and candy had been heaped beside small statues of Armina. Kyra paused to rescue an orange that had rolled free from its porcelain plate, before her gaze caught on a nearby building.

"Goddess," Kyra said. "What's that?"

It was a massive structure that took up the full length of a street. There were three floors in total, each room marked with painted shutters. Guards were positioned beside barred double doors, glinting adornments embellished over the threshold.

"What a color scheme," Enna noted. Aside from the bronze metalwork above the doors and the silver chimes for Kashan that hung from the windows, every inch of the building was painted in red. The roof blushed maroon. The walls were a deep cherry. Even the blossoming flowers drawn on the shutters were the lightest shade of scarlet.

Jin's features were acerbic as he took in the building. "It's called the House of Mourning," he said.

"It's a landmark?" Tobias asked.

"Obviously," Alara said. "It wouldn't be painted this way otherwise."

"It wasn't always this color," Jin explained. "It used to be a vacation home for the royal family. When Feng became emperor, he had it repainted."

It was an odd choice, considering the blue hues of Taijin

Palace. "Why red?" Teia said. "Doesn't that buck Shaylan's colors?"

"Feng always liked to be different. *Special.* He wanted to build something unique from any emperor before him."

For the briefest instant, something overtook the adviser's face. As he stared up at the House of Mourning, his black eyes gleamed. It was the type of rage that sent a chill through Teia—the sort of anger that left men bleeding from the inside out, crawling away from the light to exact their revenge.

Then it was gone, wiped away so quickly Teia thought she might have dreamed it. Beside her was the adviser she'd grown accustomed to, the noble with his formal ways. "It no longer belongs to the imperial family," Jin said coolly. "It's a private residence now—Yuwen sold the home after he took the throne. I don't think he wanted the reminder."

"Of his father?" Kyra said.

Jin's voice curdled. "This is where Feng came after he executed Taijin's Memory Keepers. He sought refuge for about a week, before he returned to Paifan."

Suddenly, the red finishings of the building took on a very different meaning. The group stood there for a moment more. They watched the servants bustling in a steady stream—carting baskets of laundry, hauling soapy basins of water—before Enna sighed. "Come on," she said softly. For once, she didn't try to get a rise out of Jin. Instead, she merely guided them around the House of Mourning, away from its hulking shadow.

Soon, the path had opened to a central square, where a clock tower glistened in the middle. It was a thing of beauty, painted cornflower blue and topped with a statue of a koi fish, although the rest of the square was largely deserted. A pair of old men sat hunched beside a tannery, smoking cigars and leaning heavily on sturdy canes. The apothecary in one corner appeared abandoned, its faded wooden sign creaking in the breeze.

Enna, however, wasn't deterred. She marched right up to the apothecary, shoving at its door. When it refused to give way, she muttered a curse, fished a lockpick out of her shoe, and jammed it expertly into the lock.

"Is this legal?" Jin hissed.

"Certainly not," Alara said.

"And you're all right with it?"

"You get used to it," Kyra said gloomily.

Inside, there was barely room for everyone to fit. Teia lodged herself between two wooden shelves, which were stacked with glass jars of minerals and poultices. Jin stepped gingerly over an ornate incense holder, and Tobias ducked low, stooping beneath the ropes of dried herbs.

In the meantime, Enna inspected the shelves with great care, muttering ceaselessly to herself. "Does anyone know what Lycium looks like?"

"Of course," Alara said, as she stepped forward. "Doesn't everyone?"

With the Poisons Master's help, the thief uncovered what she'd been seeking—a jar in the far back, stuffed with miniature purple flowers. "Perfect," Enna said happily. She grabbed for the lid, and gave it a quick twist to the right.

The floorboards released a groan, which echoed throughout the store. Teia lifted her left foot warily, testing the spot before her. "Did anyone else hear that?"

"If it's rats," Alara declared, "I'm going back to Taijin."

Then the floorboards in the center of the room cleaved in two, swinging down into open air. Jin yelped, backing into a pile of jars. Tobias snatched for his knife, while Kyra tensed, sparks shimmering at her fingertips. Teia remained motionless. She scrutinized the new hole in the apothecary's floor, the stretch of darkness that yawned beneath.

Enna let out a laugh. "Relax," she said, with a lazy flick of her hand. "Haven't any of you seen a trapdoor before?"

"You," Jin gasped, "are far too excited about this."

Privately, Teia thought the Society of Thieves could do away with such dramatics. *What's wrong with using a regular entrance?* she thought, as she approached the trapdoor. A rickety set of stairs had been propped beneath the floorboards, with a lantern placed on the top step. She scooped it up, ignited the wick, and descended down carefully.

This couldn't be the Society's headquarters—and if it was, the thieves must have been terrible misers. The area beneath the apothecary was largely empty, not to mention uncomfortably damp and reeking heavily of mildew. As the others followed behind Teia, Enna brought up the rear.

"I think it's that way," she said, squinting into the darkness.

Teia lifted the lantern. The light crept down the gray walls, sending a shiver through her. *Not a room,* she realized. *A tunnel.*

"Are you sure about this?" Kyra said apprehensively.

Beside her, Alara reached out. Their fight from two days before still lingered, thickening the air, but Kyra softened as Alara wrapped her pinkie around hers. "What do I always say?" she said lightly. "They'll have to go through me first."

A small smile caught at Kyra's mouth. "And if it's rats?"

"If it's rats," Alara said, "you might be on your own."

They began the arduous trek through the meandering tunnels, avoiding the dirty puddles that spotted the ground. On and on they continued, weaving and twisting, until Teia's legs were starting to ache. As they pushed through a particularly steep incline, she wondered how far these tunnels extended. At the rate they were moving, the passageways must wind beneath half of Okkan.

Just then, a familiar rumble sounded through the tunnels. Teia froze. "Enna," she said warningly.

The thief scuffed a cautious foot. "This wasn't in the instructions."

For the second time, the floor gave way, solid stone that split apart. There was an awful moment when Teia was falling—and then something smooth caught her back, a chute that propelled her onward. She was flung forward, yanked into darkness, until a gleam of light widened before her, expanding.

An opening.

She was spat out of the chute, deposited roughly on the ground. As Teia pulled herself up, groaning, she heard the rustle of murmured voices, before the whispers ascended into a roar. The noise was deafening, a mishmash of hoots and jeers and the occasional boo. People clapped their hands loudly, shrieking with laughter.

The others had landed beside her in an untidy heap. One after another, they stood, looking around them incredulously. Tobias was the last on his feet. His blade was already snug in his fist as he shifted his weight expertly, readying for a fight. "*This* is why mercenaries stay far from thieves."

They were in some kind of hollowed space, lit by blazing lanterns. The chamber was large, with wooden sides that ended in a high ceiling. Stone ledges were secured at different points along the walls. Some were empty, while others were packed so tightly that people all but spilled off each platform. There were onlookers of all ages, butting one another with their elbows, stomping their boots in devilish glee. Most were Shaylani, but there were some that bore features from other kingdoms as well. On one of the ledges, an Ismetian girl with coppery skin caught Teia's eye, winked, and drew a finger across her neck.

"Quite the welcome," Kyra said.

"I thought they didn't cut throats here," Jin said nervously.

"Quiet," Teia grunted. About forty feet up, a hidden door had creaked open. The audience calmed slightly, and the taunts faded as a girl emerged from the shadowed entrance.

She was about Yuwen's age, long and lithe, her black hair cut just below her chin. There was no platform that protruded before the door, nowhere for her to go—and yet she moved forward with the grace of an acrobat, stepping confidently into open air. Beneath her heel, a crystalline pattern began to form. It slithered out to construct a ledge, attached securely to the side of the battered wall.

Ice, Teia thought incredulously, as the girl bent her hand. A column of water distorted before her, compressing obediently into a spiny shape. In an instant, water had hardened, transforming into a high-backed chair.

The girl perched sideways onto the seat, her legs dangling over the right armrest. She flipped a serrated dagger from her belt, tossing it upward before catching it deftly.

"Welcome to the Pit," the girl said in Erisian. "My name is Amalay—leader of Shaylan's division of the Society of Thieves, Purveyor of Items, Curator of Goods. I can't wait to show you what we do to intruders."

Chapter Seventeen

Teia carried her fair share of titles, but Amalay's had to be the longest she'd ever heard.

Atop the ledge, the leader of thieves yammered on. She must have greatly enjoyed the sound of her own voice, swinging the dagger errantly to emphasize each new point.

"My thieves heard you speaking Erisian in the tunnels. You lot move like a prison wagon—all noise, no grace. You could have woken a dead man with all the commotion."

"I take offense to that," Enna mumbled.

"Not to mention," Amalay added, "what kind of spectacular idiots you have to be to infiltrate the Society of Thieves. Surely you've seen the warnings? The signs? The men that stumble around town missing all of their fingers?"

The crowd roared in appreciation. *Very descriptive,* Teia thought, as Enna stepped forward. She spread her hands, a priest rising to a pulpit. As she stared unflinchingly at Amalay, her tone was shrouded with respect.

"My name is Enna van Apt." Her name seemed to carry some weight, even in Shaylan. Several of the onlookers stopped jeering immediately. The vigorous rounds of stomping faded away. "I came to seek an audience with you."

Amalay gave her a cursory look. "Enna van Apt," she said smoothly, before gesturing out at Teia. "And just who are your companions?"

Teia wasn't eager to make introductions. Here she was, stuck at the bottom of an arena with little leverage and even less authority. Every thief in the chamber was inspecting her greedily, as if assessing how to shuck her silk robes right off her back. How would they react if they learned her identity?

"It's not important who I am," Teia said. "But you have something I need—and I'm happy to make it worth your while if you're willing to speak privately."

Amalay touched the dagger to her lips thoughtfully, tracing the tip down her chin. "Tempting," she said as she drew the blade away, "but no."

"What?"

"That's within my right, you know." Amalay's grin was sharp. "You caught me on a bad day—and I can't say I have much respect for a thief that brings outsiders into the Society."

There must have been at least a few spectators who understood Erisian. The crowd broke into scattered boos, with a few insults from the top of the chamber. Enna flushed, red creeping into her cheeks. "There wasn't exactly a messenger to post our arrival."

"Then you shouldn't have led them here at all. In the Society, we take care of our own. But whoever you've brought into our home, I can guarantee they aren't thieves."

At the snap of her fingers, a series of hidden doors flew open, leading to the empty stone platforms. Five figures walked out, one positioned on each ledge. They were clad in cheap, flowing black robes, a poor imitation of what the Naga wore in Taijin. They ranged in age and appearance, although the girl in the center immediately caught Teia's attention. She looked remarkably similar to Amalay—apple-round cheeks, a dash of freckles across her pert nose—although she was no older than fourteen. Jagged scars webbed across her forehead, kissing the right side of her face.

Amalay glanced over at the girl. Her gaze softened, just for a moment, before it returned to Teia and the others. "You'll all suffer the same fate," the leader of thieves announced. "Although it's unfortunate you've been caught in this, Enna van Apt. I've heard great things about you."

On her cue, the black-robed figures lifted their arms. A cloud of droplets appeared in the air, hovering in a swarm before clumping together. They transformed into three identical gaunt creatures, each wielding an icy sword. They were twice the height of a normal person, with a thin head wobbling on a narrow slant of a neck.

"Kyra," Teia said quietly. "Try not to use your powers."

Kyra regarded her as if she'd lost her mind. "I don't think they'd be open to sitting for a chat."

"What happened to you being a pacifist?"

The creatures sprinted forward, but it was Jin who reacted first. The adviser wrenched his hand sharply. Gaping holes split through the creatures' torsos, as if they'd been shot through with a cannon. The one on the right glanced down with a tortured moan. It lost its shape, its chest collapsing. In a matter of seconds, the others had met a similar fate.

The booing intensified from the crowd. Amalay frowned, pushing back a fringe of hair with her dagger. "It's been a while since we had someone with an affinity."

Water enclosed Jin's hands. As it wrapped around his feet, liquid solidified into blocks of ice. Amalay tipped her finger, and the adviser fell with a grunt, toppling onto his side. The icy restraints moved at her command, hauling the adviser away from the center of the arena, tethering him against one of the walls. She huffed a satisfied sigh, folding her hands to her chest.

"Now," Amalay said. "Let's try again."

The figures on the ledges raised their palms once more. Water peeled away from the floor, carrying bits of sand and gravel. The droplets pieced back together, mashing into a new form. Instead of three creatures, a single giant towered before Teia and the others. Its body was as stocky as a tree trunk, its watery torso shaking as it let out a bellow.

The girl on the middle ledge clenched her fists, and an icy scythe materialized in the giant's hands. It howled in pleasure, before lifting the weapon high above its head.

"Much better," Amalay said.

"Move!" Teia said, and they all lunged aside. The weapon came smashing down, slicing into the floor. The entire arena shook from the blow.

Enna's daggers glinted in her hands. "This is *not* how I envisioned my day would go."

"Running for our lives?" Kyra said.

"Murdered by my own group! I'm never going to live this down."

Tobias ducked swiftly beneath the giant's leg. He slashed his knife, but the blade merely passed through the creature's ankle. It barely flinched, as the crowd above whooped in approval. "Does anyone have any good ideas?"

"Stay alive?" Alara said.

"Good ideas that happen to be *useful*?"

"We need to get to Jin!" Kyra cried. "If we can free him—"

Teia rotated to where the adviser was pulling at his chains, just as Tobias shoved her out of the way. They went tumbling to the side, narrowly avoiding one of the scythe's swings. She was dimly aware of his arm cradled around her head, tucking her close to his chest.

When she opened her eyes, he was already back on his feet. Cuts raked up his forearms from where he'd skidded across the ground. "You go!" he said. "We'll cover you."

Enna groaned. "Why us?" she said. She flung one of her knives at the giant, but the blade became caught in its watery arm, suspended where its bicep might have been. As it batted a fist at Enna, Kyra drew back her hand. Before Teia could stop her, fire ripped out from her palms. It blasted into the giant, which tottered heavily on its feet. For a minute, it seemed fire might win out.

As a hush descended over the arena, the giant roared, pushing onward against the flames. The water from its torso widened, opening up like the mouth of an envelope. It folded around the flames, absorbing them whole, quenching them with a strangled hiss. Kyra fell back, panting, as the giant lifted its massive scythe.

"Kyra!" Alara shouted.

It was funny how things turned out. Back in the Archive, Teia hadn't had the strength to finish Kyra off, despite all her inner convictions about the right thing to do. But here in the Pit, surrounded by screaming thieves, she had been given a second chance—a miracle by the Goddess herself.

If she did nothing, the scythe would cleave Kyra in two. Teia's problems would be over, her concerns addressed. She could return to Erisia tonight, and never fear the Serkawr again.

Yet here was her damned conscience, resurfacing at the most inconvenient of times. Before she could fully comprehend the action, Teia had lifted her hand. As she jumped before the scythe, a burst of fire spiraled above her and Kyra, shielding them from the strike. The onlookers gasped, as the giant recoiled. The bottom of its weapon had melted, dripping with a steady *plink!*

Kyra looked dazed. "You saved me."

"Yes," Teia said. "It's a decision I deeply regret."

From beside them, Enna cursed. "Watch out!"

It was too late. The giant lurched out, faster than it'd previously been, the scythe wedged beneath its arm. Teia caught the glitter of frost, the hardness of ice, as something cold crushed into her ribs. The giant's hand had frozen over, its fingers clamped around her. Teia was lifted upward roughly, her feet dangling out into open air, her sides screaming in pain. Somewhere beneath, Tobias was yelling her name.

She was tossed onto Amalay's platform, with Kyra thrown beside her. As Teia pushed herself upright, blocks of ice encircled her hands. A sparkling chain emerged, tying her to the ledge. Next to her, Kyra had received a similar treatment.

Amalay stood. Her eyes were so brown they were nearly black. "You should have said something," she said eagerly. "I do love entertaining guests."

"I'd prefer other forms of entertainment," Teia said. "Food, drink, revelry. If you'd like a turn in these shackles, I'm happy to oblige."

The leader of thieves chuckled. "Teia Carthan, I presume?"

"What was your first clue?"

"I'd heard a rumor that Erisia's monarch was coming to Shaylan. And you!" Amalay's laugh was a rich, vibrant sound, as her focus shifted to Kyra. "There were stories that came from the Erisian rebellion, ones so fantastic I was certain they were false. My contacts across the Dark Sea swore that there was more to the rebellion's champion. She might be the face of the Dawnbreaker movement, but she could also control fire."

"Not by choice," Kyra said roughly.

Amalay clapped her hands before her. "I came to the Pit for a spectacle, and I'm leaving with a gold mine. What more could any thief ask for?"

Kyra hesitated. "What are you planning to do?"

"Isn't it obvious?" Amalay said gleefully. "You're both well worth a small fortune."

"You're going to *ransom* us?"

It was exactly why Teia hadn't wanted to reveal their abilities. In private, they might have been able to hold Amalay off. But now they were severely outnumbered, with the black-robed thieves hovering too close for comfort and the battle raging on below. Any way she cut it, the Society was clearly at an advantage.

"I can imagine a good number of groups that would pay for your services," Amalay continued, before she pivoted toward Teia. "As for you, Teia—what do you think Erisia will offer for your safe return? A portion of the royal treasury? The Morning Star itself?"

Teia didn't bother sharing that one of those two demands was currently out of commission. "Merely a portion? I'd hope I'm worth more than that."

"You have spirit. I respect that. I'll tell you what—you don't give me trouble, and I'll provide your friends with a quick death." Amalay fluttered her hand. "It's really better than what most would receive."

Forty feet below, the giant had resumed its grip on its scythe. Alara was limping badly, and the bandage around Enna's arm had been torn aside. Tobias dodged the giant, while Jin observed helplessly, still bound to the wall. A trail of blood had leaked over the floor.

Death was death, no matter how it was offered. Teia couldn't feel her fingers within the icy shackles, even as she strained against them. She glanced around her frantically, searching for a weapon, a solution.

The idea struck her suddenly, as her gaze landed on the high wooden ceiling, the beams crisscrossing the shadowed rafters. She almost laughed at the simplicity of it all, as she stopped struggling against the chains.

What was this arena, if not a tinderbox? What was she, if not the match?

Despite the bone-chilling cold, whispers of heat fluttered around Teia. She drew them toward her, commanding them onto the underside of the shackles. A thin stream of warmth worked its way into her hands. Before her, Amalay didn't notice. The leader of thieves was captivated by the fight, distracted. That would be her first mistake.

"How about I make you a different deal?" Teia said. She wiggled her index fingers, and heat blossomed at her command. "You grant me a private audience, and I don't kill your soldiers as you watch."

Amalay started to laugh. "You?" she said, her eyes finding Teia's.

Teia dipped her shoulders. "I guess that's a no."

She yanked her hands free, ice melting away. A curl of heat wrapped around Kyra, dissolving her shackles, as a second burst propelled upward. Flames danced through the ceiling beams. They threaded into the rafters, pulsing with an orange glow.

Instantly, the mood in the arena changed. Shouts bounced through the space. The thieves scattered like flies, disappearing back through the narrow doorways.

On the ledges, the black-robed figures tensed, but Teia was too quick. She sent flames dashing outward, catching each of the soldiers. They were struck from their platforms, screaming. As they hit the bottom of the arena, landing with a sickening thud, there was the audible crunch of bone, reverberating over the yells.

The girl in the center—the one who resembled Amalay—was last. As she fell, twisting in midair, Amalay staggered forward. "No!" she shouted. When she extended her hand, ice shimmered into a slide, sculpting beneath the girl. She was brought safely to the ground, the hems of her robe smoking faintly.

Amalay whipped back. An icy rod glistened in her fist. She swung it in an elegant arc, cracking Teia across the jaw. Teia stumbled, swearing in pain. She might have plummeted off the platform, if Kyra hadn't leapt to steady her.

As Kyra parried Amalay's next strike, the leader of thieves lowered her head. "How *dare* you—"

Beneath them, the watery giant had exploded. As droplets spattered throughout the arena, the girl that Amalay had saved stirred. Her robes had shifted, scrunched beneath her awkwardly. Her dark hair fanned around her, exposing what looked like an inverted triangle inked against the back of her neck.

"Amalay?" the girl said, struggling to sit upright.

"Rina!"

High above, the beams released an agonizing creak. As Amalay directed an alarmed look at the rafters, reaching out to douse the flames, Teia pushed her hand forward. She meant to grab for heat, assembling fresh threads—but then a new sensation lodged into her chest, like the heavy sparkle that came with too much champagne. She heard the murmur of water, tickling against her ears, beckoning her to listen.

It was the same call she'd had in the Archive. Teia's mind sharpened. She felt the water inside Amalay, different points lighting within her body. Some places were fainter than others, but Teia latched on to what she needed. She whispered her command, and the water rustled back.

Yes. With pleasure.

Amalay swayed. The rod fell from her grip, plunging over the edge. Her arms flung backward, before they were forced down to the ledge, suctioned to ice. She swore, trying in vain to pull free. "What are you doing to me?"

Teia stood over the leader of thieves. Pain arched through her jaw as her lips bent into a grin. "I warned you, didn't I?"

Amalay's eyes were wild. She cast another glance at the shuddering ceiling, before craning her neck to where Rina lay, groaning on the floor. "Call off your flames."

"You're worried for her," Teia crooned. "Let me guess—your sister? She looks just like you. Lovely, lovely girl." She stooped down, bending toward Amalay's struggling form. "Tell me, Amalay. Do you know what happens when someone burns? Do you know how it looks when skin starts to melt, flesh dripping off bone? Because I do. I've seen it. I've *caused* it."

"Teia," Kyra said.

Amalay gritted her teeth. *"Call off your flames."*

"Gladly," Teia said. "You give me what I came to the Society for, and nobody else needs to die."

Amalay tried once more to rise. Panic broke over her face as her arms refused to move. "I don't even know what you want!"

"That's a pity, isn't it? We could have had a conversation, before you decided to set your thieves on me." Teia curved her palm, and fire slithered through the rafters. "The Seascript."

For a second, true fear seized Amalay's expression. "The Seascript?" she repeated. "That's what you're here for?"

"Think quickly before your next answer. I'd say you have about twenty seconds before the ceiling starts to fall."

"Are you mad? If that happens, you'll kill us all!"

In response, Teia smiled. She tasted blood in her mouth, smeared across her teeth. "Maybe," she said. "But at least then you'll go with me."

Fire roared overhead, ash flaking through the air. A horrible tremor went through the arena, as if its very foundation was coming undone.

"Fine," Amalay gasped. Sweat beaded her brow. Her eyes were still fixed on Rina.

"Louder," Teia snarled. "I can't quite hear you."

"*Fine.* The Seascript—it's yours."

"On your honor?"

Amalay sucked in a breath. "Yes. On my honor."

It was time to test whatever code of ethics the Society of Thieves had in place. Teia grasped for the glinting knot of heat, unraveling the strands with a practiced hand. The flames retracted above, before vanishing altogether. The ceiling beams had been thoroughly blackened. A thick sheen of smoke filled the arena.

Teia released Amalay. The leader of thieves sprang to her feet, as graceful as a cat. She leapt immediately from the platform, icy steps forming under her feet.

Kyra came to stand beside Teia. They both gazed down as Amalay reached the base of the Pit, flinging her arms around Rina, smoothing her hair from her scarred cheek.

"Teia," Kyra said softly. Her features were drawn. A bruise rose on her temple, swelling against her eye. "How did you know Amalay would fold?"

Teia spat out a wad of blood. "Easy," she answered. "I didn't."

Chapter Eighteen

Amalay led them back into the tunnels, away from the harsh torchlight of the Pit.

She walked beside Rina, their heads bent together, their whispered discussion swirling through the passageway. They spoke in Shaylani, but Teia thought she knew their topic of conversation. Every so often, Amalay would rotate back. She'd throw Teia a furious look, as if envisioning the best way to jam a blade through her chest.

The leader of thieves might want her head, but she'd have to wait her turn. If Teia's tenuous alliance with Kyra failed, the rebel champion would be the first in line.

Ahead, Tobias kept an even pace behind the thieves. He began rolling his sleeves, creasing them at the elbow to expose tanned skin beneath. Teia's eyes caught on the long gashes that raked up his arms, angry scrapes embedded with flecks of gravel.

"You're staring."

She jumped as Alara popped up next to her. "I'm observant," Teia said crossly, massaging at her chest. "That's usually how the best plans are formed."

"Are you sure? Because I might not be good at planning, but

I do know definitions. Do you want me to tell you what *pining* means?"

"We're in an underground passageway, following two thieves who have every incentive to murder us. Is this really what you want to talk about right now?"

"Yes," Alara said without missing a beat. "And if you don't know where to start, I'd love to begin with your conversation by the cliffs—"

By the smallest of miracles, Tobias chose that moment to turn. The Poisons Master fell quiet as he slowed his stride, waiting until Teia was standing beside him. "Teia."

A flutter went through her, a glow that accompanied the sound of his voice. "Are you all right?" she said. Without thinking, she reached for his right arm, rotating it gingerly to inspect the wounds.

"Are you?" he said, tugging his arm gently from her grasp. "What happened on the platform with Amalay?"

"We had a talk."

"One that ended with her caving to your demands?"

"I can be very persuasive."

"You threatened her, didn't you?"

"Just a bit."

"That explains all the nasty looks."

"I haven't seen anything," Teia said, just as Amalay sent another bone-chilling glare her way.

She could hear the smile in Tobias's tone, sunshine breaking through clouds. "Menace," he murmured.

Alara caught Teia's eye and mouthed, *Pining.*

They rounded a corner, where Amalay shoved out at a section of the wall. A door, rendered nearly invisible against the weathered stone, swung back on its hinges. A set of crude stairs lay beyond, moss creeping over the bottom steps. At the top was another wooden trapdoor, similar to the one on the floor of the apothecary. The iron handles were shaped like daggers.

They entered a narrow circular room, lit by the warm glow of a half dozen lanterns. Rows of trunks had been stacked high against the walls, lavishly decorated with jeweled inlays, golden lids, silver initials, and—on occasion—the beautifully painted crest of a nobleman's house. There were two other floors above the one where they were standing, although the center of both had been hollowed away, allowing swirled pillars to notch upward, unfurling at the ceiling in stained glass designs.

Despite their surroundings, it was the rounded interior of the building that gave Teia pause. She frowned up at the columns, the floors that rose overhead. "Are we in the pagoda?" she said, thinking of the tiered blue structure that rose above Okkan.

"That's impossible," Jin sputtered. "That's where the Goddess's main statue is."

"Are you sure?"

"We saw it from the main road. I've *prayed* there."

She left the adviser stammering over his words as she trotted to the wall. In certain sections, patterned pieces of glass had been installed between the trunks. When she leaned forward, Teia found herself peering into another chamber, bathed in the afternoon sun. A long line of people stretched out the arched door, their eyes fixed high. One man looked straight at her but didn't acknowledge anything out of the ordinary. Instead, he simply scrunched his nose, scratched furtively beneath his arms, and continued on with his prayers.

She wasn't staring through ordinary glass. Somehow, the Society had constructed mirrors that let them monitor the pagoda, while showing nothing at all to those on the other side.

Teia wondered briefly what the mirrors were disguised as, before the answer came to mind. *The altar.* She had glimpsed the massive wall of silver that surrounded the Goddess's statue, the intricate designs hewn into metal.

Teia drew back, impressed. The thieves might lack tact, but they were undeniably effective. "We're not just in the pagoda," she said. "We're behind Armina's statue."

Jin looked positively scandalized. "Hiding here—in a place of *worship*, no less—"

"Smart," Enna said.

"Heretical."

"I'm sure the Goddess would understand."

Tobias examined the stacks of trunks. "What are all these?" he said, batting at a stray tassel.

"A rite of passage," Enna explained. "When a thief wants to join the Society, they're sent to steal a trunk. If they make it back in one piece, it's added to the collection, and they get to carve their calling card into the corner."

"Why a trunk?"

"Trunks are bulky, hard to lift. It takes skill to get away with something like that. Besides," Enna added, "who doesn't enjoy a good challenge?"

Alara tapped at one of the lids. An eagle had been stamped onto the front, its white wings poised to take flight. "Did you have to steal one too?"

"Naturally."

"From who?"

Enna smirked. "Jura Carthan," she said. "Who else?"

While they were admiring the decor, Amalay and Rina had clustered by the velvet chairs, which were positioned between the towering columns. They were speaking furiously in Shaylani, arguing in hushed tones. Amalay stabbed a finger toward the trapdoor, but Rina swatted her away.

"I'm staying," she said loudly in Erisian. Up close, her features were softer than her sister's, like a reflection within a foggy mirror. The scars across her face were oddly becoming, accentuating her enormous eyes.

Amalay hissed something back in Shaylani, but Rina shook her head. "Let them hear—I don't care. I'm not a child anymore. My decisions are my own."

Teia thought she saw Amalay's left eye twitch. "Do we have to do this now?" the leader of thieves said, also in Erisian. "We could speak about this later—"

"Later, when you can dodge my questions and pretend like this didn't happen? Most of your thieves only tolerate me because I'm your sister. How am I supposed to rise in the ranks if you keep coddling me?" Rina plopped into the chair, wedging herself against the tufted cushion. "Like I said, Amalay—I'm staying."

Amalay pursed her lips. It was obvious she wasn't happy, but Rina wasn't budging. After a moment, the leader of thieves tossed her hands skyward. She pivoted toward Teia, frost licking at the bottom of one of the columns.

"All right, Teia Carthan," she said irritably. "You demanded an audience, and I'm here to oblige. Now—what business do you have with the Seascript?"

"I'm interested in history," Teia said, and Amalay produced a hearty scoff.

"I'm impatient, not stupid. I'll give you one more chance to provide me with a coherent answer."

Teia wasn't keen on retelling her ordeal with Lehm, but she

supposed it couldn't hurt. She provided an abridged version of her various discoveries, from how Eris and Mei had raised the Serkawr together to Lehm's plans for the sea beast. Both Amalay and Rina listened intently, nodding along in unison. Kyra was silent, but Teia thought it was a start. At least the rebel champion wasn't lobbing any insults her way.

"Interesting," Amalay said thoughtfully, once Teia was done. "Commoner's flame, noble's water, the Morning Star, and the proper *shi*. Who knew that was all it took to raise the sea beast?"

It sounded like quite a bit to Teia, but she didn't bother correcting the leader of thieves. From her chair, Rina had brought her legs to her chest, her hands curled around her knees. "It reminds me of the stories our parents used to tell us."

"They spoke of the Serkawr?" Alara asked.

"They were merchants, specializing in historic relics. It's how Amalay and I speak Erisian—they used to travel the Five Kingdoms for their business." Rina bit her lip. "Although I've never heard of Mei and Eris summoning the Serkawr. I always thought the Goddess sent it as a warning when the founders fell into civil war."

"That's what we learned in Erisia too," Teia said. "But maybe Mei and Eris tried to call the sea beast after the war was over." She tipped her head. "What about the Seascript? Is there anything there about the Serkawr?"

"Our parents used to say the secret for controlling the Serkawr—and sending it back to the Dark Sea—was inside. They mentioned the book also had an incantation, which began the ritual to raise the sea beast."

Rina's tone didn't sound promising. "But?" Teia said.

"I don't know for sure. I never read it."

Amalay shrugged. "Me neither. Who has that kind of time?"

First Yuwen, and now the Society. "You stole Shaylan's most valuable artifact, and it didn't ever cross your mind to read it?"

"I'm a thief, not a scholar. Besides, the entire thing is written in old Shaylani. It's terribly difficult to read, not to mention painfully boring." The leader of thieves folded her arms. "I have to say, Teia Carthan—I'm not usually inclined to believe royals. Then again, I can't think of a single other reason why any ruler would risk their hide to seek out the Society of Thieves."

"Okkan isn't my first choice for a vacation."

"That's your loss. Have you tried the fried oysters? They happen to be excellent."

"I'm not a fan of oysters."

"Makes sense," Amalay said agreeably. "Is it true Erisians only eat broiled meat and potatoes?"

"Tell you what," Teia said. "You give me the Seascript, and I'll buy everyone here a bowl. Two, if you promise to stop wasting my time."

Amalay fluffed out her hair. "I want to help you. Really, I do. It's just that there are some—*difficulties* with what you're asking for. Wouldn't you prefer another relic? We have enough jade statues to fill up a warship."

"No doubt stolen from Taijin," Jin muttered.

Enna aimed a kick at him. "Ignore him," she chirped. "How large of a warship are we talking about?"

If Teia had wanted to peruse statues, she would have visited a sculpture garden. "What sort of difficulties?" she demanded. Dread opened in her stomach, whispering up her spine.

When Amalay grew silent, it was Rina who spoke in her place. "We don't have it," she said. Her hands fluttered nervously in her lap.

If the Society had pawned the Seascript off to the highest bidder, Teia was going to take a torch to the pagoda. "Well?" she said witheringly. "What happened to it?"

Somehow, she had already anticipated Rina's next words. "The Seascript . . ." she said. "It was taken from us."

Chapter Nineteen

Teia repressed a swear. "Taken?" she repeated. "By *who*?"

This time, it was Amalay who answered. "The Red Mountain," she grunted, and the temperature in the room dropped several degrees colder.

It was a better answer than "Lehm," but not one Teia wanted to hear. *The Red Mountain.* The name rang a faint bell. She thought back to the conversation with Yuwen in his chambers, when he'd shown her the memory of his father.

There are people who don't support my reign. The Red Mountain, for instance, would choose my ba in a heartbeat.

"The Red Mountain," Teia said, her voice tinged with disbelief. "They're a rebel group, aren't they?"

"They appeared two years back," Rina said. "They chose their name for Emperor Feng—red because of his preferred color, mountain for where he's currently imprisoned."

"Yuwen exiled his father to a mountain?"

"Cloud Mountain," Amalay answered grimly. "It's close to here—about a few hours' ride."

If Teia hadn't been so distressed, she would have found all this marginally entertaining. At the very least, the irony was inescapable. Maybe this was the fate that all Carthan monarchs were doomed to suffer—they were plagued by insurgents, both at home and abroad.

Near the trunks, Alara made a disapproving sound. "The Red Mountain," she mused. "What a ridiculous name for a rebel organization."

"Very literal," Kyra agreed.

Teia bit back a remark. In her humble opinion, *Dawnbreaker* wasn't much better. "I thought Feng was unpopular," she said instead. "Why does he have an entire movement behind him?"

"He was well-liked by some," Rina offered.

"Not by anyone with sense," Jin said scornfully.

Rina's forehead pinched. "There was a time when things were good under Feng. Tourism was high, and harvests were plentiful."

"The royal family kept their summer home here," Amalay added. "In the warmer months, Feng used to throw magnificent parties. Everyone was invited, from shopkeepers to fishermen. Workers were given a holiday. Spirits were passed out on Okkan's main road, and Feng's guards distributed sweets made in the palace kitchens."

"That's all it takes to support a tyrant?" Jin said. "A handful of parties and a pitcher of wine?"

"I'm not supporting anyone," Amalay snapped back. "There's pockets to pick no matter who sits on the throne. But you'll find Feng has more supporters than you might think—people who remember his rule fondly."

The adviser bristled at the statement. "And what about once Feng's ambitions set in?" he said. "The execution of Taijin's Memory Keepers, put to death before their children. The books he gathered from different libraries, the records he burned in town squares. Was all that waved away? Did nobody care, so long as the revelry continued?"

From her seat, Rina made a noise of disgust. The scars on her cheek glimmered in the lamplight as she peered at Jin coldly. "Yuwen hasn't been much of an improvement. He doesn't come to Okkan, and he barely leaves the palace. Even the coup that took place—"

"The one that saved Shaylan from ruin?"

"Not all of it." Rina's voice grew shrill. "People were hurt and killed. *Innocent* people, people who never wanted Yuwen on the throne in the first place—"

She broke off, her chest heaving. Teia took her in with acute interest, as Rina's leg jolted against the chair, bouncing up and down. She considered prying for more information but held her tongue. There would be time for that later. Teia had the feeling that if she interrogated Rina here, her shaky truce with Amalay would crumble.

Besides, there was plenty else to question the thieves about. Amalay was now pacing around the chamber, stomping from wall to wall—and Teia's worries were still fixed on the Seascript, no doubt locked away in some secure location.

"What you're telling me," she said, "is that the Red Mountain robbed you."

Amalay didn't slow. "Yes." The word was uttered between clenched teeth. "We think it was an inside job."

"Why would they want the Seascript at all?" Kyra asked. "Is it worth a high price?"

"Throughout our history, the Seascript has always been in possession of the current ruler. The Red Mountain believes having it offers legitimacy to Feng."

"Does it?"

"Unfortunately," Jin confirmed gloomily. "It's the reason Yuwen never spoke widely about its disappearance."

Teia had long thought her luck poor, but she'd never felt more like a miser. After the lies Lehm told the court about Teia vying for power, she scarcely needed to be associated with another rebel group. In fact, there was nothing she wanted *less* than to arbitrate who sat on Shaylan's throne.

But if Teia wanted the Seascript, there was only one way to obtain it. Marching into the heart of the Red Mountain wouldn't improve her standing with Yuwen, nor would destroying the relic once she'd read its contents. Her cousin had shown he was willing to trust Lehm; Teia couldn't risk the possibility that he'd allow the rebel leader to peruse the Seascript.

It wasn't exactly the recipe for fostering goodwill. Then again, what was another slight against the Shaylani court? Yuwen already despised her. If Teia was going to burn a bridge, she might as well set the entire foundation alight.

"Does the Red Mountain have a camp nearby?" Teia said.

The question seemed to shock the two thieves. At last, Rina drew a quick breath. "Why?" she asked.

"I'm going to send them a gift basket, of course. A bottle of Erisian ale, perhaps, and a few good loaves of bread."

"Is that some kind of joke?" Amalay said.

Out of the corner of Teia's vision, Kyra coughed. "Sarcasm," she offered.

"Very good," Alara said.

"I wouldn't waste a single loaf on those criminals," Jin said viciously. "They deserve the scraps taken from the rubbish pile."

"Oh yes," Tobias replied. "I'm sure that will bring them to their knees."

Teia kept her focus pinned on Amalay. "Not a joke," she said airily. "You can make a contribution as well—whatever you'd like, as long as it's portable. I'll deliver the basket to the Red Mountain myself, once I pay them a visit."

"We don't need you fighting our battles," Amalay said stiffly. "We have eyes on the Seascript—and a plan to retrieve it."

"And you didn't think to lead with that?" Teia retracted everything she'd thought about the thieves' effectiveness. "Where is it?"

"It's being kept in the House of Mourning."

"*The* House of Mourning?" Jin croaked.

"Is there any other?"

Teia envisioned the crimson home with its bronze filigree, splotched like a bloodstain against Okkan's horizon. "The place Feng went after killing the Memory Keepers? I thought it was privately owned."

"It is," Amalay said. "Ko Taisheng bought it. He's a merchant—one of Shaylan's wealthiest. He built his fortune purchasing empty storefronts, and leasing them out to shopkeepers at outrageous prices. Today, he owns a stake in most of the stores on Okkan's central street."

"Ingenious," Enna admitted.

"Exploitive," Kyra mumbled.

"Isn't that what I said?"

"What does he want the Seascript for?" Teia said. She pictured the worn book on display, entombed in a crystal case.

"My guess?" Amalay said. "He's safeguarding it until the rebels can break Feng out of Cloud Mountain. Once they do, they'll present it to him as a gift."

"Taisheng is part of the rebellion?"

"He's one of the Red Mountain's main sponsors. He's been bankrolling them since their inception." Amalay shrugged.

"Many merchants back Feng, you know. Taxes were lower under the old emperor. People excused it at first, but less and less as the months go by."

Jin grimaced. "Yuwen is a better man than Feng ever was."

"Better men aren't always popular," Amalay said. "In this case, it just so happens that Ko Taisheng is neither. For the sake of settling our debts, my thieves and I will take care of him."

Enna had once deafened a man for attempting to steal from her. What punishment would the merchant face for taking the Seascript? Teia hoped he was prepared to lose his hearing—maybe even his sight, if the thieves were feeling spry.

"When are you going?"

"Two days from now, on the fifth night of Kashan. On the sixth, Taisheng throws his annual banquet at the House of Mourning."

"Why the sixth?" Teia said with a frown.

"He claims it's his lucky number. *Six* in Shaylani sounds like *wealth*. There are plenty of homonyms in our language. Taisheng just happened to latch on to this one."

"I'm glad he did," Rina said. "The banquet is one of Okkan's largest events. Usually, Taisheng invites both locals and foreign dignitaries, expats who have made a new home here. There's music and spirits—and the food! The food is divine."

Alara perked up. "You've been?"

"You'd be surprised how many commoners are willing to pay for a forged invitation. We tend to keep a few for ourselves too."

"The guards don't check?"

Amalay snorted. "The guards Taisheng hires can barely be bothered to stand up straight, much less check invitations, one by one. Still, we're taking precautions. In Shaylan, it's customary to provide your workers with an evening of rest prior to a large event."

"You're striking the night before the banquet, when there's only a skeleton crew." In spite of herself, Teia was impressed. "Smart."

"We'll cover each of the building's entrances as well—one main door, one side exit, and two servant gates. But when my thieves go in, we'll use the windows below the roof. Taisheng's bedroom is on the third floor, which is where he's keeping the Seascript."

"He has a private safe?"

"He has three, including one in a hidden room on the second floor." Amalay rolled her eyes. "That renovation must have cost Taisheng a fortune, for all the good it did him. There's clearly a protrusion in the wall."

A hidden chamber sounded incredibly promising. "You're positive Taisheng doesn't keep the Seascript there?"

"It sounds like the kind of unoriginal thing he'd do, doesn't it?" Amalay said. "But I've had my thieves on the lookout since the Seascript disappeared. There's been a few occasions where they've spotted Taisheng through a window, carrying the text up to the third floor. When he returns downstairs, his hands are always empty."

"He sleeps with the Seascript in reach? Does he tell it a story before bed too?"

"He'd best not be too attached. We'll pay him a visit, take what's ours, and be in and out before anyone can call for proper reinforcements."

"You've thought this through," Teia said with begrudging respect.

"Naturally," Amalay said. "What other way is there to plan a heist?"

"Have you tried adrenaline and luck?" Tobias said. "That seems to have worked for us in the past."

Amalay scoffed. "You lot have robbed someone before?"

"We've broken into a prison," Kyra supplied. "Does that count?"

"Which one?" Rina said.

"Blackgate."

"Blackgate?"

"Twice," the rebel champion said.

"I wasn't invited for the first run," Enna groused.

"You barely agreed to go on the second," Teia reminded her. "But since you're so eager for adventure, there's a new job calling all our names."

"Excuse me," Amalay said. Her voice was sharp, teetering on a knife's edge. "You don't intend to *come,* do you?"

"I second that," Jin said.

Alara shrugged. "You clearly don't know Teia Carthan."

"Pick the most dangerous plan," Tobias agreed, "and you'll find Teia's fingerprints all over it."

"Even so—" Amalay began.

Teia smiled bleakly at the leader of thieves. "You promised me the Seascript, and I'm here to collect. If you're going, we're coming with you."

"Our routes are already formed. If we add extra people, it'll take time to replot them."

"Then I suggest we get started. Don't worry—I work best under pressure."

Amalay looked positively dumbstruck. "Mad," she professed. "Absolutely mad."

From beside Teia, Tobias released a low chuckle. "What did I say before?" he said softly. That same, rueful smile shone through his voice. Her foolish heart leapt at the sound. "Menace."

Chapter Twenty

Teia had never concocted a robbery with a band of thieves before, but she supposed there was a first time for everything.

The following days were a whirlwind of discussion, late evenings crowded around a scarred wooden table. Five thieves had been picked for the job—and although none could control water, they made up for it with a spectacular collection of weapons: glinting knives, revolvers strapped to leather belts, and one extraordinary set of pearl-handled daggers, which kept reflecting rainbows against the wall. The mood was electric, as if they were preparing for some wondrous festival, and Teia found herself caught in the hum of energy, the manic scheming that she excelled at.

Rina wasn't permitted to join the group, but that didn't stop her from trying. She lurked at the fringes of each meeting, milling about like a ghost, inspecting the crinkled blueprints from a distance. During one discussion, she even tried to debate her case, holding her head high with the loftiness of a royal. "You could use my affinity for ice," she argued. "Isn't it better to have all the help you can get?"

Amalay only gestured at the door, not unlike an exasperated instructor. "I agreed you could listen," she said. "I never said I'd let you participate."

"But—"

"Out."

With that, Rina stalked away, grumbling mightily under her breath. As Amalay watched her go, something shifted behind her eyes. A trace of sadness broke through, dancing against her brow.

"It's wrong," she murmured. "It's all wrong."

If Teia hadn't been seated beside the leader of thieves, she would have missed the comment altogether. But when she glanced around curiously, nobody else appeared to have overheard. Kyra and Jin examined the House of Mourning's blueprint. Enna tested a piece of silver between her teeth, and Tobias compared weapons with two of the thieves, their blades laid side by side on one of the empty chairs. Even Alara was distracted. The Poisons Master was prodding at a vase of pale blue flowers—a former table centerpiece, which had been moved aside in preparation for the meeting. She was inspecting the petals with great interest, as if assessing how to brew her next toxin.

"Amalay?" Teia said slowly. "What is?"

For a second, the other girl was a thousand miles away, her gaze fixed on a distant point. Then she focused on Teia again, shaking off any of her concerns. "Nothing," the leader of thieves said brusquely. "Let's get back to logistics, shall we? The Seascript isn't going to steal itself."

It was late into their last night of preparation when Amalay dismissed them, satisfied that she'd drilled the plan into everyone's heads. Most of the thieves cheered, eager to crowd into one of Okkan's alehouses. "You should come," one of them said to Enna in Erisian. "See how many drinks you can put away."

Enna grinned. "Is that a challenge, Hsien? We both know who's going to be crawling home."

He roared with laughter, thumping Enna on the back. As the others began to swarm closer, taking bets on the outcome, Teia slipped out the door. She didn't need to go to the alehouse to realize who would win. With Enna's tolerance, Hsien would be lucky if he was coherent enough to stand.

She ascended the wooden stairs, climbing steadily toward the top of the pagoda. Most of the windows lay outside the space that the Society had claimed. Yet there was a single square opening positioned on the third floor, with a rope ladder stored beneath the sill, one end attached to a sturdy iron hook. When Teia leaned out the window, she could see the statue of Armina that was installed on the roof, her hand raised toward the inky horizon.

It took a few tries to toss the ladder at the correct angle and hook it on to Armina's fingertips. Teia had watched several thieves do the same just the evening before, with bottles of rice wine dangling from their pockets. She gave the ladder a cursory tug, testing her weight, before sliding her foot on the bottom rung. Gingerly, Teia began to climb, keeping her eyes high above.

The roof had a wide main ridge, which stretched on opposite ends of the Goddess's statue. Teia maneuvered herself off the ladder. She perched on the beam, her legs resting on the roof's golden tiles. Up here, isolated and alone, she could appreciate the sprawl of Okkan—lanterns that blazed on every corner, people trickling into the pagoda, eager to pay their respects.

It was easier to survey the city than consider what lay beyond. Past the glittering buildings and silver decorations were the imposing black cliffs, the sand that ceded to the Dark Sea. When Teia thought of the lapping waves, a shiver ran through her. Was the Serkawr somewhere within its depths, prowling for its prey? Was it asleep right now, curled in a restless slumber, sensing it might soon be needed?

The rope ladder shook against the iron hook, breaking Teia from her stupor. Someone was climbing up, albeit none too gracefully. A second later, a head crested over the edge of the roof, braid ruffling in the wind. As Kyra hauled herself onto the last rung, she paused.

"Teia?" she said. "What are you doing here?"

"Same as you, I imagine."

"You're avoiding the alehouse?"

"Why bother going when I know Enna will trounce them?"

Kyra settled onto the ridge beside her. Teia tensed, wondering if she was about to be shoved off the roof, but the rebel champion merely drew her knees to her chest. "It's pretty here," she said. "I like that I can see the stars."

"Jin said certain constellations become more visible during Kashan."

Kyra squinted upward. "I think that's one of them." She pointed to a pair of stars clustered side by side. "It's called the Birds of Paradise."

"You know astronomy?"

"A little. My da had a colleague at Bhanot University. She would come over with her maps and books, and chart the night sky on our kitchen table." Kyra smiled. "Da didn't understand it. Said he always preferred rocks."

She considered the constellations, which twinkled far out of reach. "Did you know the stars shift depending on where you are? In Ismet, we used to watch the sky—me, Alara, Tobias. I don't know what we were waiting for, what we hoped we might find."

Teia's stomach dropped. "Kyra—"

"In the mornings, we would buy a copy of the newspaper. We'd bring them to the libraries and ask for a translator. We . . ." Kyra swallowed before continuing, "We learned about what you did in Erisia. How you freed anyone imprisoned in Blackgate for protesting. How you abolished the use of torture."

"The changes that Jura made weren't right. They never were."

Kyra stared out at the Dark Sea. "You didn't have to overturn them, Teia," she said gruffly. "Who would have questioned you if you'd kept them in place?"

Nobody. In Erisia, the kingdom's monarch was left unchecked, the Crown a source of unlimited power. If Teia had decreed that Jura's policies should stay, she doubted there would have been much outcry.

"I didn't have to," Teia agreed. "But I wanted to."

"Why?"

It was strange how things turned out. She and Kyra had never known each other without false pretenses—not really, not in a way that mattered. But maybe it was the circumstances that had brought them here, under the shimmering watch of a thousand stars. Somehow, this felt like neutral territory, a tepid return to equilibrium.

For everything Teia had done, she wanted Kyra to know that she spoke the truth.

"Because your voices were in my head," Teia said hoarsely. "Yours, Alara's, and Tobias's." Her heart contracted, pulsing against her chest. Each breath was lanced with an exquisite pain. "Because when I told you I could be a different kind of ruler, I meant it."

A shaft of moonlight fell upon Kyra's face. An eternity passed, then another, before she eventually spoke again. "I'm so angry at you, Teia—*still*, now, after all this time. Every day I wake up, and

I'm afraid I'll be stuck like this forever, that there will be nothing left but this hole inside me. I feel hollow. I feel *empty*." She took in the masses below, people wreathing through the shuttered shops, children nestled against their parents. "It was easier before to call you a liar. Sometimes, I wish it had stayed that way."

A knot caught in Teia's throat. She started to speak, when Kyra laced her fingers together. "Did I ever tell you how Lehm and I first met?"

She vaguely remembered the story Kyra had once told her, back in the opulent halls of the Golden Palace. "You'd just discovered you could control fire. After Lehm sought you out, he acted as your mentor."

"It's true," Kyra said. "He did. But before all that—before he ever proposed the Dawnbreakers—I asked him to kill me. I begged for it."

"You . . . *what*?"

"Did you know I burned someone, that day I came into my powers?" Kyra's chin was lifted, even as her voice shook. "It was a girl I worked with at the tailor's shop. She didn't do anything wrong. She tried to calm me down. And when she touched my shoulder to ask if I was all right . . ." Her eyes were overbright as she drew another breath. "When Lehm walked through my door, I thought it was a blessing. The Goddess might have forsaken me, but at least she'd sent a solution."

The ache in Teia's chest expanded. She wanted to lunge for the rebel champion, to fold her into a hug. Instead, she sat numbly in place, ice spreading through her lungs as Kyra went on. "He didn't mention the Dawnbreakers at first. In the beginning, he spoke about my powers—how Armina had chosen me for a reason, how fire was a gift, one that had never been granted outside the royal family. If nothing else, it was something to be proud of." Kyra's sigh was muted. "After that, he told me about his sister."

"His sister?" Teia echoed. She could recall a sketch of a young woman that Lehm had kept in his study, framed in a wedge of crystal.

"Her name was Hanne. She was killed in student protests against Ren, when Lehm was just a little boy. The way he spoke about her . . ." The rebel champion shook her head. "She believed in a different form of government, and paid for it with her life. How was that fair? How was that *just*?"

"It's how he recruited you to the Dawnbreakers."

"Even then, I was skeptical. I asked if he'd drag me in chains if I refused. And you know what he said?"

"That he wouldn't force you to go?"

"That if I followed him, I'd always have a choice. I remember how he looked, saying those words—like he believed in me. Like he knew I could make a difference." A tear slid down Kyra's nose. "Teia—the notes you found in Lehm's study. What he plans to do with the sea beast."

Wordlessly, Teia nodded.

"You told me. I know you did." Kyra exhaled tremulously. "I didn't want to believe it. I still don't."

"He gave you purpose," Teia said. "He saved you."

"For what reason?" the rebel champion said back. "At what cost? He wants to raise the Serkawr, Teia. *The Serkawr.* I've heard the legends—everyone has. And he's going to use me to do it."

There was no proper way to cushion the blow. "Yes," Teia said simply. "He will."

"But *why*? His sister—everything he told me—"

"People change, Kyra. Hearts and minds and all that comes with it. Sometimes, all we can do is watch."

The rebel champion wiped her eyes with the sleeve of her shirt. When she spoke again, her voice grated against her throat. "You're a good ruler, Teia."

"Kyra—"

"You *are*. The things you've done for Erisia, the changes you've made. I didn't think they could happen without the Dawnbreakers. And I . . ." She glanced down at her palms. "I won't help Lehm summon the Serkawr. I need you to know that. No matter what he says, no matter what he does."

"I know." Because Teia did, truly. This conversation on the roof was an admission, a reminder of where Kyra had come from. But even in the Archive, locked in battle, Teia had known the depths of the rebel champion's character.

Kyra Medoh had never been a monster.

Chapter Twenty-One

According to Amalay, it was the perfect night to rob one of Shaylan's wealthiest men.

When Teia stepped out of the apothecary, the sky was overcast, with the moon hidden behind a clump of gray clouds. The weather was humid, carrying a dampness that chafed against Teia's skin. Aside from a few gulls that preened atop the clock tower, the central square was utterly deserted.

Teia must have looked particularly grim. To her left, Enna nudged her arm. "Cheer up, Boss," the thief said. "We'll have the Seascript in a few hours. That's good news, isn't it?"

"It's news," Teia said. "I'm not celebrating until I have the book in my hands."

"Easy enough," Enna said confidently. "Amalay was like a drill sergeant. At this point, I could rehearse the plan in my sleep."

"Kyra *was*," Alara teased. "Kept me up until dawn, mumbling about what entrance she was posted at."

Kya blushed. "I did not."

"It's all right, Champion. I didn't mind. You said other things, too, which I found much more interesting. How my hair smells like rosemary and lavender. How you liked my outfit from the day before, especially with the ribbons that kept coming undone at the waist—"

"Alara."

"Don't worry—I found it all very endearing. In fact, if you want to see just what else those ribbons can do, I'm happy to show you later—"

"Alara."

"I didn't know that color existed," Jin said, fascinated, as he studied the red of Kyra's cheeks.

Enna's gaze was bright with anticipation. "We'll be fine," she informed Teia. "Men like Taisheng are ripe for the picking. I could do this job with my eyes closed."

"You realize that's exactly what someone says before things go horribly wrong."

"At least this is better than Blackgate," Tobias said. "Nobody is trying to kill us yet."

"Wonderful," Teia said sullenly. "What more could anyone ask for?"

"A boatful of jewels," Enna said.

"A private garden," Alara provided.

"A cottage back in Erisia," Kyra said dreamily. "Somewhere with lots of trees and a meadow nearby and plenty of places to read."

Teia dismissed the suggestions with a dip of her shoulders. "Well, what *I* want is to stop Lehm from raising the Serkawr and eviscerating the Five Kingdoms—so I need everyone to reevaluate their priorities, if only for tonight."

Behind them, Amalay had climbed free from the apothecary's trapdoor, holding it aside for the remaining thieves. They were dressed in fitted clothing, identical to what Teia and the others wore—black jackets, matching trousers, and hooded cowls, each drawn firmly over their lower faces. The mood had sobered significantly from the previous night, but there was an excitement that lingered, crackling through the group.

Amalay examined her thieves. There was no hint of the girl who'd wavered at the sight of her sister's retreating back. Instead, her eyes were clear, radiant with a fierce sort of joy. When she breezed out into the central square, her slender hand flashed in five directions, each pointing to a different street.

They fanned out without a word, although Teia glanced at Enna. The thief pulled her cowl up, hiding her face, and yet Teia understood the quick slant of her head, a hidden message before she darted toward the leftmost street. *Don't worry.*

It was easier said than done. There were a hundred ways for a plan to go awry, but far fewer paths to success. As Teia crept into a separate alley, she kept close to Hsien, the wiry thief who'd challenged Enna to drinks the night before. She'd heard he had needed to be carried home after the events of the alehouse, a trail of spittle dangling from his lips. Now, though, he was undeniably light on his feet, treading around stray pieces of trash, slowing to make sure she caught up.

They were approaching the House of Mourning from varying points—one thief guarding each of the four doors, while the fifth remained on lookout, stationed atop a nearby roof. Once Amalay received a signal, she would enter from the windows, sneaking inside to rain hell onto Ko Taisheng. After much debate—including a heated argument where a set of pens had been lobbed through the air like projectiles, spattering ink over the wall—it was agreed that Teia's group would be divided the same way, with Enna accompanying Amalay into the House of Mourning.

Teia and Hsien loped through the alley, pressing onward until he held up a bony arm. The House of Mourning's red walls towered ahead. She could see the cheery glow coming from Taisheng's chambers, the window where Amalay and Enna would enter. Beneath that, Teia caught the slight outcrop of space, which protruded on the home's second level. It bulged unevenly from the middle floor, marking the hidden room.

Goddess. Amalay had been right—the architect really *had* done a shoddy job.

They snuck around the side, sticking to the shadows. A simple wooden door was set against the building, the first of the two servants' entrances. Farther ahead, at the end of the main street, Teia glimpsed the second arched door, outlined in a violent shade of crimson. Tobias would be just a few alleys away, surveilling the scene with his assigned thief.

"This is it," Hsien said. He began to rummage about in the leather pouch attached to his belt, before extracting a long metal flare.

"We're early," Teia said. They were keeping time with the peals of the central square's clock tower, which could be heard faintly from where they were crouched.

"Better that than late. There was one job when my timing was off. I missed a signal, blew the con. Amalay gave me a beating so bad it knocked one of my teeth loose." He opened his mouth to demonstrate, wiggling his molar proudly. "See?"

"And you still follow her?" Teia said.

Hsien shrugged. "Amalay's a good leader," he answered. "Prickly and quick to anger, but smart. Loyal. She paid off my debts when the loan sharks would have broken both my legs." He snapped the two pieces of the flare together, attaching the joints in rapid succession. "Now her sister? That's another story."

"Rina? She's been trying to learn, hasn't she?"

"She's too nosy, that one. Always skulking around, asking useless questions. If she wants to earn her stripes, there are better ways to do it." Hsien finished assembling the flare, before presenting it to Teia admiringly. "Pretty, isn't it?"

"You're sure these flares are silent?"

"Positive. We get them custom-made. Now, we just have to wait a bit longer. Once the bells chime, we'll light the wick, distract the guards, and Amalay will be on her way."

"If you say so."

Hsien chuckled. "Amalay is the best there is. Trust me. You'll get your Seascript, and we'll take a few of Taisheng's fingers. Everyone's happy, and all's well that ends—"

His words dissolved in a choked cry. Hsien's eyes widened. A trickle of blood leaked from the corner of his mouth. He toppled with a surprised expression, smashing into the cobblestones. Teia saw an icicle protruding from his back, right between the shoulders.

Instinct took over. Teia dropped the unlit flare, stooping low as something whistled over her head. She spun around, gaze narrowed against the darkness.

The woman on the far side of the street was in plain black robes, a silver sash bound around her narrow waist. Her head was rotated away, showing only one side of her face—pale skin, scarlet lips. She looked like she hadn't seen the sun in years.

Is this the Red Mountain? Teia thought wildly, as she reached for fire. *Did someone tip them off?*

Then the woman turned, and Teia's blood went cold. Even

from this distance, she caught the dragon tattoo inked across the woman's temple. It snaked down her cheek, the tail reaching to her jaw. A sign of allegiance to the emperor—a symbol of dedication to Yuwen.

The Naga smiled. She lifted her arms, and the world vanished into a blank of white.

Chapter Twenty-Two

Snow filled the air, persisting against the warm spring night. Under different conditions, snow in this weather would have been a miracle. Yet any wonder was lost on Teia, as the flakes pressed closer, dimming her vision. She went stumbling sideways against the blizzard, trying and failing to keep hold of heat, the threads evaporating against her fingers.

From her right came a rush of movement, a whirl of black fabric against the piercing white landscape. Teia feinted as the Naga's weapons cut through the air, slender axes fashioned entirely from ice. As Teia backed up, still half-blinded by the snow, she managed to coax a lick of heat around her finger, brightening it into a flame.

A halo of fire ricocheted outward. The Naga fell back, surprised. She was unharmed, the flames glancing off the icy shield she'd summoned before her, and the blizzard dissipated, fading without her concentration. When the Naga locked eyes with Teia, her gaze was flat and calm, the look of a hunter that circled its prey.

What was the Naga doing here? Was Yuwen nearby as well? Was *Lehm*? But of all the questions that surfaced, one loomed large as Teia treaded backward, keeping her attention on the pale-faced woman.

How many other guards had tracked Teia to Okkan?

Serrated pillars of ice shot up around her, their points gleaming like knives. They split diagonally through the alley, creating jagged patterns that crisscrossed the gray walls. Teia lurched aside, but she knew immediately that she'd been too slow. Pain danced down her thigh. One of the spikes had torn through her trousers, blood welling from the gash.

It's fine, Teia thought furiously. *I'm fine.*

The Naga didn't slow. She sprinted forward, her body rotating gracefully around the columns she'd created. A cloud of droplets shone before her. They spun themselves in a silver swirl, elongating in shape. The Naga twisted her fingers, and the icicles raced toward Teia.

She cast fire before her, melting the shards. For a moment, Teia and the guard faced each other, panting, separated by the orange flames. The Naga leered in contempt. Teia thought she saw her smile, before the woman flung out her hand.

An icy formation crackled to life beside Teia, solidifying close to where she stood. As she dove aside, another burst crystallized just inches away. Panic ripped through her, terror pounding at her skull.

She's going to freeze me alive.

She tripped over something soft, and went skidding hard to the ground. When Teia pushed herself upright, she found she'd landed on top of Hsien's body. The icicle was still embedded in his back. The flare he'd assembled rested close by, the trigger beaming silver.

Teia scooped up the flare, just as the Naga hurled through the fiery barricade. She had coated herself in a layer of ice, which evaporated as she exited the flames, sloughing off her skin. As she slashed her arm out, frost imploded next to Teia. She rolled aside, countering with fire. The Naga deflected each blow. She was nearly upon Teia now, that dragon tattoo shining against the firelight.

Teia waited as long as she dared, until the Naga was mere feet away. As the woman sauntered toward her, her features alight with triumph, Teia straightened. The flare was clutched in her hands, pointed directly at the Naga.

"Take care," Teia growled, as she sent a spark into the wick.

The flare slammed into the Naga, shredding through her side. The woman screamed—a long, wailing sound that cut off in a gurgle. She fell, twitching, blood pooling onto the cobblestones beneath her.

Teia rose unevenly. She was about to limp to the Naga—put her out of her misery—when a shout came careening through the narrow streets, dappled with pain.

Tobias.

Teia left the Naga to bleed out on the stones, as she doubled back toward the main street. The House of Mourning looked on, a silent spectator against the night. As Teia raced down the alleys, counting them as she went, she could feel fire unraveling at her back, heat cording up her arms. If something happened to Tobias, she would paint all of Okkan red with blood.

The alley had just come into sight when something punched out into the main street, writhing in midair before retracting hastily. Teia stopped short, apprehension souring her stomach. Were those *tentacles*?

While the Naga that fought Teia had been gifted with ice, the guard facing Tobias had an entirely different affinity. Water twined around her, rising above her head like a nest of vipers. At her command, the tentacles of water shot out, moving with such force that they split through a nearby crate, aimed straight for Tobias.

The thief he'd come with had already fallen, her body limp as Tobias wove through the tentacles. When his blade whistled up in a metallic arc, one of the tentacles flopped to the ground, sliced cleanly in two. The Naga shrieked. She jerked back haphazardly, as the severed tentacle melted into a puddle.

When Tobias saw Teia, a smile crooked at the corners of his mouth. "What took you so long?"

He was hobbling, favoring his left leg, but she was relieved that he bore no other injuries. "Are you admitting you need help?"

"I'm not admitting to anything," he said, as another swirl of water pelted toward them, missing Tobias by inches. The lash fell through one of the walls bordering the alley, breaking apart the wooden boards. Splinters went flying, glass shattering from a ruined window. As the coil came spinning their way, Teia sprang forward.

She twisted out with a handful of flames, managing to grasp one of the coils. Water evaporated at her touch, sizzling in the air. The Naga drew back, the tentacle quivering dangerously. It pulsed erratically—once, twice—before sprouting a new end.

Like a worm, Teia thought with disgusted fascination, as the lash came careening toward her once more.

She grabbed for heat, sharpening it before her. When she sent fire spinning toward the Naga, the woman merely flicked her fingers. The tentacle retracted toward its mistress. It shielded her from the flames before snaking back out, wrapping around Teia in the span of an instant.

Water filled her nose and mouth, burning her throat. She felt her feet lift off the ground as the tentacle widened in form, ballooning in size. She was trapped within a cocoon of water, air squeezing from her lungs. Darkness rushed in, as Teia thrashed within the sphere.

All of a sudden, the chrysalis softened around her, liquid losing its shape. Teia spilled out onto the street, coughing furiously. When she glanced back, the Naga was sprawled on the ground. A bloody hole had punctured through her chest, right above the apex of her heart.

A hand stretched toward Teia. She looked up to find Tobias, his stormy eyes trained on hers. Above, the clouds had parted at last, a strip of moonlight cleaving into the alley. He was caught in its glow, his face half in shadow. It was an image that deserved an artist, a sculptor—someone far more talented than she—to capture that breathtaking sense of beauty.

"Who are they?" Tobias said, as he helped Teia up.

"The Naga—a group of the emperor's guards. They're only supposed to answer to Yuwen."

"Are you sure? It seems like there's been a change in leadership." He passed something toward her, a red bracelet of glass beads. The golden charm was etched with an upside-down triangle.

Teia's mouth fell open. She took the bracelet from Tobias carefully, evaluating the charm. "Is this . . ."

"A mountain?" His tone was bleak. "I'd say there's an overwhelming resemblance."

"The Red Mountain."

"Yes."

Teia could feel the beginning of a headache setting on, as she stowed away the bracelet. "The Naga are sworn to the emperor. What's one of them doing with a rebel group's symbol?"

Tobias's face was grim. But before he could respond, his expression contorted, racked with pain. A hiss slipped between his teeth. When he collapsed, folding without another sound, the side of his shirt was doused in red, stained crimson with blood.

Teia's heart seized. Fear blazed through her, as she whipped her head to the opposite end of the alley.

It was the Naga she'd encountered—the pale, lovely woman who controlled ice. Somehow, she had dragged herself three streets over, her innards leaking out between clamped fingers. Yet with her free hand, she'd managed to launch a spate of icicles, each daggered with a razored edge.

Rage engulfed Teia, drowning her in its midst. She stepped in front of Tobias, blocking the next wave of projectiles before advancing on the Naga. As she stalked forward, flames rippled before her like a shield. She saw her own silhouette reflected in the woman's pupils, gleaming with orange fire.

There was a prickling against her skin, scratching feebly at her arms, her legs. The Naga was trying to encase her within ice, but Teia knew it didn't matter. She'd never felt fury like this before, a black river that swelled in her chest, a rift in her soul which had broken apart.

Teia Carthan would show just how monstrous she could be.

She stopped before the Naga, who plunged a hand into her robes, undeterred. The guard withdrew a curved metal dagger—a final alternative, in case ice ever failed.

This time, it wasn't heat that Teia summoned, but water. As the Naga leveled the knife, Teia reached into the depths of her anger, the current that swirled within her. She knew what she was listening for, recognition sparking within her veins. Water awoke within the Naga—glimmering points, like stars against a velvet night.

The Naga's body pulled taut, her knees locking. The woman grunted in surprise. She tried to move, but her limbs were fastened in place. Teia closed her fist.

The Naga's hand rose slowly, the knife resting at the tip of her own throat. A sweat broke out over her forehead, distress flashing in her eyes. She said a few words in Shaylani, a garbled plea, but Teia only smiled.

Good.

When the knife speared through the Naga's neck, the woman fell forward, dead before she hit the ground. Teia didn't hesitate. She bent down, rooting about in the guard's robes. When her grip closed around something smooth, Teia's hands shook. The beaded bracelet she withdrew was identical to the one Tobias had shown her, set with that same golden charm.

She jammed the bracelet into her pocket and went sprinting back to Tobias, kneeling beside him. His pulse was feeble against her fingers. There was blood everywhere, glistening against the cobblestones.

"Tobias," she growled. "Don't you dare die on me here."

The words had barely left her lips when footsteps rang from the main street. Teia bolted up, grasping for a flame—but it was Jin who dashed into the alley. A scratch mottled his cheek. His jacket had been badly ripped, the cowl missing from his face.

"It's Lehm," the adviser gasped. "He's here in Okkan—and he has Kyra."

Chapter Twenty-Three

They staggered back to the apothecary, with Tobias steadied between them.

Blood leaked over Teia's shirt as Tobias's head lolled against his chest. His breathing came in labored fits, rattling in his throat, his feet dragging under him.

She knew it was risky being out in the open like this, but Teia was beyond caring. Let the Naga come. She would set them aflame, every last one, before stacking their charred bodies in the cobbled streets.

When they stumbled through the apothecary's arched threshold, Jin supported Tobias while Teia grabbed for the jar of purple flowers. When she turned the lid to the right, the trapdoor sprang open, its two halves falling aside with a muffled crash.

Amalay was already below, sitting on the floor at the base of the stairs. Cuts winnowed down the right side of her face, as if she'd been seized by the hair and thrown roughly to the ground. She looked exhausted, resting her head against the bottom step, although she lurched upright when she saw Tobias.

"Is he . . ."

"Get me a healer," Teia snarled.

They plunged through the tunnels, winding into the darkness

until Amalay brought them to a stop. She pushed against another hidden door, embedded into stone. When it creaked aside, the leader of thieves ushered them into a brightly lit room, before calling out in Shaylani.

Enna was waiting on one of the plush chairs. She was badly bruised, with a long gash running along her forehead. "Goddess," she swore, her green eyes landing on Tobias. "What happened?"

"The Naga," Teia said, as a wizened man in ivory robes came bustling from the kitchen. He was carrying a steaming pot of tea, although he nearly dropped the tray when he caught sight of his visitors. Amalay spoke to him rapidly in Shaylani, and the man ducked his balding head. He set the tray down hurriedly, before gesturing them into an elegant hallway, where several chambers had been sectioned from the main room.

When he pushed open the sliding door to the infirmary, a string of silver charms chimed in harmony. It was dimmer here, with candles blazing in the corners and an earthy smell lingering in the air. Rolls of bandages had been arranged beside large jars of dried herbs. A stone mortar glinted next to a basin of water. Lacquered cabinets had been bolted into the wall, their doors cracked open to reveal a variety of tinctures.

Teia and Jin heaved Tobias to the metal table in the center of the room. When Teia stepped back, the elderly man stooped forward, a scalpel in his fist. He peeled back the soiled remains of Tobias's shirt, observing the injury in a fascinated manner, before dumping an entire bottle of orange liquid onto the cut. When the poultice touched his skin, Tobias let out a groan, his brow relaxing slightly.

"Anesthetic," the old man said in rough Erisian. He poked at the mess of the wound, nodded with satisfaction, and pointed his shrunken chin at the door. "Out."

Teia planted her feet. "I'm not going anywhere," she said, but the man shook his head again.

"Out," he said, with more insistence than before. His focus was locked on the injury. As he placed two fingers on the edge of the wound, Teia felt herself staring. At the man's touch, Tobias's blood had begun to clot. Red droplets rose gently in the air, twinkling against the candlelight.

"Teia," Amalay said softly. "Yir is the best healer we have, but he needs to concentrate."

Teia hesitated, before she spun around without another word, stalking out of the room to reenter the main space. A roar had filled her ears. She was dimly aware of Amalay behind her, explaining the principles of Yir's powers to Enna and Jin.

"His affinity is healing. It's a miracle, really. I've seen him unclog arteries and slow blood flow. Once, he even created new pints of blood—"

Was that supposed to be reassuring? Tobias was inside the infirmary, still as death, because of a mistake Teia had made. She pictured the Naga who'd controlled ice, her black hair framing her face. *I should have killed her slower,* she thought bitterly.

The main door to the room swung open, bringing in the dampness from the tunnels. Two more people tottered inside—Alara and the thief she'd been paired with.

"Was anyone else ambushed by a super soldier?" Alara said dazedly. "Because I'd like to make sure I wasn't seeing things."

"You're unharmed?" Amalay gasped.

"You doubted her?" Enna said.

"It's just—you don't have any affinities."

Alara straightened the abandoned teapot. "I have brains, which are arguably more useful. It wasn't hard to lure the soldier into a building. I've been developing this gas, you see. Very toxic—*very* potent. It travels surprisingly well, once I found out how to inject it into smoke pellets."

The thief beside her muttered a few sentences in Shaylani, before sinking into a nearby chair.

"What did he say?" Alara asked.

Amalay eyed Alara with renewed respect. "He says you fight like a demon," she said. "That the skin came right off the Naga's bones."

The Poisons Master bowed her head. "Thank you," she said. "Now—are Tobias and Kyra back yet? They'll be thrilled to know this works. Tobias, especially, since I almost murdered him in Ismet, testing the toxin in the place we were sharing." When she was met with silence, Alara frowned. "What is it?"

Jin glanced at Teia. She returned his stare, stone-faced, until he gulped audibly. "Tobias is in the infirmary," he stammered. "And Kyra . . ."

He trailed off helplessly, and Alara's features twitched. "Jin," she said. "You have ten seconds to tell me what happened, before I empty my entire vial of acid on your head."

"The side door is in view of the main gate. I saw the Naga attack her."

"You didn't help?"

"I tried!" he protested. "But they were too fast. They forced her into the House of Mourning. Lehm met them at the door."

"Lehm?" Alara repeated. "Why would he take Kyra to the House of Mourning? Isn't that the Red Mountain's territory?"

"That it is," Teia said flatly. She reached into her pocket, and brought forth the red bursts of beads she'd taken from the two Naga. They made identical tinny sounds as they smacked onto the tile, the golden charms glimmering prettily.

Amalay picked up one of the bracelets. "This is the Red

Mountain's symbol," she said hoarsely, examining the inverted mountain in the center of the charm. "Where did you get it?"

"Off the two Naga that ambushed me and Tobias," Teia said. "It seems they aren't as loyal to the emperor as everyone claims."

Jin gaped. "They wouldn't. Their allegiances—"

"Don't speak to me about allegiances," she growled, raking her bloodied hands through her hair. "There are clearly Naga who are part of the Red Mountain—guards that back Feng to reclaim the throne but who've remained in Yuwen's service, biding their time."

"Why would they do that?"

"Why wouldn't they? They can pass knowledge to the Red Mountain about Yuwen, maybe sow dissent within the imperial ranks. Really, the possibilities are endless."

"And Lehm?" Alara demanded. "What does he have to do with any of this?"

"He's playing both sides to get what he wants. Didn't you say he traveled from city to city in Shaylan, seeking out information? Maybe he was also meeting with Red Mountain contacts—convincing them of his usefulness, selling them lies about helping Feng regain power. Think about it. During this time, he learns which Naga are part of the Red Mountain. Then he infiltrates the Shaylani court. He turns Yuwen against me—"

"So he can win over the nobility, and convince one of them to help raise the Serkawr."

"Right," Teia said. "And sometime after we escaped Taijin, Lehm goes to Yuwen. He persuades my cousin dearest to lend him a contingent of Naga—makes up some excuse about how he knows me best. With help from guards with affinities, *surely* he can track us down."

"He only requests Naga who are allied with the Red Mountain," Enna said slowly.

Teia bobbed her head. "Or maybe there's also a traitor in upper command, who ensures that the right guards go along with Lehm. Either way, it's the perfect cover. Lehm gets Naga who are loyal to him, at least tangentially—and Yuwen is none the wiser, since he authorized the guards to go."

Jin wavered on his feet. "Yuwen wouldn't," he said feebly. "A Shaylani emperor has never given up control of the imperial guards."

At this, Teia barked out a laugh. "You don't see the way he looks at you? You don't notice how his breath catches, how he walks like he's in a dream? He would part the ocean if you asked. He would drain the sea. He probably jumped for joy when Lehm said he would lead the Naga to find you."

Jin's mouth clamped shut. A blush had risen on his neck.

Enna swore. "Son of a bitch," she said. "How is Lehm still one step ahead of us?"

"Don't worry," Teia said. "It gets worse."

"Worse?"

She beckoned toward Amalay. "The Red Mountain has had the Seascript for months, haven't they?"

The leader of thieves nodded reluctantly.

Teia blew out a breath. "If that's the case and it's been sitting in the House of Mourning, I'd bet good money that Lehm has already read it."

"You think they allowed that?" Amalay said.

"They trust him enough to let him keep Kyra inside. At this point, I'd say it's possible that Lehm knows *where* to raise the Serkawr, along with any of its weaknesses."

Enna scrubbed at her face. "That *is* worse," she conceded, at the exact moment that Alara pivoted for the door. The thief glanced at her inquiringly. "And just where are you going?"

"Isn't it obvious?" the Poisons Master said. "I'm going to get Kyra back."

Enna flew across the room. She wedged herself squarely in the other girl's path, blocking the way out. "Lehm has her, Alara. He's not going to give her up because you *ask*."

"He will once I'm through. Although he might not be able to see after what I'm going to do to him."

"You can't go back out there," Amalay objected. "Who knows how many Naga are with him?"

"It doesn't matter. They should say a prayer when they see me coming." She glared at Enna. "Get out of my way."

The thief didn't move. "No."

"Enna—"

"You go out there, and the Naga will rip you apart."

"I stay, and that's what I'll do to every single person in this room." Alara's gloved hand drifted toward her belt. Her voice rippled with a menacing edge. "One more time, Enna. *Get out of my way.*"

"Everyone, shut up," Teia snapped. Her head had started to pound. She longed for the visceral pain that came with a punch, the sharp ache that followed. She wanted a fight—to burn down all of Okkan—but there was something she needed to take care of first.

When she shifted her gaze to Amalay, rage bubbled inside her. There were little warnings that had been there all along, messages she had chosen to ignore. Teia should have known. She should have been more cautious.

"Someone gave us up," Teia spat. "One of your thieves."

Amalay's face remained neutral. "Is that an accusation?"

"It's a fact. It can't be a coincidence that the Naga knew just where to strike."

"Not a single one of my thieves would have given us up to the Red Mountain."

"Wouldn't they?" Teia said. "Have you spoken to Rina recently?"

The chamber went quiet. The thief who'd buckled into the chair sat straight up, as Amalay's eyes gleamed. "Be careful what you say next," she said sharply.

"I'm happy to pick simpler words, if that makes it easier for you to understand." Teia lifted a hand to the back of her neck. She'd known the Red Mountain's symbol on sight—the inverted triangle, identical to the ink she'd seen on Rina when the girl had been knocked aside in the Pit. "Don't tell me you've never seen your own sister's tattoo?"

Enna's jaw dropped. "Amalay?" she said.

"Yes, Amalay," Teia bit out. "All those meetings, when we were reviewing the plan—did you know you'd be sending us to slaughter? Did you know your own sister was a traitor?"

It's wrong. It's all wrong. Wasn't that what Amalay had said that night, as she'd watched Rina stomp from the room? And even before that, as she described how the Seascript had been stolen in the first place: *It was an inside job.*

The leader of thieves was silent, balancing on the heel of her foot. Teia pitched forward, seizing the front of her robes. She was going to set the other girl alight—and she would enjoy every minute of it. "Tell me, Amalay," she said. *"Did you know?"*

When Amalay raised her gaze, her features were defiant. "I had my suspicions. I've had them since the Seascript went missing."

"And where is Rina now? Wandering around the pagoda, copying blueprints for the Red Mountain?"

A hint of shame fluttered against Amalay's face—there one second, gone the next. "After we were attacked, I sent my thieves to look for her."

"And?"

"She's gone." The confession came in a whisper. "They're scouring the tunnels, but I don't think they'll find her."

Well, that settled things, didn't it? It was almost a relief for Teia to welcome heat in, the threads that whirled around her. But as fire kissed her fingers, leaping onto Amalay's robes, someone yanked her back. A hand clamped down on her wrist, stiff, unyielding.

"Don't do this, Boss," Enna said. Her voice was quiet, meant for Teia alone.

"Let go of me, Enna."

"This isn't a fight we can afford to pick. You kill her, and we'll be running from Yuwen, the Red Mountain, *and* the Society."

"I can live with that."

"But can Kyra? Can Tobias?"

Tobias's face rose before her, creased with pain. Teia spun away from Enna with a wordless growl. Amalay was standing several feet away, her arms limp at her sides. She looked smaller somehow, shrunken into her lanky frame.

"Rina is my *sister*," she said miserably. "You had a brother, didn't you?"

"Half brother," Teia said, adding a silent *Good riddance* to the end of her sentence. "But you're free to call him whatever you want, so long as you fix this."

"*Fix* this?" Amalay said. "What do you want me to do? Storm the House of Mourning? Demand Kyra's return?"

That would be a start, Teia thought. "You're going to send your spies back out—every scout at the ready, every thief who's at your disposal. You're going to tell me if Kyra Medoh is still there. You're going to let me know if she's been moved or if Lehm leaves or if so much as a servant exits the building."

"I've done all I can," Amalay argued. "I've tried to help you get the Seascript. But with the Naga now involved—"

"You didn't help me get shit," Teia snarled. "But here's what *I'll* do if you don't confirm Kyra's location. I'm going to set Okkan's pagoda on fire first. I'm going to burn the damn thing to the ground, one rafter at a time, until there's nothing left but ashes, until the entire city knows the Society has been using it as a base. And once I'm done, I'll hunt your sister down myself. It doesn't matter where she is or who she hides behind. I'm going to find her—and when I do, I won't just kill her. I won't just torture her. I'll reinvent pain, so she can learn what it means."

Amalay paled. Maybe she, too, understood that Teia meant what she said—or perhaps she was imagining the scene in the Pit, with Rina far below, surrounded by the corpses of her fellow thieves. "If you threaten her again—" she said wanly.

But Teia no longer cared. If she stayed here another moment more, she was going to douse Amalay in flames. "Don't test me," Teia warned. She stormed toward the hallway, Enna following close behind with a worried expression. "Or do, if you're tired of living. There's nothing I enjoy more than a fight that I'll win."

Chapter Twenty-Four

Teia didn't manage to shake Enna off until she reached the middle of the corridor.

When the thief retreated reluctantly, Teia pressed her back to the wall. Every breath squeezed against her ribs. The infirmary's door was just steps away, but she was tethered in place, unable to continue. Drops of Tobias's blood dotted the floor. She could smell the medicinal tang of whatever poultice Yir had selected drifting from the other side.

She couldn't bring herself to push aside the door, to see Tobias lying on that table as the healer attempted to stitch him back together. Teia didn't consider herself a coward—and yet if she walked into the room, she would go to her knees.

She retreated slowly, her footsteps heavy. The bitter scent of herbs faded. She grasped for the first door she saw, the silver handle giving way beneath her. When she flexed her fingers, the lamp on the table sputtered, before brightening with a yellow glow.

She'd come across a spare bedroom, with a woven mat folded in squares, tucked beneath a feather pillow and a quilted duvet. Even here, there was evidence of Kashan—strands of silver chimes that dangled from the ceiling. A miniature of Armina hung above the dresser, positioned beside a small painting of Mei. The Goddess's eyes drilled into Teia. She considered fleeing back into the hallway, but someone appeared behind her.

"Teia?" Jin said.

Teia didn't move. "What?"

Hesitation seeped into his voice. "Alara decided to stay," the adviser said.

"Good."

"She wants to come up with a plan."

"Excellent."

A pause. "Are you all right?"

"Better than I've ever been."

She thought her tone would have been enough of a hint. But instead of leaving, the footsteps creaked across the room, before stopping beside her. Jin stood next to her in quiet observation, his head tipped toward the dual images of Armina and Mei.

"Is there something else?" Teia said, exasperated.

"The others sent me to get you."

"Why you?"

"Enna said you were least likely to set me on fire." Jin adjusted his spectacles. "I told her I didn't think that was true."

"And what did she do?"

"She said to go anyway, or she'd jam an ice pick through my throat."

This brought a reluctant smile to Teia's lips. "Typical Enna."

"She's loyal to you."

"I pay her retainer. She puts on appearances."

"It's different than that," he insisted. "I can tell."

Teia peered at Jin. "Isn't it the same for you?" she said. "For me and Enna?"

"You and Yuwen."

He fiddled with his fingers, tugging at the joints. "What you said back in the main chamber . . ."

"You've known about how he feels, haven't you?"

The adviser faltered. He nodded.

"And you don't return those feelings?" Teia said. She didn't believe her own statement, not for a minute. She could picture the scene in the pagoda clearly, how Jin had brushed the flower from Yuwen's hair. There had been heartbreak in that look, one second spanning eternities.

Jin twisted at the long trail of his sleeves. "It's complicated."

"How so?"

"We can't be together." The words came out in a jumbled torrent, as if he'd waited years to say this exact sentence. "Not now, not ever."

"Because he's the emperor?"

Jin's posture sagged. "Because of what happened in Taijin Palace," he said coarsely. "Because of what Feng did to my parents."

And just like that, Teia understood. It was like a missing piece had snapped into place, a wayward tile that completed the mosaic. Jin had been cagey about what his parents had done in Taijin, the occupation they'd had that allowed him to grow up with Yuwen. Teia had assumed they were scholars or instructors, who'd met with an untimely demise.

But she could recall how Yuwen had deflected the conversation when the topic of Feng arose. There was the disdain in Jin's voice, too, when he'd spoken about the House of Mourning—how he'd railed against Feng to Amalay and Rina, citing the former emperor's long list of crimes.

And what about once Feng's ambitions set in? The execution of Taijin's Memory Keepers, put to death before their children.

"Your parents were Memory Keepers," Teia said.

Grief seeped into his face. "They had served in the palace for years," Jin said. "They knew Feng. They were friendly with him."

"It didn't matter."

"Nothing did. Feng had them killed anyway, along with a hundred other Keepers in the palace." Jin's chin trembled. "People say it was madness, you know—that Feng only overstepped his power in his later years. But I think that hunger was always there. He just finally decided to act on it."

She scanned his cropped black hair, searching for that telltale streak of white. "And you?" Teia said. "You're a Memory Keeper as well, aren't you?"

He patted at his scalp, running a hand over his roots. "It's an inherited affinity," he said. "I wasn't offered much of a choice."

"You escaped the purge."

"I was overlooked. My affinity didn't present itself until much later, close to when Feng began the executions." Jin grimaced. "Yuwen shielded me. He lied for me. He smuggled in ingredients for dye when my hair turned white. Even in the aftermath, once Feng was exiled, Yuwen kept my secret. I didn't want the court to know my affinity. I still don't."

"Why?"

Jin looked down at his hands. "It's easier this way. I never received proper training, and there's no guarantee I could preserve memories correctly. Besides . . ." He sighed. "I don't need the reminder about my affinity—that I inherited what made my parents a target."

"Yuwen protected you," Teia said. "When he deposed his father—"

A note of anger crept into Jin's voice. "It wasn't the executions that moved Yuwen, Teia. Three months passed between then and the coup."

Her lips parted. If not the slayings of a hundred Memory Keepers, the enormous loss of Shaylan's history, what had pushed Yuwen over the edge? What had caused him to expel his father, banishing him to the confines of Cloud Mountain?

She had every intention of prodding the adviser for more information—but before she could, the door wrenched open. Amalay's slender form hovered in the hallway. She didn't step inside, as if afraid crossing the threshold would trigger some sudden attack. It was, Teia thought, the first smart choice she'd made all day.

"Teia," she said gruffly, as her eyes darted up to the portrait of the Goddess. "I have news."

Teia would have preferred the company of a shrew. But if the leader of thieves was here, it could only mean one thing. "Well?"

"My scouts came back from their rounds through Okkan. I have more information on Kyra and Lehm."

Chapter Twenty-Five

They sat in a disjointed circle back in the main chamber, perched on mismatched seats and low-set ottomans. The thief who'd accompanied Alara into the room was gone, no doubt sent away to join the search for Rina. A heavy table had been dragged from the kitchen. Three corners of a weathered blueprint were tacked to the polished wood, while the fourth was held down by a teacup, which left wet rings across the map's tattered edge.

Teia had studied plenty of maps over the past few days, all capturing various rooms of the House of Mourning. Yet whoever created this had outdone themselves, sketching everything in meticulous, obsessive detail. The dimensions were marked in cramped numbers, along with the placement of each door, window, and alcove. There was even a count of the exact number of steps, squashed beside a rendering of the grand staircase.

Enna whistled. "I need to hire a new cartographer," she said. "Start importing my maps from Shaylan."

"You have a cartographer?" Jin said.

"You don't?"

"The Society's blueprints are all made to order," Amalay said. "Hours of work—weeks of labor."

"Wonderful," Enna said appreciatively. "Can you do Erisia's Central Bank next?"

The leader of thieves brandished the glinting end of a hairpin, using it as a pointer to tap down on the map. "As far as we know," Amalay said, "both Kyra and Lehm have remained inside. I have thieves watching every exit of the House of Mourning, but they say there's been no movement."

Alara's nails dug into her palms. "Why is he keeping her there?"

"If Lehm is working with Taisheng and the Red Mountain, he'll have free rein of the building. Saves him the trouble of having to commandeer a separate location."

Teia inspected the blueprint. "He hasn't tried to move her yet?"

"No," Amalay confirmed. "There are no carriages set up, no wagons at the ready. In the stables, the horses have all been watered and tacked. If they plan to leave, they aren't in a rush."

A divot formed between Teia's brows. If Lehm had both the Seascript *and* Kyra, why not head straight for the safety of Taijin, or else move to the location where the Serkawr needed to be summoned? Why stay in Okkan, hiding in plain sight?

"You're sure nobody is feeding you false information?" Teia said.

"Yes."

"As sure as you were that Rina isn't a traitor?"

Amalay skewered the tip of the hairpin into the blueprint. "On my honor," she grunted, "this is where Kyra and Lehm are."

Her honor didn't seem to be worth much nowadays, but Teia supposed they were low on options. "Let's say Lehm stays in the House of Mourning," she said. "Where would they hold Kyra?"

"She could be anywhere," Alara said hopelessly. "The building is enormous."

"It is," Amalay agreed, "but there's really only one viable option. Tomorrow is the sixth night of Kashan—and Ko Taisheng will be hosting his banquet."

"Still?"

"To cancel would be the talk of the town. Taisheng has his appearances to keep up."

"Never underestimate a vain man," Enna said.

"Or a stupid one," Teia said. "It'll work in our favor. That means the House of Mourning will be busy with servants. And once the guests come—"

"The entire first floor will be flooded with people," Amalay finished. "Lehm couldn't keep Kyra there if he wanted to."

"She needs to be somewhere isolated," Alara said. "Probably a smaller space too, which can be heavily guarded."

"The second floor," Jin said. He surveyed the blueprint, and tapped at a spare bedroom. "Here?"

"No," Enna replied.

"I was asking Amalay, not you."

"You asked a general question, and I'm giving you an answer. Lehm wouldn't keep Kyra there. There's too many windows, too many points of escape."

Jin glanced at Amalay. "She's right," the leader of thieves said. Her tone was almost apologetic.

The adviser huffed. "Well, what about there?"

"Too close to the kitchens," Enna said swiftly.

"Here?"

"That's the size of a wardrobe. How are you supposed to fit a person in there?"

"Are you going to make me keep guessing?" Jin said. "Or are you going to tell me where you think she's being held?"

"I don't know. Are you going to continue picking laughable options?"

"I'm doing my best."

"What about the hidden room?" Teia said.

Jin blinked. "What hidden room?"

Enna gave Teia an approving nod, as she pointed to a chamber off the smaller staircase. It had been crammed beside the wall, slotted behind a storage closet on the second level. "Amalay told us about it when we first arrived at the pagoda," she informed Jin haughtily. "Weren't you paying attention?"

"I was preoccupied with all the other revelations," he snapped back, "including the fact that the Seascript had been stolen—*again.*"

Alara traced the outline of the hidden room. "That's where Lehm is keeping her?" she said.

"In all likelihood," Amalay agreed. "It's away from any windows, and near the back of the home. Rumor has it that Taisheng had it soundproofed."

"Nobody to hear her call for help," Teia observed.

"Good," Alara said. "That means no one will hear Lehm, either."

Jin gnawed at his lower lip. "How are we going to get inside?" he said. "Through the windows again?"

Teia looked to Amalay. "You and Enna were attacked by the Naga on the roof, weren't you?"

"Yes."

"Then it's a compromised location. They'll be expecting us if we go the same way."

"So what are we supposed to do?" Enna said. "Climb down the chimney? Waltz in the front door?"

"I'd prefer the second," Jin said.

"We all would. But unless you want to be strung up on the spot—"

"Jin's right," Teia interrupted. She was staring at the map, the front gate outlined in blue ink. "Maybe walking through the front is the right solution."

Enna burst into laughter. "Are you feeling all right, Boss? Did you happen to miss what I said about being strung up on the spot?"

"Not at all. But tomorrow night, there will be plenty of people entering the House of Mourning."

Amalay set down her hairpin. "The banquet."

"Kashan is only nine nights long," Teia said. "It'd be a shame if we missed *all* the celebrations."

"You want us to impersonate party guests?" Alara said. "We don't have invitations—or *outfits*."

"Which one is more important?" Jin said.

"I wouldn't be one to talk with those shoes," the Poisons Master sniffed, and the adviser shuffled his feet self-consciously.

Teia flattened out one of the map's raised creases. "Rina said there are normally foreign guests in attendance at Taisheng's event, which should account for Enna and Alara." She pointedly ignored Amalay, who flinched at her sister's name. "And if I'm remembering correctly, the Society turns a healthy profit forging party invitations. I'm sure there are a few to spare."

"That can be arranged," Amalay said grudgingly. "Ko Taisheng won't be roaming the building, either, if that's any consolation. During the banquet, he spends all his time on the ground floor, entertaining guests. By the end of the first hour, he's typically incoherent."

"What about the Seascript?" Enna asked. "Are we making a run for that as well?"

"What's the point?" Alara said. "If I were Lehm, I'd have put it through a shredder."

Jin gasped, as if visualizing the shredder's gleaming metal teeth. "The Seascript," he wheezed, "is a national treasure."

"It's a liability. If you think Lehm cares more about some relic than his chance to raise the Serkawr, you clearly haven't been listening."

Teia had to admit that Alara had a point. Yet some stubborn part of her hoped the Seascript would be snug in Ko Taisheng's safe—the merchant might not mind treason, but perhaps he drew the line at destruction of property, particularly if it was his own.

For all Teia had heard about the Seascript, there were secrets inside to be exhumed, pieces of Shaylani history to be laid out before them. If she wanted to stop the Serkawr, she knew implicitly where the answer lay.

"Alara and I will enter the House of Mourning to find Kyra," Teia said. "Enna will look for the Seascript."

Amalay folded her arms. "And me?"

"You're coming?"

"Not for you," the leader of thieves retorted. "But if Rina is anywhere, she's inside the house. If we reach Kyra, she might know where my sister is."

If they ran into Naga within the building, they might be able to use Amalay as a distraction. The thought cheered Teia slightly, as she turned back to address the leader of thieves. "If you insist."

Jin assessed the blueprint. "What about me?" he said. "Should I go with Enna?"

Teia shook her head. "You'll be outside on watch."

"What?" he said indignantly. "I want to help—"

"Your face is too recognizable."

"And yours isn't?"

"There aren't many people outside of you, Yuwen, and the governors who have seen my face. But if anyone identifies you inside, they might cause a scene."

His shoulders fell, but he didn't argue. Amalay might not know the adviser's true identity, but Jin must have realized what Teia was trying to say. There could be officials in attendance, ones who might have met Jin before. If the adviser was spotted at the House of Mourning, chaos would undoubtedly ensue.

"Cheer up," Enna said smugly. "I'm happy to wave to you from a window, if you happen to feel lonely outside—" Before she could finish, a shiver went through her. Any good humor drained from her face.

Jin hesitated. "Enna?" he said.

The cut on her forehead glistened. "I don't feel well," Enna said with a wince. She wobbled, her eyes rolling back in her head. As she swayed dangerously, Teia bolted upright, helping the girl balance.

She placed her palm to the thief's forehead, before withdrawing it quickly. "She has a fever," Teia said. Her voice scraped against her ears, panic heavy in each word.

"Yir is with Tobias—" Amalay began.

"I didn't ask for Yir, did I?" Teia snarled. "Alara—here, take her other arm. You must have something to help with this in your belt."

The Poisons Master barely came to Enna's chest, as she draped the thief's arm around her carefully. "I have a few things, Teia—but I specialize in poison, not medicine."

Amalay stepped forward. "I can get Yir," she tried again. "See if he can help."

"And let Tobias bleed out on the table?" Teia said, shouldering past her. "Get out of my way. She needs to lie down."

It was nearly fifteen minutes before she and Alara were able to return to the main chamber. Jin and Amalay were waiting, deliberately positioned on opposite ends of the table. Amalay had no reaction, but Jin jumped up instantly, his robes askew. "How is she?" he said.

"She'll be fine," Teia said tightly. If she worried about Enna, too, she was going to concave, her chest cracking apart. "Her cut was infected, but Alara gave her a sleeping tonic."

"She'll be out for the next day," the Poisons Master said, straightening her belt. "She needs time to recover."

Jin laid his palms flat against the table. "Does that mean . . ."

He didn't have to finish. They were now two people down in an already dire situation. But Teia couldn't afford to dwell on the cards they'd been dealt. Taisheng's banquet was taking place the next night. By her calculation, they had less than twenty-one hours to plot what came next.

"The Seascript will have to wait," Teia said.

On the blueprint, the rooms contorted in shape. They took on strange forms, shadows shifting into something new. Somewhere in the building's depths, Kyra Medoh was waiting.

"Now," she said. "Where were we?"

They stayed up planning through the remainder of the night, ironing out details, unfolding and refolding the blueprint until it had split down the center. It was well into morning before Teia sat back in her seat, satisfied. As the others hobbled off to bed, yawning into their sleeves, she scanned the map once more, evaluating the rooms.

When she heard a shuffling behind her, Teia glanced back.

She thought it was Alara, or maybe Jin—but her heart nearly stopped when she saw Tobias. He was accompanied by Yir, who flashed a gap-toothed smile. The old man seemed exhausted, but tremendously pleased with himself.

"He's fine," Yir said, before thumping himself on the chest. "Best of the best."

He stumped out of the room, humming a disjointed tune. Teia watched the healer go, rooted to the spot, before her attention returned to Tobias. A tremor quaked through her. Her mouth went dry, sentences evaporating on her lips.

He walked forward in two steps, and swept her into his arms. His left hand tightened at her waist, his right cupping her hair. His head lowered to the curve of her neck, as if dropping down in prayer.

"Don't you *ever* do that to me again," Teia growled.

She felt Tobias's shoulders shake with quiet laughter. They broke apart slowly, like the world might shatter if they moved any faster.

"Have you slept?" he said gently.

Did he think she'd be slumbering away while Yir tried to piece him back together? "Who has time for that?" Teia said.

"Normal people. It would do you some good."

"Doing good doesn't agree with me. It tends to ruin my appetite." She inspected him closely, unable to believe he was truly there, alive and well, his eyes shining down on her. "How are you?"

In response, he lifted the torn hem of his shirt. Fire raced up Teia's cheeks. Her gaze traced the taut muscle of his hip, etching down the hard planes of his stomach. The wound had cut through the space just beneath his bottom rib. It had been sewn shut in a neat line, black stitches resting against tanned skin.

"Yir drew me a diagram of exactly what he fixed," Tobias said wryly. "He was very proud."

"He should be. When you fell in the alley . . ." She didn't want to recall the image of him lying in his own blood. "Anyway," Teia finished haltingly. "I'm glad you're all right."

Tobias took a seat at the edge of the table. "Teia," he said softly. "I never thanked you for what you did."

"For hauling you back to the Society?"

"For the decree you gave me at the cliffs."

The parchment she'd gifted him, which returned the Highlands to his care. Out of all the decisions Teia had made on the throne, that had been one of the easiest. It had always been meant for him, one way or another.

"Thank me if we survive," she said. "You can give me a tour of the Highlands."

His grin was mischievous. "You wouldn't like the mountains," Tobias said thoughtfully. "But I'd take you to the docks, the path that leads down to the water."

She was vaguely affronted by the statement. "I can like mountains."

"You were muttering to yourself the entire way up Niisha. Kept grumbling about how much you despised nature."

"You noticed?"

"With you?" he said. She could have basked in the warmth of his voice, the room brightening, her pulse stuttering out in fits. "Always."

She held back her smile, examining the paperwork strewn on the table, hunting for a proper distraction. "Has anyone told you about all that's happened yet?" Teia said.

"We didn't get the Seascript?"

"And Rina's a traitor."

Tobias blinked. "Rina's a *what*?"

She explained what had transpired while he'd been with Yir, before outlining the plan to retrieve Kyra from the House of Mourning. When she'd finished, Tobias shook his head. "Goddess. You've been busy."

"Any questions?"

"Too many. I wouldn't know where to begin."

"You can draft up a list later in the day. Give it to us afterward, when the rest of us return—"

Tobias let out a cough. "What do you mean *the rest of us*?"

"You can't be serious. You almost *died*, Tobias."

"And?"

"What kind of argument is that?"

"A sound one."

"To who? Someone who's never strung together a proper sentence?"

"You can't expect me to sit here and do nothing."

"Not nothing. You'll have your list of questions to compile, won't you?"

It was an idiotic hill for Teia to die on, so irrational that a younger version of herself would have been disgusted. Logically, she knew that Tobias should come. He was on his feet, walking steadily. He was their best fighter, even without powers. Not to mention the injury that had almost taken his life seemed several weeks old, rather than just a few hours. Whatever magic Yir had conducted in the infirmary had worked.

But when she thought again about him crumpling in the alley, pain shuddered through her. She wouldn't see him hurt again. She couldn't.

Tobias softened. "Teia," he said. "I'll be fine."

"You don't know that."

"I do."

"How? Have you mastered death now? Accomplished the impossible?"

"Do you think that's going to scare me into staying?"

"It should," she said. "I thought you didn't have a death wish."

"Consider this an exception." His voice was quiet. "Didn't I once tell you that I'd go where you did?"

She remembered the memory as clear as any—how he'd promised to venture with her into Blackgate when they were still in Erisia. He'd agreed despite his misgivings, despite his convictions that neither of them would make it out alive.

I would have followed you into fire.

"I suppose," Teia said miserably. "But does it have to be here?"

Tobias simply laughed, the sound blossoming out into the room. "Astronomical odds, unlikely chances, and a plan that's all but impossible?" he said. "I wouldn't miss it for the world."

Chapter Twenty-Six

From this angle, the House of Mourning was haunting at night. Whorls of red paint brightened beneath fat clusters of lanterns, which cast the entire street in a crimson glow. The cranes on the doors appeared ready to take flight, and the metal castings on the wall positively gleamed, providing a burnished contrast to the rest of the home.

As Teia slipped into the colorful swirl of partygoers, she was immensely glad for the flow of people. It seemed half the city had arrived at the event, as guests entered the building in an endless stream. Most came on foot, dressed in their best finery, although several arrived by carriage, which caused an enthusiastic chatter to arise from any onlookers.

There were foreigners in attendance as well—people from other kingdoms, floating among the Shaylani partygoers. A K'vali woman with bright violet eyes waved her hand, and a breeze stirred behind her, primping her black curls over her shoulders. When a Dvořákian tapped his fingers together, his metal rings rearranged themselves, shifting orientations until the man was satisfied.

As the crowd swelled behind her, Teia quickened her pace, eager to reach the guards inspecting invitations. She, Amalay,

Tobias, and Alara were staggering their entrances, using the chimes from the clock tower, which rang out every fifteen minutes in a great peal of bells. Jin, too, was listening for the sounds, tracking their progress from the roof he'd been stationed on. If they weren't back by four chimes, he'd been told to return to the apothecary and retrieve reinforcements.

"What kind of reinforcements?" he'd said glumly, as they all readied themselves to leave.

"Ideally?" Teia had answered. "Someone strong enough to carry our bodies back."

There were a handful of guards stationed by the door, checking envelopes before allowing people through. One gestured at her, his attitude one of absolute boredom. She drew forth the invitation tucked into her cloak, smiling prettily. The parchment was made of a thick starched paper. The top was embossed with a red wax seal.

She had been concerned that Lehm might have circulated sketches of her to each of the House of Mourning's guards. But either the rebel leader had been distracted, or the security was as sloppy as Amalay had said. The man who held Teia's invitation merely nodded, yawned, and beckoned her inside.

As Teia blinked hard, adjusting to the lighting, she found the House of Mourning's interior was also cast in red, from the folding screens by the walls to the overstuffed velvet love seats. Latticework dividers segmented the space, and guests milled about behind each of the separators, tossing back drinks or speaking languidly with their neighbors.

Behind her, the door opened once more. She was relieved to find Tobias had been waved through, his invitation disappearing into the pocket of his robes. Beneath the lantern's light, she caught the broad outline of his shoulders, tense beneath the fabric.

"Is there a problem?" she said. "You look disappointed."

"I'm waiting for a caveat. This seems much too pleasant to be one of your schemes."

"What's wrong with just enjoying the atmosphere?" she said, as she shimmied out of her cloak. She draped the heavy gray fabric against the crook of her elbow, revealing the delicate dress beneath.

The Society kept entire trunks full of spare robes—skirts embroidered in silver and gold thread, tunics edged in tiny pearls. Teia had initially selected a more practical choice, but Alara had balked at the prospect.

"*That's* what you want to wear?" the Poisons Master had said.

"It's a tunic, Alara, not a wheat sack."

"Are you sure? It looks like it could pass for either."

Teia had watched as Alara marched to the trunks, throwing back the lids with steadfast determination. As she began rifling through the tubs of clothing, the pile of discarded robes grew at an alarming rate.

"You do realize this is a rescue mission?" Teia had said.

"It's a *party*," the Poisons Master had responded, "and I'll be damned if I let Kyra see me looking disheveled." She'd chucked a filmy skirt at Teia, glitter chafing against her skin. "Look alive, Teia. We have work to do."

Teia had rejected several of Alara's suggestions before settling on an ice-blue dress so pale it was almost white. Near the skirt, the color dissolved into a deeper shade, giving the impression of waves in motion. At the last minute, Alara had thrown a silk robe to her as well, with pink flowers embroidered down the sleeves.

"Pulls the whole outfit together," the Poisons Master had said with a wink. "You can thank me later."

Thank you, Alara, Teia thought now. As she met Tobias's eyes, she suddenly saw immense value in their detour through the Society's trunks. Something danced in his gaze, an emotion that she couldn't decipher. Warmth expanded in her belly, a glow that curled within her stomach.

Any clever remark faded from her mind. Maybe it was the adrenaline buzzing through her, the lively cadence of music that poured from the House of Mourning's inner chambers. For some reason, tonight felt different from all the others.

"What do you think?" Teia said. Her fingers found the sash knotted around her waist, the ribbon that spilled toward the hem.

He followed the movement of her hands, trailing the length of her skirt. "Ask me later," he said.

"Nothing to say?"

"Nothing to say *here*." His voice darkened to a rasp. "I don't think it's wise to tell you what I'm thinking right now."

It was a relief to look away first, to rebury whatever tangled thoughts had swirled to the surface. Teia flagged down a nearby server, who carried a tray lined with small silver glasses. She nodded her thanks, lifted two of the glasses, and gave one to Tobias.

He eyed it with obvious amusement. "What's this?"

"It's a party," she replied. "We should seem like we're having fun."

"I'm having fun."

"You look like you're about to stab someone."

"Isn't that what I said?" he answered, with the grim joy he normally reserved for fights.

She rolled her eyes at him, before scrutinizing the rest of the room. Despite scouring the floor plan in meticulous detail, Teia had underestimated the size of the space. The more dividers she and Tobias passed through, the more partygoers appeared. By the time they sailed through the third wooden separator, people were everywhere, packed so close it was difficult to move.

"There," she murmured. On one of the love seats, a Shaylani man was enthusiastically toasting an Ismetian couple, holding a bottle of clear liquid up to both women. She assumed the man was Ko Taisheng—no other person was dressed head to toe in red, down to the garnets looped around his pudgy neck—but he wasn't her focus tonight.

Beyond the drunken guests and scattered servers was a staircase, its carpeted steps flanked by a carved wooden banister. A pair of guards stood at the base: a tall, thin man who towered over the crowd, and his shorter companion, with a graying beard and uneven tufts of hair.

Close to the stairs, an alcove had been hollowed into the wall, its rounded top decorated with motifs of mountains. Teia and Tobias wedged into the shallow space. She wondered how much time had passed, and if the next set of bells was close to chiming. The House of Mourning was louder than she'd expected, ringing with lively conversation. Would the clock tower be audible above all the noise?

She peeked furtively over Tobias's shoulder, back toward the guards by the stairs. Yet Teia must have stared a second too long. The tall guard sharpened his gaze, and Teia's pulse ricocheted, beating out an unsteady tempo.

"Ah," she said, as she ducked back behind Tobias. "We might have a problem."

His voice took on a note of warning. "Teia," he said. "What did you do?"

"Why is it always the assumption that I did something?"

"Experience."

"Slander."

She chanced another glance at the stairs. The guard who'd noticed her was speaking brusquely to his companion. When the shorter man nodded, the first guard started forward, one hand positioned on the silver hilt of his blade.

Now she was certain something was wrong. "Tobias," Teia whispered. "We have to go."

"What happened?"

As quickly as she could, she told him what she'd observed. Tobias swore, before lowering his head back toward her ear. "We can't leave," he murmured. "The guards won't rotate for another hour, and it's almost two bells. If we don't get up those stairs, we're going to miss our chance."

The tall guard was nearly upon them. Teia could see the top of his head, bobbing over the oblivious partygoers. *What do we do?* she thought furiously. If they were stopped and interrogated, their plan would be thrown into disarray. Yet Tobias was right—if the two of them left now, there was little chance they'd be able to steal past the guards again without being recognized.

They couldn't fight, couldn't afford to make a scene. Teia's heart pounded within her chest. There had to be some other way to escape this mess, to make the guards think they were harmless.

"Teia," Tobias hissed. And in that instant, she was struck with an idea. It was one born from absolute insanity, a thought that sent a blush creeping into Teia's cheeks. She was suddenly painfully aware of how close together she and Tobias were, his hand brushing featherlight against hers.

Strangely, Teia found herself thinking about a very different time, a memory that refused to dim. There had been a night in the Golden Palace when Tobias had visited her room, just before their second run through Blackgate. They'd sat on the windowsill, talking about what was to come—their fears and hopes and dreams of the future. When she'd glanced over at him, the weight of the world had lifted, if only for a minute.

It had been a terrible time under terrible circumstances, but Teia could recall the way she'd felt, hope glimmering through her veins. She'd wanted him then, on that windowsill in the palace, framed beneath the stars. She wanted him now, selfishly, *stupidly,* in spite of everything that she'd done.

Was it madness that compelled her to look at him? Was it that same ridiculous sense of hope? She must have made some sort of sound, because Tobias's jaw tightened with concern. "Teia?" he said. "What is it?"

For the past six months, she had fallen asleep each night to the image of his face, the unearthly beauty that might be her undoing. *I should have told him back in Erisia,* she thought. *I should have had the courage.*

The footsteps grew closer. Tobias bit out a curse. And Teia seized hold of whatever bravery she might have left, stretching high to press her lips to his.

A shock tore through her, before she pulled away in a panic. A thousand thoughts burned through her mind, each more garbled than the last. *I've made a mistake,* she thought with absolute conviction. Before her, Tobias's expression was inscrutable.

What was the best course of action to explain away what had happened? An excuse? A joke? Was it possible to set herself aflame? "Tobias—" she started.

Then he was kissing her with such force that her shoulders thudded against the wall, his palms cupping both sides of her face. It was like feeling the brush of fire for the first time, the type of heat that seared straight through bone. Teia gasped. Her lips parted to meet his, hands knotting into his shirt. He groaned at her touch, a shiver coursing through him, and a spark ignited within Teia, cleaving through her chest.

It was extraordinary what a kiss could do. In the span of a heartbeat, any coherence had seeped from Teia's brain. She could have stayed there forever, tucked within the alcove, when someone cleared their throat. She wondered distantly if she'd misheard, before an irritated voice followed, speaking a brisk line of Shaylani.

Goddess. The guard.

The guard behind Tobias appeared more annoyed than suspicious. As he studied her flushed cheeks, Teia knew what he was thinking: Here were two partygoers who'd hidden away for privacy, taking advantage of the alcove for a stolen minute alone.

As if to confirm the theory, another voice sounded out, oozing with disgust. Amalay melted out of the haze of silken dresses. She played the role of a dignitary surprisingly well, with mauve silks that tumbled down her figure, pooling at her feet like a waterfall. By her gestures, it was clear what she was implying—that she, too, had been forced to witness the events of the alcove, to the point where it had ruined her disposition.

Teia thought it was all a *tad* overdone—did she have to keep pressing her hand to her forehead, as if she were about to faint?—but the guard seemed to sympathize. He was nodding along to Amalay, his back to Teia and Tobias. She took advantage of the seconds they'd been given, flitting out of the alcove with Tobias, hurrying toward the stairs.

The lone guard who'd remained had shifted away from the banister. He was listening intently to a golden-haired girl, who was giggling loudly, fluttering a silken fan before her face. She was speaking rapidly in Erisian, and while it was clear the guard didn't understand a word she was saying, his attention kept drifting down to her impressive neckline.

Over the guard's shoulder, Alara gave Teia a small nod. Then she resumed gesturing with her free hand, the fan snapping open and shut with each twist of her other wrist.

Let's go, Teia mouthed to Tobias. They hurried up the stairs, which bent around a bloodred corner, shielding them from view. Tobias was quiet as they moved into the wide hallway, but she saw a smile tugging at his mouth. His dark eyes drank her in.

"Teia," Tobias said. "That kiss wasn't just for the guard, was it?"

With the smirk he wore, he damn well knew the answer. Teia could feel her face warming once more, her spine tingling where his hand had fit above the small of her back.

"I'm sorry," she said, in case she'd crossed some hidden line, stepped over the point of no return.

His grin grew wider. "Why?" Tobias said back. "I'm not."

Chapter Twenty-Seven

Two bells had begun when Teia and Tobias rounded the corner. The upstairs corridor was no less grand than the first floor, with a collection of objects—vases, bonsai plants—scattered artfully on ornamental tables. It was far dimmer here than in the room below, but Teia saw even the bonsai's leaves had been dyed bright red.

What a commitment, Teia thought dryly. She could appreciate keeping to a theme, but this was downright obsessive.

Doors were starting to emerge to their right, built directly into sliding latticework panels—yet neither Teia nor Tobias stopped until they came to the end of the hall. The painting they paused before was enormous, extending clear down to the floor. It was bedecked in cranes, with the birds soaring over a set of mountain ranges, their wings skimming the snowcapped peaks.

"Taisheng couldn't have picked something more subtle?" Tobias said.

Teia gestured to the red furnishings around them. "Something tells me subtlety isn't his strong suit," she answered, before reaching out carefully, feeling along the edge of the frame. When her fingers brushed against a small circular button, Teia pursed her lips. "Ready?"

Tobias's knife glinted by his side. "As I'll ever be," he said.

As the painting swung back, they both rushed into the hidden room, with Teia's flame illuminating the space. The chamber was largely bare, without any of the furnishings that the rest of the house enjoyed. A single safe hunched in the corner, built directly into the wall. In the center of the room, a girl sat in a high-backed chair, with two Naga hovering behind her. Both guards were still, with circles of red beads ensnaring their wrists. Instead, it was the girl who reacted first, lifting her head toward Teia.

"Hello there," Rina said. The scar on her face shone in the firelight. She was dressed in robes of deep crimson, rubies sparkling against her hair. "I was wondering when you would arrive."

"Rina?" Teia said.

The thief was expressionless. "Let me guess—my sister sent you?"

"If you think I'm going to answer that, you're about as dumb as you look."

"I'm not taking insults from you." Rina stabbed a finger at Teia. "You tried to kill me. You threw me from a *platform*. And even then, Amalay allowed you to stay."

"Maybe you should learn to watch your step. It can be dangerous being so clumsy."

Tobias lifted his blade. "Your sister has honor," he said to Rina. "She keeps her promises."

"She's a fool. Indecisive, overly cautious."

"She doesn't act rashly."

"She doesn't act at all," Rina growled, the declaration spilling out in an angry stream of words. "At least the Red Mountain isn't afraid of retribution."

"They clearly aren't very smart, either, if they're allying with

Lehm," Teia said. "Why don't you save us all the trouble and tell us where Kyra is?"

"You're too obvious for your own good. I knew Amalay would think this is the room where we were keeping her. I'm sure she was analytical about it too. Did she say the hidden room made sense because it was more private than the others? Away from any exits and far enough from the banquet?"

"Is this why you like the Red Mountain? Because they listen to you talk?"

Rina's fingers bit into the cushioned armrests. "I joined because of Feng," she said, each syllable dripping with reverence. "He would have brought us glory throughout the Five Kingdoms—he still will, when he's restored. He'll be the best leader Shaylan has ever had, better even than Mei."

"You follow a weak-willed man, Rina. A man who remains in exile at Cloud Mountain. A man who was overthrown by his own son—"

Rina slammed her palms together. A tendril of ice spun outward, crashing toward Teia, as the two Naga whirled into motion. Water solidified in their hands, swords cast with an eerie blue light. Tobias met them where they stood. He swept out his leg to catch one off balance, slicing his blade at another's knee.

Rina rocketed for Teia, who dodged an icy blast. She ducked behind a nearby chair, lifting it high. It froze under the other girl's touch. As Rina cast it aside angrily, jagged spikes of ice shot up from the floor. Each was as large as a bookcase, armed with a daggered point. Teia lurched back, bursting out the door, sprinting into the corridor.

Rina was inches behind. A thin spear of ice materialized in her grasp. "Do you have any idea what Yuwen has done?" she howled. "What his men are capable of? What his coup cost me?"

Teia snapped her fingers. Flames stamped up Rina's tunic. She shouted in alarm, her focus shifting to her robes as Teia unleashed another burst of fire. Rina went hurtling to the floor—and then Teia was on top of her, clubbing down with a handful of flames. At the last moment, Rina lifted her arms. A barrier of ice expanded between them—glittering, translucent, and utterly ineffective.

Teia's blow shattered the shield, sending fragments everywhere. Heat filled the hallway, threading into a molten flame. She pulled apart her palms, a fiery sphere brimming between her hands. Her next strike wouldn't miss.

"No!"

The voice came from the end of the corridor, so full of fear that it brought Teia to a halt. Amalay staggered into view, the hem of her lovely dress wrinkled, her chest heaving from exertion. "Teia," she said. "Don't."

"Amalay—"

"I know what she's done. But please—*please*." Her tone was strained. "If you spare her, the Society will be in your debt. *I'll* be in your debt."

It wasn't compassion that moved Teia, so much as what Amalay promised. Teia hesitated—and sorely regretted it a moment later, when something cold pummeled into her. She was thrown off Rina, landing in a heap by the wall. Frost clung to her clothes from where Rina had struck her, sending her teeth chattering in an uncontrollable fit.

Blearily, she watched Amalay hurry to Rina. The leader of thieves stooped beside her younger sister, but Rina yanked back abruptly. "Don't touch me!"

"Rina—"

"You just had to meddle, didn't you?" She flipped onto her feet. "You couldn't bear the thought of leaving me be."

"The Red Mountain is using you," Amalay said. "They recruited you because they wanted the Seascript."

Rina's laugh was shrill. "I *suggested* stealing the Seascript, Amalay! They asked me to prove myself, and I did. They respect me. They appreciate my knowledge. And, unlike you, they'll actually take action against Yuwen."

"I told you that the right time will come—"

"When? You always talk about protecting me, but you failed when it mattered the most. You always do." She brushed her knuckles to the scars, glittering white against her cheek. As she spoke, a swirl of ice shimmered at her back, flexing eagerly into the air.

"Rina," Amalay whispered, "don't do this."

Rina shook her head. "I'm done listening to you," she said.

Ice ricocheted at Amalay, who deflected it with a wave. The leader of thieves braced her feet against the floor. She drew her arms up high, and snow churned above her head, a storm that brewed in the middle of the scarlet corridor.

"Fine," she said, with the bleak determination of someone prepared to win a fight. "Come on, then."

They clashed in the center of the hallway, sending ice pelting in every direction. Frost crept across the floors. Snow tore against the walls, as Teia dragged herself upright. From where she'd fallen, she glimpsed Tobias battling the two Naga in the hidden room. One sent a crush of water his way. He sidestepped the torrent, before leaping to his right. They could have been dancing, the room as their stage, metal glinting through whorls of water.

Teia stood shakily. But just as she prepared to rush back into the fray, she paused. Dread tingled beneath her skin, a sense that someone was watching her. Slowly, she rotated toward the end of the hall, in the direction of the main staircase.

Three additional Naga had emerged. Scarlet beads hung before the black collars of their robes, displaying their allegiance to the Red Mountain. They scrutinized her silently, hands clasped at their backs.

Standing before them was a man, the pale angles of his face unmistakable, his silver hair gleaming like a beacon. A weathered book rested on his upturned palm, the cover long faded with age.

"Hello, Halfling," Lehm said. "I was told you were looking for this?"

Chapter Twenty-Eight

All around Teia were sounds of a fight, and yet Lehm's voice was as clear as if he were standing beside her. The icy ridge of his tone was unchanged, a gaping cold that froze any response.

The Seascript was a massive clip of parchment, with tattered leather bindings and a cracked, peeling spine. There were different layers to the book, its closed pages shifting in color, denoting where new information had been added throughout the years.

It didn't *look* like something that might doom the Five Kingdoms, but Teia had learned appearances were often deceiving. She forced herself steady as she said, "You already know what's inside, don't you?"

Lehm chuckled. "I've always been a voracious reader. Did my traitor Dawnbreakers mention that I taught myself Shaylani, just so I could discover more about the wonderful history here?"

"Of course," Teia said. "There's so many positive lessons to be learned in a place called the House of Mourning."

"Not to worry, Halfling. I've learned *plenty*." Before she could react, he'd flicked a lighter in one hand, holding it up to the Seascript with the other.

There hadn't been much hope before. From the instant Teia discovered that Lehm had allied himself with Ko Taisheng, she'd known the rebel leader would read the relic. Yet Teia stumbled forward anyway, a strangled cry rising in her throat. She snuffed out the flames, but it was too late. As the Seascript's outer edge blackened, Lehm wrenched to the left, hefting the text back toward the Naga. One of the guards caught it deftly, her palms rippling with a sheen of water.

Within seconds, the Seascript was soaked through, its soggy remains flaking to the carpeted floor.

The stench of smoke fanned into the corridor, as Teia suppressed a swear. "I thought the Seascript offered Feng legitimacy," she said to Lehm. "You convinced the Red Mountain to let you destroy it?"

"It's funny what an extended talk can do to broaden someone's worldview. In the end, should the current emperor fall, Feng hardly needs a *book* to return to the throne." His gaze was hollow. "My apologies, Halfling. Were you wanting to read that?"

"I don't need it," Teia ground out. It wasn't a lie, not exactly. The Seascript wouldn't be relevant once she split Lehm's head from his body.

She reached out, grabbing for the heat around him. But just as in Taijin Palace, Teia encountered a strange film of moisture, which prevented the rebel leader from burning. She pushed at it cautiously, but the barrier held, heat dissipating as it met his skin.

If he wouldn't burn, perhaps he could drown. She prodded at the water within his chest. Again, an odd resistance shoved back, wrestling against her. Someone sensed she was trying to tamper, someone with far more control than she had. One of the Naga, in all likelihood, who kept a persistent watch over Lehm's shoulder.

She thrust back with all her might, striving to break the invisible hold. Faintly, Teia sensed those gleaming points that dotted Lehm's blood, the spots where water still listened to her.

She narrowed her concentration, and Lehm exhaled sharply. His arm lifted of its own accord, a puppet attached to a string. "You've discovered a new trick."

"And you've finally made friends. I'd say we've all bettered ourselves in Shaylan."

"The emperor is generous with his resources. When I explained you'd been sighted in Okkan, he allowed me some of the Naga's best fighters."

"You took a spate of guards who were already part of the Red Mountain, and used me as an excuse to bring them out of Taijin. Does Yuwen know you've allied yourself with this kingdom's rebels too?"

"I'd never do such a thing," he said, as he struggled against her control. "Is it my fault if the House of Mourning's owner happens to be an acquaintance? What he does in his spare time has no bearing on me."

"For his sake," Teia said, "I hope one of his hobbies is redecorating. He's going to have to lay down new floors after you cut your own heart out."

She guided his fingers, commanding him to grasp one of the swords on his waist. The Naga behind him shuffled in alarm, but Lehm gave a small shake of his head. "Easy," he snarled at Teia. "If you kill me now, you'll never hear what I have to say."

"I'm not interested in unsolicited wisdom."

"Oh? And what if I told you a hundred ships are prepared to sail on Erisia unless I return to Yuwen, safe and sound?"

Teia paused. "You're lying," she said, but her uncertainty soured the space between them, drifting into the corridor.

"About Yuwen?"

"About all of it."

"Am I?" He lifted his free hand and withdrew a heavy piece

of parchment, holding it up for her to see. The stamp of the royal family—a dragon clutching a pearl—was pressed in the corner. The words were written in both Shaylani and Erisian, penned in blue ink. Teia treaded closer, skimming the first sentence.

I, Li Yuwen, Emperor of Shaylan, Son of the Dragon, order that the Shaylani fleet sail immediately upon the kingdom of Erisia.

Teia's stomach tightened. She wanted nothing more than to flay the smug smile off Lehm's face. "Yuwen is going to invade Erisia?"

"He has no other choice," Lehm said, the sentence laden with mock sympathy. "His adviser, kidnapped. His visitors in court, brutalized. And with Erisia's own ruler accused of aiming for the Shaylani throne, before fleeing into the night—" He clicked his tongue. "I'd say the young emperor has every right to strike, don't you?"

"You talked him into this."

"I merely planted the seed. Better to act first than to have his throne ripped out from under him. He's so very scared, you know. He's set to journey to Okkan soon, so we can reconvene in person." Lehm let go of the decree. It fluttered between them, landing face up on the floor. "Now—are you going to release me? Or will the Shaylani fleet be sent off by morning?"

She did so reluctantly, keeping her eyes on the announcement. "What do you want?"

"Nothing more than peace." He sighed wistfully. "How I long for all of us to get along."

I'm going to burn your corpse and dance on your grave, Teia thought. But what she said was "And what does Yuwen long for?"

"Unfortunately, the emperor would like more drastic measures taken against you. He's requesting your presence at Okkan's cliffs in three days' time, right before dawn."

"He wants an apology?"

"He wants you publicly lashed and dragged through the streets of Shaylan." Lehm tapped a finger to his chin. "Or was that my suggestion? It's been such a busy week—it's so very hard to remember details."

"You have Kyra already. Why not return to Taijin and finish what you came to do?"

"What's the point in a victory if there's nobody there to enjoy it?"

"You're here to gloat."

"I'm here to *win*—although I'm glad we're having this conversation now. It would have been tactless to post a declaration of war without at least offering you the chance to spare your kingdom."

"Only for you to decimate it with the Serkawr?"

He chuckled humorlessly. "So crass," he chided. "You remind me of your brother when he was alive."

"Half brother. And if you came all this way to reminisce about Jura, I suggest purchasing your passage back to Erisia. His mausoleum is open to mourners at the Splendid Graveyard."

"Excellent," Lehm said. "Perhaps that's where they'll inter your remains as well, once Yuwen is through with you."

He snapped his fingers, and the Naga to his right pivoted away. She glided down the hallway to dip around the corner, her cloak billowing behind her. She was back a second later, with a thrashing figure in her grip. The Naga shoved the boy toward Lehm, who pulled back the captive's hair, forcing his face into the light.

In spite of herself, Teia's eyes widened. A gasp slid from her lips. "Jin?" she said.

Chapter Twenty-Nine

The adviser should have been monitoring the perimeter of the House of Mourning, keeping watch over the flow of guests into the party. Instead, here he was, a fresh bruise smarting above his eye, his face bloodied down to his jaw. A rag was wrapped around his mouth.

"The restraints have held up well enough," Lehm said, tapping at the cuffs that encased Jin's wrists. "These are on loan from the palace. It's a special type of metal found in the Shaylani mines, which prevents a person from connecting to water."

"Have you considered writing books, Lehm?" Teia growled. "Perhaps your ramblings can finally reach someone who cares."

"You could do with some appreciation." Lehm's eyes glittered. "There's quite an important element to these cuffs. If rumors are true, they were used in the coup that brought down Yuwen's father."

Teia surveyed the restraints. A lock was set beneath them, welded directly into metal. "Does Yuwen know you're manhandling his adviser?"

"The boy's tried to run more than once. We had to take more drastic measures. I'm sure all will be forgiven once we deliver him back to the palace." Lehm brought his hand upward. His thumb brushed one of the gashes on Jin's cheek, before digging into the wound. The adviser released a muffled cry. "Although come to think of it, I never promised Yuwen what condition he'd be in. It's hard to make guarantees, given who captured him in the first place."

Teia watched as Lehm pulled back his hand, his fingers now coated with Jin's blood. "Do you ever tire of invoking my name?" she said.

"Oh, not at all. In fact . . ." He unsheathed his blade, the silver edge glinting against the lantern light. Languidly, he nestled it against Jin's neck, right beneath the adviser's chin. "Come, Halfling," Lehm crooned. "You want Yuwen's adviser, don't you?"

Before Teia could answer, a burst of water split the space between her and Lehm. They were both knocked aside, with Jin thrown out of Lehm's reach.

A body had fallen to the floor, draped over the hidden room's threshold. It was one of the Naga who had rushed Tobias—her final blow must have gone wide, sending the blast that had separated Teia and Lehm. The guard's arms were twisted at jarring angles, her throat carved open in a scarlet grin.

Tobias sauntered down the corridor. The blade of his knife beamed red, as he offered a careless smile. "So," he said, as he wiped the weapon clean of blood. "What did I miss?"

"Rennert," Lehm bit out, snatching for his fallen sword. "After I took you into the Dawnbreakers—after everything I helped you achieve—this is how you repay me?"

"You didn't take me in, I sought you out. Don't pretend you ever cared for me."

"At least I know where my morals are, boy. You're the one allying yourself with a Carthan, after what her brother did to your parents."

Tobias's gaze hardened. "Don't you dare speak of my family," he spat.

"Just an observation. You should know who you're in bed with." Lehm lifted a brow. "I mean that statement quite literally."

Tobias started forward, but Teia shifted before him, planting herself in his way. She returned Lehm's stare, coldhearted and unflinching, heat stinging at her fingertips. "I wouldn't be one to talk of family," she said. "What would Hanne have to say?"

Rage descended on the rebel leader's face. He surged with uncanny speed, his blade snapping outward. Teia redirected the sword with an arc of fire, but it was like Lehm had anticipated the move. He twisted, hacking his weapon sideways, deflecting a strike from Tobias.

"You want to know what my sister would say, Halfling?" Lehm said. "Would this be before your father's guards shot into a crowd of peaceful protestors? Before the bullet hit her in the eye, and went straight through her skull? Before I looked down at my shirt, and saw bits of her brain spattered on the front? When she fell, she was still holding my hand."

When he came at Teia again, she ducked, sending fire his way. The flames missed, leaving a charred black splotch on the painted ceiling, just above where the three Naga were standing.

Lehm wove around Teia, slipping a second blade free of its sheath. She felt a sharp burst of pain in her arm. The tip of the sword had slashed open her sleeve, silken shreds of fabric floating down to the floor.

"Is that all they teach royals?" Lehm said. "I'd have expected better."

Somewhere in the distance, three bells had started to ring.

He fought with deadly precision, power rippling behind each movement. Teia flung a pillar of fire at the rebel leader, which he spun back to evade. She coaxed the flames into a circle, pulling them high, trapping him in its center. Lehm burst through a second later, both swords crossed before him. She jumped aside as he landed, his blades plunging into the spot where she'd once been.

Tobias cut forward with his knife. Lehm blocked the attack with one sword as he jabbed out with the other. When Tobias managed to dodge the thrust, Lehm pressed in close, the hilt of his right sword bashing upward. It caught Tobias on the shoulder, and he stumbled back, swearing heavily.

"You fight like a sellsword," Tobias said, sweat reflecting off his brow.

"There's so much you don't know about me, boy. Who do you think I came up with when I was younger?"

Back in the Golden Palace, Teia used to eavesdrop on meetings about the Dawnbreakers. She would listen for hours as scouts read aloud reports penned by the military's best generals, describing Lehm and the skirmishes he'd fought in. *He moves like a creature from the old myths,* one commander had written. *Like he crawled out from somewhere no being should survive.*

Back then, Teia had thought it was all an exaggeration—but now, she understood what the generals had meant. Despite dividing his attention between her and Tobias, Lehm held the advantage. And even if they did manage to survive him, there were the Naga stationed behind the rebel leader, fresh soldiers who awaited orders.

He was toying with them, pushing them to the edge to see when they'd break.

He was smiling as he stalked forward, the tips of his blades scraping against the carpet. But before Lehm could attack, he paused abruptly, swords lifted in midair. Something creaked ominously above the Naga, a groan that reverberated through the corridor. "What—"

The ceiling collapsed in a shower of warped wood, crushing one of the Naga, sending the other two bolting aside. Three figures crashed to the second floor, along with the corpse of another black-robed guard, one Teia didn't recognize. His brown eyes were open, unblinking. His skin was covered with hideous boils, which dribbled a sulfuric yellow pus.

Enna van Apt rose gracefully from the carpeted hall, as if she made a daily habit of plummeting through ceilings. Her grin was notched from steel. "Surprise," she said.

A smile pulled at Teia's lips, while Tobias's expression remained even. Only Jin showed any kind of shock. He'd fallen onto the ground, where he'd freed himself of the gag. As he gaped up at Enna, he scrubbed at his face with shackled hands, like he didn't quite believe she was there. "I thought you were ill."

For the barest second, Lehm's gaze darted to the adviser's. But before the rebel leader could speak, Enna smirked at Jin. "Wouldn't you know it? It seems I've made a remarkable recovery."

To the left of the thief, Alara dusted off her rose-pink robes. "Glad to know my cellulase solution works," she said thoughtfully, prodding a chunk of wood with her foot. "I was having trouble getting the formula right."

"Too much acid?" Enna said.

"Too strong of a smell. I'd hate to leave a fight reeking of sulfur."

Kyra stood on Enna's other side, balanced atop a melted piece of plaster. There were angry red marks around her wrists, but she flashed Alara a proud look. "It's brilliant. *You're* brilliant."

Lehm rotated toward Teia. Disbelief melded across his face, seeping into his features. "How did you . . ."

"I hedge my bets, Lehm," Teia said. "Maybe you should do the same."

When they had reviewed the places where Kyra might be held, Teia had had her doubts about the hidden room. The chamber might be isolated, but there were several other spots that met the same criteria—the bedroom, for one, where Ko Taisheng had once kept the Seascript. Besides, Cornelius Lehm had never been one to favor an obvious solution.

So when Teia had crafted her plan, she'd added in a contingency. After entering the House of Mourning, she, Tobias, and Amalay had gone to the hidden room, just in case Kyra really *was* being kept there. At the same time, she suspected that if the rebel champion was stashed in some other part of the building, Lehm would temporarily leave her side to confront Teia himself, bringing along the lion's share of his forces.

Teia had known men like Lehm all her life. He'd come too far not to gloat now.

As soon as she'd seen him with the Seascript, Teia had known her calculations were correct. After that, it was a matter of distracting him with a fight, while Alara searched the rest of the house for Kyra—with the help of Erisia's best thief, who could jimmy any lock.

From behind Teia, there came a stilted cry. She pivoted back to find that the blizzard had stopped. In the middle of an icy burst, Rina was curled on her side, unconscious. Amalay stood over her, sadness heavy against her features.

"I'd say it's time to go," the leader of thieves said brusquely.

From the yawning hole in the ceiling, skeins of rope were being tossed down, secured at the top with studded iron hooks.

Cowled figures slid down in pairs, maneuvering with catlike grace. They made no sound as they landed on the floor, so that not even the carpet shifted beneath their feet.

"Thieves?" Lehm said.

"Did I forget to mention?" Teia said. "You're not the only one who's made friends in Shaylan."

Enna opened her palm, revealing a series of sparkling pellets. When she threw them down, the world disappeared in a gray shroud of smoke, just as a *bang* rang from the hidden room.

Teia was already halfway to the chamber. The explosive that Tobias had planted after dispatching the Naga had detonated, cleaving a hole in the side of the House of Mourning. Dust mixed into the air as she leapt from the second floor, grunting as she hit the cobblestones, her shoulders aching from the brunt of the fall. She could hear the others behind her—Enna whooping with glee, Jin running awkwardly, his wrists still cuffed before him—with Amalay the last to follow. She threw up her hands, sending a layer of ice over the hole, sealing Lehm and the Naga within.

But even with the smoke and the chaos and the clamor of thieves, Teia heard the rebel leader's parting words, howled through the ice, pushing out into the balmy night.

"I'll give you three days to return Kyra and give yourself up at Okkan's cliffs. *Three days,* Halfling—and if not, Shaylan will declare war on Erisia."

Chapter Thirty

Teia tried to stay positive, but everything around her was falling apart.

Despite the promise of new stars during Kashan, the constellations were hidden behind a mass of clouds. Teia and the others plunged into the unyielding darkness, creeping past jumbled collections of wooden buildings, stopping only so Enna could pick the lock on Jin's shackles, which they left in a nearby alley. Covered fruit stands and half-mended fishnets assumed monstrous shapes. Faint voices sounded in the distance, but it was impossible to tell whether it was guests from the banquet, drunk off revelry, or the surviving Naga, out for their heads.

Three days, Halfling—and if not, Shaylan will declare war on Erisia.

At the end of one of the streets, they came across a shrine to Armina, which rose before a towering gray wall. A statue of the Goddess rested upon a silver podium, framed by a painting of the sea. Amalay reached over offerings of oranges and sweets, setting two of her fingers into the Goddess's upturned palm.

Almost immediately, there was a click. A section of the wall creaked outward, revealing a hidden door.

"One of my private safe houses," Amalay said, waving them through. "I acquired it a few years ago at auction."

"You *bought* something?" Enna said.

"Certainly not. I robbed the deed's auctioneer, and threatened to drop him off the cliffs if he mentioned anything had gone amiss."

"You know," Kyra said, "that's not normally how someone acquires property at auction."

"Do most people actually go in and place bids?" Enna asked, disgusted.

"By definition, yes."

"Goddess. How *boring*."

The safe house had clearly once belonged to a noble, or perhaps a splendidly wealthy merchant. The door opened to a flourishing garden, with another statue of the Goddess rising in the middle of a shimmering blue pool, the Serkawr twined over her bare shoulders. On the other side of the courtyard, a wooden entryway led to a spacious parlor. A dining set had been arranged by the wall, with seven matching seats bordering a lacquered table.

They dropped promptly into the chairs, sitting around the table in stunned silence. With a sigh, Teia lowered her forehead against the smooth surface. Now that they were away from the House of Mourning, the bruises had begun to settle, aches that lingered beneath her skin. Her elbow smarted from where Lehm had nicked her, dried blood crusting her ripped sleeve.

From across the table, she heard Jin clear his throat. "Enna," the adviser said dazedly. "When we left for the House of Mourning, you were asleep. The fever you had . . ."

"Like I said," Enna told him briskly, "I recover fast."

"But—"

"If we're going to talk, how about we dissect what Lehm was saying back there?" The thief cleared her throat loudly. "Teia?"

Begrudgingly, Teia lifted her head. "He said a lot of things. You'll have to be more specific."

"He said . . ." Enna hesitated. "He said Shaylan will go to war with Erisia if we don't return Kyra."

"He said *what*?" Alara demanded.

"Maybe it's a bluff," Kyra said thinly.

Enna folded her hands before her. "When has Cornelius Lehm ever bluffed about anything in his life?" she said angrily. "If there's one thing the bastard does, it's follow through on his promises. I remember when he tried recruiting me to the Dawnbreakers."

Even Teia hadn't heard this particular story before. "You turned him down, didn't you?"

"In less polite language. He asked two more times, before telling me I'd regret the slight. Found out where my ma lived and sent bruisers to her home, day and night. There was a tabby she had raised, a little orange one that liked to sunbathe in the windows. They skinned it open, and nailed its head to the door." The thief grimaced. "Tell me—does that sound like a man who's known to bluff?"

Kyra visibly drooped. "It doesn't," she admitted. "I was just hoping otherwise."

It was admirable, Teia thought. Lehm must have kept Kyra bound in the House of Mourning—there were welts rising against the rebel champion's copper skin, where the soapstone cuffs had rubbed her wrists raw. Yet despite all this, Kyra remained someone who searched for goodness, steadfast in her beliefs, her hand stretched into the abyss.

Deep inside, Teia knew what the rebel champion longed to find. If Kyra held on to that endless optimism, maybe the man who'd given her purpose—the one who'd set her on a path to greatness—would somehow return.

Admirable, but delusional. Teia probed at a chipped spot on the table. She was scrounging for ways to deflect the question about war when Amalay rose to her feet. The leader of thieves kicked at the sturdy legs of her chair, hands shoved deep into her pockets. "Why not just assassinate this Cornelius Lehm? He seems like a pathetic scrap of a man."

"Excellent description," Enna said.

"Someone was protecting him in the House of Mourning," Teia said. "He doesn't burn, and he can't drown."

"I guarantee he's not immune to poison," Alara offered. "If I can sneak into the House of Mourning—"

"You're not going back there," Kyra said sharply.

"It was just a suggestion."

"I wouldn't be surprised if Lehm took extra precautions with food and drink," Teia said. "He'll probably seal off the building, make it impossible for anyone to exit or enter."

"He knows our strengths," Alara grunted. "Maybe he'll do us a favor and die of thirst."

Enna nodded at Tobias. "What about you?" she said. "I thought you were unmatched in fighting."

"*Almost* unmatched," he said with a scowl.

Amalay slammed her palms on the table. "There must be another way. Anything can be done if we have enough *shi*."

The Shaylani word was distantly familiar. Despite the misery welling through her, Teia glanced up. "Doesn't *shi* mean location?"

"It's a homonym."

"Which means?"

"A homonym? A word that's spelled the same, but has different definitions—"

"I know what a homonym is," Teia snapped. "I meant the word you just said. *Shi.*"

Amalay shrugged. "People usually use it to refer to a location. But it can also mean *time.* It's a more highbrow way to say things—if they heard me, my thieves would laugh me out the door." She cocked her head. "Are you all right? You look like you're about to faint."

Teia certainly felt like it. All at once, she was recalling the conversation she'd had with Yuwen and Jin in the palace's pavilion, which seemed like a full eternity before. When she'd first told them about the Serkawr, Yuwen had explained the value the Seascript might possess.

There are stories that say the sea beast can only be summoned at the proper shi.

Yuwen had translated *shi* to *location.* Yet all along there had been a double meaning, one the emperor might not even have considered.

Was this why Lehm had kept Kyra in the House of Mourning, rather than take her back to Taijin? Could he have discovered that the Serkawr didn't just need to be called forth at a location, but a *time*?

For a second, hope fanned in Teia's chest. Then it was gone, snuffed like a flame. This new piece of knowledge hardly did her good now, when faced with the ultimatum Lehm had given her.

War.

It was a deceptive word—short and clipped, rolling easily off the tongue. But when Teia rested her chin above clenched knuckles, she could envision every ounce of destruction, the many horrors to come. The first war between Shaylan and Erisia had devastated both their kingdoms. The second might very well destroy them.

When she had stepped into the House of Mourning, Teia thought she'd been prepared for Lehm. She'd sworn not to underestimate the rebel leader—and yet he had kept her in check, his foot toed over some invisible line. She hadn't anticipated his declaration, this new era that was set to begin.

If she kept Kyra away from Lehm, Erisia and Shaylan would devolve into war. If she handed the rebel champion over, Lehm would summon the Serkawr, with the knowledge he'd gleaned from the Seascript. Either way, both options were the same—calamity beyond belief, carnage through and through.

"Boss?" Enna said.

They were waiting for a reply, expectant, anticipating. They looked to her as if she had a solution, like she'd somehow devised a scheme to free them from this mess. It was too much—it was all *too much.* When Teia opened her mouth, her voice caught in her throat.

"I need a moment," she said, before scraping away from the chair and lunging out of the parlor.

She didn't know where else to go, and so she ended up back in the courtyard, where the moonlight reflected off the glistening surface of the pool. Water lapped at the Goddess's bare feet, but Teia was drawn to the Serkawr, slithering over her arms. Questions hummed in her mind, refusing to allow her rest. Was it better to doom her kingdom to war? Or was it a kinder mercy to allow the sea beast to rise? She peered up helplessly at Armina, searching for some sliver of guidance, but the Goddess was as silent as ever.

"Teia."

She didn't turn. "Leave me alone, Tobias."

He ignored her pointedly. As he came to stand beside her, Tobias raised his gaze to the statue of Armina. She bore down on them blankly, her lips locked in that indulgent smile.

"I used to pray to her," he said quietly. "After what happened to my parents, when I was recovering from the injury Jura gave me. I would keep spare candles under my bed, smuggled from the nearby temple. When everyone had gone to sleep, I'd light a candle and ask for a sign."

"Did it work?"

"In a way. Eventually, there were whispers in the Highlands about a warehouse bomb planted in Bhanot. Someone had painted an image of a rising sun over the rubble."

"The Dawnbreakers."

"They were what I needed at the time. Lehm . . ." He traced the scar on his neck. "I never liked him. But I always thought he was smart. Capable."

"He's won, Tobias." Defeat tinged each word, drifting into the night. "I don't know what to do. At this point, it's easiest if we return to Erisia."

"You want to flee?"

She hated the astonishment in his tone. This had all been a gamble—the trip across the Dark Sea, the journey through Shaylan. She'd flipped a coin and watched it land. Sometimes, the only thing left was to accept a loss.

"What else can we do?" Teia cried. "If it's war either way, I'd rather be home. Fortify our defenses, hold him back however we can. Here, Lehm has the Red Mountain. He has the Naga."

"What does it matter? Kings have armies, and still lose their thrones." Tobias's voice was somber. "Teia. If you want to go, we'll go. Back to Erisia, back to the Golden Palace. But if there's anyone to outwit Lehm, it's you."

"You said it yourself. He's smart, capable—"

"Plenty of people are both. But you?"

"Are you saying I'm neither?"

"I'm saying you're beyond either quality." There was pride in his face, glimmering at the edges. "Teia, you're conniving and cunning and brilliant to a fault. There's not a single person in the Five Kingdoms who's been able to withstand you. Jura. Yuwen. Rina."

Despite the enormity of their situation, her breath hitched. Something stirred within her chest. "And you?" Teia said, before she could stop herself.

"What about me?"

"You seem to have withstood me just fine."

If she wasn't careful, she'd drown in the blue of his eyes, the dark shine of the sea against a brewing storm. Tobias leaned down, his lips brushing by her ear.

"Teia Carthan," he murmured. "You were always meant to be my ruin."

If their kiss at the banquet was a wildfire, this was the mighty pull of a wave, dulling Teia's senses, dissolving her bones. That same glow reignited in her stomach, flaring down her body. His mouth was at her neck, her jaw. His clothes smelled faintly of smoke, remnants of the explosion at the House of Mourning.

The House of Mourning.

She moved away abruptly. He glanced at her, surprised, before a smile crept over his face. "You have an idea, don't you?"

Lehm had beaten Teia bloody, and yet she remained upright, swaying and bruised but still on her feet. War might be knocking at her door, her downfall on the horizon, but it would have to wait awhile longer.

The Seascript was gone, reduced to ashes, scattered across the House of Mourning. Aside from Cornelius Lehm, there was only one person left in the Five Kingdoms who knew its contents. It was the same man who'd owned the scarlet home first, the one heralded by the Red Mountain's members.

She hadn't answered Tobias yet, but he knew her well enough to guess her thoughts. "That's my girl," he said quietly. In the shadow of Armina's statue, beneath the snarl of the Serkawr, his hand found hers, fingers entwined for just a second.

When he let go, the heat of his touch remained. It comforted her, even as she strode toward the parlor.

It was time for her to have a conversation with Amalay.

Chapter Thirty-One

When Teia rushed back into the parlor, Amalay was alone at the table. She nursed a cup of tea, looking very much like she wanted to drown in its depths.

"Where are the others?" Teia said.

"Off to bed, in various states of dejection."

"And you?"

"I'm trying to wallow here, thank you very much." The leader of thieves glowered at Teia. "But apparently you don't have the decency to leave me in peace."

"If I remember correctly, you were the one who invited us here."

"I'm fulfilling a debt. Didn't I say I'd owe you if you spared Rina in the House of Mourning?"

Teia settled into a nearby chair. "Rina," she said shortly. "How is she?"

Amalay drew a finger along the rim of her teacup. "The thieves I sent into the House of Mourning just returned with her. She's in the Society now."

Teia thought of the cowled figures that had rappelled down from the ceiling, clustering around Lehm and the Naga. "You didn't trust Lehm not to torture her for information."

"I don't trust anyone, least of all an Erisian man who seeks to raise an ancient sea beast."

So Teia had something in common with Amalay after all. Teia straightened the edge of the purple cushion. "What happens when your thieves discover that Rina is a traitor?" she asked.

"They won't find out," Amalay said. "Not yet."

"You aren't going to tell them?"

"She's my sibling."

So was Jura, Teia thought. She was decidedly unsympathetic to matters of familial strife.

When Amalay noted Teia's reaction, frustration knotted in her face. "Rina wasn't always like this," she said fiercely. "It was only after she went to Taijin, when Feng had a lottery for new attendants."

Teia stiffened, as stories of the former emperor flooded her mind. "Did he . . ."

The leader of thieves shook her head wearily. "It was Yuwen's men, on the night he deposed his ba."

Do you have any idea what Yuwen has done? What his coup cost me?

"There was no warning about the coup, you know," Amalay continued. "No preemptive message for the servants to flee. When the fighting began, guards from both sides ransacked the palace. A group of Yuwen's soldiers found Rina—she saw his symbol pinned to their chests. She pleaded with them, tried to make her case. But they were too far gone, crazed with bloodlust. When one of them took out his knife, she didn't even have a chance to defend herself."

A wave of nausea pressed at Teia's stomach. Rina's scars made sense now. "That's why she joined the Red Mountain. She wants revenge for what happened during the coup."

Ice snaked along the side of the teacup. "The Red Mountain is hardly a solution. Fools, the whole lot of them. And my little sister is the greatest one of all."

"But you'll protect her."

"She'll hate me for this now. I know she will. But if she needs a hundred more years, then that's what I'll give her." Amalay rubbed at her eyes. "Is this what you wanted to speak with me about, Teia Carthan? To listen to me bemoan the only family I have left?"

If Teia's plan didn't work, Amalay and Rina wouldn't have one year, much less a hundred. They were all living on borrowed time, minutes wrested from Lehm's grasp.

She intended to steal all that back.

"Amalay," Teia said. "What do you know about Cloud Mountain?"

It was well past four in the morning when Teia gathered the others in the parlor.

They came reluctantly, dragging their feet, stumbling over the long hems of the silk trousers they'd borrowed from the safe house's dressers. Alara curled into a plush chair, as Kyra sat on the ground, resting her head against the Poisons Master's leg. Enna cracked the joints in her neck lazily. Jin wrapped his hands around a steaming porcelain cup, taking the occasional bleary sip.

Only Tobias looked fully awake—no small feat, considering he'd been up with Teia for most of the night, helping her parse through what Amalay had provided on Cloud Mountain. From his spot by the wall, he gave her a small nod.

Alara sifted her fingers through Kyra's dark hair, which fell in shining waves down the curve of her back. "Well, Teia?" she groused. "What was so urgent that it couldn't wait until morning?"

"It *is* morning," Teia said.

"It's dark outside, and I'm running on fumes. Even the birds haven't woken up yet."

"Some birds are nocturnal," Jin said. "Owls, nighthawks—"

"List another bird, and I'll empty my entire tin of acid into your tea."

Jin placed a protective palm over his cup.

Kyra glanced around. "Where's Amalay?" she asked.

"Running an errand," Teia answered.

"Oh," Alara said, in a matter-of-fact way. "So she's killing someone."

"Or stealing something," Enna said. "She should have taken me with her."

"When we're done, I'm sure she'll bring you to all of Okkan's best spots," Teia said. "You can rob a guarded carriage. Fleece nobles to your heart's content."

"Carriage robberies are beneath me."

"That's fine, as long as infiltrating Cloud Mountain isn't."

Jin dropped his cup. Liquid seeped into the rug as he stuttered, "What did you just say?"

Teia had expected such a reaction. She'd gotten as much from Amalay hours before, after she'd shared her intentions around Cloud Mountain. When she was done speaking, Amalay had stared back at her in disbelief. "What?" she'd said, before dissolving into a fit of chuckles, smoothing her hair behind both ears. "I see. This is some kind of joke, isn't it?"

It might have been, coming from anyone else. But Teia

Carthan was no stranger to madness. If her best plans were devised under pressure, cultivated beneath the brunt of a sword, then this was her magnum opus. Her back was against a wall, but she'd sawed herself a door. All that was left to do was walk through it.

"Things have been different in Shaylan," Teia said. The admission stung both her tongue and her pride, but she forged on, unwilling to falter. "I don't have the contacts that I do in Erisia. I don't have the resources that Lehm does. But what I *do* have is knowledge. Knowledge of my enemy, knowledge of what he wants. Lehm took the Seascript before we did. He read it. He knows how the Serkawr can be summoned."

"I'm sorry," Kyra said. "Is that supposed to be a positive thing?"

"Not to mention," Teia added, "that Lehm has Yuwen licking his boots. He's earned enough respect in the Shaylani court that he's allowed to command a portion of the Naga."

"Those Naga are traitors," Enna said quizzically. "Guards who are loyal to Feng and the Red Mountain, not Yuwen."

"But my cousin doesn't know that. And if Lehm is held in such high esteem, surely there's at least one courtier who can provide him with noble's water."

"I still don't see the good news," Jin said.

"Not good. Useful." Teia turned toward the rebel champion, who blinked back at her, confused. "Kyra, you have commoner's flame. That means you're the last thing he needs to raise the Serkawr."

"Um," Kyra said. "That doesn't make me feel better."

"Are you suggesting we commission a ship and sail to the farthest corner of the Five Kingdoms?" Alara said. "If so, I've heard K'val is lovely this time of year."

"It's winter there," Tobias said.

"I'd rather face some snow than be embroiled in a war."

"About that," Enna said. "Before we all flee to parts unknown, did we happen to forget what Lehm is threatening us with if we don't give him Kyra?"

"I didn't," Teia answered. "But why did he give us seventy-two hours to do so?"

"Narcissism," Tobias mumbled.

"Insanity," Alara replied.

"He likes to draw out the moment," Jin said, rubbing absently at the swelling on his wrists.

Teia leaned back in her seat. "All of the above," she acknowledged. "But no matter what we think of Lehm, he's also not an idiot. Why give us such a specific time frame to return Kyra—and at the cliffs, no less? Lehm knows we're in Okkan. He could have given us one day, so why did we get three?"

Kyra's gaze lit on Teia. "He's waiting for something," she said slowly.

That was more like it. "Exactly," Teia said. "And what's at the end of these three days?"

"Complete destruction?" Jin asked.

"The fall of the Five Kingdoms?" Enna provided.

Tobias batted at one of the dangling silver strands from the ceiling. "The end of Kashan," he said. "Nine days of celebration come to a close."

Jin bit down on the inside of his cheek. "You think the festival is linked to summoning the Serkawr?"

"I don't think it's a coincidence," Teia said.

"And your solution is atop Cloud Mountain?"

"You and Yuwen said it yourselves—since Feng killed Taijin's

Memory Keepers, he's the only one who has knowledge of the Seascript."

"But if Lehm already knows how to raise the Serkawr," Alara protested, "what's the point of seeking out Feng?"

"Because of what else the Seascript might contain. In Taijin, Yuwen said the book might explain how to stop the Serkawr. When we first arrived at the pagoda, Amalay and Rina mentioned the same thing."

"This is a frightening number of hypotheticals," Enna pointed out. "It could be nothing but a rumor."

"Or an opportunity," Tobias said.

"An opportunity to lose our heads," the thief snapped back, and he conceded this with a shrug.

Teia waved away Enna's concerns. "Amalay said that the Red Mountain has been trying to break Feng from his exile for years. At the very least, getting inside the mountain is doable."

"What about after?" Jin said.

"After that, we just need to find our way to Feng."

"You make it seem like a stroll through the market."

"Who knows? It could very well be just that."

"Somehow I doubt it."

Kyra rested her cheek against the curl of her fist. "These members that the Red Mountain sends in," she said. "How do they tend to leave?"

"In pieces, more or less," Tobias said.

"I'm sorry I asked," Kyra muttered. "Teia, let's say we survive whatever traps are put in place to keep out intruders. You want to walk into Li Feng's exile, and—what? *Ask* for a summary of the Seascript?"

"Aren't you always the one saying I should try asking nicely?"

"A homicidal ruler imprisoned inside a mountain might be where I draw the line."

"I'll take care of Feng," Teia said. "In the House of Mourning, Lehm revealed his hand. He's shown us what he's willing to do. Up until now, we've been playing a game without knowing the rules. This is our chance to get back on the board."

She found each of their eyes, one after another. The silence wore thin, until Enna grinned. "We're beginning to make a habit of breaking into prisons," she said. "Why can't we ever infiltrate somewhere different?"

"A sweets shop," Kyra said.

"Or an alehouse," Alara mumbled.

"Is this what you do for fun in Erisia?" Jin said. "Goddess—we're *doomed*."

Chapter Thirty-Two

They spent the following two days drawing up plans, rehearsing how exactly they might confront Feng, before setting off that final morning. A fine mist had blanketed Okkan, draping over its sprawling buildings and spiny statues, the central road that swarmed with people.

When Amalay met them in the early hours, she brought a wagon on the brink of collapse. The back wheel wobbled dangerously, fitted with several broken spokes. Dust covered the floor, along with a few stray feed sacks and a heavy black tarp, rolled up tightly and shunted into the corner.

Teia prodded one of the spokes cautiously, before inspecting the creatures hitched to the wagon. "Mules?" she said.

"Shaylan's pride and joy. They'll draw less attention than a pair of horses, in case the Naga are searching for us."

"I see," Teia said, eyeing both animals apprehensively. "Which is the pride, and which is the joy?"

Amalay crossed her arms. "I borrowed them from a local turnip farmer," she said. "They're rowdy, but they get the job done."

Tobias brushed grit away from one of the feed sacks. "Somehow, I don't think *borrowed* is the right word to use."

Meanwhile, Kyra was patting one of the mules. It flicked its long ears at her fondly, nuzzling her way. "I like them," she said happily.

"Speak for yourself," Jin said. He seized the hem of his robes in his fist, right before the other mule could chomp down on it.

"They would make nice coats," Alara mused. "The color wouldn't be too bad either."

"You could start a new trend in Erisia," Enna piped up.

"I *could*. That would be spectacular, wouldn't it?"

"Don't you dare," Kyra said. She began scratching under the first mule's chin, and it tipped back its head, clearly pleased with the attention.

The mules might be more inconspicuous, but it didn't take long for Teia to regret the decision. She and the others had wedged themselves within the wagon, covered by the tarp, as Amalay drove them out of Okkan. To say the ride was bumpy was an understatement, as the wagon bounced violently over fresh potholes, before beginning the steep ascent up the mountainous path. The mules were as unruly as Amalay had promised, once skidding so suddenly that Alara clapped a palm over her mouth, moaning that she was going to be sick.

They'd brought an odd assortment of rations from the safe house—dried strips of fish, soft golden buns, flaky pastries packed with sweet red beans—but nobody had the stomach to eat. Eventually, the road evened out, far smoother than before. Teia dozed with her head next to Enna's, her shoulder chafing uncomfortably against the hard wooden slats.

When she awoke, the wagon had come to a halt.

She blinked hazily as Amalay threw back the tarp. A fresh breeze whipped through Teia's hair. She sat up in the wagon as grogginess gave way to sheer amazement.

They had stopped at a winding bend, set far enough into the trees that they'd be invisible from the road. Before Teia, mountains stretched far beyond where the path ended, rising like the fingers of a hand grasping toward the sky. Clouds shrouded their base, so that each peak seemed to float atop a misted sea, draped in thick patches of greenery. Somewhere in the distance, a bird warbled out a song.

Amalay grinned. "It's not a bad view, is it?"

"Beats the inside of a wagon," Teia answered. When Amalay went to help the others out, Teia ventured as close to the path as she dared, ready to spring back at the first sign of trouble. As she scanned the lush scenery, she saw a rope bridge about fifty feet above, stretched between their cliff and the adjacent mountain. It was precariously flimsy as it wobbled in place, missing a half dozen boards, shedding nails with each gust of wind.

"It's *beautiful*."

Kyra had come to a stop beside her. She hadn't seen the bridge, her eyes settling instead on the mountains, the swirls of clouds that painted the air. "I didn't know places like this existed."

"This wasn't what you saw when you lived in Set?" Teia said ruefully.

At the mention of her rural village, Kyra let out a laugh. "Set barely had hills, much less mountains. This . . ." She trailed off, her voice thick with wonder. "I do think about Set, you know. I want to go back someday. But when I remember home, it's always memories of Bhanot."

Teia could picture the clamor of Erisia's capital, the harried merchants and mishmash of shops that bordered the narrow streets. An ache rose in her chest. She thought of the deal she'd made with Kyra, the promise she'd extended in exchange for her cooperation. "When this is over, we'll all return to Bhanot. You, me, Alara, Tobias, Enna. We'll take the finest ship we can find, and stuff ourselves with wine and cheeses."

Kyra shook her head, but she was smiling as she said, "Goddess, Teia. Are you becoming an optimist?"

"Never. I'd sooner leap off this cliff." Teia paused. "What's the first thing you'll do when you're back?"

"After I go down to Carfaix Market and eat every pastry in sight? Send in an application to Bhanot University."

"Your father taught there."

"It's where I want to be, if they'll have me. I liked the sciences when I was younger. Maybe I'd specialize in geology like my da—or move into a different field entirely. Art, literature. I've always wanted to learn how the poets see the world." Kyra grinned. "It doesn't matter. I'd have as much time as I would need to figure things out."

Wisps of clouds drifted before them, coiling around the mountains. "That's why we're here, isn't it?" Teia said. "All this for a little more time."

"Don't forget the preservation of the Five Kingdoms."

"That's a close second."

Kyra gave her a sideways glance. "What about you?" the rebel champion said. "What will you do once we're home?"

Immediately, an answer kindled on Teia's tongue, a wish she couldn't bear to part with. Hope fluttered inside her, sparking against her blood.

Just a year prior, when Teia had considered life under Jura's thumb, her entire world had been tinted in gray. She had taken living at its simplest definition, survival for the sake of seeing another day. Back then, she'd thought she'd known what would come next—the years trudging on, limping ahead with no solace.

Except everything had changed once she'd met the Dawnbreakers, the road fracturing before her. When Teia looked back at the wagon, she saw Alara had plucked a prickled stem from the ground. She brandished it at Enna and Tobias, her arms thrown back in glee, no doubt regaling them with its many poisonous properties. Enna clapped her hands together in exaggerated appreciation, while Tobias stood over them both, looking deeply unamused. When he noticed Teia, though, he sent her a quick smile. His dark eyes softened briefly.

Once, the future had seemed like an awful thing. But now, a sliver of light framed the tunnel, an unseen promise that nudged her onward. The rebel, the Poisons Master, the thief, the champion—somewhere deep inside, Teia knew they were the reason she'd crossed the Dark Sea. She'd choose them again and again, through fire, through water, through the horrors of their pasts and whatever lay ahead.

Happiness can be found outside of crowns and thrones.

Teia wanted more than she could say, and her heart felt fit to burst.

She lifted her chin. "Ask me again tomorrow," Teia said to Kyra. She took note of the rope bridge once more, already estimating the shortest distance to reach it. "I'm going to need Lehm's head on a pike first."

They left the mules tethered within the grove and trekked the rest of the way to the rope bridge on foot, sticking to the dense shrubbery that lined the main path. When Amalay held up her hand, they ducked behind a pair of overturned logs, pressed shoulder to shoulder against one another.

Four gray-robed soldiers were cluttered around the bridge's moss-covered posts, staring unblinkingly down the road. Behind them, Cloud Mountain was so tall that Teia couldn't see its peak. On the other end of the bridge, she glimpsed a door sculpted into the side of the mountain, shaped like a rising wave.

"Are we sure that's the only way in?" Kyra whispered.

"In or out," Amalay said. "Unless you've suddenly learned how to fly."

She raised her fingers high and gave a shrill whistle. The guards by the rope bridge instantly relaxed. One slouched immediately, while another huffed in relief, scratching at his hair. His nails were filthy, rimmed with crusts of dirt.

"Just as I promised," Amalay said, as she guided Teia and the others out of the underbrush. "Making the switch was easy. There's not a person alive my thieves can't impersonate."

"What about a barber?" Alara said, assessing the thieves' stringy hair.

"Vex was a barber before he joined the Society."

"Clearly not a good one."

"What was that?"

"He must have been incredibly good," Alara said cheerily. "I love the fringe."

Teia studied the liveried uniforms, with silver swirls of embroidery that danced down the hem. They were far too detailed to have been hasty impersonations. "And the actual soldiers?" she said.

"Stripped them naked and tipped them off the bridge," one of the thieves replied, revealing a mouthful of yellowing teeth. "One was still screaming when he fell."

"You *what*?" Jin yelped.

"Very methodical," Kyra said, looking somewhat ill.

"You can say a prayer on our way up to Feng," Teia said to them, before turning to glance at Amalay. "You'll keep anyone clear of the bridge?"

"Only for a few hours. After that, a new squadron of soldiers comes by to replace the old ones. My thieves won't stay for that fight."

"I don't expect them to."

"You do realize that the guards will cause trouble when they find the bridge abandoned? They'll know something happened to the old unit. I wouldn't be surprised if a message goes directly to Yuwen."

"Good. That's what I'm counting on."

Amalay gave a quick shake of her head. "Mad," she muttered. "Absolutely mad."

"Not too loud," Enna said. "Teia will take it as a compliment."

Teia faced the bridge. It didn't seem like it would survive a strong gust of wind, much less multiple people. But when she tapped her foot gingerly on the first board, it held, groaning heavily as she adjusted her weight.

"I won't venture in to collect your bodies!" Amalay called after her. "I'll wait for them to wash into the current, like all the rest of them."

"Don't bother," Teia responded, her voice ringing out to reach the leader of thieves. "When I leave, I intend to walk out the front door."

Chapter Thirty-Three

Crossing a bridge had never taken so long.

The ropes that twisted along both sides had all but deteriorated, the ragged ends fluttering in the air. In the center, several planks had rotted through completely, with one sagging perilously from a fraying cord. Through the gap in the boards, the yawning gorge was visible through a thin layer of clouds. Beneath that, a glistening slice of river ran far, far below.

When Teia finally reached the ledge on the bridge's other side, she was covered with sweat, her legs shaking. Every muscle in her body had tensed as she kept her back to the door, waiting for the others to join her.

Kyra was steps behind, strained but resolute. Then came Alara, her eyes fastened to Cloud Mountain's door, and Tobias, who strode across the bridge with a locked expression, his lips pressed tightly together. Jin stumbled over the rift, rolling his gaze skyward in prayer. Last of all was Enna, who seemed to be greatly enjoying herself. She moved so effortlessly that she might have been on a midday walk, sashaying through some well-pruned park.

"That was fun," Enna said brightly, as she glided gracefully onto the ledge. "Good way to stretch the legs."

"You need new hobbies," Jin said.

The door to Cloud Mountain had been rendered in incredible detail, as if swirled straight from the sea. The wave drew back in the center, crowned with a layer of foam. There was no handle, no lock. Instead, a little dish jutted out from the middle of the wave, with faded Shaylani characters notched along the rim.

Jin bent down. "'All who enter pay the price in blood.'"

"How morbid of you," Alara said.

"Yes, Jin," Kyra said anxiously. "We're not inside yet. Right now, you can relax."

The adviser blushed. "Not me," he said, pointing at the bowl's weathered rim. "That's what it says."

Teia examined the chiseled words. "Yuwen was feeling ominous, wasn't he?"

"Cryptic as well," Tobias deadpanned, as he pulled his knife from its sheath. He ran the blade along his palm, before holding it over the dish. Blood trickled into the stone bowl, but nothing happened. The door remained as immovable as ever.

Teia frowned. "Maybe the blood has to come from a Shaylani."

She gestured for the knife, and Tobias extended it toward her reluctantly. Teia pressed her hand against the blade, suppressing a grunt of pain. As blood welled against the cut, she held it above the dish. Fat red drops spattered downward, until the bottom was coated in scarlet.

A creak came from beneath the door. Something whirred and clicked, gears shifting into place. The blood within the dish disappeared, absorbed straight into the stone. The wave parted in half, splitting aside to reveal a great swath of darkness.

Enna sucked in a breath. "It's not too late to turn back," she said, nodding toward Amalay and the thieves, who were keeping watch on the opposite side of the bridge. "I'll bet my spare cottage in the Highlands that our good fortune's about to end."

"Good fortune is for the unprepared," Teia said.

"You have a spare cottage?" Jin said.

Enna shrugged. "I have three. Sometimes it's good to get away from the city."

"Plenty of birds to rob in the countryside," Tobias said.

Jin glanced at them incredulously. "I'm sorry," he said, pushing his spectacles up his nose. "We're about to storm Cloud Mountain—home of an exiled former emperor—and the two of you are making *jokes*?"

"I'd never joke about my properties," Enna said, her tone scandalized. "Do you know how much work upkeep is?"

They filed into the mountain, following one after another. When the wave door slammed shut, plunging them into darkness, Teia summoned a flame. It illuminated an enormous cavern, wider than any of the Golden Palace's banquet halls. Puddles of water pooled on the cracked floor. A crude set of stone stairs snaked upward from the center of the room, the misshapen steps leading to another door.

Alara adjusted her belt. "Is that it?" she said eagerly. "This is excellent. At this rate, we'll be back in time for supper—"

The flame drifted higher, and Alara's voice petered out. The ceiling glistened, reflecting strange bits of light. Metal plastered the top of the chamber.

"What *is* that?" Teia breathed.

"Stylistic choice?" Kyra said.

"Excuse me," Jin said. "Does the ceiling feel *lower* to anyone?"

The metal in the cavern shone brighter, fire dancing off its surface. And slowly, carefully, one of the pieces began to *move*.

It peeled away from the ceiling, wobbling in the air. As it rotated toward them, its razored edge glinted. This was no decorative panel by some overzealous architect, but a sword without a hilt, one that righted itself despite having no master.

It wasn't just a single blade, either, as dozens of metal fragments separated from stone. They came in all shapes and sizes, broadswords and knives and the arched blades of scythes, gleaming in the firelight, spinning on their sides, swinging around elegantly to point at Teia and the others.

Alara swallowed. "Everyone else is seeing this, too, right?"

Kyra raised her hands before her, fire rippling between her palms. "I thought we were going to be back in time for supper?"

"Are those really what you want your last words to me to be?"

The blades stilled, hovering for a long moment. Then they shot outward as one, hurtling at an alarming speed.

"Move!" Teia said. She sent fire upward, knocking a handful of blades off course. They simply picked themselves up and cut toward her once again, twice as fast as they'd been before. She hurled herself down as the blades impaled themselves into the opposite wall, quivering violently.

"Remember what I said about our good fortune ending?" Enna bellowed. She skirted around a scythe, which readjusted sharply to slice back in her direction.

"Are you really trying to gloat *now*?" Jin said.

"I just thought I'd make a point!"

"A *point*? Is that supposed to be another joke—"

Tobias struck out with his knife, aiming at one of the blades. "The swords!" he shouted. "You have to deflect them!"

"What do you think we're trying to do?" Kyra snarled, as she parried a blow with a spurt of fire.

Tobias feinted, before slashing sideways. A blade that would have taken off Teia's head went flying, clanging directly into another. Both pieces of metal hit the wall hard, before lying still in a heap. "No! You have to deflect them into each other!"

Teia sent flames roaring outward. Jin released a whorl of water. Enna squeezed herself between two knives, jerking her dagger up to send the blades crashing together. Metal fell around them, littering the ground—until at last a narrow path stretched through the remaining weapons, a crooked line that led to the steps.

"Go!" Alara said.

They sprinted for the stairs, their feet slipping over deadened pieces of metal. When Teia reached the top step, she shoved at the door, her pulse ricocheting against her chest. It gave way, mercifully, swinging aside as she and the others dashed through. Enna brought up the rear, her green eyes wide. She bolted inside and heaved the door shut, just as a half dozen blades slammed into stone.

Teia panted furiously. Above, her halo of flames lit the space they'd just entered, the ceiling blissfully empty of any swords. They had come across a passageway, sloping so steep it was nearly vertical. Another door was positioned at the very end.

Enna doubled over. "What—was—that?"

"A swordfight without a swordsman," Jin wheezed.

"That would be poetic, if we weren't almost sliced to ribbons."

"Ribbons is an understatement," Alara said. She nursed a nasty scratch along her forearm as she dug around in her belt. When she extracted an ointment from one of the pouches, she smeared some against the cut, before pressing the tin toward Tobias. "Here."

He accepted it wordlessly, wincing as he dabbed it against the cuts on his calf, his shin, the side of his neck. "How was Yuwen able to manage that?" he said. "Controlling water is one thing.

But in the Five Kingdoms, only the Dvořákians can manipulate metal."

Nobody had a sufficient answer. "Well," Kyra piped. "At least we made it out."

"In case you haven't noticed," Enna snarked, "we're still stuck in the heart of a murderous mountain."

"It's not so bad here, is it? If the swords were the worst of it, then we'll find Feng soon—"

Before she could finish, she was lifted off her feet. An invisible force thrust her toward the wall, a blow that would have broken her neck if Teia hadn't grabbed her around the legs. With a mighty yank, they tumbled into a tangle of limbs, both gasping.

Kyra rolled painfully onto her back. "Never mind," she groaned. "I take back what I said."

Teia pushed herself upright, twining threads of heat into her hand. *I'm getting tired of this damn mountain,* she thought, as she scanned the length of the hallway. Just like the other room, there was nobody else here, no attacker ready to swing.

The heat around her evaporated, as another blast of wind tore through the corridor, its wail deafening. Teia was wrenched into the air, suspended like an autumn leaf. She twisted sideways, swatting out blindly with fire. Between flickering bolts of flame, she saw the wind wreak havoc, shrieking with glee, pummeling the others like dolls.

"I'm beginning to miss Blackgate!" Enna howled, as she writhed furiously against the wind.

"We need to shield ourselves!" Alara yelled. "Jin—water—"

The wind carried away most of her words, but Jin nodded in understanding. The adviser clamped his palms together. Water appeared on the floor of the hallway. It fought against the wind, stalling, before rising as a barrier, bisecting the passageway.

Teia fell, her bones rattling from the shock. Around her, the others had landed as well, while Jin strained against the gale. When the adviser contracted his hand, water curled around them, enveloping them in the center of a hollow bubble. The wind screeched in fury, but the water held its shape. Droplets blew everywhere, soiling Teia's clothes, soaking her hair.

"This way!" Jin shouted. Through gritted teeth, he pushed along step by step, inching up the passage's incline. The water held back the worst of the wind, sculpting around Teia's group in a protective barrier. She was freezing cold, her teeth chattering, her eyes narrowed against the gale.

When the door finally came into reach, Jin's watery cocoon unfurled on the side. Teia grabbed for the door's silver handle. She yanked it back and they toppled through the threshold, collapsing into darkness.

Teia's ears rang with the sudden silence. She stood shakily as Kyra cast a new flame. They had come to another empty chamber, this one twice as large as the room with the blades. Yet Teia wasn't fooled as she spotted the next door, lined in silver, twinkling reassuringly against the light of the fire.

First metal, then wind. She had a sinking suspicion that she knew what was coming, a prediction cobbled from their last two trials. Apparently, Yuwen had spared no expenses when building his father's exile.

"Be careful," she warned, just as a low rumble split through the chamber.

"What was that?" Alara hissed.

"Do you really want an answer?" Tobias said.

"You're right. I'm happy to live in ignorant bliss."

The sound came again, like the mountain itself was expressing its displeasure. A tremor shook the earth. The ground quaked. It crumbled beneath Teia's feet, loose stones skittering in a shower of rubble. Tobias lunged for her, swearing.

Her fingers slipped through his grasp as the earth gave way beneath her, breaking into a newfound gorge.

Shit, Teia thought, as she felt herself pitching downward, weightless, hand still outstretched, desperately seeking a hold as she plunged into the rift.

Chapter Thirty-Four

She struck the ledge on her back, landing so hard that she released a gasp. Adrenaline seared through Teia, accompanied by a sharp twinge in her side. She knew instantly that something had cracked. A rib, maybe two.

Maybe three, she thought grimly. She prodded at the area delicately, and pain crackled through her. She let out a strangled hiss.

"Goddess," someone rasped to her left. "I can't wait to get off this mountain."

Tobias had fallen beside her, wincing as he rolled upright. Some ways away, on the jutting corner of the ledge, Kyra was sprawled at an awkward angle, her arms flopped limply beside her. "I hate it here," she announced glumly.

In spite of the ache in her side, a smile ticked at Teia's lips. "Kyra Medoh," she said lightly. "You *hate* something?"

Kyra sat up. Other than a myriad of scrapes and bruises, she seemed no worse for wear. "Please," she said defensively. "I hate a lot of things."

"Like?"

"People who take advantage of others. People who abuse their power." She paused. "And spiders. I really don't like spiders."

It was the smallest consolation to realize that they hadn't fallen straight to the center of the mountain. Thirty feet up, the two doors were in sight, one on each end of the chamber, although the earth between them had crumbled away. Teia, Tobias, and Kyra were stuck within the crevice that had been created—and while Enna could have scaled the jagged rock walls, Teia was certain that she lacked the same talent.

"Teia!"

Jin, Alara, and Enna were huddled at the top of the gorge. They were peering down with identical horrified expressions, although Enna's gaze kept drifting to the chasm beyond the ledge. Teia hesitated. When she pivoted back, creeping closer to the stone outcrop's brink, her eyes caught on something that flickered below.

The bottom of the rift opened into a river of fire.

Molten liquid snaked along, bubbling ominously with a red-orange glow. Massive stone wedges bobbed on the surface. Flames lapped around them, sputtering in wild fits.

A tendril of the fiery current lifted toward Teia curiously. It wove toward her, as if sensing her presence. When she stretched her hand forward, molten liquid doused her fingertips.

"I don't believe it!" Kyra exclaimed, lurching toward Teia. "That's magma. *Magma.* Do you know how rare this is?"

"Almost as rare as being thrown into a rift?" Tobias said.

"I'd bet rarer," Kyra said promptly. She poked at the magma in Teia's hand, swatting impatiently at her sleeve as it burst into flames.

There was something to be said about Kyra's unwavering positivity—perhaps a life lesson that could be gleaned, for someone far more philosophical. But as Teia took in the magma, all she felt was a renewed spurt of loathing. She would have traded this scientific miracle for a rope and a grapple.

She searched the stream of fire for inspiration. It wouldn't have been accurate to claim there were regular strands of heat here, loose and uncontrolled. Instead, millions of interspersed threads had been layered like a blanket. She caught sight of the ones that controlled the tendril, which swished out at her obediently. It wriggled in her direction, before dipping back into the magma.

Teia grappled cautiously for the threads. Gently, she called the tendril back to her. This time, when the magma lifted, it brought a small, molten chunk of rock at its end, setting the stone in Teia's palm.

Oh.

"Teia?" Tobias said, alarmed, as she stiffened, eyeing the enormous pieces of stone that floated in the fiery current. An idea jabbed at her mind. She glanced back up to the top of the chasm.

Kyra straightened from her spot on the ledge. "You're planning something, aren't you?"

"Am I?" Teia mumbled.

"It's the same look you had before you told us about Blackgate."

"The first time or the second?"

"Both."

That was good to hear. Teia was nothing if not consistent. "Get back," she commanded, before drawing a deep breath. She opened her palms wider, reaching for more threads. They flew firmly into her grasp, nearly overflowing from her hands. She gave them a solid yank, willing them to rise.

Someone screamed. Pillars of magma erupted, ripping massive slabs of rock from the molten river. Teia clenched both fists, dragging her palms downward. The columns readjusted in height. As they did, the wedges balanced atop each pillar teetered slightly. The stone chunks were thick enough that the bottoms dripped red, while the tops remained slate gray.

The stones formed a crooked path upward, leading from Teia's ledge to the silver door.

"Teia?" Kyra gasped.

Her limbs seemed to double in weight, the strain dragging her down. The rocks were too heavy—she couldn't keep this up for much longer.

"Go!"

She watched blearily as Tobias and Kyra raced for the silver door. The strands of heat resisted Teia now, fighting back as she struggled to keep control. She began running, leaping clumsily from stone to stone. The door was open, a beacon in the distance.

But she couldn't cross to safety—not yet. If she stepped out of the chamber, she might weaken her connection to the threads of heat. Already, they were slipping from her fingers, melting back into the bubbling river below.

Teia pivoted, wrenching against the strands that begged to go free. She was eye level with Enna, Jin, and Alara now, but they were still stuck on the opposite side of the rift, separated by the open gorge.

Teia set her jaw. She drew her hands higher, and forced the fiery columns upward.

The stone slabs lifted, buoyed on the pillars of magma. Now, they extended a bridge from one door to the next, a way across for the others. *Hurry,* she tried to say, but her voice no longer worked. Her vision had waned, the world disappearing. Everything was crushed beneath the sweltering pain in her torso, as the threads bucked at her touch. Faintly, she heard someone shouting her name.

"Teia, they've made it!"

"Teia—you have to go!"

Go, she thought, and it was that word that propelled her to move. She pitched herself toward the silver door, a lovely, hazy splotch before her. The connection to heat was dissolving. Behind her, the stones were splashing back into the magma below, the river exploding in molten bursts.

As Teia felt the last threads snap, the pillar under her melting away, she leapt from the slab she stood on. Pain licked at her ribs, her legs shuddering under her. She slammed into Tobias's chest, his arms wrapping around her protectively as he yanked her over the threshold.

"I have you," he gasped, his voice muffled against her hair.

The silver door clanged shut. For a second, encased within the inky darkness, it was easy for Teia to pretend she and Tobias were alone—truly alone, without the weight of obligation or the threat of their demise. Tobias's arms were locked around her. She could hear his heart pounding as he groaned softly, pressing his lips to the top of her head.

"Teia," he rasped. "Do you ever tire of making me frantic?"

She released a wisp of a sigh, a sound so quiet that she barely registered it. "Never," she said back, just as Kyra lit a new flame.

As Teia and Tobias stepped away from one another, Enna jostled forward, hands planted on her hips. "I didn't know you could do that," she said admiringly.

"Neither did I," Teia admitted.

"You manipulated magma!" Kyra said. *"Magma!* Do you know how incredible that is?"

"Better than controlling both fire and water?" Alara said wryly.

"Better. *So much better.*" The rebel champion jostled eagerly from foot to foot, before adding shyly, "Maybe one day you could teach me?"

"If we ever find another current of fire," Teia promised, "you'll be the first to know."

Kyra beamed. "I'm searching for one the minute we get back to Erisia."

At the mention of a second cache of magma, Jin chanced a nervous look around. They were at the start of another passage-way, which slanted up in an austere gray ramp.

Teia began plodding forward. "The ground isn't going to collapse, if that's what you're worried about."

"There are worries I've discovered here that I didn't even know existed," Jin said. "Swords that move of their own accord, earthquakes that come out of nowhere."

"Don't forget murderous winds," Tobias said.

"This is *definitely* worse than Blackgate," Enna proclaimed.

But as powerful as Yuwen was, Teia didn't think he would have been able to construct Cloud Mountain's fail-safes alone. "Metal for Dvořáki," she murmured, naming the kingdom that resided in the far north, where an endless winter covered the twinkling, thatch-roofed villages in powdered sheets of snow.

Kyra tugged at her braid. "No, Teia," she said patiently. "This is Shaylan."

"Do we think she hit her head?" Alara said.

"Tell her to do it again," Enna chirped. "Maybe she'll forget she already paid my commission."

"I'm perfectly sound of mind," Teia snapped. Enna's fee currently cost a good chunk of the royal treasury; doubling it might actually send Erisia into bankruptcy. "Think about the different trials we've had to face, the elements that have worked against us."

Tobias's thumb ran over the scar on his neck. "The K'vali

control wind, don't they?" he said thoughtfully. "And the Ismetians earth?"

"No ordinary person would be able to build what we just went through," Alara objected. "Yuwen would have had to gather the most powerful people in each kingdom."

"Not just that," Teia corrected. "He would have needed their rulers."

She didn't know how Yuwen had done it—persuaded leaders from three kingdoms to alter the inside of Cloud Mountain, transforming it into a place of no return. None of the rulers were at war, but it wasn't as if they were *friendly*. She couldn't remember the last time they had even been in the same room together. It was much easier to send an ambassador, in case the meeting ended in a grisly way.

She glanced at Jin, who dipped his shoulders helplessly. "Yuwen constructed Cloud Mountain without me," he said. "All I know is that he was thorough."

"*Too* thorough," Enna grumbled.

"The emperor puts great attention to everything he does."

The thief rolled her eyes. "Lucky us," she said.

"What about the Shaylani trial?" Alara said. "Could it have been the blood Teia gave at the entrance?"

"That was too easy," Tobias said. "A precursor, rather than a trial."

"Maybe they thought the other precautions were enough." The Poisons Master paused. "What about Jura? Would he have helped with this? The magma . . ."

"Magma is a naturally occurring material," Kyra said. "It could have been unintentionally triggered when the rift opened."

"Besides," Teia said firmly, "Jura wouldn't have helped with Cloud Mountain." Of this she was certain. There was no fathomable way that Jura Carthan would assist a Shaylani, much less lend his services for *free*. Her half brother would have thought it beneath him.

Alara blew out a breath. "Does that mean we only have one more trial left?"

"Shaylan's," Jin said morosely, a scrap of water threading between his fingers.

Enna touched a hand to her forehead in prayer. "Let it be something nice," she said. "A pool of water we have to swim across. A spa with a dozen attendants."

Tobias snorted. "You think Yuwen's trial would be a *spa*?"

"Out of all the things that have happened today, do you really think that would be the most unlikely option? Maybe he wants us presentable to meet his father."

"I doubt it," Teia said flatly, as she imagined a deluge of water rushing out from the walls, drowning them in the stone walkway.

"You never know," Enna said, as they rounded the bend. Eerie green lights were beginning to creep down the corridor, shimmering from iron sconces installed on either side. "I, for one, will be channeling happy thoughts."

Chapter Thirty-Five

It wasn't a spa.

When they turned the corner, they found themselves at the rectangular mouth of a cavern. The ceiling stretched high above, drenched in shadows. The room was empty, save for a single pedestal nailed to the center of the floor. An iron door was affixed to the rounded wall, which Alara pulled on cautiously. It didn't budge.

"I don't suppose you could pick the lock?" she said to Enna.

The thief rapped expertly at the door. "There's nothing to pick," she said, gesturing to where the lock should have been. "Do you have an acid that can eat through metal?"

"Still in development," Alara said seriously. "I didn't think to bring it along."

"Then does anyone have a spare battering ram? Because unless one of us can walk through doors, I'd say we're stuck."

"Not quite," Teia said. She beckoned at the pedestal, sparkling beneath the lantern light. "Have you seen what that is?"

Silver swirls made up the base of the structure, which stretched up to support the lithe surface. A dragon with sapphire eyes had been chiseled into the top, framed by an interlocked pattern of tides.

Enna blinked. "That reminds me of the Archive's stands for the memory spheres," she said, and Kyra blushed magenta, before mumbling an apology to nobody in particular.

A minuscule line of words had been carved below the dragon. "What does this say?" Alara asked Jin, who stooped toward the characters.

"'Remember who you wish to free,'" he read. "'Remember why he must remain.'"

"Yuwen likes his riddles, doesn't he?" Tobias said.

Teia wholeheartedly agreed. After all this, couldn't her cousin have left a more specific set of instructions? She treaded closer to the podium, searching for hidden clues. The dragon's eyes seemed to follow her with its jeweled stare, as she repeated the message to herself.

Remember who you wish to free. Remember why he must remain.

She straightened, her mind chipping away at the puzzle before her. "Yuwen built all this for Feng. Whoever comes to seek him out needs to remember why he's been locked away."

It was, she admitted, an ingenious idea. The person freeing Feng was required to deposit a memory. A *negative* memory, if Teia's interpretation was correct—a reminder why he should stay in exile. And unless Cloud Mountain's visitor was well acquainted with the former emperor, they hardly had enough knowledge to produce what was being asked. It would be impossible to venture past the final door.

Kyra hesitated. "We need a memory to move forward?" she said.

"That's my best guess."

"What kind of memory?" Jin asked.

"Based on this? The reason why someone loathes Feng."

Enna's groan was tortured. She dropped to the floor in a dramatic heap, her back sliding down the pedestal. "Oh, perfect," she said. "So all this was for nothing?"

Teia's brow creased. "How so?"

"Did you happen to forget the crucial part about needing a memory? We can't move on, which means we can't ask Feng about the Seascript. At this point, we might as well go back to the room with the blades, and let them notch *failure* onto our foreheads."

"Why our foreheads?" Alara said. "Why not our backs? At least that's less visible."

"Does it matter?" Tobias asked. "You'd be dead either way."

"There's no reason to have a closed casket at my funeral."

Teia had no intention of etching anything into her face, pessimistic declarations or otherwise. "We're not going back," she informed Enna. "And we certainly haven't failed."

"Did you suddenly develop an affinity that I don't know about—" Enna cut off abruptly, her eyes flitting to Jin. Her voice grew hushed. *"Oh."*

Kyra gawked at him. "You're a Memory Keeper?" she said.

The adviser looked like he wouldn't mind disappearing into the floor. "Not technically," he mumbled. "I never received any formal training."

"But you can withdraw a memory."

"Extract." He nodded unhappily. "Yes."

"And you hate Feng. You've made that clear."

"I . . ." He trailed off, staring hard at a spot on the stone wall. "There's no other way to get through that door, is there?"

"No," Teia said. "There isn't."

His expression wavered, shattering like panes of glass. Jin's shoulders slumped, even as he took a deep breath. "All right," he said, with the despair of someone approaching an executioner's block. "All right."

When he tapped his temple, water engulfed his hand in a second sleeve. Jin drew his fingers forward, and the water pulled slowly away from his skin. It shaped into a gleaming sphere, shining with a metallic tint. When he placed it atop the pedestal, a hum came from the center of the podium.

The sphere widened, rising into the air. Images unfurled on its rippling surface.

The memory showed a flourishing courtyard—groves of trees that dripped with fruit, fresh flowers bursting into bloom. Taijin's main gate could be seen in the background, with Niisha Mountain cresting over the wall. Crowds pressed in on all sides, kept back by Naga wielding weapons of water. Some of the onlookers were crying, sobbing into handkerchiefs or wailing indecipherably. One woman fainted and was promptly carted away by a guard.

There were about a dozen prisoners in the center of the courtyard—Shaylani men and women who knelt before a wide dais, their arms cuffed solidly behind them, streaks of white curled in their hair. The oldest was a wrinkled man, his tunic too large for his bony frame; the youngest was a girl around sixteen years of age. And there, at the very end, were two people who knelt in crinkled robes, their lips moving in silent prayer.

Jin was his parents' son through and through. He'd gotten the soft curve of his cheeks from his mother, and his sloped nose from his father. Within the memory, the scene shook, like the adviser was lunging at the protective wall of Naga. "Ma! Ba!"

His father didn't move, his head bent low, but his mother twisted back. Her face was shaded with fear. "Jin," she whispered.

From the dais, there came a round of exuberant clapping.

Two seats had been arranged on the ornate platform. The first was a hulking red throne, engraved with the motif of a soaring dragon. Li Feng leaned forward in his chair. His beard was flecked with silver, brushing down to the golden beads on his waist. When his eyes swept over the prisoners, they were flat and cold.

Beside him was a boy, gripping the sides of his seat. He was clad in magnificent robes, jade pieces winking out from the embroidery. *Yuwen,* Teia realized with a shock. He didn't look at the prisoners as Feng raised his fist.

Spikes of ice materialized in the air, sharpening to a point. The shrieks from the crowd grew louder, as the Naga struggled to hold them back. The memory trembled once again, as Jin hurled himself against the guards. "Yuwen!"

Yuwen only glanced away, his jaw rigid, his knuckles white against the silver armrests.

"Yuwen!"

Feng's hand fell. The spikes shot forth with deadly accuracy.

The sound of Jin's scream pierced through the memory. For an awful instant, Cloud Mountain was alive with his grief, the chamber ringing with his cries. Teia could feel the anguish that seeped into the air, the weight of his parents' last moments, the terror compressed into the courtyard.

The memory folded back into a sphere. It sat primly on the pedestal as Jin backed toward the wall, trembling.

"Jin?" Kyra said. When the adviser didn't answer, she rushed to him without hesitation, wrapping him in a tight embrace.

A tear traced down Jin's face. From behind him and Kyra, there came the rumble of stone. The door had opened at last, exposing a set of steps that wound into the darkness.

Jin pulled away from Kyra stiffly. "The rest of you should go," he said, wiping at his face. "I need a moment."

The rebel champion wavered. "Jin . . ."

"Please."

Nobody dared protest after what they'd just seen. Kyra gave Jin one last hug. He peered at her numbly as she started for the stairs, sending a flame to scout before her. The others matched her stride, until only Teia and Jin were left in the chamber.

The memory shone innocently above the podium, silver beaming beneath the surface. "You won't do anything rash, will you?" Teia said.

He managed a halfhearted laugh. "Like throw myself into the pit of magma?"

"Or run yourself onto a sword."

Jin shook his head. "You don't have to worry about me, Teia."

But she did—and not just because they were preparing to meet the man who had executed his parents.

"Jin," Teia said hoarsely. "Yuwen was there. He *watched*."

Something slithered behind the adviser's gaze. "Don't you know?" Jin said. "It's what he's best at."

Teia and the others were nearly at the top of the steps when Jin reappeared.

Even by the dim light of Kyra's flame, the adviser's eyes were tinged red. Yet his spine was straight as he lifted his chin toward the door, which was hewn in stone at the top of the staircase. It didn't look like something that would keep in an all-powerful emperor. Fuzzy patches of mold grew along the rough wooden surface. The handle was a tarnished brass knob.

"Who wants to go first?" Enna said.

Want and *need* were two vastly different scenarios. With a pang of regret, Teia squeezed past the others, treading up the slippery stairs warily. When she touched the door, it fell open immediately, swinging back without resistance.

"It's not locked?" Kyra said.

This was exactly what Teia was afraid of. After the many events of Cloud Mountain, she'd learned Yuwen didn't do anything by chance. Surely there was some other nasty surprise that awaited them, an attack that would make the others feel like carnival tricks.

But there was no sudden ambush, no tsunami sent to drown them. The parlor they entered was fit for a noble, curated with a designer's eye: embroidered rugs, beautiful rosewood fixtures, calligraphy scrolls expanding down from the walls. Feng's fondness for red was present even here, deep in the heart of Cloud Mountain. The result wasn't as dramatic as the House of Mourning—there were odd splashes of green everywhere, from the rug to the table—but most of the furniture came in deep hues of maroon.

Aside from the color, the only other abnormality was the threshold they'd crossed. When Teia glanced down, she realized the space beneath the door had been hollowed out. It ran blue with water, the color so vibrant it hurt to look at. Water fed upward along the sides of the door. It formed a protective barrier through the full length of the threshold, a continuous pattern that refused to break.

"What *is* that?" Teia said.

Jin frowned. "I don't know."

"Never thought I'd see the day," Enna said. "The emperor's own adviser, not knowing something?"

"I know plenty of things," Jin said. "But interior design doesn't happen to be my forte."

Teia shushed them both impatiently. From beyond the parlor's ornate opening, a figure had come into view.

He walked with a limp, aided by a cane topped with a silver dragon. His once-handsome face had lost any youth—heavy brows faded to gray, forehead weighed with wrinkles. Yet his eyes remained as they'd been in Jin's memory: a dark, bitter shade of brown, alert and sharp as they flitted over the group.

When they landed on Teia, Feng went rigid. "Calla?" he said. His grip on the cane tightened.

"Not quite," Teia said back. "Hello, Uncle. I can't say that it's a pleasure."

Chapter Thirty-Six

The first thing Feng did was wave them inside. The second was fix a pot of tea.

There were just enough seats around the wooden table for all of them, and they sat gingerly on soft green cushions before steaming porcelain cups. Kyra reached for hers, but Alara stopped her with a well-positioned kick.

Feng chuckled. "Don't worry," he said, as he picked up his cup and took a deliberate sip. His Erisian was better than most nobles in the Golden Palace. "I'm scarcely able to cultivate poisons here."

Kyra glanced at the Poisons Master for confirmation, who shook her head firmly. "False," Alara muttered testily. "You can cultivate poisons anywhere."

Feng peered over the painted rim of his cup. "So," he said briskly, gazing at Teia. "A Carthan back in Shaylan. I never thought I'd see the day."

"You'd be surprised how often I've gotten that reaction," Teia said.

"Your ba was charismatic. I'll give him that much. Fed my older sister every dream she could imagine, and whisked her off to some faraway land." He surveyed her carefully. "Is that a quality you've inherited, Teia Carthan?"

"Charisma?"

"Being a dreamer."

"I dream of many things. Meeting my estranged uncle happens to be at the top of my list."

He gave his cup a practiced swirl. "Your wit comes from Calla, you know. She could always think on her feet."

"It seems she was many things that you aren't." Teia pushed away the porcelain pot. It scraped loudly across the table as she continued. "I didn't come all this way to make small talk, Uncle."

"Oh?"

"I need information on the Serkawr."

His thick brows lifted in surprise. "The Serkawr?" Feng said lightly. "What would I possibly know about that old myth?"

"More than most, considering you read the Seascript, before killing every Memory Keeper in sight."

"Ah, well. It was a long time ago—"

"It was just over two years ago," Jin snapped. He seemed to be physically restraining himself from leaping for Feng's neck. "*Two years.* Barely anything at all, to someone with empathy."

Feng put down his cup. "Jin, is it? I thought I recognized you. You were one of my son's friends, always running around underfoot."

"I'm Yuwen's adviser now, a member of his court. And my first official recommendation was that you should swing from the end of a rope."

The former emperor flinched at the mention of Yuwen's name—a tiny, shuddering movement that caught Teia's interest. Before she could consider the matter, Feng had risen from his seat, water expanding from his back like a set of tentacles. One of them slammed into Jin, forcing him off his chair, pinning him to the ground. The adviser choked beneath the lash, as Feng's expression tightened in fury.

"You're in my house, boy. You'll do well to treat me with some respect."

Kyra sprang to her feet. Alara grabbed at one of the powders on her belt. Even Enna tensed, her fingers wrapped around her dagger, but Teia didn't move. She listened to the garbled sounds of Jin struggling, and tipped an inch back in her chair. "So leave," she said.

That, if nothing else, caught the former emperor off guard. "Excuse me?"

"You heard me. You saw us walk through the door. You know we've cleared a path through Cloud Mountain." She gestured to the entryway. "What are you waiting for, Uncle? If you're so eager to amass some respect from Shaylan, then leave. You can head back to Taijin, pander to your handful of followers there."

The tentacle retracted from Jin's throat. Feng rotated toward Teia. From certain angles, rage digging into his features, he bore an astounding resemblance to Jura. "Insolent girl."

She curled her hands inward. Fire illuminated the space between them, embers shimmering in the air. "Insult me again and I'll set you aflame—you and this miserable place where you'll spend the rest of your existence." Teia's smile was hard. "You *can't* go, can you? The water around the door—it prevents you from leaving."

It was an educated guess, but one she was fairly confident in. What other reason did Feng have for entertaining them at all? Why hadn't he plowed past them when he first realized they had entered the parlor, flinging himself through the open door?

Feng's teeth clenched. "It senses me. It *knows* me. And when I try to walk through that damned door, it transforms into a barrier, one so pressurized that I can't break through."

"Yuwen built you a prison. I'd expect him to be exhaustive."

One of the watery tendrils smashed down on Jin's empty chair, splintering it in two. "He wouldn't have had a fraction of his success if those fools hadn't aided him."

"The rulers—the ones from Dvořáki, K'val, and Ismet."

"Traitors."

"Debatable." The flames pulsed wider, keeping Feng at bay. "You must tell me the secret to drawing such ire, Uncle. Whose family did you insult to have them all hate you so deeply?"

"I wouldn't waste my breath on them, much less any words. But the threat of conflict will always scare the weak minded."

Teia paused. "The threat of conflict?" she repeated.

Feng's lips bent into a smirk. "My illustrious son didn't share the reason for my imprisonment?"

"Aside from the book burning, the massacres, and the terrorization of your own people?" Teia's heart thudded loudly in her ears. Slowly, her mouth dry, she said, "You were planning to invade the Five Kingdoms."

"I was," Feng said. "I would have started with Erisia first. Made my way up to Dvořáki, then down to K'val and Ismet. Oh, it would have been a glorious thing. The ships were ready, the crews assembled. And then my son—my damned son."

The tentacle came down again, snatching the chair's fractured back, flinging it into a cabinet. Teacups shattered behind the sparkling glass.

"Everything was for him," Feng growled. "Everything I did, every plan I made. He would have inherited an empire. He would have been a god."

I would have started with Erisia first.

Yuwen hadn't explained *why* he'd exiled his father, had he? He'd alluded to a combination of reasons, but not this one. Jin, too, had been deliberately evasive when he'd spoken of why Yuwen had overthrown Feng.

It wasn't the executions that moved Yuwen, Teia. Three months passed between then and the coup.

Yuwen might have waffled on the right thing to do, but eventually, he'd taken a stand. And when he'd imprisoned his father, he'd done so not just for the good of Shaylan, but for the Five Kingdoms. For *Erisia*. A burning sensation pierced through Teia's stomach. Without even knowing, she had owed her cousin a debt.

"Yuwen didn't want to be a god," she snarled, noticing how Feng recoiled again when she spoke his name. "He only wanted to be your son. Now, he's the Emperor of Shaylan—a *good* emperor, with the kind of heart both you and I could only wish for."

"Is that why you came to Cloud Mountain?"

"I'm happy to repeat myself, since exile seems to have stolen your memory. I'm here for information on the Serkawr. Whatever was in the Seascript, whatever its weaknesses might be."

"And what will you offer me, in exchange for my knowledge?"

"My wholehearted appreciation. You give me what I need, I say thank you, and then I'm going to leave. Stroll right through that door and stop a war from annihilating the Five Kingdoms."

"What makes you think I'd lift a finger to stop that? As far as I'm concerned, the Five Kingdoms can burn."

"Not on my watch," Teia said. "I enjoy being among the living."

Feng flung out his hand, and water overtook the flames that separated them. Both Tobias and Kyra started, but Teia caught the rebel champion's gaze. She gave a minuscule shake of her head as Feng leveled his arm. A barrier of solid ice warped around him, Jin, and Teia, sealing them inside a gleaming tomb.

"I'll kill you for the insubordination," Feng said, spittle flying from his mouth. "And then I'll do away with your friends, starting with Yuwen's adviser. Who will know? Who will be left to bear witness?"

"You do that, and we'll both meet death with nothing to show."

"I have nothing now."

"And your son?"

"My son is a traitor. A boy who stole my throne, who lives with no consequence."

"A boy who's been so manipulated that he's given up control of the Naga."

Feng ground to a halt. "You lie," he said harshly, before making the same argument Jin had, back in the Society's base. "Never in Shaylani history has an emperor relinquished control of the Naga."

She pointed down, and Feng swiveled back. On the floor, Jin had spread his hands. A silver memory sphere floated toward Feng. The former emperor accepted it reluctantly, opening one palm to allow the water to settle.

The memory showed the Naga in the House of Mourning's red hallway, their black robes billowing behind them. Lehm was in the center with a thin-lipped smile, as he signaled the guards to stop.

Feng hefted the sphere higher. "Who is that?"

"Cornelius Lehm," Teia said. "The very man who's trying to summon the Serkawr."

While Feng watched the memory, she inched closer to Jin,

who set his hand against her temple. Teia had already held the memories in her mind, the moments she needed the adviser to extract, and a second silver bubble bloomed before Feng. There was Yuwen in his chambers, sadness weighing his features, projecting his own sphere of his father.

"You think he doesn't remember you?" Teia said.

Steps away, Feng watched the scene, thunderstruck. The images reflected in his dark eyes, as the memory changed. Within the sphere, there was Feng descending from his carriage, parting his arms, waiting to draw his son into an embrace.

"You think he doesn't care for you?"

Another shift. In the memory, Feng painted a toy dragon green. As he brandished the paintbrush happily, he held up the toy for Yuwen to inspect, beaming ear to ear.

"You think he doesn't miss you?"

"Enough," Feng said gruffly. Then, as if he'd managed to regain his senses, he glared vehemently at Teia, his tone feverish. "How did you know?"

Technically, some of the scenes were memories within memories—snippets Yuwen had shown Teia when he'd first told her about the Archive. But that wasn't what Feng was saying. Not really. The former emperor wore the exhausted demeanor of a soldier on the battlefield. She'd seen that look before, the ruptured soul of someone prepared to bend the knee.

He wanted to ask how she'd learned his weakness.

Teia thought of the memory she'd seen in the Archive, with Feng's final minutes on the throne. She thought of his reaction when his son was mentioned. She thought of the splashes of green in the parlor, an homage to Yuwen's favorite color.

"If you don't help us," Teia said quietly, "Yuwen will be the first to die."

"Is that a threat?"

"A promise. I won't touch him—not on my life. But you'll find there are far worse players than me."

"Lehm."

"Yes."

The memory had started once more. Feng took in the images—his son, lit by lamplight in his chambers, holding the swirling sphere like it might break.

"You're your father's daughter," he said bitingly. "A Carthan to your bones."

"I'm many things. A villain, a fiend, a ruler, a monster who lurks in the dark and preys on your fears." Teia tilted her head. "Is that supposed to be an answer?"

Feng swept his hand through the memory. "Fine," he said, as it burst into mist, scattering down in tiny, fluttering pinpricks. "What exactly about the Serkawr do you want to know?"

Chapter Thirty-Seven

They sat back at the table, righting chairs and cups that had been overturned in the fight. The ice wall had thawed with a flick of Feng's hand, although large puddles now pooled on the floor. He viewed them impatiently, before tensing his fingers. Water evaporated straight off tile, leaving the surface sparkling clean.

"Tell me," Feng said. He settled comfortably into his seat, with all the authority of a monarch. "How familiar are you with the Serkawr?"

"It's Armina's pet," Teia said. "A creature who lives in the Dark Sea and is bound to carry out her will."

"And its history in the Five Kingdoms?"

There was all she'd discovered recently about Eris and Mei raising the Serkawr together, but Teia simply regurgitated what she'd learned in her many years of schooling, hammered home by sour-faced instructors in the Golden Palace. "When the Divine Five received their powers, they fought a civil war for control of the kingdoms. The war only ended when the Goddess sent the Serkawr as a warning."

Feng smirked. "I'd forgotten about that drivel," he said. "It's what they teach in Shaylan, too. Every child in the Five Kingdoms must have their heads full with that nonsense."

The former emperor spread his hands. Twin spheres of water swirled above his upturned palms, before molding into the scaled torso of a serpent. "The Serkawr," Feng said. "A creature ingrained in the foundation of the Five Kingdoms."

The serpent broke apart into two figures. The taller one had a short gray beard. A fur cloak sprouted around his shoulders to settle down his back. The shorter woman had a slight build, with curved eyes and a narrow face. They circled one another, two predators evaluating their competition.

Teia frowned. "This isn't a memory, is it?"

"No. But I find it easier to show what's in the Seascript, rather than explain. You'll see it's a rather messy story."

"Visual aids," Kyra said earnestly. "Very helpful."

The former emperor indicated up at the man. "That's your kingdom's founder," he said. "Eris the First, as he's described in the Seascript. And that"—Feng beckoned at the woman—"is Li Meisan. Mei, informally. According to the book, they were at each other's throats from the moment they met."

"If they hated each other," Teia said, "why raise the Serkawr?"

Feng looked marginally impressed by her knowledge. "Why does anyone do anything?" he said. "Power."

Teia recalled her conversation with Jin and Yuwen in the pavilion, their debate over how the sea beast would cede control to Lehm. "I've heard about an incantation, which begins the ritual to bring the Serkawr ashore. Is that true?"

He nodded. "Think of it as a summons, a way to bind it to a master—or in Eris and Mei's case, masters." Feng flexed his hand, and the watery shapes broke apart into droplets. When the liquid re-formed, it showed a group of hooded figures approaching a tall set of cliffs. The rugged structures were oddly familiar, craggy shapes that rose against the shore of the Dark Sea.

Okkan, Teia thought. Within the watery display, fog billowed out between the cliffs. The woman at the front threw back her hood. It was Mei, cradling a small box between her hands.

"What is she holding?" Kyra breathed.

"*Shenxiansa.* I believe the Erisians know it as the Morning Star."

The back of Teia's neck prickled. "That's not possible," she interjected. "The Morning Star was left behind after the civil war."

"My dear niece," Feng intoned. "What makes you think there was ever a civil war at all?"

The watery forms continued to move, undeterred by the conversation below. Mei lifted a wrapped item from the box. She handled it with reverential care, as she tugged back the scrap of fabric.

Teia had only seen drawings of the Morning Star: captured within the Golden Palace's dust-laden tomes, or else displayed in paintings on the throne room frescoes. Yet even here, fashioned from water, the jewel was unmistakable—red as blood, cut with four points on each side.

Eris stretched out greedily, his hand already glimmering with a flame. But he'd no sooner touched the jewel than he yanked his fingers away. Several hooded figures closed in on him, berating him angrily, while Mei stared down at the Star in shock. A hairline fissure now snaked through the center, barely visible to the naked eye.

Teia jolted upright. "What was that?" she said.

"One of the attendants described the incident later," Feng said dismissively. "It's laid out in the Seascript, in dreadfully banal prose. When Eris reached for the Star, a direct flame was too much for the jewel. Cracks began to appear on the surface."

A sudden, throbbing hope jabbed at Teia's chest. "Did they, now?" she said.

"It's all alleged, of course. The attendants were lowborn. They wouldn't know their heads from their asses."

Teia didn't bother informing her uncle that Eris himself had also been a commoner. "Fascinating" was all she said. In Feng's projection, the jewel had now been arranged on a cairn of rocks. Eris and Mei stood on opposite sides of the mound, their lips moving with a soundless invocation. As if to mirror the activity below, a single star shone directly overhead, its light slanting upon the two founders.

Teia's mouth fell open. She thought of the prediction she'd made about the end of Kashan: how the Seascript showed the *shi* that the Serkawr would be raised—not just *where* but *when*. The answer had been before her all along, in the silver decorations that fluttered down from every building in Shaylan, sculpted pieces of metal shaped like stars.

On the final night, everyone stays awake to see the last star before dawn, which glows with a blue tint. The entire kingdom comes together, if just for one day.

The Morning Star, along with the last star before dawn. Even a poet couldn't have written a more fitting conclusion.

Mei lifted her hands. After a moment, Eris did the same.

A crest of water folded around the bottom of the gem, followed by a crown of flames. The jewel was enclosed with a halo of water and fire. It beamed with a shining luster, gleaming from the inside out. It seemed to pulse. It seemed to *glow.*

The scene shifted once more. Gone were Eris and Mei, the hooded figures who'd gathered around them like ravens. The twinkling star above had vanished, replaced by muggy gray clouds, as a battle raged on the rocky cliffside. Bloodied flags and snapped blades had been embedded in the dirt. Soldiers screamed, clawing at their mutilated faces. Below, bodies jostled in the surf.

"What is this?" Teia demanded, as a man's corpse lay on the ground. His lower half was gone, ripped clean in two.

"This," Feng said, "is the aftermath of the Serkawr."

A scaled leg descended onto the body, crushing it beneath its foot. The watery shapes quivered, as if struggling to show the sea beast in its full form.

Feng dropped his hands. The battle dispersed back into liquid, congealing in an untidy ball. "I promised you what I know," the former emperor said. "Well, Teia? Is it everything that you hoped for?"

Teia's mind spun with all she'd seen, her brain chiseling over what she previously knew. "There was no civil war," she said delicately.

"History is always being rewritten. *History* says the Morning Star was left behind by the Goddess once the war supposedly concluded. But why would the end of infighting possibly merit such a gift?"

Enna frowned. Teia wondered if she, too, was mentally combing through the scriptures, her faith shaken by the images Feng had shown them. "The Star was supposed to be a reward for their deference."

Feng's response was a scathing scoff. "Of all the ways for Armina to offer her favor, do you think that's the explanation that makes sense?" he said. "If you believe the Seascript, the Goddess wanted to bestow greatness to mankind. Once the Divine Five were given their powers, Armina also granted them the Morning Star. Her chosen champions had braved her trials and earned their reward. They'd proved themselves *worthy.* The jewel was a physical representation of all they'd endured."

"Eris and Mei took advantage of it," Teia said.

"Power calls to everyone. Both founders just happened to answer its summons." Feng laid the ball of water on the table, rolling it back and forth idly. "The Morning Star was always meant as a conduit, a way to call forth the Serkawr in a time of need. The sea beast wasn't some plaything. It was an extension of Armina, a loyal servant who'd long done her bidding. Summoning it required not one but two elements, to ensure greed didn't overtake any single person."

"Should have made it three," Alara said.

"Or all five," Jin murmured.

"Better yet," Tobias offered. "Armina should have cast the Star into the sea, after she saw what Eris and Mei did."

Feng sneered. "What do you think happened once the Serkawr was stopped?" he said. "The Star disappeared—it wasn't seen for another two centuries. Eventually, it washed onto Ismet's shores, before finding its way into Erisia's coffers. In the meantime, Eris and Mei kept their heads only because of their powers. They stifled news that they had summoned the Serkawr, killed most witnesses to the scene. They claimed their two kingdoms had fallen into battle, and that the Goddess had sent the Serkawr to dissuade any further fighting."

"The other founders believed that?" Kyra said incredulously.

"People will believe anything if given the chance."

Teia cleared her throat. "One more question," she said.

"Just one?" Tobias put in. "I have several."

Teia ignored him. "The Serkawr," she said to Feng. "How was it stopped after it was summoned?"

Feng began to laugh. "After it was summoned?" he echoed,

before he bent over the table, howling with mirth. It was a long minute before he finally recovered, wiping at his eyes. "Divine intervention," he said.

"We're a bit short on that."

This sent the former emperor into another fit of hysterical glee. "History is often incorrect," he said, "but at least one part was accurate. When Eris and Mei summoned the Serkawr, it was only at the Goddess's mercy that the beast was recalled back to the Dark Sea." He chuckled humorlessly. "If I were you, I would start praying. Because unless Armina returns to the Five Kingdoms, there isn't a force alive that can stop Cornelius Lehm once he raises the Serkawr."

Chapter Thirty-Eight

Feng's cheerful bit of wisdom lanced through Teia's skull. She pushed away from the table, her thoughts clattering about loudly.

Divine intervention. If that's what things came to, they might as well slit their own throats. Teia had no intention of ever pinning her hopes on the Goddess—not when her mind lingered on the crack within the Morning Star, the fracture that came from the heat of Eris's flame.

Suddenly, a vigorous thud rang from the main door. Everyone froze, as Teia peered over Feng's hunched form. Shadows adorned the room's gilded entryway.

"Do you have rats here?" Kyra said.

"Inside a *mountain*?" Jin said.

"Goddess, I hope not," Alara muttered, hiking her feet onto the edge of her seat. A vial was clutched in her gloved fist.

For a second, the shadows pulled back, retreating—and then three figures burst into the living space, robes settling in black plumes of silk, dragon tattoos circling their brows. Before anyone could react, one woman extended her arms. A circlet of water hurtled at Feng, its jagged edges hardened to ice. The bladed wheel raked over the table, leaving deep gouges in the wood.

"Naga?" Feng bellowed, as he dove aside. "You brought Naga *here*?"

The Naga at the end—a skinny man with a gap-toothed leer—scuttled sideways. With one hand, he raised a great pulse of water, forcing Teia's group back. In the other, he twitched his fingers, a puppet master and his marionettes. Six lions made of water reared up from the floor, their ears flattened against their skulls. One let out a growl, its tail swishing between its legs.

"Oh, lovely," Tobias said. "One for each of us."

The lion nearest to Teia pounced.

She brought up a shield of fire, knocking the beast aside. Feng was several feet away, battling the other two Naga. In his prime, the former emperor must have been an incredible fighter. Even now, his abilities dulled by his time in Cloud Mountain, he moved like smoke, slipping between the blows with ease. He countered the strikes with great pillars of ice, which rammed into the ceiling and overturned furniture.

One of the Naga—the shortest of the trio—wielded dual sabers of water. As she brought them down, the blades lengthened into spears. The tip of one gashed open Feng's cheek, and he shouted in fury. The former emperor stretched outward, pressing his fingers to the Naga's forehead. The woman tripped, falling with a crash. Her entire head had become encased with ice, which shattered as she hit the ground.

The Naga who'd corralled Teia's group screamed. He stabbed a finger forward, and three of the lions instantly changed course. They sprang at Feng. He batted them aside with a growl, spikes of ice shooting upward to impale the creatures. They softened back into liquid, before evaporating into mist.

It should have at least been a minor victory. But Feng stumbled, before catching himself against the wall. He reached up to the cut on his cheek, which was tinged with an odd shade of green. His fingers came away bloody.

Alara gasped. "The Naga—they've poisoned him."

"With what?" Teia said.

"It's hard to say." Alara squinted. "Judging by the color? Worshid. Highly toxic. Fast acting. Usually fatal."

"So they're not after us?" Tobias snarled. He was flat on his back, grappling with one of the lions, his blade gleaming as it stabbed into the beast. "That's a nice change of pace."

Feng was slower now, and the final two Naga jumped at the advantage. Aside from the three remaining lions, which prowled a tight circle around Teia's group, she and the others were unguarded, the living space's exit mere steps away.

"We have to go," Teia hissed. "Quickly, before the Naga notice—"

Kyra was already grabbing for fire. "Teia. We can't leave Feng."

"I thought you drew the line at homicidal rulers imprisoned inside mountains."

"If we go, they'll kill him."

"And if we don't, then the Five Kingdoms fall. Is that what you want, Kyra? Is that the choice you'd like to be remembered for?"

In that instant, the former emperor looked up. He'd been beaten down to his knees, bleeding profusely from an assortment of wounds. One of the Naga had slashed through his eye. The other bore down on him with a whip made of water.

Yet for everything Teia had heard about Feng, his expression was calm, as serene as the surface of a lake. As one arm raised to fend off the barrage of attacks, a smile settled on Feng's cracked lips. She wondered who he thought her to be, surrounded by the wreckage of his exile. His older sister, back from the dead? Or perhaps his son, the boy he'd loved and lost, the only one left who could move the mad emperor.

In the end, she thought that was why he drew his next breath, fighting to rise against the blows. "Go!" he boomed, and wrenched his arms upward.

The room dropped in temperature. The lions froze over at once, with one caught midleap. Ice swarmed over the Naga before Feng. There was a single choked scream, cut off by the pristine crackle of ice, jagged bolts scraping the ceiling. The black-robed guards had both been captured within, preserved like bugs in amber.

Through the sheets of ice, Feng lay motionless. His eyes were blank. Blood dribbled from the cut on his face.

Teia didn't stop. What more was there to witness? She sprinted for the door, with the others in tow. It was only when they were back in the dim stairwell, the wooden door shut firmly behind them, that they dared pause to rest.

Kyra drew a shuddering gulp of air. "Feng sacrificed himself," she whispered.

"He didn't do it for us," Jin said.

The rebel champion toyed with the end of her braid. "What now?" she said. She sounded very young, her voice uneven. "We find Amalay? We leave Cloud Mountain?"

On the other side of the door, the former Emperor of Shaylan was dead. And in just a few hours, two kingdoms would be at war.

Teia started down the stairs. She wiped a smear of blood from her forehead. "Now," she said steadily, "we're going to meet Lehm."

Chapter Thirty-Nine

It was the final night of Kashan, and someone was going to die.

By the time they'd made their way down Cloud Mountain, clattering along in the mule-drawn wagon that Amalay had left for them, the Shaylani army was waiting by Okkan's cliffs. No less than a hundred soldiers were stationed in tidy rows of ten. These were the fighters without affinities, marked by their filmy gray robes. Most looked apprehensive, while a few appeared downright terrified, clasping the hilts of their swords.

Yuwen and Lehm were positioned in the front. They were flanked by two lines of Naga—Teia counted fourteen of the black-robed guards in total. As the wagon screeched to a halt, stopping at the edge of the dense forest, Lehm's stance drew taller. His knuckles rested against the swords on his waist, as his empty gaze clung to Teia.

All this for me? Teia thought. Really—the rebel leader had outdone himself.

From the spring seat, Enna cast a shrewd glance over her shoulder. "Are you sure about this, Boss?" the thief said. "If you're so eager for death, a dagger in the chest would do just fine."

"Tempting," Teia said, as she hopped nimbly from the wagon. "I prefer my knives in the throats of my enemies."

Alara climbed down with the elegance of a royal, her boots treading against the soft dirt. "Amateurs," she said gracefully. "Blades are too clunky. Poisons are much better."

Meanwhile, Kyra was studying the silent rows of soldiers. "They're prepared," she said, as she worried at her bottom lip.

"So are we," Teia answered. The salt air mingled with the scent of brine. It called her back to the ocean, to the sea, as someone brushed at her hand, the barest whisper of skin on skin.

"You'll be careful?" Tobias said.

Teia smiled. "I always am."

Above, a shimmering blue star flickered in the sky, signaling the end of Kashan. Teia was squarely within Lehm's deadline as she approached the cliffs—Kyra and Jin on either side, Enna, Alara, and Tobias behind her. They were mere steps away from the jutting black ledge, the place where every Shaylani royal came to stir the tide, to prove their worth.

Teia couldn't part the waves. She couldn't split the sea. But she had a message to deliver all the same, and she wasn't one to be denied.

Yuwen was beautiful beneath the twinkling light of the stars, a fairy-tale prince borrowed straight from a story. His long hair fluttered in the breeze. He lifted a hand, as if to embrace her, the sleeves of his blue robes falling back from his wrists. At his sides, the Naga stiffened, threads of water looping around their arms, twirling against their hands.

It would have been more intimidating had Teia not watched two men freeze to death inside a mountainous prison. If she was going to be met with a show of force, then she'd be glad to return the favor.

When Teia raised her arms, a fiery arch crested overhead, dazzling against the onyx sky. For a second, the black cliffs of

Okkan were bathed in a spectacular glow. A fearful whisper rustled through the soldiers, as they readjusted their weapons and gaped up at the flames. One of them shuffled nervously into Lehm, who promptly shoved the soldier away in disgust.

Yuwen's military might have been awed, but the emperor was unmoved. His face darkened as Teia's flames shrank away, melting into gray tendrils of smoke. "Is that why you came, Cousin? To show my soldiers some party tricks?"

"You're the one threatening war."

"You've left me with no other choice. You and your companions kidnapped Jin—"

"I wouldn't be so quick to speak, with the man you're entertaining. But since you're so concerned about the company *I* keep, you'll be thrilled to hear about Lehm's new alliances."

Yuwen's brow lowered. "Lehm's alliance is with me," the emperor said. "We have a shared interest in bringing you to justice."

A laugh blistered against Teia's chest. "Yuwen," she said. "If the world had any sense of justice, neither of us would be having this conversation."

To the emperor's left, Lehm gave a short nod to one of the Naga. Teia had been expecting something to that effect, and so her hand swept out, heat swirling between her fingers. Fire catapulted through the air, meeting the lash of water that careened toward her. The coil burst open, scattering the crowd with droplets.

"Not so fast," Teia crooned. "I'll say when it's time to strike."

"Control yourself," Yuwen snapped to the Naga. "Teia Carthan seems to think she possesses some indisputable proof of her innocence. If she wants to act the fool, I'm happy to oblige."

"Not my innocence," Teia said. "But certainly not Lehm's, either. Why don't you check the inside of his coat?"

Yuwen raked a furious glare her way, but she didn't miss the tautness in his posture. She had issued the emperor a challenge, a request that would cost him no effort to grant. How would it look to his soldiers if he denied her now?

He rotated to Lehm apologetically. The rebel leader gave a practiced scoff, before heaving aside the folds of his greatcoat. "This is her attempt at stalling," Lehm said scornfully. "The Halfling knows I have nothing to . . ."

His voice tapered as Yuwen withdrew his hand. Somewhere at Teia's back, she heard Jin gasp.

The emperor gripped a scarlet circle of beads in his fist. They glinted as he held them aloft, allowing the golden charm to dangle beneath the starlight. From where Teia stood, twenty paces away, she could see the inverted triangle stamped in the center.

"Lehm." Yuwen's tone had gone flat. "What is this?"

For the first time, Lehm seemed truly shocked. His eyes went to Teia, before he composed himself hastily, clearing his throat with gusto. "That isn't mine, Emperor."

"Then how did it come under your possession?"

"A trick. One orchestrated by the Halfling, no doubt—"

"How? She hasn't come near you since she arrived. And unless you're suggesting she magically transported this bracelet into your pocket—"

Lehm wet his lips. "Emperor," he said. "I can assure you that this is all a misunderstanding."

"This is the symbol for the Red Mountain, Lehm." Each word was louder than the last, as anger overtook Yuwen's face. "These are the people who would see me fall, who'd give my throne to another. *Tell me again how this is a misunderstanding.*"

As the rebel leader grew silent, no doubt searching for the correct thing to say, Teia dared raise her gaze. Yuwen's army watched on, captivated by the scene before them—and there, in the center, was the soldier who'd staggered into Lehm, her gray robes draped around her.

Amalay met Teia's eyes, a smirk dancing against her lips.

Good, Teia thought. The leader of thieves had played her part well, sliding into the ranks as the soldiers assembled on the cliffs, planting the bracelet with a quick sleight of hand. And while Teia had considered asking Amalay to gut Lehm where he stood, she had decided against it. There were too many risks involved with an assassination attempt here, before a dozen Naga with a range of affinities.

No. It was better to wait, to bide her time. Teia had been patient all through Shaylan. What was a little longer, to put Lehm in the ground herself?

"It's not just his affiliation with the Red Mountain, Yuwen," she called sweetly, and both the emperor and the rebel leader pivoted sharply toward her. "Why don't you ask Lehm what compelled him to commit regicide?"

"Regicide?"

"Your father is dead—murdered at Lehm's command."

A growl slipped through Yuwen's lips. "Ba is in exile in Cloud Mountain."

"There's nothing there anymore but corpses. Lehm sent assassins after Feng. He was afraid of what your father knew about the Seascript."

Teia hadn't yet discovered *how* Lehm had persuaded the Naga to kill the former emperor. After all, weren't the black-robed guards with him loyal to the Red Mountain first? Didn't they yearn for Feng back on the throne?

She might not have the answers she wanted, but it didn't matter—at least not here. As soon as Teia spoke, she knew her words had the desired effect. Lehm's eyes blazed with fury. His teeth gnashed together as he said, "This is what Teia Carthan does, Emperor. She lies. She sows distrust—"

"So send for a Memory Keeper," Teia said loudly. "I witnessed Feng's death in Cloud Mountain. I can take a room in Okkan until I'm able to show you the memory."

She didn't miss the alarm that flitted across Lehm's face. Jin might be a Memory Keeper, but Yuwen would never reveal the adviser's secret before so many people. The only other option was for the emperor to send word to someone else—and in the days it would take a Memory Keeper to travel, Kashan would be long over.

Yuwen paused. "If a Memory Keeper would dispel any doubt—"

"Emperor," Lehm said. "You believe this nonsense?"

Yuwen's fingers remained clenched around the Red Mountain's bracelet, his cheeks pale but resolute. "Jin stands freely beside Teia—without chains, without restraints. In all my life, I've never known him to be a poor judge of character. Perhaps he saw something I didn't."

Teia appreciated the vote of confidence, although it was a tad too late now. "Yuwen," she said. She had one more thing to tell him, one final piece of the story. "Before you welcome Jin back with open arms, there's something else you should know."

"Which is?"

She didn't hesitate as she spoke her next statement. "Your adviser," Teia said. "He's a traitor."

Chapter Forty

Teia watched as the sentence took root, carrying over the raging surf to reach the emperor. Yuwen's forehead creased. Emotions careened across his face, flashing like cards within a magician's deck—shock, rage, disbelief.

"Jin, a traitor?" Yuwen said. He gave a quick laugh. It came out strained, worn thin in the middle. "That's impossible."

"He's been reporting each of our moves back to Lehm—sabotaging our progress. He helped facilitate your father's death in Cloud Mountain."

"No. He wouldn't."

"And why is that?"

"Jin isn't just a member of my court. He's not just my adviser." Yuwen's voice held the ache of someone who was willing to hear lies, who would accept any story to detract from the truth. "He's my friend. My *closest* friend. I'd trust him with my life."

"I wouldn't be so quick to make that declaration," Teia said. But as she opened her mouth to say more, a barrier of water descended toward her. She sent her flames overhead just in time. The water evaporated, sending a great puff of steam upward—but through the shroud of gray, Teia glimpsed Jin on the other side, his expression wrought with steel.

"Don't," he said.

Beside the cliffs, Yuwen's features dimmed. "Jin?" he said.

Teia's laugh was biting. "Don't *what,* Jin?" she challenged, as the steam started to clear. "What are you afraid I'll say? I was planning to begin with Cloud Mountain, and how you left open the door in the room requiring a memory. Handy way for Lehm's Naga to bypass the final trial, don't you think?"

"You knew?"

"I've had my suspicions about you since the Archive. How did Lehm know when we were set to arrive? If the Naga stationed there were traitors, why would they only strike you over the head? It would have been far easier to kill you and leave no witnesses behind." Teia shrugged. "After that, when we left Taijin, I've never seen a sane hostage fight so hard to stay. But I didn't confirm your loyalties until Kyra was captured."

"How?"

"Why would the Naga take her but allow you to escape? Why not bring both of you along? After that, I decided to test my theory. When we went to rescue Kyra, I fed you a half plan to see what would leak back to Lehm."

Jin's gaze narrowed. "When we went into the House of Mourning, you had me run the perimeter."

"Yes."

"You didn't want me inside."

"It wouldn't have been sporting to have you report *all* my whereabouts back to Lehm. Although I have to say—it was a bit *too* convenient when he happened to bring you out as a hostage."

Jin rubbed at his jaw. "And Enna?" he said. Teia remembered his stunned expression when the thief had emerged from the ceiling rubble. "When we were making plans to infiltrate the

House of Mourning, I'll bet she wasn't actually ill. The cut on her head, the supposed infection—"

"It's called *acting*," Enna said. "Maybe if you were better at it, you wouldn't be in this position."

After Teia had incited a fight with Amalay and stormed from the room, Enna had followed her into the corridor. It had given them a precious few minutes of privacy—enough time to cobble together a hastily whispered plan, before the thief had returned with her orders. She'd sent Jin to go find Teia, then briefed the others about the adviser.

After they'd made a great show of Enna being ill, Teia had emphasized they would target the hidden room. Jin hadn't suspected that Enna was pretending, nor had he known Teia wanted to search the rest of the house for Kyra. While Teia, Tobias, and Amalay caused a scene on the second floor, the thief had helped Alara rescue the rebel champion.

Jin cleaned off his spectacles, before setting them back on his nose. "Why not just kill me?" he said mildly. "Why go through all this?"

"Because I keep my enemies on a short leash," Teia said. "As long as you were with us, it meant Lehm needed something."

Gone was the tremulous scholar, with the shy, flustered demeanor. Teia had the unsettling feeling that she'd underestimated the adviser, this boy who'd been sculpted through tragedy.

"Lehm was right about you," Jin said, as he wiped his palms against his shirt. "I was foolish to think a wave would stop you."

This she hadn't known. In her mind's eye, Teia pictured *The Inferno*, the golden masthead and crimson sails dwarfed by the billowing wave. The screams of the crew, the shriek of water—the quiet that followed within the ink-black sea.

"My ship," Teia said, as anger clawed against her. "*You* sank us?"

"You have no idea the things I've done," Jin said. "Who do you think has been shielding Lehm each time you've met?"

He twisted his palm, and a watery bolt struck Teia in the ribs. She skidded backward, crashing into Alara. In a matter of seconds, liquid had snaked around all of them. Teia and the others were imprisoned within a hollow, swirling dome, as water melded to Jin's will.

"Right on cue," Enna declared. "Another disastrous plan."

"Are all thieves this helpful?" Teia retorted. "I said we'd confront Lehm, didn't I?"

"What you didn't mention was that we'd be trapped inside a cage, while that turncoat of an adviser runs free outside."

"A dome," Teia said.

"Semantics," Kyra muttered.

Teia stretched gingerly for the dome, before snatching her fingers back. The water that surrounded them spun at a furious speed, so fast that she feared she might lose her hand. "Then let me be completely clear," Teia said. "Once we break out of this—"

"If," Enna mumbled.

"*Once* we break out of this," Teia insisted again, "Kyra will run for the Star, just as we discussed."

"And everyone else?" Tobias said.

Teia's grin was caustic. "Easy," she said. "Everyone else will raise hell."

Outside the barricade, Yuwen had staggered forward. He moved like a man who'd been shot, away from the Naga, away from the safety of his soldiers. "Jin," he croaked. "Say it isn't true. Say this is all some mistake."

"Yuwen—"

"Please." The word was little more than a whisper. Yuwen reached out a trembling hand, his fingers skimming Jin's cheek.

The adviser took a shuddering breath. "We can go back to Taijin. We can fix this."

When Jin looked up at the emperor, his expression went flat. "Yuwen," he said. "There is no *we*."

He wrenched free, gravel crunching beneath his feet. "How dare you," Jin said. *"How dare you.* All these years—all this time. There were moments when I thought things could be different. I'd hoped—" The adviser broke off violently as a shiver tore through him. Then, more quietly, his voice almost inaudible: "I'd hoped."

"If this is because of the Memory Keepers—your parents—"

"You don't deserve to mention them!" Jin bit out. "The two of us came up together, Yuwen. It was always you and me, for as long as I can remember. Lessons, meals, banquets. We would sneak away during those awful speeches and go to the gardens. We'd race wooden tops and then lie on our backs. We'd count the stars, just to see what number we could get to."

"I remember," Yuwen whispered.

"We spent hours together. *Hours.* There were entire days when I didn't leave your side. And all I needed from you was one minute of compassion. One minute for you to say something—*anything.*"

"Jin—"

"You watched them die!" The sentence came out in a scream, ricocheting over the cliffs. "You sat there on your beautiful throne, and you watched your ba kill my parents. You watched and you waited and you did nothing."

"I was scared." Yuwen's tone broke in a sob. "I was different then. Younger—more afraid."

"You think my family wasn't scared when they were taken to the courtyard? You think I wasn't scared when I supported you in the coup? I told myself that once Feng was gone, things would be different. I would mourn, and I would survive. I would make myself whole." Jin's eyes glistened. "That was my mistake."

Yuwen was shaking now. "I'm sorry," he said. "I'm so sorry—"

"Sorry doesn't bring them back. *Sorry* is the word of cowards, who only leave damage behind."

"Jin." The name came out low, pleading. "Jin, please."

Back by the rugged cliffside, there came a slow clap. "What a pity," Lehm said coolly, his voice raised above the surf. "Heartbreak is never easy, is it?"

Yuwen turned back toward the rebel leader. Tears glittered on his cheeks. "Keep him silent," he thundered to the Naga. "I don't want to hear another word."

At the emperor's command, the Naga reacted with astounding speed—but only a handful moved toward Lehm, before they were met halfway by the other black-robed guards.

Yuwen faltered. "What—"

The three lone Naga—the ones who must have still been loyal to Yuwen—didn't stand a chance. Two had their throats skewered immediately, while another drowned where he stood, writhing on the ground. In an instant, the man's garbled cries faded away. The remaining eleven Naga swerved to Yuwen, their faces smooth and expressionless.

"Stand down," the emperor ordered, panic flecking his tone. *"Stand down."*

They ignored him, dividing deftly into two groups. Four of the Naga doubled back toward the gray-robed soldiers, who hefted their weapons unsteadily. When the Naga lifted their arms, a great rush of water spun outward. The gray-robed soldiers were trapped within a spinning vortex, a waterspout that rose from dry land. In the center, Teia caught sight of Amalay, who looked like she sorely regretted masquerading as someone without affinities. If they lived through this, Teia suspected the leader of thieves would demand added payment for her troubles. The favor from the House of Mourning could only stretch so far.

The seven other Naga focused on Yuwen. When they steadied their hands, water slithered forward, solidifying midair into chains made of ice. The restraints wrapped around Yuwen. He broke the first set easily, ice shattering to pieces—but more draped over him, until Yuwen plummeted to the sand. He was dragged down by the weight of the chains, his arms pinned behind him. From where Teia stood within the dome, it looked like the emperor was bowing.

"Teia!" Kyra's voice had taken on fresh urgency. She was inspecting the dome's ceiling with outright fascination. "Do you see that? There's less water pressure here. If we combine our flame, we can break out of this. Here, this way—"

Teia shook her head. "No," she said. "Not yet."

"*Not yet?* You want us to wait until Lehm kills Yuwen?"

"He won't."

"And you're a sudden expert on Cornelius Lehm?" Alara said.

"Trust me," Teia replied. Even through the rippling water, she could see the rebel leader's triumphant smirk. "What he's doing now is all for show."

A strand of hair had fallen loose across Yuwen's forehead. "Lehm," he panted. "What is this?"

The wind pulled at the neat lines of the rebel leader's coat. He treaded toward the emperor, observing the chains that bound him. "Do you believe in fate, Yuwen?"

"You bastard. When I get loose—"

"Because I don't," Lehm said. "I never did. And then I came to Shaylan, and met Jin here in a filthy alehouse, right on the outskirts of the capital. The poor boy was near drowning in spirits, stinking of rice wine, so drunk he could hardly stand straight. But when I got him on his feet, do you know what he said he wanted?"

"To be left alone?" Yuwen said. "To escape the likes of you?"

"Far from it," Lehm said. "What your adviser asked for was vengeance—a chance to right a wrong. And I said I could provide that, so long as he helped me."

"And the Naga?" Yuwen spat, as he strained against the chains. "How did you turn most of my guards?"

"I courted the Red Mountain—quite a few of your guards keep split allegiances. But the Naga I sent into Cloud Mountain to kill your father? The ones who are here now, keeping you in your proper place?" Lehm nudged at the chains with his foot. "They've declared their loyalty, Yuwen. Not to you or Feng or the Red Mountain—to *me*. They tire of a young emperor, lost in the past, unable to govern. They want someone with vision."

"Is that why you orchestrated this? To steal my throne? To stage a coup?"

Lehm's laugh scraped through the air. "Why, why, why. It's an eternal obsession, you know." A mocking edge crept into his voice. "Lehm, why did you start Erisia's rebellion? Lehm, why did you journey to Shaylan? Lehm, why go through the trouble of uniting us on these wretched, empty cliffs?"

He unsheathed one of his swords, tapping it lightly to the ground. "Because I can," Lehm said. "Because I'm able. Because I was born with no powers, no wealth—the son of two failed merchants, who swore he'd become more. You think I'm here for something as mundane as a *throne*?" He placed his blade beneath Yuwen's chin, forcing the emperor's head upward. "You lack imagination. What I want is going to reshape the Five Kingdoms."

Yuwen gritted his teeth. Teia wondered if he was thinking of their conversation when she'd first come to Shaylan, the warning she'd given him about Lehm.

"The Serkawr," Yuwen said.

Lehm's mouth lifted. "I'm glad we're finally in agreement," he said, as he withdrew the sword. An angry red mark had opened against the soft of Yuwen's throat. "I didn't come to Shaylan for the scenery, did I?"

At Lehm's command, one of the Naga flexed his fingers. Sheets of ice stacked into the dirt, so thin they resembled slips of paper. The ice righted itself, assembling into a structure—a triangular base atop a flattened surface, repeating until a tower as tall as a man's chest was built.

Lehm shifted his hand into his coat. And when he brought it forth, Teia couldn't help but stare.

For something that had been the source of so much trouble, the Morning Star was smaller than she'd expected. It glimmered innocently in Lehm's hand, flashing tantalizingly in his grip. As he stepped forward to place it atop the tower, icy prongs shot up, holding the jewel upright.

"I call forth the Serkawr," Lehm said. His face was incandescent beneath the light of the blue star, his eyes wide and empty. As he spoke, his voice seemed to deepen, assuming an unearthly quality. "I ask for what's mine."

At Lehm's words, the jewel began to glow. It pulled free from the ice to climb into the air, revolving slowly as it did. Its edges were tinted with a brilliant luster.

"Teia," Kyra hissed.

"Not yet—"

Yuwen thrashed against the chains. "You hate me that much?" he said to Jin. "You'd see the world kneel to the likes of him?"

For the smallest moment, Jin wavered. Then his expression hardened, shuttering closed. "I trusted you, Yuwen. I *loved* you, from the moment I understood what that meant. But when I look at you, nothing ever changes. I see the boy who stood aside during the executions. I see the boy who did nothing as he sat atop his throne." He stepped toward the Morning Star. "Let the world be remade. Mine already fell two years before."

Water swirled above his open palm. He sent it spiraling straight for the jewel.

"I am what you made me," Jin breathed. "And by my hand you'll fall."

Chapter Forty-One

Water surged toward the Morning Star. As it wrapped around its base, cradling the jewel in a churning embrace, the Star gleamed brighter. A light pulsed from the center of the gem, a heart come alive.

"Kyra," Teia said. *"Now."*

They moved as one, directing twin flames toward the top of the dome. Water showered down on them, dusting their heads. Teia felt her fire sputter as she dug in her heels. The water resisted, fighting with all its might.

And then they broke through. The dome sloughed away, water drizzling down as mist. Shouts of alarm rang through the cliffs. The Naga tore their attention away from Yuwen, as Teia sent a bolt of fire toward them. One of the Naga absorbed it easily, conjuring a watery barricade that doused the flames.

Five Naga peeled away from Yuwen. They ran for Teia, but Tobias reached them first, catapulting over one to slash another with his knife. Alara withdrew silver pellets from her belt, no doubt filled with a noxious assortment of poisons. Enna skirted out of the way of each attack, avoiding the Naga like they were ungainly signposts.

Teia held back the guards that fell upon her. She parried blow after blow, until a Naga happened upon a lucky strike. His icy longsword ripped a bloody gash into her leg. Teia cursed. She crumpled as the man aimed a steady hand. A coil of water shot forward, scrabbling like a disjointed finger. It lifted Teia around the waist and threw her to the ground, before another tentacle drove into her throat.

Teia's vision blurred. Black spots erupted behind her eyes.

"Stop!"

Despite the pain, Teia managed to move her head. Kyra was standing beside the icy podium, her braid whipping sideways in the bitter wind. When she lifted her hand skyward, something glistened between her fingers.

The Morning Star.

Through the haze, Teia had the faint notion that she was going to kill Kyra. What was she *doing*? Hadn't the entire point of their distraction been so Kyra could destroy the Star? Why was she hesitating now, so close to the end?

"Teia!" Tobias shouted. She heard other cries, too, voices that she knew belonged to Enna and Alara. But the Naga had regrouped, assembling in a new formation. The others were kept away, as someone chuckled beside her.

Teia couldn't see Lehm, but she could hear the triumph in his voice, his sword scraping against his sheath as he returned it to his waist. "Hello, Kyra," he said. "I was wondering when you would act."

Kyra's eyes fell on Teia, who was wrenching at the tentacle pressed into her neck. "You'd raise the Serkawr," Kyra said, as she turned back to Lehm. Fire ignited within her palm. The Morning Star became trapped in a circle of flames. "I can't let you do that."

"I'd imagined as much," Lehm said silkily. He seemed entirely unbothered by the Star, smothering gently within Kyra's grasp. "It's one of the things I admire about you."

"That I'm here to stop you?"

"That you've always been one to play the hero. I knew it from the moment I arrived at your miserable little village. Do you remember? You were huddled in a corner of your home, surrounded by those charred walls. You called yourself a monster."

"Shut up."

"You said you never wished for your powers. And when you told me to stay back, I said I could help you. That, together, we could transform the Five Kingdoms."

"Shut up."

"I believed in you then, Kyra. I still do. But that's the thing about heroes. They have their weak spots. They're predictable. They have *morals,* which I find refreshing."

As if reacting to Lehm's words, the watery lash pushed harder against Teia's throat. She couldn't help it: a terrible sound rose from her chest, as Kyra's head snapped upward. "Teia!"

"I'll tell them to stop, Kyra," Lehm purred. "Or have you really changed so much from that girl I met in Erisia? Are you prepared to watch her die before you, as you stand there and do nothing?"

"Lehm—"

"It's a simple decision, really. You were so *angry* just a few weeks before. You hated Teia. You swore you'd have her head. She took away the first cause you'd ever fought for. The Dawnbreakers were extinguished because of her. Why not return the favor? Why not allow her death to come to pass?"

"Lehm, please."

"You know," he said thoughtfully, "I've been called a great

many things in my life—insults that would bring a lesser person to their knees. But I'm true to my word, no matter what some may say. Didn't I promise you'd always have a choice?" Lehm gave a dry laugh. "So I'll ask once more, Kyra. This isn't Alara. This isn't Tobias. Do you really think Teia Carthan is worth the Five Kingdoms?"

Kyra must have responded, an answer that was lost to the wind. A second later, the pressure on Teia's throat eased. She rolled to the side, gasping. Her fingers dug thin tracks into the dirt.

"As I said," Lehm mused. "Predictable."

When she managed to lift her head, Teia's heart dropped.

The Morning Star floated over Lehm's palms, now topped with a red halo of flames. The light that shone from its center had brightened. It was blinding to see, a splash of sunlight beneath a velvet sky, its glow matching the star that hovered high above.

The light within the jewel flashed once, twice. It resembled a lantern calling home a ship, a lamp lit for a weary traveler.

Somewhere in the depths of the Dark Sea, a keening rose from the water.

It was an ancient sound, the kind of growl that reached into the very center of the earth. Lehm's pale eyes glistened. "At last," he murmured. "At last."

From the beach below, a flock of gulls burst outward, flapping their wings desperately. They cawed in fright, as the waves lengthened. The tide grew larger, swelling against the surf. In the horizon, bubbles foamed against the churning water, as something broke through the waves, blotting out the moon.

After centuries of slumber, the Serkawr had risen.

Chapter Forty-Two

Not a single image of the Serkawr had done it justice.

Its head was as large as a ship, long horns draped with whorls of algae. Ridges protruded against the narrow slope of its snout, dipping down toward a long, thick neck. Its teeth dribbled poison, which spattered a muddled sheen into the water. Glittering spikes covered the sea beast's hide. Instead of a fiery red, as Teia had always seen in paintings, its scales were burnished a molten shade of gold.

Lehm let out an exhilarated laugh. He pushed the Morning Star away from him, and it levitated in the air, emanating its dazzling aura. Lehm didn't seem to notice as he stepped forward, a strange smile dashed across his lips.

"Kill them," he said.

It was Lehm's voice, but not, imbued with an awful rasp that resembled metal on stone. The Serkawr swung its massive head. Its yellow eyes thinned to slits. A forked tongue flickered between its teeth, as it broke through the surf with terrifying speed, pulling out of the water with ease.

The sea beast had *wings*.

Not a single story had ever mentioned the Serkawr could take to land, sea, *and* air. It was surprisingly graceful for something so large, its wings iridescent, shimmering like bolts of silk. A moment later, the Serkawr landed on the cliff. Its hind legs pressed close to the forest, blocking the sole path of escape. Entire trees were leveled beneath its feet, water pooling from its torso.

"Goddess," Kyra swore.

"Say her name again," Enna said. "I hope she's listening."

The Serkawr shot outward like an arrow. It went first for the Naga who'd corralled the soldiers without affinities, ripping the guards apart. When the vortex that had boxed in the gray-robed soldiers dissipated, the Serkawr's massive tail lashed out. Amalay flitted gracefully out of the way, but the other soldiers lacked her sense of self-preservation—or perhaps were just foolishly brave. They brandished spears and daggers, which the Serkawr shook off as a mere inconvenience. It snapped up four soldiers, and flattened another two beneath its massive tail. Then, seemingly bored, it turned, setting its gaze on Teia and Kyra.

"Yes," Lehm said. *"Kill them all."*

The Serkawr charged. The Naga keeping Yuwen down were in its path, and so the sea beast surged toward them first. As the guards conjured chains to keep the beast away, the Serkawr wrenched its neck upward, breaking through the ice. One woman started to run and was knocked aside with a flick of the sea beast's tail. The Serkawr stalked forward, poison dripping from its jagged mouth. The Naga made a sign of prayer before it lurched out, crushing her body between its jaws.

Even if Teia wanted to run, there was nowhere left to go. The forest had been mangled, broken branches and mutilated stumps littering the path. Any who tried to flee—gray-robed soldiers, Naga with affinities—were targeted by the Serkawr. The sea beast tore through both armor and flesh, friend and foe.

It was the sight of Lehm, calm amid the chaos, drinking in

the scene, that stunned Teia to action. "The Star," she gasped, as the jewel glittered red above the rebel leader's shoulder. "If we can reach it—"

"You think we can break Lehm's connection?" Tobias said. "Send the Serkawr back to where it came from?"

"We don't have much of a choice, do we?"

"And if we can't?" Enna said.

"Then we'll meet in the grave either way," Alara said. The Serkawr arched its neck up, away from the soldier it had just devoured. Gore smeared its mouth.

Teia sought the threads of heat around them, the swirls of orange and yellow that fluttered through the air. But what she felt first was the call of water, a primal instinct that flashed through her. "Go," she hissed, as the Serkawr crouched with a snarl. "I'll buy some time."

Kyra tensed. "Teia—"

"Go!" she said again, just as the Serkawr lunged.

Teia had never been especially sentimental. She couldn't afford to be, what with danger lurking behind every corner of the Golden Palace. Yet as she stared down the rampaging creature, its hot breath steaming against her skin, the stink of rotting flesh putrid in the air, Teia thought she heard her mother's voice, whispering in her mind.

The ocean is in our blood.

She reached out to the glowing pinpricks within the Serkawr's veins—but it was like trying to hold up the decaying foundation of a building. Teia screamed, a sound yanked from deep within her, as she clenched her fists. She sank to her knees, her muscles trembling, drawing breath through the searing pain.

Obey me.

The Serkawr ground to a halt. Its colossal leg twitched once, twice. Teia felt a thundering twist in her chest, as if her heart were bursting free. She clenched her fists harder, keeping her attention on the glimmering points of water.

Obey.

The sea beast roared. It jerked forward abruptly, and Teia's hold disintegrated. She fell, unable to stand, agony raking up her arms. As the Serkawr pitched forward, a figure swept before her, one hand extended outward.

Yuwen. With the Naga who'd restrained him either dead or in combat, he had freed himself of his chains. When the emperor pulled his hand high, water slammed into the Serkawr, forming a pillar that smashed into its side. The sea beast screeched as Yuwen steadied his palm toward the Dark Sea. Far below, there came the mighty growl of water assuming a new form.

A second figure rose from the sea, soaring out above the cliffs. It was smaller than the Serkawr, made entirely of water, with the body of a snake and crooked, tattered wings. It dove downward in a flurry of mist, wrapping around the Serkawr's leg. The Serkawr bellowed, snapping out blindly with its teeth. Yuwen's creature melted into droplets, re-formed around the sea beast's neck, and started to squeeze.

"No!" Jin cried. He leapt forward, but Teia hurled herself at him, throwing the adviser off balance. Beyond, Lehm was locked in battle with Tobias and Enna, while Kyra sent a wave of flames toward the Star. The air around it seemed to repel any attack, an invisible shield that encased the jewel.

The Serkawr. How was it stopped after it was summoned?

Divine intervention.

The Serkawr shook off Yuwen's creature. It spread its wings to rise into the air and plunged back into the Dark Sea. For a brief instant, everything was quiet.

Then the sea beast tore upward from the growing tide. As it loomed above them, its shadow blanketing the face of the cliff, the Serkawr released a torrent of water from its mouth. The wave swept over dry land, washing soldiers and Naga alike straight off the cliff. They were pitched over the edge, screaming, as the Serkawr landed on solid ground once again.

Yuwen's creature rushed at the Serkawr, but the sea beast was accustomed to it now, prepared for an attack. It bit out at the creature, severing its leg. As the Serkawr's jaw split through water, its enormous tail swished, spikes protruding from the end.

Teia spotted the spikes—and yet Jin didn't. She saw her chance. When the adviser bludgeoned upward with water, she shoved back with her flames. He deflected, just as she'd expected, but the force of her blow sent him stumbling straight into the Serkawr's path.

The spikes gouged through his torso, flinging him into the air. Jin landed on his stomach, his arm twisted beneath him. He glanced up in time to see the Serkawr's tail come crashing down.

"Jin!" Yuwen screamed.

Jin was a traitor, a spy, a mole who'd fed information back to Lehm. But as Teia watched, she had to admire his courage in whatever version it might appear. In his last seconds, Jin didn't defend himself. He merely sighed—a small, soft sound.

The adviser died in water and silence, a smile etched across his bloodied mouth.

Chapter Forty-Three

Yuwen collapsed to his knees, as a pulse rippled through the battlefield. Somewhere behind Teia, she heard a familiar voice yell her name, shouting for her attention.

One of the surviving Naga bore down on Kyra. He jabbed out at her, water surrounding his fists like a bulky pair of gloves. She fended him off with fire, but he stooped beneath her arm. Kyra was thrown into a shallow gulley stamped out by one of the Serkawr's footprints.

Before the Naga could deal a killing blow, Teia drew back her hand. Fire quivered in her palm as she sharpened her aim. A sphere of flames landed at the Naga's feet. He was blown back in a fiery explosion, crumpling in a broken crush of limbs.

Teia rushed to Kyra. As she helped the other girl up, the rebel champion grabbed for her wrist. "Teia," she said. *"Look."*

The Star remained suspended in the air, but the light within had softened. Its luster had reduced to a fraction of what it'd once been.

Hope scalded in Teia's chest. "Maybe the shield around it has weakened. If we both use fire—"

"There's a chance we could break through," Kyra finished. Her chin was bloody from where she'd been struck by the Naga, but she managed to beam at Teia. "See? I knew you were becoming an optimist."

They hurried over to the Star, taking care to keep out of Lehm's line of sight. Together, they raised their hands, and fire swelled before them, spiraling at the gem. *Please,* Teia thought, as the flames scorched a blinding shade of orange. *Please.*

Nothing happened. The invisible shield around the gem held.

"Dammit," she growled, before squaring her shoulders, calling for more threads of heat. *"Again."*

They sent fire forward once more, but to no avail. The jewel gleamed mockingly, as Kyra released a breath. "What about using both fire and water?" she asked, sweeping back loose wisps of hair. "Would that work?"

It was worth a try, considering how the Serkawr had been raised in the first place. This time, when Kyra pushed forward with fire, Teia grasped for water. Outside of internal manipulation, she'd only ever been able to control small quantities—and so she repurposed the liquid from nearby puddles, directing it at the gem. It all but bounced off the Star's shield, as fruitless as Kyra's flame.

The rebel champion threw up her hands. "I don't understand," Kyra said, frustration coloring her tone. "The gem's light faded. Lehm must be getting weaker—"

And just like that, Teia understood. "No," she gasped, as she thought of Jin's final moments, that serene smile flashing across his face. "It's Jin. He's dead, Kyra."

She regretted the words as soon as she spoke them aloud. Teia saw the exact moment that realization sank into the rebel champion. Her brow furrowed, creasing with determination.

"Kyra," Teia said. "Kyra, no—"

"You see the Star, Teia. Jin helped raise the Serkawr. If the gem dimmed when he died, maybe something will happen if I—"

"Maybe." The word fell heavy from Teia's lips. "It's speculation at best. The Star losing its light could mean nothing at all."

"But what if that's the key? What if it's how we stop Lehm?"

"And if it isn't?"

Kyra squeezed her eyes shut. "You think I want this?" she said softly. "I want to go back to Bhanot, to start my studies, to visit the vendors at Carfaix Market. I want another ten years, or twenty. I want to be *home.*"

"And you can do all that," Teia snarled, "once we find out how to break through the Star's damn barrier. We don't know that sacrificing yourself will work—"

But Kyra was looking past the gulley, to the chaos that raged around them. "You're right," she said. "But who would I be if I didn't at least try?"

Before them were the bloodied remains of corpses, torn to pieces, bodies strewn across the once-lovely cliffs. The Serkawr writhed, battling the watery creature Yuwen sent forth. The emperor had risen, tears dripping down his chin. Tobias and Enna grappled with Lehm, while Alara darted through the chaos. Chains of explosives rang out amid the cries of the injured.

It wasn't enough. Teia knew it as well as anyone. They were only prolonging death, keeping it at a distance. In a matter of minutes, they would be overwhelmed. There was nobody coming to save them, no sudden intervention from a coldhearted Goddess.

"Kyra," Teia said.

The rebel champion was already turning away. Her hair had come loose from its braid, unraveling around her shoulders. "Tell Alara I'm sorry," she said. "That we'll meet again in the next life."

With that, she was gone, swallowed into the chaos.

Teia swore. She clambered to her feet, threading through the corpses and soldiers, the broken blades embedded within the soft-packed dirt. She could feel each step against the beat of her heart. In the background, the Serkawr screamed. She skidded aside as the beast thudded sideways, one wing folded beneath its torso.

Teia scanned her surroundings frantically. Finally—*finally*—her focus caught on a lone figure perched close to the crumbling edge of the cliff.

Teia lunged. She caught Kyra's hand in hers, before the other girl could push herself forward. The rebel champion glanced back. Overhead, the sky had lightened slightly, the blue star fading fast—and yet Kyra Medoh was as she'd always been. A champion. A hero.

"Teia," she breathed. "It's all right. You can let me go."

She couldn't. How could she? Everything was blood and noise and pain—and yet the world had become surprisingly quiet, shrinking down to two people.

Kyra had been a rebel. She'd been an enemy. But now, inches away from the steep plunge of the cliff, the waters of the Dark Sea frothing below, something within Teia cracked open. If she allowed her fingers to loosen, if she met fate where it stood, nothing would ever be the same again.

If that meant the Five Kingdoms would burn, Teia would light the first flame herself.

"Kyra," Teia whispered. "Please."

But Kyra's dark eyes merely lifted. She took in Tobias and Enna, before settling gently on Alara, her shock of golden hair, the scrape along her cheek.

The Poisons Master must have sensed something was wrong. When she saw Kyra standing at the cliff, she began running, a shout rising in her throat. *"Kyra!"*

Kyra's gaze returned to Teia. Her lips drew back in a smile. "Teia," she said. "I'll be fine. I promise."

Then she was wrenching away from Teia with uncanny strength, her boots dislodging loose chunks of stone. As she leapt over the edge, there was a second when time seemed to still.

Kyra Medoh disappeared into the waves below.

Chapter Forty-Four

Teia knew the many ways a heart could break.

They were lessons she'd amassed throughout her life, moments that refused to leave her. Calla, pale as snow, a linen sheet drawn over her face. Ren, drooped on his splendid throne. Jura, setting her alight in the palace's gardens, his features bright with glee.

But now, on Okkan's mighty cliffs, Teia felt something shatter. She barely heard Alara as the Poisons Master stopped beside her. "Teia," she said tremulously. "Is she . . ."

Teia didn't answer. She didn't trust herself to. She thought of Kyra, the first time they'd spoken. The earnestness she carried, the smile she wore. Her insufferable belief that goodness existed—that it would continue to prevail against the odds, even in the darkest of places.

Grief reverberated through Teia, gnawing into her ribs. Yet it was anger that hauled her upright, keeping her on her feet.

Kyra might have preached compassion, but Teia had no such morals. She was going to blot Lehm's name from history.

It couldn't all be for nothing.

She was already running, rage kindling against her bones. Her eyes found the Morning Star as a breeze hummed through the cliffside. It wove through the crowds, tasting of salt and sorrow. She could have sworn something shifted over the bloody scene, invisible threads severed by a knife.

The Star still hovered high, but the unearthly glow had gone out.

Lehm realized this at the same moment as Teia. His sword slipped an inch against Tobias's, his eyes widening in disbelief. He staggered toward the jewel, but Tobias brought the hilt of his knife up, smashing it into Lehm's nose. The man howled in pain, blood pouring down his chin, as Teia leapt as high as she could, an arm outstretched for the heavens themselves. Above, the blue star of Kashan had nearly vanished, clinging to its last rays of light.

"I call forth the Serkawr," she whispered, her pulse blazing, her fist closing around the gem. "I ask for what's mine."

For a long moment, nothing happened.

Then lightning carved into Teia's body. She slammed to the ground, her fingers clasped around the jewel. Warmth spread up her arms, her legs, the length of her spine, sharpening to a tremendous heat. Her ears echoed with a terrific roar, the sound drowning out her surroundings.

The Serkawr lifted its head, spikes flashing against its scaled back.

The flame within Teia grew brighter. She was lit from within, made anew, each of her muscles bathed in a smoldering light. When she moved her hand, she felt the sea beast's strength at her fingertips. It bent to her will, as easily as a dream.

"Stop," she said, and the word magnified against her tongue, cresting out toward the sea. The Serkawr paused. Its yellow eyes trained on Teia.

She had never known power like this. What were kings and

queens, the petty squabbling that rose from meaningless disagreements? Temptations sang against Teia's tongue, marbling her veins. How could she return to Erisia after this? What was one throne, when she could claim all five?

She was the world, and she would bring down the stars.

Dimly, she heard Lehm's shriek. He flew toward her, blade in hand, but Teia flicked her fingers. The tip of the Serkawr's wing came crashing down. It pinned Lehm in place, his sword skittering away. He writhed furiously, before casting his glare up at Teia.

"Typical of a Carthan," he panted. "Your father, your brother, and now you."

He was trying to goad her, to push her to some further reaction. And maybe it would have worked, just a short time before. But now, when Teia looked at Lehm, she wondered how she had ever feared him. He didn't matter. He never had. Blood dripped from his broken nose. He was tiny within the Serkawr's grasp, a shrunken version of a once-great leader. A fool of a man, who had learned what it meant to lose.

He was struggling harder now, perhaps sensing what was to come. Dread seeped into his expression. "And what happens after this?" he said. "You lock the Star away. You give all this up. Is that something you're prepared to do?"

She must have hesitated for a second too long. Lehm pressed on, eager to continue. "I know how you feel right now. That rush of power, like your very bones are on fire. Like you could cross the Dark Sea in the span of a heartbeat. How will you go back to the way you were before? Will you return to a palace with a stolen throne, knowing who you might have become?"

Images of cheering crowds and fluttering banners flooded Teia's vision. They mirrored the ache that had stirred when she'd seized the jewel, the knowledge that the Serkawr would bow to her command. What was she destined for, if not to rise? She had carved her own fate from fire and blood. It was only natural she'd arrived where she was now.

This was power. *She* was power.

But even as a thrill surged up her spine, a pestering whisper bloomed in Teia's mind. Not at first—but slowly, surely, like the waves persisting against a rocky shoreline. It was a voice that remained firm and steady, beaming through the crush of noise.

Somewhere, far in the distance, beneath the battle and the tide and the horror of the cliffs, was Kyra Medoh. Teia could almost hear her laugh—and in that instant, it was as if the two of them had returned to the roof of Okkan's majestic pagoda, the wind nipping at their robes. The city lay below, hypnotic in its beauty. Kyra tipped her head, her gaze level, her braid curled down her back.

You're a good ruler, Teia.

I am, Teia thought. She felt the first light of morning kiss her face, warm against her tearstained cheeks. *I've always tried to be.*

Perhaps there was a time when she'd have made a different choice. Yet here on Okkan's cliffs, Teia glimpsed her future—the years she'd been gifted by Kyra, the decades she might still have. And although the path onward diverged, splitting cleanly in two, there was only one Teia was willing to walk.

She didn't need the Serkawr—its call to power, its whispers in her ear.

Teia Carthan knew who she was.

She smiled, leaning down to where Lehm had fallen. The corner of his bloodied lip twitched. He thought she was accepting his offer.

"Of all I could become," Teia said, "I'm happy to be your undoing."

She lifted her hand, and he followed each movement, terror reflecting in his eyes. *Good,* Teia thought, as she pointed toward the rebel leader.

"Take him," she said to the Serkawr.

The sea beast shot out. Its razored teeth sank into Lehm's chest, spurting thick trails of blood. The rebel leader let out a shrill scream as Teia gestured to the Dark Sea.

"Back," she told it, and the Serkawr obeyed. With a flap of its wings, it rose high above, Lehm clamped between its jaws. As the sea beast surveyed her, Teia could have sworn it nodded. Then it sliced gracefully into the churning waves, vanishing with hardly a sound.

"Teia?"

The Star was still clenched in Teia's right fist. When she unfolded her palm, she saw her reflection in its surface, distorted in red. For a second, that same temptation flickered once more, teasing at her chest.

She pulled for a thread of heat, then another. A flame erupted in her open palm, engulfing the Morning Star. The gem warmed against her skin. A crack appeared in the center, crisscrossing the one from centuries before. Another fissure snaked through the top, wrapping around one of the points.

On the horizon, the sky had brightened to orange. The water calmed against the surf, as Teia closed her hand. When she opened it again, the Morning Star was little more than a heap of shards, the flame burned to ash.

Below, the black waves lapped on, as if nothing had ever happened at all.

Chapter Forty-Five

It proved impossible to recover Kyra's body.

After they had taken inventory of any survivors, Amalay returned to the Society to retrieve her healer. While they'd waited for reinforcements, Teia and Yuwen had maneuvered down the steps carved along the steep cliffside, until their shoes sank into the golden sand. At Teia's request, the emperor dredged the waves, sifting through the sea. Yet at long last, even he was forced to admit defeat.

"There are plenty of bodies, but none of them are hers."

Teia was under no delusions that Kyra might be alive. But this felt like added insult to injury, a final blow to the girl who'd wielded fire, whose corpse now lay within a watery grave. "You can't find her?" she said.

"The waves say she's gone."

The waves needed to improve their method of communication. Bodies didn't just disappear. "Gone where?" Teia said. "Washed out to sea? Carried farther along the coast?"

A frown was permanently notched into Yuwen's brow. "If I had to guess?" he said. "Back to Armina—somewhere neither of us can follow."

Was that supposed to be a comfort? Of all the ways for the

Goddess to make her presence known, Teia could scarcely think of one less effective. But when she raised her gaze, Yuwen had moved away from the ocean. He faced the craggy pull of the cliffs, where the remnants of his army were tending to their wounds or else seeing to their dead. He seemed about to speak again when the drum of hoofbeats clattered above, announcing Yir's arrival. The Society's healer had come to save as many as he could.

From the cliff's ledge, Amalay peered down at them. She looked at Teia, nodded, and dipped out of sight, moving as effortlessly as a shadow.

Yuwen cupped a hand over his eyes. Teia hadn't thought it wise to share the leader of thieves' true identity, and so she'd simply said Amalay had friends in Okkan, healers who might be able to assist the wounded.

"It's kind of her to help," the emperor said.

Teia thought of the vessels she'd promised Amalay in exchange, each loaded with a small mountain of valuables. "She's very selfless."

"And susceptible to bribes?"

"You know about that?"

"I'm observant." He paused, unraveling the torn silk of his sleeve. "Why?"

His grief would come later, the anguish of losing both his father and the boy he'd loved. Yet for the moment, Yuwen's demeanor was composed, his concern focused on his surviving soldiers. *A good emperor,* Teia had said to Feng, when she'd confronted him in Cloud Mountain. She'd meant it then. She still did now.

"We're blood, Yuwen," Teia said. They were all they had left of family—two rulers from opposite ends of the Five Kingdoms, alone on their glittering thrones. "Will you return to Taijin?"

"As soon as I can." Yuwen stared out at the endless expanse of water. "If you'd like, you're welcome to stay. You and all your companions, for as long as you might need."

"I have to return to Erisia. Although I do need a new ship."

"You can have your pick of the fleet. I'll send word ahead to ready a crew."

She murmured her thanks as the waves rolled into the surf. Teia loosened her breath, deliberating, before she added, "Perhaps next time, you'd like to come to the Golden Palace?"

The smallest smile graced his face. "I'd enjoy that very much."

With that, he shuffled back to the stairs. From the beach, a different set of footsteps rustled behind Teia. Alara, Tobias, and Enna had stepped onto the sand. The Poisons Master's expression was distant, her robes clutched around her shoulders. "You didn't find her," she said. She didn't sound surprised.

"No," Teia replied quietly. She wished there was some way to comfort Alara, to provide the warmth that Kyra had always exuded.

Teia had seen death before. On more than one occasion, she'd wrestled her own life right from its grasp. But this felt different, a tear in her chest that she'd carry for the rest of her days. It hurt to breathe. It hurt to draw air, weighted with the knowledge of what led to this moment.

The Poisons Master lowered her chin. Tears trembled in her eyes. "She was too good for us," she said. "She didn't belong here, no matter how we tried to keep her."

For once, Enna was solemn. "She'll be missed," the thief said gruffly. "People like her are hard to find."

"No," Tobias said. "People like her are once in a lifetime."

Alara drew a shaky breath. "And what about the rest of us,

stuck in the aftermath?" she said. "I don't know how to say goodbye. I never have."

The hot scorch of tears pressed into Teia's throat. Instead of speaking, she reached out to squeeze Alara's hand, before bowing her head low.

One by one, the others did the same. It was a warm morning, not a cloud in the sky, the sun beaming onto their backs. A beautiful day, by any other standards, as the breeze kissed Teia's face. *Take care,* she thought, as she lifted her eyes high, toward a flock of birds soaring over the sea—a prayer for the girl who'd given everything. *Take care.*

She didn't know if there was another life beyond this one. But in this instant, Teia dared to hope. She would wait. She would be patient. And she would endure the decades, the ebb of time, until she and Kyra met again.

Enna's sigh was gentle, almost lost in the surf. "Back to Erisia, then?" she said. "I'm assuming Yuwen will provide a ship."

"You were eavesdropping?" Teia said.

"It was either learn how we're getting back, or assume we're swimming across the Dark Sea."

"I'm not going," Alara said. Her voice was ragged as she gripped the pouches on her belt. "I can't. Not yet. Not when everything in Bhanot reminds me of her."

"Where will you go?" Tobias asked.

"I'm not sure. I just need some time away."

Teia had been anticipating something along those lines, but the answer still came as a blow, leaving her breathless. "Are you certain?" she said. When Alara nodded, Teia spread her hands. "I can have Yuwen charter another vessel for you. Whenever you're ready to come back, Erisia will be waiting."

"And all of you?"

"No shortage of nobles to rob in Bhanot," Enna said. "You know where I'll be."

"Me as well," Tobias said. "There are . . . family matters that I'll be attending to."

"In Erisia?" Alara said.

"In the Highlands."

She didn't question him, didn't push for an answer. Alara's gray eyes were clear, focused despite the pain. "Until next time?"

"Until then," Teia said, as she hugged Alara fiercely.

All of them had been made and remade by the journey behind them. What had begun in the frantic sprawl of Erisia's capital had ended here on the glistening sand, brought before the famed cliffs of Shaylan. But Teia had no doubt she'd see Alara again. She knew it with certainty, just as she did the pulse of her heart and the hiss of a flame.

The Dark Sea stretched ahead, the weeks of voyage to come. Yet in the confines of her mind, Teia could envision what came next. On the other side was Bhanot, with its patchwork of homes and wind-weathered buildings, the untidy streets that she'd memorized as a child, the markets that never grew quiet. The Golden Palace rose from its center, its spiraling turrets crowned in gold. It was whispering her name, calling her back.

At long last, Teia Carthan was going home.

Chapter Forty-Six

ONE MONTH LATER

If there was anything consistent about the monarchy, it was the piles of paperwork that awaited Teia's return.

She had gone through a full ten sheaves of reports, papers scattering loose from a teetering stack on her desk, documents so smeared with ink that they were nearly illegible—and still there was more to do. Scouts hounded her on their latest discoveries. Officials quibbled about tariff rates. On one particularly humid morning, the Minister of Tourism trailed Teia from chamber to chamber, waving a file in his veined hand, espousing the importance of building new fisheries.

"Geralt," Teia had said, as patiently as she could. "You think tourists sail to Erisia for the *fisheries*?"

The minister had been dumbfounded. "Why, of course, Highness. Why else would they come here?"

When she finally managed to escape the clamor, it was to receive visitors to the Golden Palace, commonfolk and nobility alike who asked for an audience. As Teia strode into the throne room the following morning, her red robes fanning behind her, she found General Samos Miran already inside. His face was characteristically dour. His hair was beginning to thin, a subtle hint at his age.

"General."

"Highness. How did you sleep?"

"How do I ever?" she answered, settling onto her throne. "What's your opinion on fisheries, Miran?"

The general adjusted the medals on his chest. "Is this Geralt again?" he said scornfully. "He spoke of nothing else while you were away."

"Then I'm grateful to have missed as much as I could." Teia sat tall against the velvet upholstery, straightening the crown atop her head. "We're ready for the visitors?"

"They're waiting for you outside." Miran hesitated. "Highness. If I may be so bold."

He might as well. "Yes?"

"You haven't spoken much of your travels."

"There's hardly been the time."

The general reached up, tugging at the patch over his missing eye. "And Lehm?" he said. The name echoed through the room.

If there was any comfort to what had happened in Shaylan, it was that Teia knew exactly what became of Lehm. "Dead and gone," she said. "He won't be troubling us again."

"Are you certain?"

"On my life."

This seemed to satisfy him, if only for a minute. "How did you convince the Shaylani of his deceptiveness?" Miran said. A faint note of admiration shone in his voice. "Lehm can be tricky, devious. I feared . . ."

She gave him a small smile. "Don't worry, Miran," Teia said. "I didn't."

Nobody would ever know the sacrifice that Kyra Medoh had

made, miles away on the black cliffs of Shaylan. They wouldn't realize they were alive because of her—her selflessness and her optimism, her relentless pursuit of decency.

I hope you're well, Teia thought, just as she had every day on the journey back to Erisia, just as she would every day until the end of her days. She wasn't foolish enough to believe in miracles, but she wondered if there might be an exception—that, somehow, her words would reach wherever Kyra had gone, delivered to where they needed to go.

Teia steadied herself, loosening a breath. "You can send in the first visitor," she said to Miran, who bent in a bow.

As he pulled open the door and exited the chamber, a boy walked through the ornamented threshold. Teia's pulse began to race. A glow flashed through her veins, warming her from the inside out.

The Lord of the Highlands bowed his head. "Highness," he said.

Nobility suited Tobias Rennert. His dark hair was tidy, save for a single strand that fell into his torrential eyes. The scar on his neck shone in the light, threading into the silver collar of his robes.

She hadn't seen him since they'd disembarked the ship that Yuwen had offered—a sturdy, elegant vessel, with a wooden dragon at the prow. The Erisian dockmasters had nearly fainted when they'd seen Teia on a ship that flew Shaylani colors, but she hadn't minded. Blue complemented her. It always would.

"Tobias," she said, as he crossed the room in a matter of steps. He held out a cream-colored envelope, which she accepted hesitantly. The parchment was heavy, weighted. Their fingers brushed, just for a moment, lingering beneath the paper.

"I was once asked," he said, "if I would extend you a visit to the Highlands."

She broke open the pale gray seal, embossed with the St. Clair symbol of a hound against the moon. "I don't know," Teia said slyly. "Some say the road is treacherous between here and the mountains."

"No more so than any other. I know plenty of shortcuts."

"Unmarked roads, filled with bandits and thieves?"

"I'll say a prayer for any that have the misfortune of meeting you."

She couldn't hold back her laugh. "And what would we do while I'm there?"

"That depends on how often you plan to come. But the first time, I'll take you to the harbors. We'll watch the ships, walk the docks. I'll show you the best sweets shop in all of Erisia. They sell every flavor of tea cakes you could imagine."

"That could be dangerous," she warned him. "The treasury happens to be *very* full."

"You'll clear the shelves?"

"And the storerooms. You have no idea what you've unleashed."

"Menace."

"As expected." She sat back against the throne. Almost casually, Teia said, "Enna will be dining here tonight."

Tobias grinned. "And leaving with the silverware in her bag, no doubt."

"She did that two evenings ago. I think she's angling for the plates next—wants to complete a whole dining set before the Winter Holiday."

"The glassware and bowls?"

"Tables and chairs too. Why not be efficient?" Teia paused.

Her heart felt ready to implode as she took in the boy before her. "Will you stay?" she said quietly. "It's a long journey back to the Highlands."

At this, she was rewarded with a crooked smile, the one she'd never tire of. Tobias stepped onto the dais. He reached for her hand. Gently, his lips pressed against her knuckles, his gaze holding hers.

"Always," he said. "For as long as you'll have me."

A sharp burst of knocks rang from the door. The next visitor was ready, adhering to the strict schedule that Teia's pages had put in place. She offered Tobias an apologetic look, but he merely laughed, a spool of music that careened through the room.

"I'll leave you to it," he said, as he moved toward the door. She caught one last glimpse of him before he slipped into the hallway, gilded in the sunlight slanting through the arched windows.

The page boy hovered by the threshold expectantly, prepared to bring forth the following visitor—and yet Teia gave herself another moment, watching the light dance across the golden walls. It stretched over the tiles, bathing the frescoes on the ceiling, the paintings of her country's past monarchs. One day, she would be up there as well, beside the image of her father, beside all those who'd come before her.

When she was ready, the Queen of Erisia lifted her hand.

A new day had dawned over her kingdom.

Acknowledgments

I never thought writing an acknowledgments section would make me emotional, but here we are. As I'm sitting here, drafting these words, all I can think about is Teia's story—how proud I am to share it with the world, how happy I feel that she's now with readers, and above all, how much I'm going to miss her. Truly, this has been the end of a very long road. Without the people mentioned below, none of this would be possible.

Kelly van Sant, my wonderful agent. There have been so many moments throughout this journey when I didn't think this story would ever come to light, much less be a completed (!!) duology. Thank you, thank you, thank you.

Kevin Norman, I'm so lucky to have found Teia Carthan's #1 fan—someone who both understands her story and is one of her fiercest advocates. These past couple of years have been absolutely everything. I will always be thankful that these two books brought us together.

Tegan Tigani—I've said it once, I've said it a thousand times. Having you as my editor has fundamentally shaped this book for the better. Thank you for your keen eye, your attention to detail, and your evergreen knowledge on boats.

The entire Girl Friday team—Kim Kent, Katherine Richards,

and Paul Barrett, in partnership with Kelly Frodel, and Tiffany Taing—has worked tirelessly behind the scenes. Thank you for everything you've done for this book. A huge thank-you as well to the Lavender PR team—Brittani Hilles, you are an absolute gem and I'm so lucky to have worked with you. In addition, thank you to everyone at Bindery, which continues to uplift authors and help them shine, all while putting out an amazing catalog of books.

Dan Funderburgh, you are an artistic genius. This cover—and the last—blew my mind. Thank you for lending your incredible talent to this story.

Publishing is an industry of highs and lows, and I will always be grateful for my writing friends, who've kept me sane throughout this book. To the Sinking Barn group chat—Sarah Street and Nessa Le, there's nobody else I'd prefer to share one (1) brain cell with. Lilian Li, I always have the best time yapping with you, even if we get absolutely zero writing done. S. Hati, please move ASAP so we can hang out in person (but also stop hurting me with your gorgeous prose). Tammy Kung, who is technically publishing adjacent, and was one of the first to read *Tempest's Queen* with her outrageously funny commentary. Thank you also to Kay Synclaire, Susan Morris, Laura Samotin, KS Shay, and Maddie Martinez for the laughs, talks, and hangouts, both in person and online. Finally, Margaret Rogerson—thank you so much for your kindness when I first went out on submission several years back. Being able to beta read your novella literally altered my brain chemistry.

To the booksellers who've championed this book, thank you for taking a chance on Teia. It really, truly means the world. Every time I walk into a store and see my book (!!!) on a shelf, I become giddy all over again.

Andrew, who saw me in full gremlin mode when I was first drafting *Tempest's Queen*, and still cooked me dinner every night. You're undoubtedly my better half (also I'm sorry about what happens to Kyra).

To my incredible friends, who have literally done everything to support this book (*Inferno's Heir* book club will always be a core memory). Whenever I write about found family, I'm writing about you.

To my parents—thank you forever and always for everything you've done for me. Mo, you (unfortunately) make me laugh more than anyone else. My extended family, who've enthusiastically championed this cause, even when I fumble my explanations of what my books are about. And to my grandparents—in anything that I do, I hope to make you proud.

Finally, to anyone who's read *Inferno's Heir.* Sometimes on bad days, I reread the messages you've sent, and it reminds me why I continue to write. This book will always be for you.

Thank You

This book would not have been possible without the support from the Violetear Books community, with a special thank-you to the Associate Publisher members:

Akcole26
AndiiSwagg
Ashley Odriozola
booknerdcharlie
Christian Bellman
Courtney Doerr
Cristina Rowe
Dani Paez
Fowzi Abdulle
Holly Blakemore
olivia8397

About the Author

© Andrew Cui

TIFFANY WANG studied communication and international relations at the University of Pennsylvania, and she's currently wandering her way through New York City. In her spare time, she enjoys browsing bookstores, hunting for a quiet place to write, and snacking on a questionable amount of Cheetos. She is also the author of *Inferno's Heir*.

Violetear Books is an imprint of Bindery, a book publisher powered by community.

We're inspired by the way book tastemakers have reinvigorated the publishing industry. With strong taste and direct connections with readers, book tastemakers have illuminated self-published, backlisted, and overlooked authors, rocketing many to bestseller lists and the big screen.

This book was chosen by Kevin T. Norman in close collaboration with the Violetear Books community on Bindery. By inviting tastemakers and their reading communities to participate in publishing, Bindery creates opportunities for deserving authors to reach readers who will love them.

Visit Violetear Books for a thriving bookish community and bonus content:

violetear.binderybooks.com

KEVIN T. NORMAN is a Latinx creator from Los Angeles, California, who combines humor and his love of reading to create content focused on education, social justice, and all things bookish. He has a combined TikTok and Instagram following of over 390,000. In 2022, Kevin was chosen as an LGBTQ+ Trailblazer, a title awarded by TikTok to only twelve creators from the US for their work with the LGBTQ+ community.

@KEVINTNORMAN (IG AND TIKTOK)